Unending ...
for Modern ... W9-AQX-668

modern women

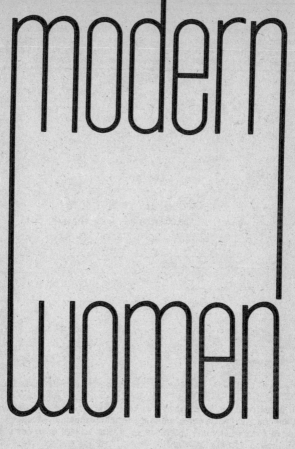

RUTH HARRIS

ST. MARTIN'S PAPERBACKS

For Michael Harris with love.
For Tom McCormack with thanks.

MODERN WOMEN

Copyright © 1989 by Communications Resources International, Inc.

Library of Congress Catalog Card Number: 89-35114

ISBN: 0-312-92272-8

Printed in the United States of America

St. Martin's Press hardcover edition published 1989
St. Martin's Paperbacks edition/September 1990

10 9 8 7 6 5 4 3 2

I

NOVEMBER 22, 1963

"You certainly can't say that the people of Dallas haven't given you a nice welcome."

> —Mrs. John Connally, Jr., to President Kennedy in the motorcade in Dallas

"Jack! Oh, no! No!"

> —Jacqueline Kennedy, several moments later

1
JANE

AT first she wasn't sure what happened. If anything.

Wearing a phony press badge with a fake name borrowed from Ian Fleming, Jane Gresch was seated on the window side in the first row of the first press bus accompanying John F. Kennedy's presidential trip to Texas. Because of a mix-up in scheduling, the bus was farther back in the motorcade than planned. As Jane gazed out the window at the sparse crowds that had turned out to see a president much too liberal for local John Birch tastes, she thought she heard a car backfire.

From behind the tinted bus window, Jane saw, as if in a silent film, a stir of uncertainty ripple through the crowd. She noticed several people turn and begin to run away from the motorcade. A young mother pushed her two children to the ground and, using her own body as a shield, flung herself on top of them.

Then the bright daylight receded and Jane's view was blocked as the bus went into the shadows of the Dealey Plaza underpass.

"What happened?" Jane asked. She turned to Owen Casals, her date for the weekend, who was sitting next to her in the aisle seat. Tall Owen. Dark Owen. Lean, handsome, work-all-day, fuck-all-night Owen.

He stood up to get a better view of the scene in front of them.

"The president's car sped off. Really barreled away," he said, turning to Jane. He looked alarmed. Owen, too, had heard the sound. Rifle fire, he thought, although he immediately rejected the idea. It was impossible. Along the banks of the Yalu River, yes, but not here in America.

Originally a police reporter like his father, Owen had risen through the journalistic ranks swifty. At thirty-two he was a star in his world, a general assignment reporter for *Newsflash* magazine. Owen traveled constantly covering the hot stories—and President Kennedy's Texas trip promised heat.

The local Democratic party's bitter infighting had prompted what was hoped to be a fence-mending presidential trip. Adlai Stevenson, citing the ugly mood in the Lone Star state, had advised the president not to go. The warning added an edge of danger to the story. Mrs. Kennedy, known to dislike politicking and politicians, had accompanied the president, contributing a bracing jolt of glamour and sex appeal. Dallas promised to be the kind of story on which Owen had built his career.

When the bus came out of the underpass, Jane saw a policeman jump his motorcycle up over the curb, dismount, and scramble up the grassy bank. As he disappeared from her view, Jane thought she saw him reach for his holster. The bus stopped for a moment and a lone reporter got off and ran after the policeman. Then it started again and continued at a leisurely motorcade pace toward the Trade Mart where the president was scheduled to speak.

"Something really serious, we'd hear sirens. Cops and Secret Service would be all over the place. This bus wouldn't be crawling along," Owen said. He had decided that the noise he had heard was probably a motorcycle backfiring. The driver of President Kennedy's limousine had certainly heard the same sound and, trained to act first, think later, had undoubtedly jammed his foot on the accelerator and peeled out.

"Just act like you belong," Owen advised Jane, leaping out of his seat as the bus pulled up to the Trade Mart. Even if nothing had happened, Owen wanted to be the first to report it.

Scores of tables had been set up in the huge function room of the Trade Mart. The speaker's podium, where President Kennedy was about to address the crowd, was draped in red, white, and blue bunting. American flags stood by the speaker's podium and bouquets of hundreds of yellow roses stood at the head tables. The organist was warming up with a few bars of "Hail to the Chief."

Everything was ready, but suddenly everything ceased. Hundreds of Texans in the middle of a rubber-chicken circuit lunch stopped eating. Jaws stopped in midbite. Forks hung suspended in midair. Water glasses poised midway between table and mouth. Jane could see eyes open wide in surprise, heads shake in doubt, mouths open in O's of disbelief as the rumor spread through the room.

"Is it true?" a man in a business suit and ten-gallon hat asked Jane. He glanced at her press badge and, thinking she might know something, grabbed her urgently by the arm. "Did someone shoot the president?"

"Shoot?" Jane replied. A feeling of chill she had pushed away earlier returned. Jane remembered the stir in the motorcade route crowd—an uneasy and frightened ripple similar to the wave of movement that was sweeping the banquet room.

Before Jane could say another word, Owen grabbed her by the arm and propelled her into the surging mob of journalists that pushed through the banquet hall and up the stairs into the second-floor press room. Just as Jane and Owen entered the room, an official-looking man put down a telephone.

"The president's been shot," he said, his face turning white. "He's at Parkland Hospital."

2
LINCKY

ON November 22, Lincky Desmond did what she almost always did for lunch. She left the office at twelve thirty and went out for a brief walk and a breath of fresh air. Then she stopped at the deli for a tuna sandwich that she would eat at her desk while working on a manuscript.

The fact that she had been sleeping with her boss didn't mean that Lincky worked less. In fact, it meant that she worked more. There were two reasons. The first was that Lincky didn't want Hank Greene to think that she would use their personal relationship to take advantage. The second was that Lincky didn't want anyone in the office to suspect the affair by noticing that she was goofing off and not getting chewed out about it. Hank Greene, after all, was known as one of the most demanding bosses in publishing.

The first thing that struck Lincky was that the deli, usually frantic at lunchtime, was eerily quiet. The customary frenzy was notable by its absence. The waiters were not shouting orders at countermen. Dishes did not clatter noisily and silverware did not bang against stainless steel counters. The customers, too, were silent. They had stopped eating, stopped talking. Lincky would have thought that she had suddenly gone deaf except for the sound of a portable radio turned up high.

"The president is dead. That's a confirmed report." The announcer kept repeating the words over again and again. "The president is dead. That's a confirmed report."

Lincky was confused.

"President?" Lincky asked, turning to the Brooks Brothers–suited young executive who stood in the line behind her. "President of what?"

"Kennedy," he said. Lincky noticed that his skin was ashen. "They got Kennedy."

Irrelevantly, it struck Lincky that with his charcoal gray suit, rep tie, and horn-rimmed glasses, he didn't look much like a Democrat. Even before the impact of the news fully sank in, Lincky ran out of the deli toward the office.

As she hurried down Third Avenue to 45th Street in the clear, gloriously sunny late autumn weather, Lincky still didn't quite know whether or not to believe what the man in the deli had told her. President Kennedy dead? He was so young and so vital. Dead? It was incomprehensible. Yet that was what the man had said.

Lincky saw people standing on the sidewalks, huddled around portable radios. Traffic had come to a halt. A bus, its doors open, stood empty, abandoned in the middle of Third Avenue. Knots of people were gathered around automobiles listening to car radios through open doors and windows. A large crowd had gathered in front of a discount store window where banks of television sets showed grim-faced reporters and anchormen.

Half walking, half running, Lincky realized that something momentous really had happened. Part of her wanted to stop and join the people clustered in groups. The other part, the dominant part, wanted to get back to the office. She wanted to see Hank. She wanted to be with him. She wanted to share this moment with him.

The Henry Greene Literary Agency's fourth floor offices were deserted. Everyone was out at lunchtime, particularly on a beautiful late November day, sure to be one of the last nice days before winter and darkness took over the city. Looking for Hank, Lincky went down the corridor to his modest corner office. Like everyone else, Hank was still out. Unable to be with Hank physically, Lincky did the next best thing. She sat down in his chair, smelled the familiar odor of his cigarettes and soap, and took comfort from these signs of Hank's presence.

More prepared now to confront the terrible news, Lincky turned on the portable radio in Hank's office. Every station had broken into its regular programming for the same bulletin from Texas:

"President Kennedy is dead. He was shot today in Dallas by an unknown assassin."

It was only then, when she first began to truly comprehend the dimensions of the tragedy, that Lincky realized that not once since she had heard the dreadful news had she thought of her husband.

3
ELLY

AS dumb jobs went, selling shoes in the Pappagallo boutique in Georgetown was one of the dumbest. As impossible customers went, this one, Elly had long since decided, redefined the species. Her name, although not nationally prominent, was fairly well known in Washington. Her husband was an upper-echelon lawyer in the attorney general's office. It was said on the Georgetown dinner party circuit that she and her husband had the perfect marriage: he had the brains and she had the dough, piles and piles of it.

She also had a blond lion's mane bouffant hairdo that she flew to New York every week to have set and teased at Kenneth's, a wardrobe of Jackie Kennedy look-alike A-line dresses, and an overly emaciated figure to offset her overly developed bank account. Her existence proved that it *was* possible to be too rich and too thin. She reeked of Shalimar and insatiability.

She was exactly the kind of spoiled, materialistic, self-centered woman Elly McGrath had been brought up to despise.

Seven pairs of suede and patent leather shoes were scattered around the pearl gray carpet of the boutique. Three pairs were pumps, four were T-straps. Three were black, the rest were various shades of cream, tan, rust, and brown. Elly was on her knees on the floor, helping her customer slip her long, bony feet into and out of them. The woman had been parked there for an hour and a half unable to decide which color and which style she wanted.

Floundering in a morass of indecision, she inspected each style carefully, lingering over each one in turn. Under her breath, she debated the merits and debits of each style and each color, arguing with herself over its present and future usefulness, flattery, and fashion quotient. The microscopic examination did not seem to help her make up her mind. Nor did the fact that she had repeated the exercise on the two previous afternoons.

"I don't know. I'll have to think about it," the woman said.

She motioned to Elly to put her own shoes back on and got up, ready to leave. As Elly collected the shoes strewn over the carpet and began putting them back into their tissue-lined boxes, the stock boy suddenly burst out of the stock room.

"President Kennedy's been shot!" he said. "He's dead!"

For as long as she lived, Elly never forgot that at a moment of national crisis she had been on her knees, trying to sell shoes to a selfish and self-obsessed woman who greeted the announcement of the president's assassination with an angry sigh.

"I suppose that means my dinner party's off for tomorrow night. And Ethel *promised* that she and Bobby would be there," she said, her thin, predatory hand with its blood-red nails on the open door of the boutique. "Jesus Christ! Why does everything have to happen to me?"

Elly was jolted by the assassination and her customer's self-centered reaction. She was wasting her life, her time, her energy. Where were her brains? Where were her values? Where were the ideals with which she had been brought up? Elly was appalled at the way she had been spending her time and energy.

"I'm quitting," Elly told her boss an hour later. She was in tears.

"You're just upset. Why don't you go home for the rest of the day? Come back tomorrow," replied Janice Kellen, the boutique's owner. Elly was an excellent saleswoman, the best Janice had ever had. She didn't want to let her go.

"No. You've been nice to me and I've enjoyed working here, but I realize that it's the wrong place for me," Elly replied.

It was an impulsive, emotional decision that Elly couldn't really afford. She had very little money and no idea about what she was going to do next other than that it was damn well going to be more constructive than selling shoes. Making her way home through a stricken city, Elly comforted herself by remembering that she still had the only things that really mattered to her: her friends and her family—and, maybe, if she really got lucky, the man she had her heart set on, Owen Casals.

II

FROM CONFORMITY TO CAMELOT/1957–1963

Love and marriage,
Love and marriage,
Go together like a
Horse and carriage.

—from "Love and Marriage" by Sammy
Cahn and Jimmy Van Heusen

4
JANE

Nice girls don't!

—Fifties injunction

"Says who?"

—Jane Gresch

PLAIN Jane?

Never!

Ever since she could remember, Jane Gresch had hated her first name. It was so ordinary, so *boring*, so exactly the absolute opposite of her. Jane Gresch was no Plain Jane and she wanted to make sure everyone else knew it, too. Just because her birth certificate said "Jane" didn't mean for one minute that she had to go through life with a name that didn't suit her and so, starting in the fourth grade, Jane had fiddled around with the spelling of her name. It was a case of orthography as identity.

Jayne. Jaine. Janey. Jain. Janie. Jayn.

She wanted to find a name that fit her, a name that was special, dramatic, unique, a name that would make other people notice and pay attention. Sometimes, she traded the *i* for a *y*. At other times and in other moods, she inserted an *e* while at still others, she imperiously deleted it. She transposed letters and otherwise changed, dropped, and restored spellings in a search for the name that would tell the world that *this* was no plàin Jane, no plain vanilla, no middle western, middle-of-the-road, white bread Miss Nobody.

Jane varied the look of her written signature as frequently as she changed the spelling of her name. She experimented with signatures ranging from huge to microscopic. She tried oversized initials followed by tiny letters. For a time she adopted a spiky, neurasthenic scratch. She spent hours perfecting the best imitation of cursive italic she could manage and varied *that* with a bold, careless, I've-got-more-important-things-to-do scrawl. She dotted *i*'s with circles and crossed *t*'s with wings. She owned pens with thin and thick nibs and with slanted points designed especially for calligraphy. She favored, at different times and in different moods, inks in her favorite colors of green, fuchsia, or crimson.

Jane was determined to stand out. If she hadn't wanted to be a famous writer for as long as she could remember, she would have wanted to be an actress. Trying new experiences, daring to be unconventional, passionately flinging herself into her emotions seemed to Jane as natural as breathing or—as she would tell interviewers later when she had become not only famous but, for a while, notorious—as natural as sex itself.

Jane was tall, big boned, and fleshy. She had impossible-to-manage light brown hair, lively hazel eyes that sometimes looked blue, sometimes green, a generous, mobile mouth with large, square teeth, and a smoky Lauren Bacall voice.

Born in 1941, she grew up in postwar St. Louis, a city with fewer than a million people, a thriving but provincial center of agriculture and manufacturing. Her father worked as a freight dispatcher for the Wabash Railroad and her mother, whose mother had written romance stories for the penny press, was a housewife. Jane's grandmother had aspired to be a Midwestern Margaret Mitchell but settled for writing for money to support her charming but improvident husband and children. Jane felt that she had gotten her way with words and sense of drama from her maternal grandmother.

"There's a long literary tradition in our family," said Jane, loftily smoothing over the nitty-gritty details.

Jane had had sex on the brain for as long as she could remember. Or at least, that was what she said and what, after a time, she came to believe. She had first learned about the power of sex, she would tell reporters, as a four-year-old who had danced on the dining room table the day her baby brother, Robert, was brought home from the hospital. Aunts and uncles and neighbors had come over to see the newest addition to the Gresch family.

"I took one look and saw how everyone was oohing and aahing over him and I knew I had serious competition. No one was paying the slightest attention to me," Jane said. "I knew I had to do something. I wasn't just going to stand there and fade into the wallpaper!

"I pretended to be just as interested as everyone else. I cooed and drooled over Bobby. Then, when I decided that enough was enough, I got up on the dining room table and began to dance. No one even looked up. They were still exclaiming over Bobby.

"I wasn't getting anywhere but I wasn't going to give up either. As I danced faster, my skirt began to whirl out. I suddenly remembered how everyone always laughed when I turned somersaults and my skirt flew up over my head. Still standing on the table, I stuck my behind straight up in the air and raised my skirt over my head. Suddenly, as if by magic, people turned away from the baby.

"My mother told me to put my skirt down. She said I was being naughty but she was smiling. My Uncle George laughed and so did my father. My grandmother scolded me but I noticed that she was laughing, too. Everyone was paying attention to me. They had forgotten all about the baby.

"From then on, I always knew how to get people to pay attention to me. From the time I was four years old, I deliberately set out to be a star."

She also became her brother's devoted protector and benefactor.

"Jane acts like a nut a lot of the time but she's never let me down. Not once," he said.

Reminiscing about her St. Louis childhood, Jane would tell reporters that she had been the vamp of her class, a Midwestern man-trap, a home-grown femme fatale. When she discovered that women had breasts, she had stuffed the chest of her Shirley Temple doll with tissue paper, giving the skipper of the good ship *Lollipop* a Mae West shape. It was Jane who looked up the word "penis" in the St. Louis public library's medical dictionary and she who shared its meaning with the other girls in her class. And not only the meaning of the word, but the use of the member itself.

"They don't just pee out of it. They put it into you!" an eight-year-old Jane told a bug-eyed Amy Sheridan and a dubious Wilma Elbaum in the privacy of the treehouse Jane's father had built for her in the branches of the big oak in the Gresches' back yard. Jane had pulled up the ladder behind them so that her thrilling revelations would not be interrupted.

"They do? Exactly *where* do they put it?" asked Amy, agog with the startling new information. It added a provocative dimension to her own forbidden, nocturnal explorations "down there" where her mother said she should never but never touch herself or allow anyone else to touch her.

"That's silly. They can't put it anywhere. It's a tiny little thing and it wobbles when they walk. I know. I've seen my brother's. I saw my father's twice, too," said Wilma dismissively before Jane could answer. Wilma wore thick glasses with marbleized pink plastic frames and approached life with the detached curiosity of a scientist.

"It's not always tiny," said Jane, putting Wilma the know-it-all in her place. "It gets big when they're excited."

"If you're so smart, tell us what excites them," said Wilma. Wilma had never seen such a thing as a large penis and she intended to expose Jane's lies for what they were: a way of getting people to pay attention to her. Poor Amy tended to be far too credulous.

"Us!" replied Jane triumphantly, having the last word. "Women. We can make men crazy. They go wild. They're in our power."

Jane had her first opportunity to exercise that female power when she was twelve and Gene Schuble was fourteen. It was May, late on a Tuesday afternoon, after school and before dinner and homework. Mothers were in the kitchen preparing supper. Fathers were still at work. Children were outside playing in the fresh air. Jane and Gene were on the Schubles' front lawn.

With dark hair, pale skin, and heavy eyelids, Gene resembled a young Elvis Presley, a bit of luck Gene played up by greasing his hair and wearing it in a high pompadour in front and a slick D.A. in back. At fourteen, he was an all-American car freak. He worked in the neighborhood Esso on weekends and wore grease-stained jeans as proud emblems of his chosen profession.

Gene bragged that he knew every automotive model on the road not only by sight but by the very sound of its engine. Gene liked to display his formidable knowledge by closing his eyes and turning his back to the street. Without looking, he would listen carefully to the sound of the motor and announce out loud the make and model of every car that passed. The boys were impressed, none more than Gene. The girls were mostly indifferent.

Jane, who lived two houses away, was an exception. She was Gene's fairly willing audience and fact checker. The game was Gene's favorite and Jane agreed to play it in exchange for the loan of Gene's bike whenever he wasn't using it. Because that particular Tuesday was a warm, almost sultry, typical early summer St. Louis day, Gene stretched out full length on the lawn while Jane sat facing the road in order to confirm Gene's automotive genius.

"A Fifty Dodge," Gene said as the first automobile in the

afternoon's exercise passed. When Jane didn't validate his announcement immediately, Gene hesitated, made uncertain by the silence. Finally, he changed his mind. "A Chevy?"

Jane still didn't answer. Her mind wasn't on cars. It was on the fascinating lump that had suddenly appeared in Gene's trousers. It hadn't been there a moment ago. Like a mountain rising unexpectedly from the sea, it had simply appeared. Where there had been nothing, there was suddenly something. Something, Jane instinctively knew, that had to do with the power women had over men.

"Jane!" said Gene, irritated at the long silence.

"You were right the first time," Jane said absently. The fact was that in her fascination with the state of Gene's trousers, Jane hadn't noticed what make the car was. Hadn't noticed and didn't care.

"You should have told me right away it was a Dodge," Gene gumbled, annoyed at the loss of face.

When Jane began to mumble an apology, Gene told her to shut up. Another car was coming and he wanted to concentrate. He wanted to get the make and model right. He had a reputation to uphold.

"Shhh!" he said, concentrating as the second car came nearer.

Gene was pretty sure it was a Buick but he never got the word out as Jane, unable to resist a second longer, put her hand out and touched the lump.

"Jesus Christ! Get your hands off me!" Gene blurted, turning scarlet and rolling over as he pushed Jane's hand away. He scrambled to his feet and fled. He ran along the driveway toward the back door and the safety of his mother's kitchen.

That evening, Gene walked over to Jane's house to watch the *Texaco Hour of Stars*. In the darkened living room, Jane noticed with a sense of triumph that Gene had completely changed his mind about where her hands ought or ought not to be.

Jane and Gene "fooled around," as they put it, from that memorable May afternoon on, when automotive games were forgotten and other, more compelling games, presented themselves. Whenever they could find privacy, Jane and Gene explored each other's bodies avidly, adventuresome young Christopher Columbuses sailing in uncharted but entrancing seas. They always stopped short of intercourse.

Conventional Wisdom, that dreary troll, held that Nice Girls Don't. Jane, ever unconventional, took the prohibition as a challenge. She was longing to go all the way. She had read that the earth moved. Jane wanted to find out more about that. Was it like one of the earthquakes she had seen on television? Did buildings crack and drinking glasses jump around on kitchen shelves? Would just the part of the earth she personally occupied tremble? Would she be the only one to know? Or could other people tell, too? Jane didn't know and she was dying to find out.

Gene, quite maddeningly, refused.

"Jailbait," he sneered, turning Jane down.

"I'm fifteen. We can do it now," Jane informed Gene on the day after her fifteenth birthday. She was unusually intense, even for her.

"Fifteen is practically sixteen," Gene agreed, disposing of the age issue. He was seventeen and walking around with a permanent woody. If any time was right, now was definitely it.

"We can do it in the treehouse," Jane suggested, a venue she had decided on the year before. "I'll pull the ladder up."

To Gene's profound humiliation, he came the instant his penis touched Jane's wiry pubic hair. He lay there in stricken silence. He wondered if there was any chance that Jane might not have noticed.

"You didn't even get it in!" Jane said. She had waited ages! For this?

"I was just warming up," Gene said, annoyed at Jane. As

his anger mounted, so did something else. His cock, Gene noticed, was getting stuff again. "Jojo never lets me down."

This time Gene got it all the way in, and this time he did not come so soon.

"How was it?" Gene asked when he was done. His pale skin was flushed, his pompadour, like Jojo, temporarily deflated. Gene felt he had done well and he expected recognition for his accomplishment.

"So-so," said Jane. She had not yet learned to tell men that they were wonderful no matter what. She had not yet found out about the prickly relationship between men and their pricks. She had felt something, that much was definite, but she wasn't sure exactly what. She felt sort of hot and congested down there, but she wasn't transported like the heroines in the sexy novels she devoured. The earth hadn't moved, although Jane noticed that the leaves on the branch above them *had* stirred a little. Wilma would have sniffed and said it was the breeze. Jane, ever the optimist, was willing to give Gene the benefit of the doubt.

"We can try again," offered Gene magnanimously, confident now in good old Jojo.

It was not an offer that Jane refused. Not then and not ever, she always bragged.

Sex made Jane feel good. Sex got Jane the attention she craved. Sex was a way of dancing through life.

5
JANE

1 9 5 9 :

[It's] not writing at all—it's typing.

—Truman Capote on Jack
Kerouac's work

FROM 1957 to 1961, the years that Jane spent at the University of Missouri, the choice was between hip and square. Square was white bread, the white picket fence, Eisenhower, suburbia and the emblematic American family of four: Mom, Dad, one son, one daughter. Square was panty girdles and gray flannel suits, Pat Boone and Debbie Reynolds, Percy Faith and the *Saturday Evening Post*.

"For drones," said Jane.

Hip had all the glamour—and all the danger. Its centers were on the edges of the continent. On the East Coast, Greenwich Village was a patchwork of Brendan Behan bars, coffeehouses reverberating to the beat of bongo drums, experimental theaters, and hole-in-the-wall art galleries. San Francisco was the West Coast capital of hip. North Beach poets agitated against the restraints of rhymed quatrains while bearded, sandal-wearing authors were creating the literature of bebop.

On both coasts, pot, pacificism, anarchy, group gropes, and a romanticized portrait of "spades" all bubbled together in the roiling kettle labeled hip.

It was a choice that, because of geography, age, and sex, Jane did not have to make, although she did take to wearing peasant blouses and dangling silver earrings as a badge of her sympathy to all things creative and artistic. She also let her hair grow and wore it in an untamed frizzle.

"You look like a beatnik," commented an awed and respectful Amy.

"You look like you need a comb," said Wilma.

"I consider that a compliment," replied Jane, refusing to be put on the defensive by Wilma's lack of imagination.

From her distant vantage point in the Midwest, Jane was attracted to hip because of its air of open sexuality and because the beatniks were the first group she had ever heard of that actually seemed to think that writers were important.

The problem was that Jane could not identify with any of the heroes of hip because they were all male. Defiantly, muscularly, undeniably male. Their testosterone-crazed, alcohol-fueled writing had undoubted energy and excitement, but to Jane these poets and novelists of macho were totally irrelevant to her own experience. She did not want to be a female Jack Kerouac. She wanted to be an American Françoise Sagan.

"Young, sexy, and famous," she told Wilma, confiding her dream.

Jane wrote her senior thesis on the differences between *Bonjour Tristesse* and *Aimez-Vous Brahms?* and got her accustomed A. For a creative writing course she wrote a novella about a college girl who "accidentally" kills her father's young mistress in a skiing mishap over the Christmas holidays. The plot was unshamedly swiped from *Bonjour Tristesse*. So was the title: *Bonjour, Santa*. And so was the European point of view about sex.

"Immoral! A married man sleeping with a girl young

| 24 |

enough to be his daughter?" said Lucy Ann Pierson, who taught the course. She showed *Bonjour, Santa* to Lionel Sanderson, the head of the English department.

"Amoral!" he told Esther Rowd, the dean of women. Professor Sanderson was upset by a reference to sex play in a ski lift.

Jane's efforts eventually almost got her kicked out of school, so offended were certain members of the faculty and student body. The comments ranged from "disgusting" to "repulsive" to "shocking." The novella and the scandal surrounding it also gained Jane a highly satisfactory campus notoriety.

"I'm a cause célèbre," she told her mother proudly.

"Is that good?" asked her mother.

"Of course. It's exactly what I want," said Jane, pleased at the proof that her talent for attracting attention had not deserted her.

While Jane dreamed of being a famous writer and occasionally wondered what it would be like to be a girlfriend of a famous beatnik writer, she lived her daily life in a comfortable Midwestern world of conservative values and aspirations that any Beat worth his grass and guitar would have sneered at as hopelessly square.

Other than what would become a lifelong penchant for shawls, fringes, and handcrafted jewelry, all that Jane consciously got out of the hip movement of the late Fifties and early Sixties was the conviction that New York—specifically, Greenwich Village—was the most stimulating place in the world. San Francisco never really entered into her dreams because, compared with New York, it seemed like a small town. If Jane ever left St. Louis—not that she was planning to—one reason would be to get away from smallness.

As the lyric of the time went, Jane enjoyed being a girl. Sort of. She religiously shaved her legs, plucked her eyebrows, and skipped dessert. She set her hair every night before she went to bed. Even though she followed all the advice in the fashion magazines, nothing, including using flat beer as a setting lotion, ever gave her sparse, lank hair the slightest bit of body. A dorm-administered Toni one dateless Saturday night was a disaster that caused her already thin hair to break off and fall out.

The only problem that bothered Jane more than her impossible hair was her impossible body. No matter how many desserts she skipped or how long she subsisted on cottage cheese and black coffee, her hips never became truly svelte and her ass never shrank below what she considered balloon proportions. The most that ever happened was that after a week of puritanical dieting which Calvin himself would have admired, Jane would get so crabby and shaky that she would run out for a hot fudge sundae in self-defense.

Jane found herself in a perpetual, irreconcilable dilemma. If she ate, she felt good but looked lousy. If she didn't eat, she looked better but felt awful. She hated herself for her inability to control her body any more than she could control her hair. Big ass. Big thighs. Why, oh why, she asked herself a million times, had the Rubenesque body ever gone out of style?

Doing what everyone else did, Jane played the field during freshman and sophomore years. However, being Jane, she played harder than most. She fell in and out of love with record-breaking frequency and emotion-shattering intensity. She was a self-declared victim of love, a fool for love, a love addict and a love junkie. She thought that each love would be the last love and that every love was destined to be the great love—until the next love came along. What her grandmother had written about in discreet hues of lavender, Jane lived, day in and day out, in violent shades of purple.

Along with furnace blasts of passion, sex was the great lure that Jane had to offer and she was generous, for those days, in the way she offered it. She got a reputation on campus for putting out, a reputation Jane embraced.

"Virginity is for the timid," she declared grandly in her smokiest voice. "I'm not promiscuous. I'm passionate."

Passion, Jane thought, was the answer to everything. Passion, she thought, was the very reason for living.

Despite her flamboyant and outspoken rebellion against the sexual constraints of the times, in senior year, right on schedule and right along with almost everyone else, Jane got pinned.

The happy pinner was Nick Kandaris, a recent graduate of the St. Louis School of Pharmacy. He was the third of five children, a dark-haired, serious-minded, handsome young man. His feet were solidly on the ground, his future carefully mapped out in his mind. He wanted a wife, a family, and financial security. He was willing to work hard to achieve his goals and in return expected to reap the rewards of happiness and wealth.

Jane met Nick at the Municipal Theater during the intermission of the roadshow production of *The Diary of Anne Frank.* Nick was attending the play with his cousin, a classmate of Jane's. As Jane entered the theater with her current love, the bearded announcer of the campus radio station's jazz program, Nick noticed her. She was hard to miss in a long, flowing, very low-cut dress of purple crushed velvet accessorized with lacy tights, rhinestone-buckled shoes, dangling silver earrings, and a multicolored shawl shot through with glittering threads. With her ripe figure and unruly hair, she looked like an Italian art-film queen.

"Who's that?" asked Nick.

"That's Miss Round Heels, the campus punchboard. She was almost expelled," the cousin explained, adding, "She writes dirty stories and says they're art."

A voluptuous lady pornographer? To Nick, that meant one thing: she probably put out. As the house lights dimmed, he asked for an introduction.

"You'll be sorry," warned the cousin, settling back to enjoy the play.

Already besotted with hormonal intoxication, Nick paid no attention.

6
JANE

"All my life, I've known better than
to depend on the experts. How
could I have been so stupid as to let
them go ahead?"

—John Kennedy on the
Bay of Pigs disaster

AT intermission the introduction was made. The attraction was mutual, immediate, irresistible. Nick was no fool. He knew an energetic, uninhibited sexpot when he saw one—particularly one who was such a live wire that even he could almost see the sparks.

Jane wasn't blind either. She recognized a starry-eyed emotional slave when one crossed her path. Especially when he had long, dark eyelashes, blue velvet eyes, satiny olive skin, and dazzling white teeth. Not to mention six feet of athletic body stretched over superbly proportioned bones. When the play was over, Jane left with Nick.

"What happened to your date?" asked a slightly dazed but delighted Nick when Jane took his arm.

"I told him I met someone," Jane said gaily, acutely aware that Nick's well-formed mouth seemed born to be kissed.

"Just like that? What did he say? Wasn't he upset?" Nick

asked. Despite the flattery, Nick didn't entirely approve. He was by nature an orderly person, unaccustomed to sudden changes of plans, a stranger to caprice.

"Sure he was upset. He said he'd die without me," Jane said. She didn't seem the least bit disturbed.

"He did?" Nick looked at Jane for a moment. He wasn't sure if Jane was teasing him or not.

"Just because he said he'd die doesn't mean he will. He'll go home, smoke a joint, and play a John Coltrane record. He'll recover," Jane said calmly. She'd been through her boyfriend's melodramatic routines before.

Ex-boyfriend, from the way things looked, Nick reminded himself, reeling slightly from the speed with which things had progressed.

"Together we will turn the earth to paradise! Oh, what you will be to me and what I will be to you," whispered Jane as she and Nick left the theater and headed for the street. She was impressed by her own romantic words, overcome with the poetry and promise of it all.

"I knew what was going to happen between us the moment I saw you," breathed Jane in her low, sexy voice, as they sat in Nick's car after the play and headed for an Italian restaurant.

Nick's heart pounded so hard and so fast at Jane's romantic words and promise of erotic ecstasy that he was afraid she could hear the sound. He cleared his throat loudly and tried to concentrate on his driving.

Jane sat close to Nick, wedging him so far over that the door handle spiked uncomfortably into his side. Not that he particularly noticed. Jane's hand was on his knee. Her warm, moist breath in his ear sent shafts of painful-pleasurable electric shocks down the length of his entire body. From brain to groin, he was enveloped in waves of heat and desire.

At the Villa Sorrento, Nick asked for, and got, a corner table.

Before the antipasto was served, Jane's hand was on Nick's

thigh. Over the eggplant Parmesan, it drifted upward toward his cock. By the time espresso arrived, Jane's tongue was deep in Nick's ear.

"Let's get out of here. Let's go someplace where we can be alone," Jane whispered.

Gesturing for the check, Nick laid down some bills. Unable to wait a minute longer, forgetting all about the change, Nick and Jane fled the peering customers, the red-flocked wallpaper, and candles stuck in straw covered Chianti bottles for the privacy and darkness of the parking lot.

They threw themselves into Nick's car and flung themselves on each other. They ripped off their clothes as they covered each other with wet kisses and hot hands.

"Oh, Jesus," Nick kept saying, barely able to believe the rapture that had magically, undeservedly, come his way. "Oh, Jesus."

"Jane," Jane corrected. "My name is Jane."

Even though more than half blinded by raging sexual fever in the early days of their romance, Nick and Jane had their occasional moments of clarity. Earthbound himself, a typical Capricorn, one of his sisters said, Nick had an inchoate longing to live more fully and richly. Jane's world throbbed with life, change, and drama, and when Nick was with her he felt truly alive. He was dazzled by her words, observations, and emotional intensity.

"I've never met anyone as interesting as you. You feel things twenty times more deeply than anyone else," he told Jane.

Nick was enthralled by the kaleidoscopic range of Jane's passions and enthusiasms. He wished that he could achieve for himself some of her unfettered emotional freedom.

"I know I keep things in too much. It's much healthier to let go a little," he said, hoping that Jane's example might be an inspiration to him.

Jane, for her part, was attracted to more than just Nick's handsome good looks. She admired his common sense and steadiness of purpose. Knowing how erratic she could be, Jane thought that some of Nick's stability and discipline might rub off on her.

"God, I'd love to be organized!" she said, impressed when Nick showed her how he had filed all his copies of *TV Guide* by date in case he wanted to remember when he'd seen a certain program.

Jane responded instinctively to Nick's obvious enslavement. There was, for Jane, nothing quite as irresistible as a man who made his passionate attraction and boundless adoration totally obvious. No amount of flattery was too much for Jane.

"You're a genius," Nick said, when it was announced that Jane would graduate cum laude.

"You're brilliant," he declared, when one of her short stories was accepted for publication in the *Missouri Literary Review*.

"You are wonderful. The audience loved you," he said when Jane roused a debating society audience with a defense of the suicides of two romantic heroines—Anna Karenina and Emma Bovary.

"But not as much as I love you. We were meant for each other," Nick added.

"Kiss me," said Jane.

Only Bobby expressed reservations.

"Nick's a fungus-brain," he told Jane. "All he does is sit around and watch sports on television. He's going to drive you crazy."

"Buzz off," replied Jane.

By Valentine's Day, Jane was wearing a diamond engagement ring and picking out a wedding dress. Her dreams of becoming a Midwestern Françoise Sagan had receded and, whenever anyone reminded Jane of them, she said that love came first. Her career could wait.

"Nick matters most. I can always write later," Jane declared. She no longer dreamed of adoring reviews and world-wide celebrity. Instead, she found all the adoration and celebrity she needed right at home with Nick.

Like most of her contemporaries, Jane spent most of the spring term of senior year wondering how many children she and Nick would have and what their names would be. They spent weekends house hunting and planning their future. Jane became interested in silver and china patterns and spent hours trying to decide what kind of a bedspread to buy for their new house.

"Chenille launders easily but damask is more elegant," she said, trying to make up her mind.

"I'm going to puke," said Bobby, making a disgusting sound effect to illustrate his intention.

"Do me a favor and go do it somewhere else," said Jane, ignoring his bratty remarks.

The wedding was set for the twentieth of June, two days after Jane's graduation from college. Almost everyone who knew her breathed a sigh of relief that crazy, wild, rebellious Jane would settle down at last.

"We're so glad you're going to be sensible," said Jane's mother when she and Jane went to Famous-Barr to pick out Jane's china pattern. "Daddy and I were worried about you."

"Worried?" replied Jane. She assumed that her mother was relieved that she had gotten through college without getting pregnant. Not that Jane's hectic sex life was something she and her parents discussed.

"You always had this idea about being a writer ever since you learned to read. Your dad and I didn't say anything because we didn't want to rain on your parade," said Etta Gresch, her hazel eyes, just like Jane's, level and sincere with emotion. "But it's a terrible life. My mother was always waiting for the next check. We didn't want you to struggle like she did. Now you'll marry Nick and the two of you are going to live happily ever after just the way Daddy and I have."

Etta Gresch looked into her daughter's future and saw safety, security, and stability. She looked into her own past and remembered a childhood shadowed by unending financial adversity. Her father had never held a full-time job. He had worked as a house painter, a contractor, a handyman. He dreamed of going into business for himself and making a fortune but never quite summoned the will or the energy to pull himself together. Money was always scarce.

Etta recalled the humiliation of eviction, the bleak dinners of cold cereal and water, the monthly anxieties over the rent, the light, the phone, the screaming battles over money between her mother and father. Etta's scars were still raw. She was relieved when Jane gave up her impractical dreams of becoming a writer and decided to marry Nick. With the hard-working, down-to-earth Nick by her side, Jane would never have to worry, never have to struggle, never have to bear the wounds that she herself had borne.

Etta waited for Jane to say something, but Jane, who usually had an instant answer for everything and everyone, was, for once in her life, silent.

At her mother's loving words, Jane found herself unable to breathe. Standing in the china department of Famous-Barr next to the Wedgwood display, she feared she would pass out. She felt as if suddenly all the air had been forced from the room.

"Are you all right?" Etta Gresch asked, frightened by Jane's strange expression and uncharacteristic silence.

"I'm fine," gasped Jane. She plastered over her panic with a smile and in a moment she was able to breathe again.

The moment had passed. The seizure was over. The message from the unconscious was quickly forgotten, buried in the avalanche of prewedding plans, details, and crises.

In the following weeks, whenever the conversation turned to Jane's happy future with Nick that terrifying moment at Famous-Barr would recur. Talk of the five children Nick wanted, the house and the car and the dog would start Jane's heart pounding. Her pulse would race. She would gasp for breath. Jane told Nick about her attacks.

"They're awful. I can't breathe. I'm scared I'll die," Jane said.

"You're probably being dramatic," Nick said. "As usual."

"As usual," Jane repeated with a smile. She already felt relieved. Nick's calm, the opposite of Jane's penchant for drama, was contagious. It was one of the things Jane loved most about him.

The attacks got worse as the wedding date drew closer. The periods of breathlessness lasted longer. Jane gasped for air. She was afraid she would suffocate.

"I don't understand what's the matter. I'm fine. Except when I'm not," Jane told Nick, mystified by what was happening to her. This time, he did not brush off Jane's concern so casually.

At Nick's suggestion, Jane went to the doctor. He examined her and declared her to be in perfect health. She was, he said paternally, probably suffering from a touch of anxiety, an entirely understandable bout of prewedding jitters.

"It's nothing to worry about. We'll fix you up right away," he said, reaching for his prescription pad.

Nick, now working at his father's Euclid Street pharmacy, knew all about Miltown.

"It's new. It's a wonder drug. You'll be fine now," he said confidently, handing Jane the bottle of white pills.

Except that Jane wasn't. The Miltown made Jane feel as if everything were happening in slow motion. She felt as if she were experiencing life through a hazy filter. The Miltown did nothing whatever for the pounding of her heart, the racing of her pulse, or the ghastly episodes of feeling suffocated.

"What's happening? What if I faint during the ceremony?" she asked her mother.

"You won't faint," said her mother. "Every bride gets nervous. It's normal."

7
JANE

JUNE 1961:

"Protect me!"

—Defector Rudolf Nureyev to French
police as he broke from Soviet
guards at Le Bourget Airport
in Paris

PROFESSOR Aaron Engler, head of the University of Missouri's literature department, was considered the campus curmudgeon. He was a small, natty man with observant eyes, a sensualist's mouth, and a sharp mind that could cut through intellectual slovenliness like a saber through cellophane. He habitually wore precisely pressed gray flannel trousers and navy cashmere blazers with solid gold buttons. He had no patience with fools and a waspish tongue most people found it wise to avoid.

Aaron Engler had been Jane's faculty white knight in the scandal over *Bonjour, Santa*. The brouhaha went into high gear when Lucy Ann Pierson gave Jane's novella a failing mark. Outraged, Jane submitted the novella to the campus literary magazine, which rejected it, calling it "pornographic." Jane took the rejection public with a letter to the campus newspaper comparing herself to "pornographers" like Rabelais, D. H. Lawrence, and Philip Roth.

The storm gathered momentum until Jane was on the verge of being expelled from school. At that point, Aaron Engler intervened. He called for a copy of Jane's manuscript.

"I've read *Bonjour, Santa* and find it imaginative, bold, and courageous," he told Esther Rowd in front of the entire faculty. "What's shocking about it is not the sex but the murder. And not one person has objected to that!"

Aaron Engler went on to indict Lucy Ann Pierson with the crime of harboring constipated bourgeois attitudes. He accused the editors of the campus literary magazine of attempting heavy-handed censorship.

"We are here to defend and uphold First Amendment values and to protect the right of creative people to function in an atmosphere of intellectual freedom. The University of Missouri should be proud of students like Jane Gresch," he concluded, eventually persuading Dean Rowd to drop all thoughts of expulsion.

Professor Engler also used his influence and contacts to get *Bonjour, Santa* published in the *Hawthorn Review*.

"I'm a published author," Jane said, showing the *Hawthorn Review* to anyone who came her way. She considered her printed byline the pinnacle of her life.

When the battle was over and victory won, Jane asked Professor Engler to become her campus adviser and, when he agreed, Jane met with him every two weeks during her senior year. True to his iconoclastic reputation, Aaron Engler was the only person not to offer congratulations when Jane showed up for their bi-weekly conference wearing her brand-new engagement ring.

"I thought you were different from the rest of the sheep," he said, referring to the legions of seniors who were proudly flashing their diamonds and picking names for their future children. "What are you going to call your first novel? *Bonjour, Bon Ami?*" he asked. "What are you going to write about? Dirty dishes and diapers?"

Aaron Engler's remark stung. What *was* she going to write about if she got married? Colette had never written about car pools. The ennui that Françoise Sagan suffered was not induced by trips to the supermarket. The parties that Jane Austen described did not take place on suburban patios.

If she married Nick, what *would* she write about? Prescriptions and crab grass?

Jane tried hard not to think about it too much and succeeded fairly well until Amy and Wilma, who were both already married, told her about what happened when the wedding march was over.

"Don't get married!" Amy Sheridan Barry blurted in early May. Amy had been living in Kansas City with her husband and her two children. She had come to St. Louis for Jane's shower. Amy, expecting for the third time in three years, was staying overnight and, now that the rest of the guests were gone, Amy and Jane were in Jane's pink bedroom rehashing the party.

"It's nothing but screaming babies and shitty diapers," Amy said. It was the first time Jane had ever heard Amy use an expletive stronger than "gosh!" A crimson rash of pregnancy angrily dotted Amy's fair complexion and big dark circles were smeared under her eyes.

"I thought you and Jack were happy," said Jane. Amy was Jane's opposite, always pleasant and easygoing.

"We are. As long as I do what Jack says," said Amy. "Jack earns the money and he says that because he does, whatever he wants goes. As long as I do what he wants, everything's fine."

"And if you don't?" asked Jane. She recalled that when she had spoken about going back to her part-time job at the library after their honeymoon, Nick had declared angrily that no wife of his was going to work.

"Sometimes he doesn't speak to me. Other times, he yells and screams," Amy said. She spoke in a matter-of-fact tone, delivering a first-hand report from the front lines of marriage that Jane hadn't heard before but had no reason not to believe. Unlike herself, Amy never exaggerated for effect. "I'm a prisoner. Jack's the warden. If I'm good, I get privileges. If I'm bad, I get shit."

Jane stared at her friend and felt the air begin to leave the room.

Two weeks before the wedding, Wilma Elbaum gave Jane the same advice in the same words. Wilma had eloped with Gene Schuble the previous summer in a St. Louis version of the Romeo and Juliet story. Gene was everything the Elbaums didn't want for their daughter. He wasn't rich. He wasn't Jewish. He wasn't even halfway decently educated. As for prospects, he had none.

Wilma was everything the Schubles didn't want for their son: plain, Jewish, and filled with fancy ideas of being a doctor. Wilma and Gene, crazed with sex and familial opposition, had sneaked away and gotten married. The marriage, according to Wilma, had been a disaster from the beginning.

"Don't get married," she told Jane at, of all times, a wedding rehearsal.

"But I thought you and Gene were madly in love."

"*Were*. Past tense," said Wilma from behind glasses that had gotten thicker as the years had passed. "Love is gone. Romance is gone. Fun is gone. Get married and you can kiss it all goodbye. Our parents barely speak to us. We hardly have any money. Gene works at the body shop and drinks beer after work. He gets home in a rotten mood. If dinner isn't on the table, he has a fit. If it is, nine times out of ten he doesn't like it. One time he threw the whole dinner on the floor and told me to clean it up," Wilma said. "Just be sure you don't make my mistake. If I were you, I'd live a wild life for a few years before I tied myself down."

"Can't you leave?" Jane asked, horrified.

"Where would I go?" Wilma asked angrily. She glared at Jane, defying her to answer.

"You could live with me and Nick," Jane said.

That night, Jane had her worst attack yet. She felt herself begin to gasp for air while she stood at the bathroom sink, brushing her teeth. She was thinking about what Wilma had told her. Then she remembered what Amy had said. The questions of Professor Engler's, which she had been able to forget, suddenly came back.

What are you going to write about? What are you going to call your first novel?

Jane felt lightheaded. She had a brief sensation that her mind was leaving her body and then she blacked out. When she came to a few moments later, she was on the bathroom floor. Luckily, she had fallen on the mat.

"If I had fallen on the tile, I might have hurt myself seriously," she told Nick.

"Maybe you're pregnant," he said.

As the date of the wedding came closer and closer, Jane woke up every night gasping for breath and remembering how Amy had described being a wife as being a prisoner. She was haunted by the way Wilma had found herself trapped with a young husband turned vicious. She kept hearing Professor Engler's sour tone and unanswerable questions.

Jane could no longer quite so blithely dismiss Bobby's comments about Nick as the obnoxious remarks of a jerky kid. She counted the days on her calendar and wasn't sure whether or not she was relieved when she got her period. Pregnancy would have explained her fainting spells. Pregnancy would have been the trap she couldn't escape.

"I want to postpone the wedding for a while," Jane told Nick two days before the wedding. She knew how irresponsible her words must have sounded but she needed more time. Time to think. Time to breathe.

"Postpone? The cake is ordered," Nick said, thinking that either he hadn't heard quite right or that somehow Jane had forgotten all about the cake.

Jane stared at him.

"Cake? Cake! I'm talking about my *life* and you're thinking about a fucking cake?"

"It's been paid for. I went to the bakery myself," said Nick.

Jane blinked. She looked at Nick and wondered suddenly who this man from Mars was. Bobby was right. He was a drone. Nick's plodding literalism about the cake was absolutely unbelievable. Was this someone she knew? Was this someone she wanted to *marry*?

Jane burst into tears and ran out of the room. Nick watched her go. He didn't understand. What on earth could he have said to set her off like that?

I'm going to Greenwich Village, Jane wrote to Nick later that afternoon. She took off her engagement ring and put it into the envelope along with her note.

Jane's wedding gown was hanging on her closet door. The dyed-to-match satin shoes were in their tissue-lined box. The veil was carefully arranged on the standing lamp. Jane knew that her parents might be furious but she also knew that, once they calmed down, they would realize that a canceled wedding was better than a miserable daughter trapped in a suffocating marriage.

Jane dropped the note into the Kandarises' front-door mail slot on her way to the airport. Like Nureyev defecting to the West, Jane jetéd to freedom. She'd never been on a plane in her life. She'd never been to New York in her life. Yet she was too determined to be scared, too committed to her future—whatever it would turn out to be—to turn back. All she knew was that she felt like a woman who had barely escaped a death sentence. For the first time in months, she breathed easily.

Jane's heart rose as loftily as the plane that soared above the earth. The fear of crashing never entered her mind. Neither did the fear of flying.

8
LINCKY

1 9 5 9 :

High hopes! I've got high hopes!

—from "High Hopes" by Sammy Cahn
and Jimmy Van Heusen

LINCKY Desmond was born Lincoln Ten Eyck on April 10, 1941. She grew up in Westport, Connecticut, and she was just as stylish and impressive as her name. Lincky's father was a successful wine importer and her mother, who was thirty-eight when Lincky was born, was her husband's partner in Ten Eyck Importing. Warren and Helene had been married for thirteen years when their first and only child was born. Lincky would be the heiress to the company they had built.

Lincky's parents introduced her to wine at an early age. In the European style, they served her a teaspoonful diluted with water. Lincky's father taught her to know and appreciate the grand vintages of France. Her mother was an authority on the less celebrated but well-made bottlings from smaller properties and introduced Lincky to their qualities and nuances.

"It's important to develop your palate," her mother told her. "One day you'll join us at work."

"Eventually Ten Eyck Importing will be yours. You'll need

to know about all aspects of the business," her father said, instructing Lincky in the business and financial side of his profession.

During their leisure moments, Lincky's parents affectionately competed over who could pay the most attention to her. A sports fan, Lincky's father taught her to ride, to play tennis, and to skate. He took her to baseball games, tennis matches, and horseshows.

"You're the best date of all," he would tell her, delighting in her gaiety and responsiveness. "The man who gets you is going to be one lucky fellow."

A diplomat's daughter, Helene handled the social side of the business. She entertained constantly and introduced Lincky to a wide range of people.

"I'm so proud of you, Lincky. You can talk to anyone from a baron in St. Emilion to one of the workers who brings in the harvest for him. You're comfortable in a four-star hotel *and* in a roadside café. Being able to fit in is very important in our business," her mother said, pleased with her daughter's adaptability and poise.

Lincky and her parents formed a magic circle of three. Within that charmed circle, Lincky was cherished and protected. She knew that nothing bad could ever happen to her.

From the moment that she learned her ABC's, Lincky loved to read. She went from *Babar* and *Dick and Jane* to *Wind in the Willows* and *Charlotte's Web*. She was entranced by the Pooh stories and had every title in the Five Little Peppers series on her bookshelves. She devoured every single one of the Nancy Drew mysteries and graduated from them to Agatha Christie.

Lincky's classmates called her "Miss Nose-in-a-Book."

"Better than Miss Nose-in-the-Air," Lincky replied, unruffled by their teasing.

Reading, her father told Lincky, was an indication of high intelligence. "You have a good brain. It's important that you use it," he said, urging her to develop her mind.

Lincky's mother agreed. Helene also thought that Lincky was beautiful and made sure that Lincky thought so, too.

"Those big blue eyes come from my side of the family and that thick, blond hair comes from your father's side,'" Helene told her daughter. "Even if you weren't my child, I'd think you were lovely. Just remember, though, that beauty isn't everything. Character and hard work count, too."

Lincky's parents wanted the best for Lincky and they expected the best *from* Lincky. Inadvertently, they led her to believe that failure was unacceptable.

The number of Lincky's accomplishments at Westport High rivaled the number of cashmere sweaters in her dresser drawers. She was captions editor of the yearbook, captain of girls' tennis, and maintained a straight A average. Her parents rewarded her with a bottle-green Jaguar just as soon as she got her driver's license.

Lincky's outstanding high school record was followed by further laurels at Wellesley. She received Phi Beta Kappa grades, led the tennis team to its second-best record in a decade, and worked on the campus newspaper. Her love life was less satisfactory.

Lincky was attracted to older, quite successful men. During junior year she went steady with Philip Apt, a senior at Harvard medical school who wanted her to drop out of Wellesley and move to Chicago where he would do his residency. Lincky, confronting her first conflict between love and achievement, didn't quite know what to do.

"I have only one year to go at Wellesley. I want to get my degree," she said.

"Do you love me or don't you?" Philip asked. "If you loved me, we'd get married right away and you could go to Chicago to be with me."

"I love you but what would I do in Chicago?" asked Lincky.

"Shop, keep house, gossip with the other wives," he said.

"I don't like to shop, I'm not particularly domestic, and I'm not a gossip," said Lincky. "I have a feeling you haven't noticed the first thing about me."

Philip shrugged. "Have it your way. If you don't want to go, I'll find someone who will."

"You mean I'll be that easy to replace?" Lincky asked.

"I need a wife," he said, as if that explained everything.

In her senior year, Lincky had an affair with a divorced professor who was fifteen years older than she was. Ronald Timkens was an authority on Elizabethan literature and had written standard biographies of Shakespeare and Marlowe. He was elegant, distinguished, and witty. Lincky thought it was love. Her roommate told her that it wasn't.

"He's notorious for going to bed with the prettiest girl in every senior class," Lincky's roommate told her. "My sister graduated from Wellesley two years ago and Ron came on to her, too. The minute she graduated, he dumped her."

"You mean I'm just part of a whole parade?" asked Lincky. She was accustomed to being the one and only.

"I'm afraid so."

When Lincky confronted her lover with her knowledge, he did not deny it.

"What's wrong with that?" Ronald asked. "A new crop to choose from every year is one of the perks of teaching in a girls' school."

"You don't really love me, then, do you?" asked Lincky.

"Of course I really love you. For now," he said. He had a seductive smile, a caressing voice.

"For now?" asked Lincky. She had been brought up to think that love was for always. "At the end of the year, it'll be over?"

"Let's enjoy it while it lasts," he replied.

Lincky shook her head.

"I do not intend to be this year's flavor," she said, canceling their rendezvous for that evening.

Lincky was not quite sure why her romances had gone

wrong. Had Philip Apt been arrogant or was she too indepen-dent? Was Ronald Timkens a calculating womanizer or was her own pride at fault? Like most women of her time, Lincky tended to blame herself for the difficulties she encountered with men. Her mother told her not to.

"You're special, Lincky. One day you'll meet someone who's also special," Helene Ten Eyck said.

"I hope so. I want my marriage to be just as happy as yours," Lincky said.

"It will be," her mother promised. "You'll just have to be patient."

Except for a few blind dates that didn't work out, Lincky spent the rest of senior year without a boyfriend or even the prospect of one. During leisure moments, while most of her classmates were knitting argyle socks for their boyfriends at Yale and Harvard, Lincky read.

She wept over *Anna Karenina*. *Madame Bovary* burned itself into her soul. She read *Rabbit, Run* straight through and dreamed of walking with John Updike through a crisp, sunny New England autumn afternoon. She gobbled up *The Carpetbaggers* and imagined having champagne and caviar with Harold Robbins in Hollywood. She lost herself in *Out of Africa* and had fantasies of taking tea on a veranda overlooking the Ngong Hills with Baroness Blixen.

"My collection of Modern Library Classics even outnum-bers my collection of cashmere sweaters," she told her father, laughingly commenting on her dual obsessions. "If only I had a boyfriend, my life would be prefect."

Lincky, like every young woman of her generation, wanted to get married and have children. However, molded by her parents' example, Lincky also looked forward to working. She wanted to do her share to help make Ten Eyck Importing even bigger and better.

"When you get out of college, you'll come to work for us," her father said. "At first you'll work in the office. It's not the most glamorous part of the business but it's just as essential as knowing how to choose the right wines."

To prepare for her future, Lincky took a typing course the summer after her senior year at Wellesley.

"From the *caves* and *chais* to Katherine Gibbs, I'll have all the bases covered," she joked.

Lincky and her parents spent the Labor Day weekend of 1961 at the White Elephant Inn in Nantucket. On Tuesday morning, in their annual ritual, her parents took the charter service to Idlewild, where they planned to connect with the Air France flight to Paris. Lincky would stay on in Nantucket until the end of the week before returning home.

September was harvest time in Bordeaux and Burgundy, and ever since the end of World War II Warren and Helene had traveled through the vineyards making their selections for Ten Eyck Importing. This year, knowing that Lincky would be working in the office, they went off with lighter hearts than usual.

It would be their last trip.

Lincky was still at the White Elephant when its manager, Robin Rodgers, took her into his office and informed her of the accident. The Piper had gone down. All four people aboard had perished.

"Your parents' plane crashed," he told Lincky. "I'm sorry but they didn't survive."

"Crashed? Why?"

"Engine failure," said the manager.

Failure. The word echoed down dark, forbidden corridors.

Lincky, who rarely cried, sobbed. Lincky, who always knew where she was going, was lost. She blamed herself for the accident. If she had gone along, there would have been too many passengers for the small charter. Her mother and father would have had to take the regularly scheduled plane. There would have been no crash. Her parents would have lived. Instead, they were dead and it was her fault.

"I'm all right," she told Robin when her tears had subsided. "I want to be alone for a while."

Lincky went to her room. She couldn't accept the news. She went through the two suitcases her parents had left for her to bring home to Westport. Lincky touched her mother's perfume to her wrists and put on one of her father's old sweaters. The physical evidence of her parents' existence didn't change what Robin Rodgers had told her. In her father's bag, Lincky found an almost full vial of sleeping pills. She swallowed them all and lay down on the bed. She wanted to be with her parents.

Lincky woke up in Nantucket's Cottage Hospital. Alvin Hayes was in the room. He was a spare, blond man who had been the Ten Eycks' lawyer for over a decade. With their deaths, he had become their executor and Lincky's guardian.

"That was a silly thing to do," he said in a kind way. "Fortunately, Mr. Rodgers decided to look in on you when you didn't come down to dinner. He brought you right here and the doctors pumped your stomach."

"Is that why my throat hurts?"

"Yes. You'll be fine. But you have to promise me that you'll be a good girl from now on. Just think what your parents would say if they knew. They'd think you're not very responsible. They'd think that you've let them down."

"They'd be so disappointed," said Lincky, thinking of the way her parents had always stressed the importance of discipline and self-control. "They'd be right."

"Will *you* be all right?"

"Yes."

"And you promise to take care of yourself?"

"I promise," Lincky said. She told herself to be strong and she was. She warned herself not to cry in public and she didn't. She promised her parents that she would make them proud of her and assured Alvin Hayes that he didn't have to worry about her. Lincky consciously pulled herself together and at the funeral Lincky's relatives remarked on how well she dealt with the tragedy.

"You're such a grownup," said Lincky's cousin on her father's side. Martha Rellis, who was thirty-five, was closest to Lincky in age and had come in from Utah to be with Lincky.

"Your parents would be pleased at the way you've acted," said her grandfather on her father's side, Lincky's only surviving grandparent. He was almost eighty and looked to Lincky for comfort.

"Lincky's like Helene. She knows how to act like a lady. She'll be just fine," said Helene's sister, Rosita. Rosita Tarnell invited Lincky to come to Atlanta to live with her but looked relieved when Lincky politely turned her down.

Through an Ottawa law firm, a large Canadian liquor combine approached the Ten Eyck estate. It wanted to buy Ten Eyck Importing. Alvin knew that Lincky was too young and inexperienced to run the company. He was uncertain of her emotional stability. Wanting to carry out his duty as Lincky's guardian and ensure her financial future, Alvin Hayes agreed to sell Ten Eyck Importing. He negotiated shrewdly and obtained an excellent price.

Alvin Hayes had behaved impeccably but, instead of inheriting the family business on which she had focused her future, Lincky received a check. She had money but she belonged nowhere. Her family was gone and her future had vanished. The magic circle was broken and Lincky was outside.

9
LINCKY

OCTOBER, 1961:

Roger Maris hits 61 homers,
breaking Babe Ruth's record.

LINCKY moved to Manhattan in the early fall of 1961, the same
season in which two bellwether literary works first appeared.
Franny and Zooey, J. D. Salinger's mystical novella, ran in the
New Yorker and Joseph Heller's black World War II comedy,
Catch 22, was published by Simon & Schuster.

Franny and Zooey pointed the way to the fascination with
Eastern religions and transcendental states that would charac-
terize much of the head tripping of the Sixties. *Catch 22* was
one of the first commercially successful works to capture the
antiestablishment mood and pervasive disrespect for authority
that would become another of the decade's distinguishing
motifs. The decade's assault on the traditional power centers
formerly ruled entirely by Protestant, middle-aged white men
would dovetail with Lincky's ambition and energy and provide
her with opportunities and frustrations she would not have
encountered a generation before.

The Ten Eycks' Westport house was far too big for one person and too filled with memories; Lincky decided to move to New York, where she would be surrounded by people. She asked Alvin Hayes to sell the house, and she rented an apartment on the East Side near Bloomingdale's. She opened charge accounts at the Doubleday, Scribner, and Brentano bookstores and decided to get a job in publishing.

"I like to read," she told Alvin Hayes. "I might as well get paid for it."

A job would also be a good way of staying occupied, Lincky thought. Keeping busy had always been her parents' prescription for problems and difficulties. Since her parents' death, Lincky had learned to keep her feelings at arm's length. She felt that if she could control her life, she could control herself.

Via the unexciting, nuts-and-bolts method of answering an employment ad in the *New York Times*, Lincky got an interview at *Women's World* magazine, a successful combination of the *Ladies' Home Journal* and *House Beautiful*. *Women's World* featured, according to its slogan, the three R's: recipes, renovation, and reading. When Lincky applied for a job at *Women's World*, its success and influence were at their apogee. Circulation was in the millions. Advertising revenues consistently reached new highs. The audience was middle-class, middle-of-the-road middle America.

"The book editor needs a secretary," said the personnel director, skipping right over Lincky's Phi Betta Kappa background and experience as a yearbook editor. "Can you type?"

"Yes," replied Lincky and proved it with a 55-words-a-minute demonstration.

Lincky reported for work the second week of September. Her boss, Charlie Lamb, was white haired and white bearded and had twinkling blue eyes. Lincky thought that he resembled a thin but potbellied Santa Claus, not only in looks but also in his jovial personality. She wondered if he would become a friend or even a father figure.

In his late fifties, Charlie was married but childless and his life centered on publishing. Charlie had been the book editor of *Women's World* for almost twenty years, and before that had worked as a reader and then an editor at Doubleday. His wife, whom he had met while working at Doubleday, was still employed there as a secretary in the production department.

Charlie had a good nose for fiction. Thanks to him, *Women's World* had become known for its excellent book excerpts and condensations. At the time Lincky went to work for Charlie, however, he had begun to coast. Charlie had done his job so long that he functioned on automatic pilot.

"I don't read anymore. I know from the publisher's catalog descriptions which books will interest *Women's World* readers and which won't," he admitted.

Charlie was fond of the long, liquid lunches for which publishing was renowned. He liked a martini or two and a half bottle of white wine along with his midday meal. Sometimes, when there was something special to celebrate or if he was just in a particularly good mood, he also ordered a brandy along with his coffee. Charlie was not alone in his habits and found many colleagues with whom to share the lunch dates that publishing had elevated almost to the level of sacrament.

"I think he was drunk yesterday afternoon," Lincky told Coral Weinstein, the beauty editor.

"So what else is new?" replied Coral.

Lincky quickly realized that the Charlie Lamb who went out to lunch was not the same Charlie Lamb who came back. Run-on sentences whose point was somehow lost, a tendency toward forgetting what he said or did in the afternoon, and bouts of sleepiness were all symptoms of Charlie's alcoholic intake. Lincky soon found out that if any important decisions had to be made, they had better be made in the morning when caffeine was Charlie's fuel of choice.

Without making any undue fuss, Lincky got into the habit

of arriving at work every morning at eight thirty. As soon as Charlie arrived at the office, Lincky smilingly served him a container of coffee and a punch list of projects.

"The bidding deadline for first serial rights for *To Kill a Mockingbird* is today," she reminded him.

"Larry Bodine was supposed to turn in the condensation of the Irving Stone last Friday. Do you want me to call him?" Lincky asked, speaking of a habitually dilatory freelance editor.

"The manuscript of the new Irving Wallace novel just came in. It's about the behind-the-scenes drama surrounding the Nobel Prize. Everyone's going to want it. If we want a chance, you should call Adam Carloe," she said, referring to the agent who handled the first serial rights.

Lincky became very interested in her job. She took to reading the office copy of *Publishers Weekly*, the publishing industry's trade journal. She sometimes mentioned about-to-be-published books that she thought sounded just right for *Women's World*. She told Charlie which authors had changed publishers, which books had been picked up by the book clubs and which had been sold to the movies. With no family and no boyfriend, Lincky was happy to take work home and she read every galley and manuscript that came into the office.

No one, least of all Charlie Lamb, ever sat down and told Lincky what her job should consist of. Out of a combination of interest, a determination to stand out and a search for forgetfulness, Lincky simply made it up as she went along. She saw what had to be done and, without a syllable of opposition from Charlie, went ahead and did it.

"Why do you work so hard? You don't think Charlie is going to reward you for it, do you?" Coral asked.

"Of course," replied Lincky.

"Wait till you ask for anything beside the standard raise."

"I don't know what I ever did without you, Lincky," Charlie said after Lincky had worked for him for three months. He was delighted with his fireball secretary and the more

Lincky wanted to do, the more willing Charlie was to let her do it.

"You're the greatest, Lincky. You saved my butt," Charlie would say, coming back later and later from lunch, his cheeks flushed, his nose red, confident that during his sojourn at Chanticleer, Brussels, or the Italian Pavilion, Lincky would have smoothly covered for his absence with the managing editor, fielded his phone calls, and independently drafted answers to the letters that needed a response.

In December, Charlie called Lincky into his office.

"How'd you like to go to a party tonight?" he asked. Charlie received constant invitations to publishing parties, screenings, and advertiser's functions. Almost every day, Charlie left the office at five P.M. and headed for a business-related party to continue the drinking he had started at noon.

"The Doubleday Christmas party at the Plaza? I'd love to," said Lincky, assuming that Charlie was inviting her to accompany him.

"No. I'm going to the Doubleday Christmas party alone. This one is from North Star Press," he said, handing Lincky the invitation. She had never heard of North Star Press, a small, recently established paperback publisher of mysteries, male adventure fantasies, and spy novels.

Lincky attended the North Star Press party, held in a nondescript Irish bar on Third Avenue. She met the owner of North Star, Gordon Geiger, who was enthusiastic about the future of paperbacks.

"It's a mass market medium that hasn't really begun to be exploited," he said. "Paperbacks are going to be increasingly powerful *and* profitable."

Lincky also met Ralph Weiss, a former editor who was now working for an agent, the notorious Hank Greene.

"I'm Hank's secret weapon," Ralph told Lincky when she asked him what he did.

"Is he really as bad as everyone says?" asked Lincky, who

had heard the Hank Greene horror stories that regularly circulated.

"He's not Mother Cabrini," replied Ralph.

Lincky also spent time with a writer of paperback originals named Glen Sinclair. He said that he had written over sixty books of all varieties but most of all enjoyed writing subliterate spy thrillers for lip-readers.

"Sixty!" exclaimed Lincky in disbelief.

"It's easy. Basically I'm writing for myself," he unabashedly told Lincky, thus destroying certain of her romantic fantasies about novelists and the rigors of the creative process.

"How was it?" Charlie asked the next morning. He was obviously slightly the worse for wear after the posh Doubleday blowout.

"Interesting," said Lincky. "I enjoyed it."

Charlie began to cull through the invitations and hand the ones that didn't interest him to Lincky. Exercising his prerogative, Charlie continued to go to the big, important parties for the sure-fire bestsellers, the famous authors, the Oscar-quality films, and the more glamorous ad agencies and their clients. He swilled champagne and fine scotch and stoked up on smoked salmon and caviar, all in the name of doing business.

He let Lincky go to the small-time parties no one paid very much attention to, where she contented herself with a Coke and a handful of peanuts. Lincky, happy to have somewhere to go and something to do in the lonely hours when work was over, attended every single party and found that going second class could be fun. She met young editors, reviewers, agents, authors, and up-and-coming stars in the book, film, and advertising worlds.

In January 1962, at one of the second-tier parties given to launch a book about a technical approach to investing, Lincky was introduced to a young stockbroker named Peter Desmond. The author of the book was Harry Desmond, Peter's uncle and his boss at Desmond & Desmond.

"Did Harry pay you to show up?" Peter asked Lincky. He wanted to know what someone like Lincky Ten Eyck—an attractive and well-dressed young woman—was doing there among the stockbrokers and ass kissers.

"*Women's World* pays me to come. I work for the book editor," replied Lincky with a smile, noticing Peter's blond hair, blue eyes, and handsome, strong features. He stood a shade over six feet and wore a well-tailored suit with a blue and white checked Sea Island cotton shirt and a navy and red striped tie—exactly the kind of clothes her father had always worn.

After a few more questions, Peter found out in quick order that Lincky Ten Eyck had grown up in Westport, graduated from Wellesley, and liked to play tennis. No questions were required for him to notice Lincky's huge turquoise eyes, lean, racy figure, and sleek cap of shiny hair cut in a Prince Valiant style. He also noticed that Lincky wore no wedding or engagement ring and decided that Uncle Harry's boring party had turned out not to be so boring after all.

"Would you like to leave? I have a car. We could go to the Village for Italian food," he suggested.

"I'd love to," said Lincky.

She was pleasantly aware that people looked at them admiringly as they left the room.

"What a good-looking couple!" she overheard a woman say. "They look like they were born for each other."

10
LINCKY

1 9 6 2 :

Fly me to the moon,
And let me play among the stars . . .

—from "Fly Me to the Moon"
by Bart Howard

SPAGHETTI (no one called it pasta in those days) went ordered but uneaten and Lincky and Peter sat in the Minetta Tavern on MacDougal Street and talked until almost midnight. Their conversation confirmed what both had sensed almost at first sight: that they were psychic soul mates.

"So you're an only child, too?" asked Lincky when Peter said that he had no brothers or sister.

"My mother was almost thirty-five when I was born. My parents waited a long time for me," he said.

"Mine too," said Lincky. "Did you ever want brothers and sisters?"

"Sometimes," said Peter. "But a lot of the time I liked being special."

"I know exactly how you feel," said Lincky. Then she told him that both her parents were dead.

"They died in an airplane crash on Labor Day weekend," she said.

"Poor baby!" said Peter. "How awful."

"I'm all over it now," said Lincky. She was dry eyed and spoke as if it had all happened a long time ago. "But I have hardly any relatives and the ones that I do have are scattered all over. I really wish I had a brother or sister. That way I'd feel I belonged to someone."

I wish you belonged to me, thought Peter.

As the evening continued, Peter and Lincky began to realize that they had much more in common than similar backgrounds and being only children. They liked Italian and Chinese food but found Mexican and Indian too spicy. They enjoyed Broadway musicals but not the opera. They thought that diet soda was a good idea but that powdered orange drink wasn't. They were both tennis fiends and discussed the coming U.S. Open and the fact that the Australians dominated world tennis.

"This is going to be Rod Laver's year," Peter predicted.

Lincky nodded.

"He's been runner-up the last two years. I think his turn has come," she said, referring to Laver's defeat in 1960 by Neale Fraser and in 1961 by Roy Emerson.

They discussed their tastes in popular music.

"Love Ray Charles," said Lincky.

"Hate Mitch Miller," said Peter.

Then they went on to pop art.

"Robert Indiana is interesting," said Peter.

"Andy Warhol is going to last," said Lincky.

Then television.

"Never watch it," said Peter.

"Except for Johnny Carson," said Lincky.

"Except for Johnny Carson," said Peter.

When Peter dropped Lincky off at the East 61st Street brownstone in which she had a small apartment, Peter asked her to go out with him again.

"Would you like to see Barbra Streisand? I'll get tickets for *I Can Get It for You Wholesale*," he said.

"I'd love to," said Lincky.

"Do you think Streisand is as good as everyone says?" asked Peter as they left the theater.

"Better," said Lincky.

They linked hands and Peter walked Lincky all the way up Broadway and over to her apartment. They talked about what it was like to have parents who were considerably older than their classmates' parents. They reminisced about what it was like to play alone. Lincky recalled a dollhouse and Peter remembered a set of toy soldiers.

"I invented a whole family for my dollhouse. There was a mother, a father, five children, two dogs, a lamb, a pet chicken, a cat, and a canary," Lincky said, laughing.

"My soldiers all had names and heroic deeds. They stormed forts, held off enemies, crossed rivers under fire, captured hills, and rescued their friends," said Peter.

"I've read that only children usually have intense fantasy lives," Lincky said.

"That's why you had your family in the dollhouse and I had my soldiers. We needed more people in our lives and so we made them up."

"I feel I've known you forever," Peter told Lincky as they reached her front door.

"I feel the same way," Lincky said, amazed at how much alike they were. She imagined introducing Peter to her parents and knew that they would have approved of him. *Special*, they would have said. *Just perfect.*

"Have you seen the new TWA terminal yet?" Peter asked Lincky, referring to the recently completed Eero Saarinen building. The grandson of an architect, Peter was an architecture buff.

Lincky shook her head.

"Would you like to go out to Idlewild on Saturday?" he asked. "I could show you the terminal and then we could play tennis at Silver Creek. It's a country club I belong to on Long Island."

"Sounds wonderful," said Lincky.

"Don't you know you're supposed to let the man win?" Peter asked Lincky when she beat him two out of three sets, 6-4, 4-6, 6-3.

"I don't always do what I'm supposed to," replied Lincky. "When I play, I play to win."

"That's unusual for a girl," Peter said.

Lincky shrugged. "I guess I'm an unusual girl. Is that bad?"

"No," said Peter. "It's good."

Peter Desmond came from almost the identical kind of background that Lincky did. His father was a retired Wall Street executive. His mother was the daughter of a prosperous architect. Peter had gone to Andover and then to Yale. He had gotten superior grades, was a member of the tennis team and movie and theater critic of the *Yale Daily News*. He had a Master's degree in economics from Columbia, stockbroker's licenses from New York and Connecticut, and the beginnings of a collection of original architectural drawings. He liked to point out how his experiences paralleled and complemented Lincky's.

"We're both only children. You were the daughter and heiress. I'm the son and heir. I was a good student and so were you. You were on the tennis team and so was I. You were on the school paper and so was I. We're practically twins. You're the female version. I'm the male edition. We like the same things. We share the same background. We even look alike," Peter said.

"It's amazing, isn't it? How much alike we are," agreed Lincky. "Sometimes when I look at you I feel I'm looking into a mirror."

When she was with Peter, Lincky no longer felt alone.

Their sense of identity and unity increased even more when Lincky learned that Peter had also been disappointed by his love life. He had dated frequently throughout college and in the years after. Although he had been pinned once during senior year, he had never been engaged. As he confided to Lincky in early February, none of the girls he should have married appealed to him.

"They all looked the same and they all thought the same. They wore Peter Pan collars over sweaters turned back to front and gold circle pins advertising their virginity," he told Lincky, recalling the campus fashions of his college years. "They were boy-crazy, clothes-crazy, and marriage-crazy. All they wanted were husbands who would provide three or four kids, a station wagon, a handful of charge accounts, and a country club membership. I didn't want to be that kind of husband."

"What kind of husband do you want to be?" asked Lincky.

"Yours," he replied.

Lincky was silent for a moment. She thought over what Peter had just said.

"Is that a proposal?" she asked.

"It's something we should think about," said Peter.

That night Lincky invited Peter up to her apartment.

"I want to do more than just kiss you," Peter said. Their necking had become heavy petting. Lincky's sweater was twisted up above her breasts and Peter's fly was open.

"I want you to," said Lincky. Her hand was on Peter's peter and she couldn't get over the way it was both so strong and so delicate at the same time. She caressed it as Peter's hands circled her breasts and his tongue plunged into her mouth. They were both breathing heavily and neither could wait for the moment of penetration.

"I have a rubber," said Peter.

"Don't use it," said Lincky. "I want to feel you inside me."

"But what if you get pregnant?" said Peter.

"I won't," said Lincky.

"You're sure?" Peter asked.

"Yes," she said, confident of her body and unable to wait another moment. "I need you, Peter. I need to feel you in me. I need you to be part of me."

Everything about Peter made Lincky feel better about herself. He offered the precious salve of familiarity and the priceless illusion of stability. His family was intact, his future planned. From the moment she met Peter, the sense of isolation that had haunted Lincky since she woke up in the Cottage Hospital was dispelled. When she thought about how close she had come to never meeting him, she realized how foolish she had been to swallow her father's sleeping pills.

"I hate to fail. But for once I'm glad I did," she told him.

"I can't believe you really tried to commit suicide," Peter said. Extreme measures were alien to him. So were extreme circumstances.

"My parents were dead and I didn't want to live," said Lincky. "Now I feel just the opposite."

"We'll be together all the time," he said.

"My parents were together all the time," said Lincky.

Peter smiled.

"I love you so much."

"The two of us," Lincky said. "Loved and loving."

The things Peter told Lincky about working in his father's firm made Lincky feel better about the sale of Ten Eyck Importing. Peter was the only male Desmond of his generation and the logical heir to the company his father and uncle had founded. Although Peter's future was at Desmond & Desmond, he chafed at being his uncle's employee.

"My uncle sees me as competition and he does everything he can to cut me down to size," Peter told Lincky. "I'm tired of being criticized all the time and told I don't work hard enough. No matter what I do, my uncle compares me to my father and I come up on the short end."

"You mean I might not have liked working for my parents as much as I think?" Lincky asked. She had always imagined working for Ten Eyck Importing as a harmonious continuation of her privileged childhood.

"Working for the family is a mixed blessing," Peter said.

"It's secure but they take you for granted and even though you're a grownup, they still tend to think of you as a child. They can't help it. It's natural. They're getting older and you're still young. They're getting weaker and you're getting stronger. There's nothing anyone can do about it, but still they resent you for it."

"It must be very difficult for you," said Lincky.

"It comes with the territory," said Peter. "And now that I've met you, it won't be so hard. Love makes all the difference. I never dreamed I'd meet anyone like you."

"You're my love, my family, my future," said Lincky. "I'll do anything to make you happy."

Lincky could not believe how happy she was, and how lucky. Peter was better than a brother, more than a lover. He would be everything to her.

"We'll be just as happy as my parents. Peter and I are perfect for each other," she told Alvin Hayes. "On and off the tennis court."

She did not consider it appropriate to mention that bed was even better than tennis.

Peter officially proposed to Lincky in mid-March as they danced to "Fly Me to the Moon" at a Saturday night dance at the Silver Rock Country Club.

"I don't need an airplane to fly to the moon and dance among the stars," he whispered. "All I need is you."

"And all I need is you," Lincky said, accepting his proposal.

"Remember the night we met? When we were leaving the party I heard a woman say that we looked like we were born for each other," Peter said, holding Lincky close. "I knew then that I was going to fall in love with you."

"I knew it, too," Lincky said. "When I met you, it felt like destiny. I realized then that 'only' doesn't have to mean 'lonely.' "

Lincky and Peter got married in June 1962. Lincky paid for her own wedding out of the special fund her parents had set up when she'd turned sixteen. They'd wanted, they had said so often, to give her the best wedding any girl had ever had. If only her father could be here to meet the wonderful man she'd fallen in love with. If only her mother could share her happiness and her hopes. This happiest moment of Lincky's life, like all her happy moments, was clouded with sad memories. Sweet, for Lincky, was always bittersweet.

Alvin Hayes gave the bride away. The magnums of champagne, put down by her father in the year of Lincky's birth, carried the most prestigious labels as did the clothes in Lincky's trousseau and the linens in her hope chest. Lincky and Peter's future would be furnished with the familiar comforts of their pasts.

At Lincky's request, the band at her wedding played a combination of standard ballads for the older guests and the twist music that had just become ragingly popular for the guests who were the same age as the bride and bridegroom. The bandleader, on his own, added the romantic numbers from the soundtracks of *West Side Story* and *Breakfast at Tiffany's*.

"Breakfast, lunch, and dinner," whispered Peter into Lincky's ear. He wanted to give her everything. Everything Tiffany's had. Everything he had. Everything her heart desired. Including a family. He was twenty-seven. He was ready.

11
LINCKY

1 9 6 2 :

Astronaut John Glenn orbits the
earth three times.
Barbara Walters goes to India on
Jacqueline Kennedy's goodwill
tour for the *Today* show.
Walter Cronkite replaces Douglas
Edwards on the *CBS Evening News*.
Tony Bennett makes the charts with
"I Left My Heart in San
Francisco."

WHEN Lincky returned from her honeymoon, she went back
to her job at *Women's World*. By then, she had learned that the
staff referred to the three R's as the three D's: drapes, diapers,
and diets. She had also learned that *Women's World* (like the
real world) was run by men.

According to the personnel records, Lincky was still officially employed as a secretary. Wearing her brand-new wedding ring, Lincky continued to do Charlie Lamb's typing and
filing. She answered his phone and fetched his coffee and no
longer entertained the fantasy that her boss might replace her
father.

"Usually girls quit once they get married," said Rose
Pomeroy, the managing editor's secretary. Rose had been engaged for two years and planned to marry her boyfriend as
soon as they had saved up enough to make a down payment
on a house. "You don't have to work. Why do you put up with
this crap?"

"I'm paying my dues," said Lincky, trying to be good humored about her experiences as Charlie Lamb's minion.

"You're a Phi Beta Kappa college graduate and you're doing Charlie Lamb's filing!" said Becky Reese, the assistant to the director of the test kitchen. "It's disgusting. You do the work and Charlie goes to lunch. I'm amazed you haven't shot him yet."

"I've thought of it," admitted Lincky. "More than once."

"You practically do Charlie's job for him but you're still typing and shlepping coffee, too!" said Coral Weinstein, the beauty editor. She was a slim brunette who wore her hair in a Jackie Kennedy bouffant complete with fall. "I asked Personnel if you could come over and be my assistant. They told me to go fry ice. More politely, of course. I'm sure they checked with Charlie first. He'll never let you go. That dumb he's not."

"He's promised me a promotion," said Lincky, thanking Coral for her efforts. Besides, Lincky wanted to work with books and authors, not lipstick and nail polish. "He's asked me to be patient."

Coral snorted. "If you believe that, I've got a bridge I'd like to sell you. It's in Brooklyn."

Becky and Coral were right. The longer she worked for Charlie, the more of his job Lincky ended up doing. She read books and manuscripts for Charlie and wrote the editorial reports and analyses he relied on for acquiring material for *Women's World*. She had gotten to know, at least by telephone, most of the people Charlie worked with. Lincky often bid on the books *Women's World* wanted to excerpt and condense, and she had learned how to iron out contractual problems and make sure that release and publication dates were strictly adhered to. She had even acted as a junior copywriter, painfully composing the first drafts of cover lines and inside copy blocks, which eventually appeared on the magazine's cover and on its book pages.

In return for her efforts, Lincky had received the standard five percent raise as a result of her first employment review.

"Three dollars and twenty-five cents is insulting," she told Charlie when Personnel informed her of her raise.

"I'll see what I can do," replied Charlie.

What Charlie could do was nothing.

"You're already getting the top secretarial salary," Charlie reported back, conveying what Personnel had told him.

"But I do much more than the other secretaries. You told me yourself that you didn't know what you'd do without me," said Lincky.

Charlie sighed. "We can't pay you more than we pay the other secretaries, can we?" He seemed to expect Lincky to understand the impossible position she was placing him in with her request.

"Why not? I do more. It would be only fair if I got paid more, wouldn't it?"

Charlie didn't take the bait. "We don't want there to be any jealousy among the girls," he said, in explanation of Company Policy. "If we give you a raise, the others will want raises, too."

Lincky fumed and stewed and two weeks later she went back to Charlie.

"Bob Westruff was hired at the same time I was," Lincky said. "He was just promoted to assistant furnishings editor. He has an office, an expense account, and shares a secretary with the assistant kitchen equipment editor. Why should Bob get a promotion and not me? Bob is lazy. He comes in late and leaves early."

"That's his boss's problem," said Charlie.

"And what about Larry Bodine?" Lincky said. Larry Bodine was a freelance editor Charlie often hired to condense and excerpt books. That year Larry had asked for and received a raise in his usual fee plus a listing on the masthead as a contributing editor. "You know how often Larry's assignments come back overdue. You know that you've asked me more than once to redo Larry's work. Why can't my name at least go on the masthead?"

"You're way out of line, Lincky!" said Charlie, angry at her for the first time ever. Then he calmed down. "Be patient. I'll see what I can do."

Peter advised Lincky to take Charlie at his word. He told her not to be overly anxious.

"Don't lean too hard on Charlie. He'll get mad if you're too aggressive," Peter said.

Lincky decided that Peter was probably right, and she waited almost three months before bringing up the subject of a raise and promotion a second time. She reminded Charlie of all the extra work she had done and mentioned the rewards that Bob and Larry had already received. Charlie once again asked for patience.

"There've been a number of promotions around here lately," he reminded Lincky, obliviously rubbing salt into her wounds. "The budget can only stretch so far. Just hang in a little longer."

In September, Lincky pointed out to Charlie that she had worked at *Women's World* for a year and she reminded him of his earlier promises. When she asked once again for a raise and a promotion, Charlie shocked Lincky by refusing.

"You just got married. You don't need the money," he said, justifying his refusal.

"What does getting married have to do with anything? How does needing or not needing the money enter into it? I work hard, harder than any of the other secretaries, harder than Bob and Larry. I've earned a decent raise!" replied Lincky, outraged that Charlie had actually had the nerve to smile when he told her that she wasn't going to get what she had clearly earned.

For the first time since she'd gone to work for him, Lincky did not automatically return her boss's smile. She had invited Charlie and his wife to her wedding. They had danced, feasted on caviar, lobster, filet mignon, and vintage champagne, and now he was using her marriage against her! Lincky could barely believe it.

Lincky reminded Charlie that it wasn't only a raise that she wanted. She wanted a promotion, as well.

"If I become an editorial assistant, you won't have the problem of the secretarial salary cap," Lincky continued, trying hard to remain reasonable while showing Charlie a way out of his dilemma. "I'm already doing the job of an editorial assistant. You've said so yourself. More than once."

"Be patient," Charlie said. He was dying for a drink.

"I've *been* patient!" Lincky replied. "Bob Westruff didn't have to be patient!"

"Bob wasn't a secretary," Charlie reminded Lincky.

"That's right! *He* started as an editorial assistant!" Lincky said, now openly angry. Bob, who was no Phi Beta Kappa and who was lazy besides, had started out at the level Lincky was trying desperately to rise to. The reason? One and only one. The reason every woman who worked at *Woman's World* recognized: Bob was a man. Bob had a cock. Not, Lincky thought furiously, that the qualities of aggressiveness and energy usually associated with that organ were particularly apparent in Bob's Rip Van Winkle style.

Charlie glanced at his watch. Time to leave for lunch. He got up and put his coat on, a sure sign that the conversation was over.

Santa was pissed. He asked the waiter to make his first martini a double.

"Women in the office are a pain in the butt," he told his lunch companion, Ted Spandorff, an editor at Raintree Books. "They're necessary but they're a terrific nuisance. And it's always the secretaries who are the worst troublemakers. Most of the internal problems in the office are caused by them. They either do sloppy, indifferent work and screw up everything, or if by some miracle they do halfway decent work, they constantly bitch about raises and titles."

Ted nodded sympathetically. He knew exactly what Charlie was talking about.

"Even the good ones aren't reliable. You just about get them trained and they quit," Ted said, thoughtfully stroking the luxuriant dark mustache that evidently was meant to compensate for the thinning thatch on top.

"Women! For as many years as I've worked in offices, I can't figure out what their problem is," Charlie said, still in high gear over his third glass of Pouilly Fuissé. "You know that secretary I used to think was so wonderful?" he asked Ted. "Well, she's not all that wonderful."

"Pushy" was the word Charlie used. It was a word that would follow Lincky for years.

As Lincky struggled with decades of encrusted "Company Policy," John Glenn was orbiting the earth, Barbara Walters was on her way to India with the First Lady, Walter Cronkite had moved up in the world and Tony Bennett had left his heart in San Francisco. Everyone, it seemed, had gone somewhere or gotten somewhere. Except Lincky. Back home and back down to earth in the day-to-day world of male-dominated offices all over the country in 1962, SOS was the name of the game. Same Old Shit.

Although *Women's World* was a woman's magazine, there were only two women listed on the masthead: The beauty editor and the assistant to the director of the test kitchen. Coral Weinstein, it was said, had gotten her job because of her affair with a cosmetics tycoon whose company bought half a dozen expensive pages of advertising a month. She allegedly kept her job for the same reason. The office grapevine said that if the affair ever fizzled, Coral had better start writing a résumé.

"Yeah, I'm quaking in my boots," said Coral, who thought it was no one's business except hers who she shtupped on her own time. "How come no one remembers that I worked at Estée Lauder for five years and at Revlon for five years before that?"

Becky Reese had worked at *Women's World* for fifteen years.

She had received her title four years earlier when she had staged a one-woman wildcat walkout. Becky had left the office in the middle of testing recipes for the big Christmas issue, taking along with her the entire holiday recipe file. She refused to return to work and surrender the recipes unless her name went on the masthead along with a title.

The essential testing of the directions for the apricot-chestnut stuffing and cranberry-pecan sauce, the molasses gingerbread men and cinnamon-clove sugar cookies halted. Catastrophe had struck! *Women's World* readers depended on the holiday menus they clipped from its columns. A holiday issue without recipes for Christmas goodies was unthinkable, inconceivable.

"I had them by the short and curlies," Becky said, fondly remembering her moment of power. "A fortune in food and beverage advertising was at stake. If they wanted their big Christmas issue, they *needed* those recipes. They *had* to give me what I deserved."

"I won but most of the time I think it was a Pyrrhic victory," said Becky. "I'm still in charge of mixing, stirring, chopping, peeling, counter wiping, and dirty dishes."

The director of the test kitchen, of course, was male.

Having learned that it was better to look for a job while you already had one, Lincky stuck it out. She began to work the grapevine of contacts she had made at the B-list parties.

"I could use an assistant," Ralph Weiss told Lincky.

"What does a 'secret weapon' do?" asked Lincky.

"Turn shit into Shinola. Sometimes I even turn great into supergreat," said Ralph. "Basically, I'm a ghost editor."

"I've heard of ghost writers. Never ghost editors," Lincky said.

"Hank Greene won't let a manuscript leave his office until it's in top shape," said Ralph. "That's my job."

"I didn't know agents worked on manuscripts. I thought they just sold them."

"That's all most of them do. Hank is different," said

Ralph. "Would you like to try an edit on a sample manuscript? If I like it and Hank likes it, maybe you could come to work for me."

"Sure," said Lincky. "I'll do anything to get out of *Women's World*."

"Even work at the Hank Greene Agency?" asked Ralph. He was surprised that Lincky with her cashmere sweaters and Park Avenue manners would even consider working for an outré character like Hank Greene.

12
LINCKY

NEW IN 1962:

Diet Rite and Tab
Polaroid instant color film
Lear Jet Corporation
Esalen Institute, Big Sur, California

HANK Greene was one of those people other people talk about. Lincky had heard dozens of stories about him and his three-year-old literary agency through the publishing grapevine. Everyone agreed that Hank Greene was smart and ambitious. No one, it was said, worked longer or harder than Hank Greene. No one, it was said, drove a tougher bargain for his clients. No one, it was said, was more innovative in getting better deals and better terms. No one, it was also said, was more difficult to get along with.

Hank Greene had been called the meanest man in publishing. He supposedly fired people on Christmas Eve, excoriated employees in public, and sometimes reduced the women (and once in a while the men) who worked for him to tears. He docked people for being as little as five minutes late arriving for work in the morning or returning from lunch in the afternoon. He had allegedly installed a time clock in his office just as if it were a factory. Sickeningly late hours at the Hank

Greene office were rumored to be nothing special. Late hours were merely routine.

Lincky weighed the horror stories about Hank Greene against the tales of his brains and balls in light of the fact that, despite all her efforts, her job hunt had so far been a flop. It was the old runaround: the jobs she was offered, she didn't want; the ones she wanted, no one offered.

Lincky was learning that everyone in the world wanted a secretary. Editors wanted secretaries. Agents wanted secretaries. Publishers wanted secretaries. No one wanted an assistant editor and Lincky found herself in the classic bind. She wanted to be an editor but she needed experience and she couldn't get experience unless someone took a chance and hired her. So far, except for the possibility of Ralph Weiss and Hank Greene, no one would. When Ralph Weiss sent Lincky a sample manuscript as a trial, she was determined to get Hank Greene to grant her an interview.

"Pay attention to everything: theme, plot, writing style, characterization, pace, and structure," Ralph instructed Lincky. "Then write what we call an internal report assessing the potential salability of the manuscript. Go into hardcover and paperback rights, foreign sales, first serial, book club and film possibilities. Be frank. It's for Hank's and my eyes only. After you do that, draft a letter to the author with your suggestions."

Lincky read the manuscript overnight and spent the weekend writing the internal report and an author's letter that included half a dozen editorial suggestions.

"The internal report's fine. The letter is okay as far as you went but it's not nearly enough," said Ralph when Lincky returned the manuscript, report, and letter to him.

"Can you show me what I *should* have done?" Lincky asked.

Ralph came over to Lincky's apartment the following Saturday afternoon and, consuming a bagel with cream cheese, three jelly doughnuts, and a bag of pretzels washed down with celery tonic, showed her how to work a manuscript. Lincky's half-dozen suggestions turned, under Ralph's sharp and experienced eye, into four dozen.

Ralph showed Lincky how weak construction could be shored up, how cutting could tighten, and how and when expansion could add depth, emotion, and impact. He taught Lincky about the uses of the cliffhanger, the value of the well-chosen cliché, and the techniques for creating memorable fictional characters. He gave her, in fact, a crash course on manuscript editing.

"Where did you learn all this?" Lincky asked when they were done. Lincky realized that Ralph had not merely edited the manuscript, he had transformed it.

"From Hank. He used to be a writer. He said that he wasn't all that great but that the editors he had were worse. So he became an editor for a while. He worked for Elihu Harper, who was one of the best," said Ralph, telling Lincky something about Hank Greene she hadn't heard before.

Lincky absorbed Ralph's advice quickly. She rewrote her internal report and author's letter and returned them to Ralph.

"I'll show everything to Hank," Ralph said. "As soon as I hear back from him, I'll call you."

At eight-thirty A.M. the next day the phone on Lincky's desk rang. It was Ralph. He said that Hank Greene had read her report.

"What did he say?" Lincky asked.

"He didn't say anything," said Ralph. "He grunted."

"Is that good or bad?" asked Lincky.

"If he really hates them, he eats off them. Yours doesn't have any mayo stains."

"Could I try another manuscript?" asked Lincky.

For the entire next week, Lincky read and edited until midnight or later. She wrote and rewrote her internal memo and author's letter a dozen times over on yellow legal pads. Peter could not understand why Lincky worked so hard.

"You're not getting paid," he pointed out, mystified by Lincky's industriousness. "You don't have to give freebies to Hank Greene and Ralph Weiss."

"I'm not doing it for the money. I'm doing it so I can leave *Women's World*. If I do well, I might be able to get an interview. If I get an interview, Hank Greene might offer me a job," Lincky said, looking up from a page she had covered with marginal notes. Her lipstick had worn off and she looked tired.

"You want to work for Hank Greene?" asked Peter. Working for Hank Greene was, according to everything Lincky had heard and passed on to Peter, like signing up with Attila the Hun.

"Not necessarily. But I want people to find out how hard I work and how fast I learn. That way, sooner or later I'll get the kind of job I want. If not with Hank Greene, then with someone else," said Lincky.

While Lincky was working for Charlie Lamb during the day and Hank Greene at night, she also worked on her marriage. Lincky wanted to make Peter as happy as her mother had made her father. Lincky made Peter the center of her life. She took an interest in his interests, befriended his friends, and looked forward to the day she and Peter would create a magic circle of their own.

There were no drip-dry sheets on the bed because Peter preferred pure cotton. No place mats at the table because Peter had grown up with tablecloths. No stainless steel because Peter was accustomed to sterling. No frozen dinners for Peter because, ever since she got married, Lincky had taken to reading cookbooks the way she read every other kind of book. Julia Child and Craig Claiborne quickly became her gurus in the kitchen.

On weekend mornings, Lincky made eggs Benedict, which she served to Peter while he was still in bed. She set the tray with a red rose, a split of champagne, and the latest sex manual. Their gourmet breakfasts were followed with gourmet sex.

"What are we going to do if they ever stop publishing how-to-fuck books?" asked Peter.

"I don't think we're in too much danger but if they do,

we'll think of something. I have faith in us," said the always creative and ever enthusiastic Lincky.

Night after night, Peter came home to elegant dinners of fish in white wine sauce or filet mignon in red wine sauce. Every weekend, Lincky gave dinner parties featuring boeuf bourguignon or coq au vin for Peter's clients, college friends, and Wall Street associates. Peter and Lincky joked about her mad passion for recipes with wine.

"I guess it's in my genes," she said, deglazing the calf's liver pan with red wine or adding a dash of white to steamed mussels.

As Peter had always hoped but barely dared dream, he had not ended up with a conventional wife and a conventional life.

"I was always afraid that marriage would be boring," he said. "But I've never spent one boring moment with you. Not one!"

"I'm one of the lucky few who escaped the split-level trap," he told his friends from Andover and Yale.

Peter enthusiastically applauded Lincky's initiatives with Charlie and her determination to find an even better job.

"Lincky's a secretary right now but any day she'll have a secretary of her own!" he liked to joke.

Finding his own office dishwater dull, Peter found Lincky's enthralling.

"*Women's World* is much better than any soap opera!" Peter declared as Lincky regaled him with ongoing accounts of Charlie's latest alcoholic fiascos, with wild tales of Coral's tempestuous affair with the cosmetics tycoon, and fascinating reports of the Machiavellian political infighting and backbiting among the staff.

Peter and Lincky, both only children, lavished the same kind of devoted, single-minded adoration on each other that their parents had. Encouraged by Lincky, Peter pursued his interest in architectural drawings even more vigorously.

"A Chicago gallery has some Frank Lloyd Wright drawings for sale," Peter told Lincky, suggesting they go to the Windy City for the weekend to examine them.

Cheered on by Peter, Lincky continued her search for a better job. When Lincky had reported on three sample manuscripts, Ralph Weiss called and said that Hank Greene wanted to interview her. The interview was arranged for the week between Christmas and New Year's.

"No one works that week," said Peter. "It's goof-off time."

"For most people. Obviously not for Hank Greene," said Lincky.

13
LINCKY

PUBLISHED IN 1963:

The Group, Mary McCarthy
The Fire Next Time, James Baldwin
The Feminine Mystique, Betty Friedan

HANK Greene was born playing catch-up. His was the only Jewish family in Greenville, South Carolina, where Hank had grown up and where Saul Greene, Hank's father, was the lowest-paid executive at the Eagle Paint Company. Jewish and poor were only the start of Hank's problems. Sports, not smarts, counted at school. Hank was taunted with being a "brain." Extremely nearsighted, he was the last to be chosen for teams. *Girls* were picked before Hank. Hank did not get into the college of his choice or the fraternity of his choice; nor, of course, did he ever get the girl of his choice. None of these early experiences conspired to making Hank Greene a happy man.

At the time of his first encounter with Lincky, Hank Greene was aware of only the most basic facts about Lincoln Ten Eyck Desmond. He knew that she had one of those WASP last names for a first name, that she had graduated Phi Beta Kappa from Wellesley and that she worked for Charlie Lamb, the boozy book editor of *Women's World*. Hank figured that she would be one of those uptight, lockjawed snobs he had resented his entire life, the ones who made it clear that Hank Greene was not and never would be a candidate for membership in their club.

Hank had, of course, been reading Lincky's manuscript reports all along. They were succinct and concrete in their suggestions. Any writer receiving one could not fail to improve his or her manuscript by following their suggestions. Hank was not only impressed by the quality of Lincky's work, he also liked her speed. Of all the freelancers Hank employed, Lincoln Desmond did three times as much as any of them three times as well. Ralph Weiss's recommendation was also a factor. Ralph, whom Hank had fired and rehired four times in the eighteen months they had worked together, was a good judge of talent.

Hank assumed that any girl who got straight A's and majored in English literature would be boring, bookish, and physically unattractive. He took it for granted that Lincky would be an ugly broad with glasses and greasy hair. Hank knew the type. They spent lunchtimes hunched over a book in the library at high school and college. They never had a date on Saturday night or any other night. Afterward, they became librarians or went into social work or publishing because, God knows, no one in his right mind would ever marry them. Not only did Hank Greene have no erotic fantasies about Lincoln Desmond, he would have bet the agency that no one else did either. He figured you'd have to get dead drunk to fuck her.

To say that Hank did a double take the first time Lincky walked into his office is to misrepresent Hank's reaction by one. Hank took his first look as Lincky entered his office and said hello.

He blinked and took a second look as she sat down in the visitor's chair.

He took his glasses off, polished them with his tie, put them back on and took a third look as she leaned forward, waiting for him to begin the interview. He was trying to convince himself that what he was seeing was not some red-satin-sheet fantasy come to hallucinatory life but a flesh and blood woman.

Size six, thought Hank. She wore a black cashmere sweater and gray skirt that indicated her curves without blatantly advertising them. Her shiny hair was cut into a sleek, geometric helmet and her big greenish-blue eyes were alive with intelligence. She wore a gold-and-diamond wedding ring and an expensive-looking watch on a black crocodile band. Hank Greene, permanent outcast, perpetual reject, decided right away that Lincoln Desmond was way out of his league and he hated her for it.

What, Hank asked himself in mystification, was someone who looked like a million dollars doing looking for a crap job as Ralph Weiss's assistant at the Henry Greene Literary Agency? After all, the Henry Greene Agency wasn't exactly William Morris and Hank Greene wasn't exactly Swifty Lazar.

What, Hank asked himself in disbelief, had he done to get so lucky? What, he asked himself, unable to take his eyes off Lincky, was going on here?

Lincky, nervous at the prospect of an interview with the fearsome Hank Greene, was oblivious to Hank's reaction. Instead she registered his thick glasses, pockmarked skin, smoldering cigarette, and dyspeptic expression. He didn't smile, didn't get up to greet her, didn't shake hands, didn't even say hello. What had she done wrong? Was it possible that he hated her on sight?

Lincky hoped her dark outfit wasn't too funereal. She prayed she would say the right things and give the right answers. Hank Greene represented a way out of the secretarial trap. Hank Greene also scared her half to death.

Hank opened the file on the desk in front of him. He cleared his throat and began the interview.

"What's your name?" he demanded in a gravelly, smoker's voice.

"What's my name?" Her voice came out in a squeak.

Lincky knew she sounded stupid. She felt stupid. She didn't understand the question. Lincky could read her name upside down on the front of the folder on Hank Greene's desk. Why was Hank Greene asking her what her name was?

Hank Greene shifted around in his chair. He looked annoyed.

"So what am I supposed to call you?" he asked in a crabby tone. "You don't think Hank Greene is going to call some girl 'Lincoln,' do you?"

"Lincky," she replied.

Hank grunted. "So tell me what you do at *Women's World*. Then give me one good reason why Hank Greene should hire you," he said. He leaned back in his chair and dared her to impress him.

"I work for Charlie Lamb," Lincky said, not sure where to begin. Hank Greene made her so nervous she couldn't think straight.

"I know that, for Christ's sake," Hank said, rattling her résumé impatiently. "Don't you capeesh English? I asked you what you do."

"Basically, I do Charlie's job for him."

Hank looked exasperated.

"For the third fucking time, *what do you do*? Are you an idiot or what?"

"I read, buy rights, oversee the condensations and fix what the outside editors foul up," Lincky said, her words coming out in a breathless rush. Then her mind went blank. She was too scared to open her mouth again.

"So what else? What do you do after lunch?" prompted Hank. "And don't hand me some crap like you go to publishing parties."

"I check contracts, make sure we adhere to release dates, call agents to see if we can get first look, follow up the bookkeeping department so that payments go out on time, work with the art department on the illustrations, try to write copy, search out books other magazines might have missed, keep up with sub-rights directors to find out what's coming up—"

"Stop babbling. I got the message. You work your ass off. Big deal. So far you're offering quantity. Any schmuck can do heavy lifting. I'm interested in quality," said Hank. "You any good?"

"Too good for Charlie Lamb," blurted Lincky.

Hank looked at her as if she'd put a dead fish on his desk.

"So you think your boss is an idiot and you're a genius, right?"

"No. Charlie's smart but he's lazy," said Lincky. "I want a better job."

"And you think I'm going to give you one?"

"Obviously not," said Lincky.

"Wrong again," said Hank. "Seventy-five bucks a week. You start tomorrow. You do good, you come in on time, you don't give me grief, you might get a raise in six months. Might. That means maybe."

Through her terror-induced vertigo, Lincky realized that she had the job and that Hank's seventy-five dollars represented a ten-dollar raise.

"I can't start tomorrow," Lincky said, knowing that it was probably suicidal. "I need to give Charlie two weeks notice."

"Who are you? Miss Morality?"

"Yes," said Lincky.

Something in her tone must have impressed Hank because, for the first time, he didn't have a comeback. Now that she not only had a job but had survived a confrontation with Hank Greene, Lincky relaxed enough to notice a few things about her new employer. His clothes, a brown polyester suit, nylon shirt, and a two-dollar tie, were a disaster. His hair, apparently cut by the stylist at Alcatraz, was worse. Yet, oddly enough, except for the clothes, Hank Greene had style. The man pulsed drive and intensity. The physical space immediately surrounding him seemed almost visibly charged with particles of magnetic energy. Lincky felt that his presence in any room would raise its temperature by several degrees. Even his physical liabilities seemed like assets. The pockmarks were the sexy residue of an excess of male hormones in adolescence. The thick glasses denoted exceptional intelligence. The cigarettes burned as furiously as Hank himself. No one could ever feel isolated when she was in the same room with Hank Greene. Not even Lincky Desmond.

Lincky stood up, shook Hank Greene's hand, and told him that she was looking forward to working for him. He looked at her from behind his thick glasses as if she were crazy.

"You shitting me or what? I'm supposed to be the worst slave driver in publishing."

"I don't believe everything I hear," replied Lincky. "Anyway, I also hear you're supposed to be the smartest slave driver in publishing."

Hank glared at her for a moment.

"Well, maybe there's hope for you. You got one thing right," he said. Then he picked up his telephone and waved Lincky out the door. The expression on his face was undecipherable.

Lincky left Hank Greene's office in a confused state of exhilaration and agitation. Her primary emotion was elation. She had finally done what very few women at the time managed to do: climb out of secretarial limbo. Lincky now had a title. Not a big one. Not the one she wanted one day, of course, but a title nevertheless: Reader.

Reader, Lincky kept saying to herself, savoring the word, as she walked back to *Women's World*. She was no longer a secretary. *Reader*. It felt good but like every happy moment in Lincky's life, it was shadowed. If only her parents were alive. If only she could tell them.

She would not tell them about the other emotion: the uncomfortable sense of danger evoked, not by the job, but by Hank Greene himself.

"Hank Greene? You must be kidding," replied Charlie Lamb when Lincky told him that she had gotten a new job and would be leaving *Women's World*. Even though it was just after lunch, Lincky's announcement affected Charlie like an intravenous blast of caffeine. He sobered up instantly. His florid, booze-flushed skin blanched. The alcohol-expanded capillaries shriveled like suddenly limb erections. His bloodshot eyes snapped smartly into focus. Charlie had a problem and he knew it.

"I'm not kidding. I'm starting in two weeks," said Lincky, adding that she would be happy to break in a new secretary.

"Won't you reconsider? I'll see what I can do about a raise," Charlie offered.

Lincky was silent.

"And a promotion," added Charlie.

Lincky was unmoved.

"I've already made the commitment," Lincky said. Now that it was too late, Charlie was offering to find out about a raise and promotion. Lincky thought about Becky Reese and her one-woman wildcat strike and realized that kamikaze techniques were all that the bosses at *Women's World* apparently understood.

"There's a good future for you at *Women's World* if you can be patient," Charlie said.

"The Quarter-Century Club?" replied Lincky, recoiling as if he'd held out a live rattlesnake.

"You'll regret it," Charlie Lamb said when he had finally become resigned to the fact that Lincky was leaving *Women's World* for the Henry Greene Literary Agency. "Hank Greene takes advantage of people. You'll be miserable."

"I always thought you'd work at Knopf," said Alvin Hayes, who was clearly disappointed at Lincky's decision. The only agent Alvin Hayes had ever heard of was Leland Hayward, the film star's agent who was as famous as some of the stars he represented. Alvin had never heard of Hank Greene, who, Lincky told him, was a relative newcomer with only a small agency and no celebrated clients except Owen Casals, the *Newsflash* reporter, and Kathleen van Doren, a midlist trash-meister.

"If you want to work for Hank Greene, then that's what you should do," said Peter supportively, although he too had his doubts about Lincky's decision. Knowing that doing well was crucial to Lincky and aware that the odds would be heavily stacked against her when it came to Hank Greene, Peter wanted her to realize that quitting would not be an admission of failure. "If you aren't happy, you can always leave. Everyone would understand."

"Except me."

To Lincky, quitting equaled failure and failure was synonymous with catastrophe.

Even before she officially went to work for him, Lincky had decided not to let Hank Greene bother her. Responding to the optimism naturally evoked by the New Frontier and her new job, Lincky felt extra-confident. It was the last of the Camelot years, a time when the future seemed bright and everything seemed possible. Lincky—all by herself—had taken the first step toward defining herself as a modern woman: a woman who knew how to get what she wanted without turning to a man for help. Peter was impressed. He was also slightly taken aback.

"Sometimes your independence is almost frightening," Peter said.

"Not to you, I hope."

"Of course not."

Lincky started her new job in January 1963. She said goodbye to Charlie Lamb and his three-hour lunches and hello to Hank Greene and his time clock. Lincky continued her habit of getting to the office early. She was often the first one there—except for Hank himself, who apparently lived there.

"What's the matter? Hubby kick you out of bed?" Hank growled one morning at quarter past eight when he found Lincky at her desk typing an internal report.

Lincky looked up at her employer and smiled sweetly. Ralph had cautioned her that letting Hank Greene even smell weakness was a death sentence.

"Your wife kicked you out of yours?" Lincky replied, taking a cue from Ralph Weiss and refusing to let him scare her.

Hank Greene gave Lincky a sour look and silently stalked back through the empty office to his own door at the end of the hall. That afternoon, Lincky made a point of staying at her desk until Hank Greene left the office.

"Goodnight," she said politely as he passed her desk in a shower of cigarette ashes. He did not even reward her with a scowl.

"Good old Hank!" said Ralph, who had witnessed the scene. "I hope you're not sorry you decided to take the job."

Lincky smiled and shook her head. "Coral Weinstein survived Charles Revson," she said. "I'll survive Hank Greene."

14
ELLY

1 9 5 6 :

> Of all the accomplishments of the
> American woman, the one she
> brings off with the most spectacular
> success is having babies.
>
> —*Life* magazine

ELLY McGrath grew up in a pleasant, middle-class apartment
on lower Fifth Avenue in the Greenwich Village Jane Gresch
had dreamed of from afar. Her father was a labor lawyer active
in liberal politics. Her mother was the advertising director of
Ohrbach's, a 34th Street store known for its copies of Paris
fashions.

"Whatever I accomplished, I owe to them," Elly said,
attributing her social consciousness to her father and her abilities in sales, publicity, and promotion to her mother.

"Unfortunately, I didn't get my father's legal brain or my
mother's fashion sense," she added, comparing herself to her
older sister, Margaret, who had inherited both.

Elly grew up breathing the same charged air as the avant-
garde writers, musicians, and painters who gravitated south of
14th Street. What impressed her even more than their books,
music, and art was the pervasive sense of rebellion against the
status quo that their work represented. The East 9th Street

galleries showed controversial, tradition-smashing artists like Jackson Pollock and Mark Rothko. Anarchists, Utopians, Socialists, and even Communists gathered in Bleecker Street coffeehouses to discuss their political agendas over espresso. Theaters in church basements mounted experimental plays and smoky cellars presented the newest in jazz riffs.

While Jane's Village fantasies were of art and creativity, it was the tantalizing and seemingly very real possibility of changing the world that attracted Elly.

Born in 1940, Elly came of age during the years when Jane Russell and Marilyn Monroe were the ideal, and every girl alive yearned to be a man-trap complete with rocket-launcher knockers and a handspan waist. Unfortunately for Elly, she had neither. She described her tall, slim figure as a broomstick.

"Washboard ribs and knobby knees," she said in merciless self-assessment. "No bust, no waist, no hips, no curves of any kind."

Elly tried hard to change the shape of the body nature had cursed her with. She did bust exercises until her arms quivered with exhaustion. She sent away for breast developers, hoping that each new advertised promise would be, finally, a promise kept. After thousands of arm presses designed to develop the pectoral muscles and hundreds of dollars spent on various creams, lotions, and potions guaranteed to turn a B into a C, Elly still couldn't even fill out an A cup.

"I'll be the only fifty-year-old wearing a training bra," Elly lamented to her mother.

Elly secretly feared that her string-bean figure would destine her to be a wallflower.

"Boys like boobs," she said, clearsighted and aware of her limitations even at fifteen.

As an adult, Elly viewed herself with the same astringent, slightly skewed clarity.

"I spent half of my youth in search of a cause, the other half in search of a man," she said, looking back.

By the seventh grade, Elly was an inveterate signer of petitions, joiner of organizations, and volunteer in political campaigns. In high school, Elly followed the televised Army-McCarthy hearings the way the other kids followed the adventures of *Our Miss Brooks* and *My Friend Irma*. She rooted for good-guy army counsel Joseph Welch and booed bad-guy McCarthy. She mocked his twin refrains of "Point of order! Point of order!" and "Mr. Chairman! Mr. Chairman!"

"He's crazy and dangerous," she said of the junior senator from Wisconsin. "His two henchmen are worse," she added, referring to G. David Schine and Roy Cohn.

Almost everyone liked Ike. Elly was madly for Adlai. She was crushed when Eisenhower was reelected in 1956. She told everyone who would listen that while Eisenhower was bad enough, Nixon was worse.

"What if something happened to Ike?" Elly would demand, her fair complexion flushing crimson in righteous indignation. "How would you like it if Tricky Dick were President?"

Along with the heroes and villains of the Fifties came the beginnings of the civil rights movement. Elly joined the NAACP, participated in several civil rights demonstrations, and had fantasies of traveling to the South and being a Freedom Rider. The thought that she might be arrested and even sent to jail made Elly's fantasies that much more heroic and romantic. Wanting to emulate her father's highly principled example, Elly was determined to do her share to free America from the poison of racial injustice. She was extremely proud that her first lover was black.

When Ernest Jones entered the Hudson Street Day School in the fall of 1955, he was the only Negro in Elly's class. Ernie Jones's father managed several white-owned dry cleaning shops in Harlem and his mother was a public high school teacher. The fact that Ernie's mother worked was an important facet of Elly's attraction to Ernie.

"Until you came to Hudson, I was the only one in the class whose mother had a job. All the other mothers play cards and go to Bergdorf's together. My mother goes to the office," Elly told Ernie that winter. "Between that and being practically six feet tall, I really feel like a freak."

"Until you started talking to me after history class, I was thinking about quitting Hudson," Ernie admitted. "The other kids pretend to be nice to me but I know they don't mean it. Not one person has ever invited me to their house. It's because they don't want to take a nigger home."

"Don't use that word!" said Elly. "Don't even think it!"

Ernie and Elly defended themselves by proudly playing the role of outsider. Finding strength and balm in unity, they became a defiant, disdainful gang of two.

"What a bunch of assholes," Ernie said, referring to his preppy classmates and their daily uniform of dirty white bucks, button-down oxford-cloth shirts, and khaki chinos.

"The girls are no better. They all think they're Grace Kelly with their white gloves and pageboys," sneered Elly, who wore her own strawberry blond hair in loose, shoulder-length waves.

The other kids retaliated. "Mutt and Jeff," they called Elly and Ernie. "The Oreo couple."

Their insults only drove the two closer together.

Elly and Ernie maintained high academic averages, used expressions like "man" and "cool," and made fun of popular icons like Ed Sullivan and Perry Como. They spent weekends browsing in Greenwich Village bookstores, shopping for matching handmade leather sandals and hanging around the folksingers in Washington Square Park. Ernie thought that Harry Belafonte was a sell-out and introduced Elly to the records of Mahalia Jackson and Marian Anderson. Elly invited Ernie to a rally in support of Autherine Lucy, the first black student enrolled at the University of Alabama, when she was suspended from the school for "safety reasons."

" 'Safety reasons'! Those bigots just don't want a black person at their lily-white school!" said Elly, "I think they ought to send the army and force them to take blacks! At bayonet point if necessary!"

"I don't agree. I'm with Martin Luther King. Nonviolence is the most effective weapon oppressed people can use. Gandhi proved that," Ernie replied.

After classes, when the other kids went to the school auditorium for basketball and cheerleading practice, Ernie and Elly went to the library to study. When the library closed, they went to Ernie's house to finish their homework. Elly would arrive home from Ernie's at the same time her parents got home from their offices.

When Elly's father asked her why she didn't have any other friends, Elly replied with disdain.

"Girls talk about boys and clothes. The boys talk about sports and how much money their fathers make. I'm like you. *I'm* interested in ideas," Elly said.

When Elly's mother asked her why she chose a Negro as her best—and apparently only—friend, Elly looked shocked.

"You're not prejudiced, are you?" Elly asked. "I hope Daddy doesn't hear you talk like that."

Margaret was also concerned about Elly's isolation.

"It's important to get along with your peers even if you don't like them," she told Elly.

"Why?" demanded Elly. "Give me one good reason."

"To get dates," said Margaret.

"I'm not interested in dates."

"You will be."

The Joneses lived in a big, rambling apartment on Broadway and 136th Street. When homework was done and their books put aside, Ernest and Elly explored their feelings about the world, each other and, as they grew closer, each other's bodies.

Because Ernie's father worked late and Ernie's mother did the marketing and household errands on the way home from school, Ernie and Elly had the luxury of an empty apartment and plenty of time. They lay on the bed in Ernie's book- and record-crammed room kissing and necking, tentatively moving from necking to petting, from above-the-waist to below-the-waist. Each step was satisfying but frustrating. Each step led to the next. By mid-March, finger fucking was no longer enough.

"I want to be a woman," Elly said. She was sixteen and, unlike her classmates, she regarded her virginity as a burden. There was no one she could imagine surrendering it to with more devoted altruism than Ernie Jones.

"You're sure?" asked Ernie.

"I'm sure," said Elly and guided his penis to her vagina.

"Did it hurt?" asked Ernie when it was over.

"No," said Elly, lying only a little.

Ernie's room had an entrancing view over the nearby buildings to the Hudson River but, increasingly, Ernest and Elly had eyes only for each other. Although Elly worked hard at seeming to be colorblind, she was absolutely fascinated with Ernie's physical self. She spent hours secretly studying the shape of his thick lips, the width of his nostrils, the comparative paleness of his palms, the brownish-mauve color of his penis. She could not keep her hands off his wiry, kinky hair, so fascinating was its total contrast in color and texture to her own silky blond tresses. Sometimes Elly felt that she and Ernie were physically almost different species.

"Goldilocks can't believe she's in bed with Sambo, can she?" Ernie teased.

"Don't say that! I'm no Goldilocks and you're no Sambo!" Elly exclaimed angrily, as if by saying so loudly enough and vehemently enough, reality would meekly fall into line.

Ernie did his best to collaborate with Elly in her determination to be colorblind. In the privacy of his room, their double deception was misleadingly easy to maintain. Yet no matter how conscientiously Elly and Ernie applied themselves, the outside world kept intruding.

15
ELLY

MARCH 1956:

Martin Luther King, Jr., found guilty
of orchestrating the Montgomery,
Alabama, bus boycotts, vows to
continue the protest with "passive
resistance and the weapon of love."

"MOM and Dad are taking us to Florida for spring break," Elly
told Ernest in late January of their senior year as she described
her family's plans for the coming midterm vacation. "Wouldn't
it be terrific if you could come, too?"

"That would be great! I have some money saved from my
Saturday job," Ernie said, thinking longingly of beaches and
palm trees as snow fell into the bleak gray streets outside. "I
could afford the ticket but not the hotel. I'll have to ask my
parents for a loan."

Money, Ernest discovered immediately, was not the
problem.

"Money or no money, don't you even dare think about
going! You want to drink from fountains labeled Colored? You
want people to call you 'boy' to your face and 'nigger' behind
your back?" Hazel Jones was exasperated at her son's complete
lack of common sense. "I am not going to lend you a dime."

"Then I'll sleep on the street. It's warm in Florida," said Ernie.

"Didn't you hear me? You're not going to Florida!"

"I can afford the ticket. It's my money and I can spend it any way I want!"

"Not and call yourself my son!" said Hazel.

Ernie begged, pleaded, and threatened but his mother stood her ground.

"I said no and I mean no!" she said, forbidding Ernie even to bring up the subject of the trip again. "I don't want to hear another word about it!"

William Jones agreed with his wife.

"Get down off your cloud, Ernest Jones!" Ernie's father said angrily. He wondered, not for the first time, if he and Hazel had made a mistake sending Ernie to the fancy private school that bent over backward to accept minorities. Even with the partial scholarship, the tuition was a financial struggle and William Jones feared that his son might grow up in an ivory tower. Against his own instincts, he had given in to Hazel who had insisted that the temporary financial sacrifice would one day be well worth the superior education.

"It's pure white down there. The beaches are segregated and so are the restaurants," William continued, trying to explain to his Northern-bred son that the South was a different and alien world.

"I'm not saying you'd be lynched but even that could happen," William told his son. His memories of the South were indelible. "You could be beaten up if you're in the wrong place at the wrong time or if some white man doesn't like the way you look at his daughter. Don't you read the newspapers? Black men—and women—are being attacked in the South all the time. Sometimes, they're even killed. No white jury gives a damn. And if something happens to you, they're not going to give a damn about you either!"

The united front presented by his parents, combined with the prospect of public humiliation—or worse, eventually persuaded Ernie to give up the idea of the trip to Florida. Deflated, he told Elly that his parents refused to let him go, which was the truth. Reluctant to shatter the colorblindness Elly insisted on, he lied about why.

"They said I'm too young to be going off by myself," Ernie told Elly.

Elly didn't understand why Ernie hadn't fought harder and changed his parents' minds. She took it as a sign that Ernie didn't love her as much as she loved him but when she told him that, Ernie denied it.

"I do too love you! I wanted to go more than anything!" he said heatedly. "But you don't know how stubborn my mom and dad can be. They think I'm still a baby. You know how parents are!"

It was easy to blame Ernie for not standing up to his parents. It was less simple for Elly to admit that she, too, had lied. Not by commission but by omission. What Elly didn't tell Ernie was what her own mother had said when Elly suggested that Ernie join them on their Florida trip.

"I forbid it!" Louise had said, her pretty face tight with anger. "I don't want you to get hurt and I don't want Ernest to get hurt. He's a Negro up here in New York but Florida isn't New York. Not by a long shot. Down South, he'll be just another nigger and you'll be a nigger-lover. I won't permit it!"

Elly was infuriated by her mother's language. "Nigger" was a word that had never been uttered in the McGrath household. Elly accused her mother of being a bigot and a racist.

"You're as bad as any sheet-wearing, cross-burning Ku Klux Klanner," Elly said, bursting into tears.

Louise, however, was not moved by Elly's anger or accusations or tears. She continued to refuse to permit Ernest Jones to accompany them to Florida.

Brian McGrath, torn between his liberal principles and the all-too-real potential for racial ugliness, sided with his wife.

"White people and black people have been killed down South over racial issues," Brian pointed out to Elly, reminding her of recent racially motivated murders. "I won't allow you—or Ernie—to be placed in the slightest danger."

"It's not fair!" said Elly.

"One day, things will be different," Brian McGrath said, holding Elly in his arms and trying to soothe her.

"When?" Elly asked. She bore a double burden, the sense of the everyday reality of racial hatred and the even more painful suspicion that although Ernie cared for her, he did not care enough to fight his parents to be with her.

"I don't know," he said, stroking his daughter's lovely, soft hair. "No one knows."

"Ernie? To Florida?" said Margaret. "You must be out of your gourd."

Despite Elly's disappointment over the Florida trip, as long as she and Ernest stayed in his room high above Broadway, everything between them continued to be affectionate and loving throughout the remainder of that spring. Now that she had Ernie, Elly did not feel like such a broomstick and even the flea-bite size of her breasts temporarily did not matter.

"We have each other and that's all that counts," Elly told Ernie during the Memorial Day weekend.

Ernie didn't reply.

"What are you thinking about?" Elly asked anxiously. In the past, whenever Elly made a declaration of love, Ernie had replied with a similar sentiment.

"Nothing."

What he was thinking was that Elly wasn't very realistic. Florida wasn't the only stumbling block. Whenever Elly and Ernie left his bedroom and tried to rejoin the rest of the world, they confronted head-on a whole list of things they couldn't do and places they couldn't go. They couldn't go into a hamburger joint, to the movies, or to the park without being stared at and quite obviously talked about. Holding hands anywhere in public, even on bohemian Eighth Street, was out of the question. They couldn't go to the Sweet Shoppe and play the jukebox after school like the rest of the kids. No one at Hudson invited them on Friday night double dates, Saturday night parties, or Sunday get-togethers.

Elly and Ernie felt awkward at the one Friday night hop they attended and they decided not to go to the junior prom together. Or rather, their once impregnable sense of unity increasingly undercut by social reality, Ernie decided.

"I'm sick and tired of being the class spook," he said bitterly one week before the prom, informing Elly that she should find herself another date.

On the very last day of school Elly received a second shock when Ernie told her that he was going to spend the summer in Sag Harbor where his parents rented a house.

"I thought we were going to spend the summer in New York," Elly said. She was referring to the plans she and Ernie had made all winter long. For a moment Elly thought that she must have misheard or misunderstood. She and Ernie had everything planned: Ernie was going to work in one of his father's dry cleaning shops. Elly had persuaded her parents to let her get a summer job in the Washington Square Bookstore rather than go to Europe with them and Margaret. She and Ernie would spend their free time together.

"Don't you remember? We've talked about it all spring long. How we're going to hang out in the park and go to the coffeehouses and jazz places? That's what we agreed!" Elly reminded Ernie.

"I changed my mind," said Ernie. He looked away, avoiding Elly's accusing, teary eyes and wounded expression.

Two days later, Elly learned that Ernie had another girlfriend, a Negro, whose family also had a house in Sag Harbor. It was the first, but not the last, time that Elly would be devastated by a man's rejection.

16
ELLY

THE FAB FOUR FIND AN IDENTITY:

1957: The Quarrymen (John and Paul)
1957: Ed Clayton Skiffle Group (Ringo)
1959: Johnny and the Moondogs (John, Paul, George)
1959: Rory Storm and the Hurricanes (Ringo)
1960: The Silver Beatles (John, Paul, George)
1960: The Beatles (John, Paul, George)
1962: The Beatles (John, Paul, George, Ringo)

ELLY's college years at Bennington were a series of romantic disasters. There was the Yale playwright Elly wanted who didn't want her, the Harvard political science major who betrayed her with other women, and the Brattleboro potter who talked about love but disappeared once Elly allowed him into her bed.

"I have an unfailing instinct for men who know how to hurt me," she told Margaret over Christmas vacation of junior year. "I have a perfect record. I haven't missed one."

The men Elly encountered in New York were no better than the ones who had mangled her heart in New England.

There was the young actor Elly met in the summer of 1958 in an acting class in the Village. He was moody and often sullen, yet he could also turn on the charm. Elly thought that he defined charisma. Elly spent her time in class not listening to the teacher, but staring at the actor. He had already appeared in the movies and acted on Broadway. He had received creditable reviews and was represented by a well-known agent, but it wasn't his professional promise and credentials that attracted Elly.

It was his blue eyes, blond hair, and broken nose, his tight, faded jeans, the T-shirt with the rolled-up sleeves, and the bashed-about leather jacket he wore, rain or shine, hot or cold. He exuded the arrogant certainty of sexual superiority. His swagger seemed to broadcast that he could have any woman in any room in which he happened to be.

He was simply the handsomest, sexiest man Elly had ever laid eyes on. She invariably chose him for two-person acting exercises. She loudly applauded his readings and interpretations. She followed him to the water fountain when he went to get a drink and, on Friday and Saturday nights, she waited outside the stage door entrance of the theater in which he was appearing to get a glimpse of him when he left after the evening performance.

One day, he stopped Elly after class.

"I know you've been dying to go out with me," he said. "Is Sunday okay?"

He called for Elly at her parents' apartment, temporarily leaving his motorcycle in the care of the doorman. Then, with Elly hanging on behind him, he tooled through the Village streets at breakneck pace, ending up at a cheap spaghetti joint on Thompson Street.

He was sweet and sensitive and very intense. He gazed deeply into Elly's eyes and talked about himself.

"My life was screwed up before I was born," he said, telling her about his rotten childhood in the Midwest, his stint in the marines and the forty-one days he spent in the brig. He spoke about his Broadway role as Johnny Pope, the junkie in *A Hatful of Rain*.

"It was okay but I don't really care that much about the theater. It's the movies that interest me," he said. He mentioned working with Paul Newman and Pier Angeli in *Somebody Up There Likes Me* and said that his latest movie, *The Blob*, was going to be released that fall. "I'm going to be the biggest fucking star since Brando."

When he took Elly home he didn't even try to kiss her. "You're not my type. You're too nice for me," he said.

"I could try," said Elly.

He thought for a moment, considering Elly's offer, and then thought better of it.

"Nah. It wouldn't work," he said and roared away on his motorcycle.

Steve McQueen's narcissism had been completely lost on Elly but not his white-hot sex appeal. Elly blamed his lack of interest on her lack of breasts.

Then there was the abstract expressionist painter Elly knew from the Cedar Bar on University Place. Paul Hopkins had piercing granite-colored eyes and a bony, hawklike handsomeness. Dressed in black leather and denim, he exuded sexual energy. One of his thickly pigmented, dark-hued paintings had been featured in an article on contemporary art in *Life* magazine and he spoke brilliantly and passionately about art. Night after night, Paul Hopkins was one of the centers of attention at the artists' hangout.

Elly was no less fascinated than any one else and she mooned over Paul Hopkins the way she had mooned over Steve McQueen—openly and shamelessly. She followed him with her eyes, hung on his every word, and asked adoring questions. She brought him a bouquet of daffodils when he said that flowers represented the female genitalia. She presented him with the copy of *Life* that featured his painting.

"Would you autograph it for me?" she asked.

Elly was thrilled when, one night, Paul detached himself from his audience and walked directly over to her. In the moment before he spoke, Elly felt the earth stop in its orbit. What would he say? What would he do? Why had he singled her out? Elly's heart crashed wildly against her chest as he spoke.

"Let's get out of here," he said.

Elly's heart was pounding so fast that she couldn't speak. Her silence and the blissed-out expression on her face were as much of an answer as Paul needed.

"Come on," he said, taking her arm. "I'll show you my studio."

He walked Elly up University and east on Tenth, all the time talking about the psychological links between surrealism and abstract expressionism. Quivering with sexual anticipation, Elly barely heard a word. She couldn't wait to get to Paul's studio. She wondered if he would throw her to the bed, rip off her clothes, and ravish her. She wondered if he would be gentle and loving, with an artist's hands and a poet's soul. She wondered if he would be shy and if she would have to make the first move. She thought about sweaty bodies and tangled sheets. She thought about passionate declarations of eternal, everlasting love and wondered what it would be like to be married to a famous artist.

He stopped on the block between Broadway and Fourth Avenue and, getting out a key, led Elly into a former leather tanning factory that now served as his studio and apartment. The space was bare and cavernous and smelled of oil paint and ancient hides. There was no furniture except a mattress on the floor, a standing coat rack, and a stack of orange crates pressed into service as bookshelves.

Elly sat down on the mattress as Paul opened a bottle of scotch. He poured a tumblerful for himself and one for Elly and, presenting it to her, sat down beside her. On pins and needles, Elly waited breathlessly for the touch of his hand, the touch of his lips. Instead, he continued to talk about art. Passionately, intensely. The way, Elly knew, he would soon talk of his feelings for her

He drained his glass, Elly's glass, then another glass and, after that, still another. When he finally kissed Elly, his breath reeked of alcohol. When he tried to make love to her, his penis stayed obstinately limp. Elly's soaring fantasies of sexual bliss evaporated like the fumes of alcohol. When he fell into a leaden sleep, Elly silently let herself out and went home alone.

At the Cedar Bar the next night, Paul Hopkins acted as if he had never seen Elly in his life. She finally screwed up her courage and went up to him.

"Did I do something wrong?" Elly asked.

"No," he replied. "What makes you ask that?"

Despite her romantic failures, Elly didn't give up. She dreamed of love eternal and ideal marriage, of a husband and children and happily ever after. She fell in love regularly and had her heart broken just as regularly. She was always the victim. Always the one who got left. "Ever the dumpee. Never the dumper," she told her Bennington roommate, Ethel Ivey.

Chastened by her experiences, Elly was sure that Owen Casals would be another in the long line of handsome, sexy, romantic men who got away.

Elly first met Owen in the fall of 1960 when she had just begun her senior year at Bennington. Owen, a reporter for the Boston *Herald* and author of several short stories that had appeared in *Esquire*, was teaching a course on the short story. He was over six feet tall and dark haired with intense pale-gray eyes and lean, craggy good looks. The strong, silent type, Owen Casals gave off a been-everywhere, seen-everything, knew-everyone air. He wore his clothes with Gary Cooper grace and had the kind of remote, self-contained personality that women saw as a challenge.

"Especially me," said Elly.

As was the fashion at the time, Owen Casals smoked heavily and drank with panache. He specified bone-dry martinis with English gin and knew his way around a wine list. He held his liquor well and, no matter how much he consumed, he never appeared drunk or out of control. He used his cigarette as a mating gesture, caressing it between thumb and middle finger, lit end turned inward, protectively cupped by the palm.

"I got into the habit during my tour of duty in Korea," he told Elly, explaining that at night it was essential to conceal the lit ember from enemy troops.

The hint of danger and battlefield bravery was the most romantic thing Elly had ever heard in her life. Behind his great surface sophistication, Owen Casals looked to Elly like the kind of suffering, sensitive man only the right woman could rescue from his pain. A social worker in the fields of romance, Elly had found a worthy recipient for her attentions.

Elly hung around after Owen's class, hoping for a precious word with her handsome teacher. She did everything she could think of to win his attention. When Richard Wright died, Elly gave Owen a first edition of *Native Son*. She lent him her original-cast album of Lionel Bart's *Oliver*. She brought him copies of highbrow literary journals.

"I thought you might find this story interesting. It's called *Bonjour, Santa* and even though it's somewhat derivative, the author has a fresh voice," she said, handing Owen a copy of the *Hawthorn Review*.

Elly subscribed to the Boston *Herald* and made a point of telling Owen how much she liked his articles. "I thought your piece on Khrushchev's visit to the UN was very perceptive," she said. "Even though he banged his shoe on the desk, you didn't fall into the usual knee-jerk Red-baiting and warmongering."

Owen, nine years older than Elly, knew what her adoring gaze, thoughtful offerings, and well-researched compliments meant. Although appropriately flattered, he ignored her except for a cup of coffee after class now and then.

"No wonder," said Ethel. "Those black leotards make you look even skinnier than you really are and that Kohl eyeliner completely hides your eyes. When you're not talking dance, you're quoting T. S. Eliot and Marcuse. You're not exactly a laugh a minute."

"I guess he thinks I'm a jerk," said Elly. Then she laughed. "At least I'm a pretentious jerk!"

17
ELLY

JANUARY 20, 1961:

"Ask not what your country can do
for you, ask what you can do for
your country."

—Inaugural speech, President
John F. Kennedy

ELLY and Owen ran into each other again in the early winter
of 1961. A new president—the youngest in American history—
had just been inaugurated. A New Frontier was on the horizon.
New ideas were in the air. New beginnings were on everyone's
mind. Elly was sharing a West 57th Street apartment with Ethel
Ivey and was embarked on her first job. She had worked in the
Kennedy campaign and was still floating on a victory high.

Running into Owen Casals right after the inauguration
seemed like an omen of wonderful things to come. The occasion of their meeting was a party given by Elly's employer,
Parmenides Press, to honor the American publication of Jean
Anouilh's *Becket*.

Elly recognized Owen immediately. He was just as attractive as Elly remembered. He held his cigarette cupped inward
and wore a cream-colored shirt with a striped tie, a checked
jacket, and gray flannel trousers. She wondered if Owen Casals
were still single or if he had gotten married.

Single, Elly-the-fool hoped. Married, Elly-the-fatalist was certain.

"Are you still teaching at Bennington?" Elly asked instead, going up to Owen the instant she spotted him. He was several inches taller than she was and Elly, who was usually taller than *everyone*, loved being able to look up at him. "I'm Elly McGrath. I took your short story course."

"You've changed," Owen said, taking a moment to recognize her. "What happened to the leotards and black eyeliner?"

Elly flushed.

"A youthful phase," she said. "I've got a job now. I'm trying to dress like a grownup." Elly was wearing a beige skirt, a green sweater, and a navy jacket. The skirt's hem sagged unevenly. The sweater was too big and the jacket pulled under the arms. "I'm working at Parmenides Press. We publish Anouilh. Also Pinter, Osborne, and Henry Miller."

Elly was proud to be associated—even from the galactic distance of a right-out-of-college secretarial job—with such inpeccably highbrow company.

"Still the intellectual?" Owen teased, noticing how pretty Elly was. She had wavy strawberry blond hair, china blue eyes, and a flawless, creamy complexion. He also noticed that under her unbecoming clothes, Elly had a long, lean, elegant body. Hardly any breasts, Owen noticed, but that didn't matter. Owen knew—and appreciated—the difference between quantity and quality.

"Are you still living in Boston?" Elly asked.

"I've given it up for the fleshpots of Manhattan. I left the *Herald* in July. I'm working for *Newsflash* magazine now. I'm resident hack, ambulance chaser, and pontificator," Owen said, describing his position as national-assignment roving reporter in the cynical, self-deprecatory way that made everyone including Elly realize just how good the job was and exactly how far Owen had gotten in the world.

Anyone else would have been merely impressed. Elly was awed.

"Would you like to have dinner?" Owen asked as the party began to break up.

"Are you married?" Elly asked.

"I take it you're accepting the invitation," Owen laughed, a twinkle in his eye.

Elly blushed scarlet and wished the earth would swallow her up. A fatal heart attack would also have been acceptable.

Owen took Elly to dinner at Xochitl, a funky Formica table and paper-napkin Mexican joint on West 46th Street. Over salt-rimmed margaritas, cheese tacos, beef tostadas, refried beans and bottles of Dos Equis, Owen answered Elly's question.

"I'm not married," he told her. "I'm divorced."

"I'm sorry." Elly tried to sound sympathetic, although her expression was hardly somber.

"Twice," Owen added, spelling out his marital history. He did not want to engage in any false pretenses. "I'm a lousy risk."

Elly doubted it, although she congratulated herself that this time she had the sense to keep her mouth shut.

Owen also spoke of the novel he wanted to write one day. "I've been thinking about it for years. I'd like to write a really good novel. Maybe even a great one."

"But you're such a brilliant journalist," Elly said.

"Journalism is a good way to make a living. An honorable way. An interesting way. But writing a novel serves a higher goal. A novel can express a more permanent truth."

"Well, of course," said Elly. "If you want to write a novel, you will. You'll write a wonderful one!"

"I hope so," said Owen, knowing that it wouldn't be all that easy. "I have an agent. What I need is the time to write *and* exactly the right idea."

"Who's your agent?" Elly asked, wondering if it was any of the agents she sometimes spoke to on the telephone at work.

"Hank Greene. Have you ever heard of him?" asked Owen.

Elly shook her head.

"I guess he doesn't have any authors who publish at Parmenides."

After dinner, Owen took Elly home to his apartment on West 13th Street. He didn't even have to finesse her into bed.

"My God! It's so big!" Elly said, when Owen undressed.

"I hope you don't mind," he teased.

Owen was an athletic and uninhibited lover with an unusually ardent and imaginative technique. Women had often told Owen that he had a remarkably large penis *and* that he knew what to do with it. Born to fuck, Owen liked to think. And proud of it. He saw to it that Elly's orgasms outnumbered his, a tactic his womanizing father had wisely counseled.

All Elly knew was that every one of her dreams had suddenly, magically come true. She was in bed with a famous journalist, a man a million other women would have *killed* for. He had a huge cock, hot hands, and a tricky tongue. She wished that the night would never end.

"Is it good for you, too?" Elly asked at one point, practically drowning in rapture and afraid that she was so preoccupied with her own ecstasy that she was being selfish.

Owen smiled and wordlessly answered with another thrust, another tease in and out, another climb up the mountain for Elly.

The next morning, Elly went into Owen's kitchen and brought juice, coffee, and toast back to bed.

"What are you doing today?" she asked, serving him his breakfast. "I could call my office and say that I have the flu. I haven't taken a sick day yet," she said, wanting him to know that she wouldn't get into trouble at work.

"Wait a minute! Let's not lose perspective here," Owen cautioned. "We had a nice dinner and then made lovely love. But that's all."

Elly looked crushed.

"It's nothing personal," Owen added hastily. "It's me. I

can't get involved right now. I'm hardly ever home. I travel all the time for *Newsflash*."

"We could see each other while you're here in New York," Elly said.

"I'm serious about writing that novel. I won't have much time."

"I didn't mean *every* night."

"Besides, I'm a two-time loser," he added, giving Elly what he thought was a definitive reason not to get too carried away.

"Just because a person has been divorced doesn't mean—"

Owen cut her off. "You're really going to have to leave. I interviewed Charlayne Hunter the other day and now I have to write it up," Owen said, reaching for the notes and the reading glasses that were on his night table.

Elly gulped her coffee, washed their dishes, put them back into the cupboard, and left Owen Casal's third floor walk-up. She did not want to do anything to annoy Owen. The desegregation of Southern schools was one of the biggest, most important stories of the year. And *writing*, Elly knew, was sacred.

Two and a half weeks later Owen finally called. "How'd you like to see the new Truffaut?"

"*Jules et Jim*? I've been dying to see it!" Elly said.

After the film, Owen took Elly to a basement Armenian restaurant in the East 20s for braised lamb and tabbouleh. Then he walked Elly back to his apartment and his bed.

His cock was just as big as Elly remembered, his hands as hot, his tongue as tricky. She thought of all the things he'd done to her and tried them on him.

"Do you like this?" she asked, looking up.

"Don't stop," he moaned.

It was another magic night of rapture for Elly but, when morning came, Owen kissed her goodbye lightly. "See you soon," he said, opening the door to let her out and patting her affectionately on the fanny.

He said nothing about *when* and Elly left Owen's apartment with daggers of suspense piercing her soul. She walked along 13th Street wondering what would happen next. She wondered if she'd ever hear from Owen Casals again.

Ten days passed during which Elly picked up the phone a dozen times to call Owen. A dozen times, using every bit of willpower at her command, she put it down again. One thing Elly knew: girls never called men. Never!

Just when Elly thought she was about to die of misery and Owen Casals-deprivation, he called again.

"I'm at LaGuardia," he said. "I've just come in from Boston. I'm doing a piece on the Boston Strangler. Would you like to meet me at the Parthenon? It's in Astoria. World class pastitsio," he promised, as if he had to hold out a lure.

Once again, Elly and Owen had a wonderful time in and out of bed but after that almost three weeks would pass before Elly would hear from him again. Owen Casals was a man who had been born instinctively knowing that you always left them wanting more.

18
ELLY

1960:

Come on, baby, let's do the twist.

—Chubby Checker

JUNE 1963:

"Ich bin ein Berliner."

—John F. Kennedy visiting the
Berlin Wall

FOR the next two years, Owen was in and out of New York, in and out of Elly's life. Elly tried not to make him the center of her universe. She made every effort to keep their dates in perspective and not to read more into their relationship than was there. A half-packed overnight bag was permanently parked on the floor of Owen's bedroom, ready for the next trip, the next assignment. It was a constant reminder to Elly that settling down was not on Owen's agenda.

"Men like Owen have a hundred women to choose from," she told Ethel, who was living in New York and working as a waitress as she studied sculpture at the Art Students League. Ethel, who had been married and divorced while still at Bennington, was currently living with the director of the Confederation Française. She was cheating on him with the assistant manager of the local branch of Chemical Bank and with a clerk in the art supply store on 57th Street where she bought clay and chisels.

"A hundred? Try a thousand," said Ethel.

"Elly, you haven't changed since college," her sister said. Margaret had been married for a year to a law school classmate named Lee Fremont. She was pregnant with her first baby although she hadn't yet told the law firm where she worked. Employees who got pregnant—until Margaret, they had always been secretaries—were compelled to resign. "You still radar-in on the two-timers and double-crossers. When are you going to learn?"

"Maybe Owen's different," Elly said.

"Owen's *not* different and you know it," said Margaret. "He's your perfect neurotic type."

Every time Elly went out with another man, she inevitably compared him with Owen.

"An accountant. He told me all about which kind of deductions are legal and which aren't," groaned Elly, telling Ethel about her latest blind date and mentioning that Owen had just gone to Paris with Jack and Jackie Kennedy to cover the De Gaulle talks.

"He took me to Longchamps! *Dad* takes me to Longchamps," Elly said of another would-be suitor who worked in the same law firm that Margaret did. She reminded her sister (in case she had forgotten) that Owen Casals never picked a boring restaurant.

"He's five feet eight. I *tower* over him," she told her mother, speaking of Parmenides' art director, who had escorted Elly to a Literary Guild cocktail party and had made it clear that he would like to take her out again.

No man could compete with Owen. No man had a voice as sexy as Owen's or a sense of humor as sharp as Owen's. They didn't know the kind of inside gossip that Owen knew or meet the kind of famous, interesting people Owen met. Their choice of movies wasn't as sophisticated as Owen's. No man wore his clothes with the casual chic Owen did. None talked, walked, laughed, held a cigarette, or kissed the way Owen did.

"Not to mention that not one of them is hung the way Owen is," Elly told Ethel.

Remembering Steve McQueen, Paul Hopkins, and a parade of other irresistible men who were able to resist her, Elly continued to try valiantly to give other men a chance.

"I am *not* going to get my hopes up about Owen," she told Ethel.

"You're right about Owen being my neurotic type," she admitted to Margaret. "I'll enjoy it while it lasts. It's a fling, that's all."

Despite her good intentions, Elly found herself constantly thinking about Owen. When she wasn't with him, she wondered where he was, what he was doing, and who he was doing it with. She became a scholar with one subject: Owen Casals. She tried to analzye from the admittedly scanty evidence how Owen felt about her and what her chances might be with him.

Elly poured over Owen's words like a gypsy tea leaf reader attempting to divine hidden meanings and concealed portents. She thought about the magazines on his coffee table and the books on his bookshelf and, like an anthropologist, tried to reconstruct from them the contours of his emotional life. She recalled his facial expressions, searching them for clues to his innermost feelings. She read his *Newsflash* articles word for word, looking for cryptographic messages that might reveal the secrets of his psychic terrain. She read his horoscope, Sagittarius, daily, looking for a message from the stars.

"I'm shameless," she told Ethel.

"When I'm in love, my brain turns to mush," she confessed to Margaret.

Sometimes Elly would conclude that Owen had another girlfriend and that there was no hope for her. In more optimistic moods, she told herself that he was simply working hard or out of town. From the stories that carried his byline, Elly followed Owen around: to Washington to cover the Bobby Baker financial scandal, to Arizona on a story about birth defects caused by the tranquilizer Thalidomide, to Ketchum to compose a final farewell to the man who wrote *A Farewell to Arms*, Owen's own hero, Hemingway.

Elly kept reminding herself what Owen had told her—that right now he was living for his career and the book he was planning to write one day soon. He was not interested in getting romantically involved. Not with her or with anyone. He didn't have the time. He didn't have the energy.

"It wouldn't be fair for me to get involved with anyone," he told Elly, giving her a reason for not seeing her more often. Owen's honesty, of course, only made him rise even further in Elly's opinion.

"I hope you'll always think of me as a friend," Elly told Owen one July afternoon in 1963. She and Owen were in bed. Owen's tongue was in her ear and his hand was drifting south at the moment she spoke.

"A little more than a friend, I hope," he replied, his hand lighting on her inner thigh.

"*Much* more than a friend," she said.

"Mmmmmm," he said.

Elly interpreted the sound as encouragement.

"I think about you all the time. Every time the phone rings, I cross my fingers and hope it's you. I wish we could spend all our time together. I feel like half a person without you—"

"Whoa!" said Owen. "Let's not get too carried away here."

"I mean every single thing I said. You're like a god to me. I'd do anything for you. I love you, Owen. I always have and I always will!"

As Elly spoke, Owen froze. His tongue stopped. So did his hand.

"Elly, of course I want us to be friends. More than friends. But I didn't say anything about love."

"Maybe you just need time to catch up with me," said

| 113 |

Elly. "I love you so much! I just know that one day you'll love me, too! All you have to do is—"

"Back off!" warned Owen.

He sat up in bed and lit a cigarette. The strike of his match sounded like an angry thunderclap to Elly's stricken ears. She cowered in silence.

"Didn't I tell you that I can't get involved right now? I thought you understood. I thought you weren't like other women," Owen said, shaking his head.

"Other women," Elly knew, was code for Owen's despised ex-wives. Both had made the fatal errors of being clingy, demanding, and possessive, errors Elly had vowed never to make.

"I'm *not* like other women! I'm different! I *do* understand!" Elly protested even as Owen got out of bed and reached for his clothes.

By the time Elly was dressed, Owen was at his desk, his typewriter clacking busily away. Without another word, not even goodbye because she knew how much Owen hated to be disturbed when he was working, Elly meekly let herself out of the apartment.

Almost every time Elly saw Owen, no matter how wonderfully they'd gotten along or how explosive the sex had been, she always left him with the empty, panicky feeling that she might never see him again.

This time, the feeling was worse than usual.

One week, then two, then three passed and Elly did not hear from Owen.

"What did you do? Ask him to set the date?" asked Ethel. For almost a month Elly had been moping around the apartment, refusing to go out in case the phone rang and it was Owen.

"I told him how I feel about him."

"What does that mean?"

"I told him that I love him," Elly admitted.

"*Before* he told you?" asked an incredulous Ethel.

"I had to tell him. I couldn't hold it in anymore. I wanted him to know."

Ethel shook her head. She knew that Elly was hopeless when it came to men. She had never imagined she could be *this* dense.

Margaret's reaction was identical. "Don't you know that you should always let the man be the first to say 'I love you'? You were cool enough not to call him. I assumed you knew better than to start babbling about love.'"

"I guess I screwed up," said Elly.

Margaret nodded. "It's probably just as well," she said. "Men like Owen are bad news. Especially for you."

By mid-August, Owen still hadn't called. The man who did was Vince McCullough, a red-faced, red-haired ex-newspaperman Elly had gotten to know while working in the Kennedy campaign.

"My assistant is moving to San Francisco," Vince said. Elly could practically smell his cigar smoke over the telephone. "How would you like to work for me in the White House? My office is rectangular but it's real close to the oval one."

19
JANE

Can You Type?

THERE were things that bright girls who came to Manhattan
in the early Sixties quickly learned and Jane Gresch learned
them all. She learned that the *Village Voice* had the best sublet
ads, the *New York Times* the best employment ads and that
Loehmann's in Brooklyn was the place to buy designer clothes
at rock bottom prices. She learned that anemones, which she
had never even heard of in St. Louis, were sophisticated but
that gladiolas, a staple on St. Louis hallway tables, weren't.
That white shoes were corny but that black patent went with
everything, even navy. That gallery openings were much better
places to meet men than the Museum of Modern Art and that
a job, the right job, was probably the most important thing in
life.

The right job, Jane learned, meant prestige, power, access.
The right job led to the right people. The right job led to an
interesting social life. The right job led to the next, even better

job. In New York, Jane learned, women competed even harder for the few decent jobs than they did for the few decent men.

"That's because the jobs last longer and satisfy more than the men do," Jane wrote in a letter back home to Amy.

Jane's post-engagement love life, although erratic, was not traumatic because, in those days, relations between men and women hadn't yet been turned upside down by equal rights, women's lib, and sexual freedom. In those days, men still expected to have to court a woman in order to win her. They automatically paid for dinner and never expected sex on the first date. They called for Saturday by Wednesday, weren't terrified by the thought of love and commitment, and had never heard of EST, the vaginal orgasm, dressing for success, or the biological clock. In those days, waiting for Mr. Right wasn't a life sentence. It was simply a rite of passage. Even though Jane had fled Nick, she still believed that one day she would want to marry. One day a few years from now.

Meanwhile, she treated Manhattan like a sexual smorgasbord, choosing a bit of Tom, a sample of Dick (can't let that pass), and seconds or thirds of Harry.

"You need to have experience to be a writer," she told Wilma, who had, at Jane's instigation, dumped Gene, moved to New York, and applied to NYU med school. "I'm stocking up."

Sex was different in those days. So was money—and in many of the same ways. Although people had less, what there was went further, was worth more, and had not yet become a hideously fraught subject loaded with fear and anxiety. In the early Sixties, sex made people happy and so did money. A cheapo Village studio went for $75 a month, the subway, fast and safe, cost fifteen cents and a stylish haircut at a posh 57th Street salon cost $7.50 if you went on Tuesday night when the assistants practiced on volunteers under the watchful eyes of an experienced stylist.

Just as love had not yet entered the age of AIDS, real estate had not yet entered the age of Trump. During her first two years in New York, Jane solved the apartment problem by not living anywhere in particular. Instead, dragging her suitcase behind her, she camped out at a variety of sublets. There was a garden apartment on Grove Street furnished with South Seas wicker, a tiny, boxy but sweet-smelling studio in Murray Hill located over an Italian bakery, a rabbit warren railroad flat in the 80s just off East End Avenue, a sleek modernistic cubicle on 72nd between Amsterdam and Columbus and a mirrored, leopard-skin-carpeted bachelor's pad complete with round bed and black satin sheets on Second Avenue in the low 60s.

The disadvantage of the sublets was that Jane's parents could not understand why her address and telephone number changed every few weeks. The advantage was that she got to know the city and its neighborhoods better than most people.

Jane's work life was just as erratic and gypsylike as her love life and residential life. Now determined to be Colette or maybe Françoise Sagan, Jane made up her mind that she was not interested in a career or in any job that might lead to one. To render herself unemployable, she decided that under no circumstances would she learn to type or take shorthand. When anyone asked, Can You Type? Jane could honestly and sincerely say Absolutely Not.

Jane specialized in fringe employment. "The lunatic fringe," she told Wilma.

Through the *New York Times*, Jane found a job working for an English fashion photographer who had a studio on East 18th Street. Christopher Thompson did not give a damn if Jane could type. Nor did he even mention the dread words Gregg or Pitman. He wanted Jane to answer the phone, keep his appointments straight, make sure that stylists and makeup artists were booked, calm down distraught and/or hungover models, make coffee, run out for sandwiches, and keep the plants watered.

"Also call the plumber when the loo gets stopped up, make sure I don't run out of film and chat up the fashion editors. Making sure the editors are happy is Number One," Christopher said. "They're the ones who give out the assignments," he added practically.

Jane said that it was Christopher's accent that made her take the job. It also didn't hurt that along with the job came all manner of freebies ranging from haircuts by high-priced stylists to makeup, clothes, and accessories left over from a shoot. When Christopher went back to Paris in June 1962, he passed Jane along to a society photographer who took debutante and engagement photos.

When Jane got bored with the society photographer, who was independently rich and worked only when he felt like it, she worked as a receptionist for a model agency, a gofer for a costume jewelry designer, and an interviewer for a marketing research organization. Her job was to ask housewives what brand of detergent they preferred and why. It turned out to be sort of dopey but sort of fun. At least in the beginning.

Every one of Jane's jobs had one thing in common—erratic hours, which gave Jane enough time to do what really mattered to her: write. Even as she chatted up fashion editors and interviewed housewives, Jane wrote Colette-like short stories about the life of the senses (about which she was the first to admit that she really didn't know very much) or Sagan-like tales of ennui (which she thought was probably something like boredom although she wasn't exactly sure since she had never experienced it). She sent them to the *New Yorker*, which promptly sent them back.

Jane reacted to each rejection with a fit of depression and self-disgust followed by renewed determination to *make* them publish her. How exactly she would accomplish that she didn't know. All she knew is that one way or another, she would make them want her. And if she couldn't make the *New Yorker* want her, she'd make someone else want her.

In the dog days of August 1963, in the middle of a double

depression brought on by another *New Yorker* rejection and the numbing sessions of asking housewives questions whose answers she didn't give a damn about, Jane answered an ad in the *Times* for a job as a researcher for a writer.

Glen Sinclair had brown eyes, walnut-colored hair and vampire-white skin. He was tall and thin but potbellied and stoop shouldered. He smoked a pipe and told Jane that he was a beaten man, a description Jane believed. Between his slumped posture and hangdog expression, Glen Sinclair looked like a man burdened with the problems of the world.

"I'm desperate. My researcher quit to get married and everyone else who's applied for the job has been male. I can't stand men. They're insensitive, mindlessly aggressive, and boring. They talk about sports. I hate sports," Glen said. "I like women."

He then announced that he was no artist and had no pretensions about being one. Whatever sells, he told Jane, he wrote. Since he had no imagination, he continued, he preferred nonfiction, although if an editor wanted a Western, a spy thriller, or a tale of the occult, he'd knock out one of those, too—in particular, the thrillers that appealed to his basic paranoia about his own sex. These days, Glen went on, diet books were selling like crazy. Diet books, therefore, were what he currently wrote most of. The need to keep coming up with new diet book angles was one of the things that had gotten him so beaten down. It was murder coming up with a constant flow of new ideas and new angles.

"Absolute murder," he said. "I need help. I need a researcher."

"I've been interviewing housewives about washing dishes," Jane replied, wondering if the market research she'd been doing had anything to do with book research. "What exactly would you want me to do?"

"Go to the library and take out all the diet books and all the books on nutrition. Buy the women's magazines every month and clip the diets. I work with a number of doctors. Call them up and find out the latest theories about weight loss from them. Write down anything that sounds interesting, new, or stealable. I'm always hard up for new material. Your job is to help me find it."

"I'm hired?" asked Jane in surprise.

"Sure," replied Glen, surprised that she was surprised.

Working for a writer, even a writer of diet books, was infinitely more interesting to Jane than working for photographers or asking housewives about detergents. Despite his cynical approach, Glen Sinclair turned out to be an extremely nice and very bright man. He made a good living as a writer and was the first professional author Jane had ever known.

"Did you always want to be a writer?" Jane asked, still starry-eyed about Writers and Writing.

"Hell, no. I wanted an army career. I wanted to be a pilot but my eyesight was against me," replied Glen sadly, extolling the joys of army life and the military routine with its total mindlessness and complete lifetime security. "Instead, the army assigned me to a press office in Guam. I composed the submissions to headquarters for medals. Half of what I was writing was fiction so I started grinding out stories for the pulps and here I am."

Glen Sinclair, Jane found out very quickly after she went to work for him, wasn't kidding when he said he liked women. His social life was infinitely more hectic than Jane's. Even Christopher, who was surrounded by models and regularly fell madly in love with one or the other seemed like a monk compared to Glen, who dated every single night of his life. He met women everywhere. He encountered them in banks, supermarkets, restaurants, newsstands, florists, delis, subways, and movies. He invited them to dinner and then to bed and, apparently, they rarely turned him down.

"I don't give a shit about booze, drugs, gambling, or literary respectability," he told Jane. "I like women."

Most mornings, when Jane arrived at Glen's apartment

ready to go to work, he was entertaining his date from the previous evening. Sometimes Jane saw the same woman for several weeks or months in a row. Other times, the cast changed nightly. In October, after Jane had worked for Glen for several months and felt comfortable with him, she asked him a question that had been on her mind ever since she realized the extent and diversity of his amazing social life.

"Why haven't you ever made a pass at me?" Jane asked.

"Good researchers are hard to find," he replied.

"And good lays aren't?"

"Not as hard as good researchers," he said. They laughed. Jane and Glen had become buddies. They watched out for each other. They cheered each other on and, when necessary, up. They even, in a way, loved each other.

Besides, Jane could afford to be good humored about her boss's lack of sexual interest in her because just the night before she'd met a man named Owen Casals. Even though they hadn't gone to bed yet, Jane was pretty sure that whatever problems lay ahead, sex wasn't going to be one of them.

20
JANE

1 9 6 2 :

Love, love me do
You know I love you.

—The Beatles

JANE met Owen Casals at a Friday night dinner party during the third week of October 1963 as the Love generation was gathering momentum. Both Jane and Owen were under the spell of the good vibes and good grass that seemed to be everywhere.

Sexy, sexy, sexy, thought Jane with her first glance at Owen.

Ditto, thought Owen.

The last time Owen had called Elly was late in August just after Elly had moved to Washington. Ethel Ivey had answered.

"Elly's moved to Washington. Do you want her number?" Ethel asked.

"Yes," said Owen.

Owen carried the number in his wallet. He debated about whether or not to call Elly. So far, he had decided not to. She was a great girl but she was too intense. Owen thought it would probably be better to let it die a natural death. When he went out these days, it was as a free man.

Overhearing snippets of Owen's conversation from across the room, Jane got the impression that Owen Casals lived on an airplane. He had recently been in Albany, Washington, and Los Angeles covering stories on politics and show biz. He was telling off-the-record anecdotes about Nelson Rockefeller's and JFK's sex lives.

"When he isn't boffing Happy, he'll take whatever's around. JFK is into quantity. Period."

Jackie Kennedy's charge accounts: "Bergdorf Goodman ought to name a wing after her."

James Baldwin: "*The Fire Next Time* is a brilliant book and he's a gifted writer but he'd better watch out for the booze."

He also lamented the demise of the *Daily Mirror* earlier that week.

"Fucking TV is turning us into a nation of illiterates," Jane heard him say. "Not that the *Mirror* was exactly the *Christian Science Monitor*."

Owen noticed Jane right away. She was wearing suede bell bottoms, a red silk poet's blouse, and a burgundy velvet weskit trimmed with mirrors. Her sandy hair was disheveled, as if she'd just fallen out of bed. Or might be about to fall in.

"You know what's the most interesting thing about this party?" Owen asked, going over to Jane. She was sitting on a floor cushion, a plate of food in one hand, a fork in another, and a glass of wine on the coffee table in front of her.

Jane glanced around the room briefly. People, plates, candles, a portable Sony television set, an Alexander Calder circus poster from the Whitney Museum, Azuma rattan and bamboo furniture, a Haitian straw rug. Jane's eye stopped on the silverware. Tiffany's Queen Anne pattern with rattailed knifes, Jane's Manhattan-trained eye told her.

"Marsha left her husband. Not the other way around," Jane said, referring to their hostess.

"Explain."

"When Marsha split, she took what she could carry. The silver, the portable TV. Probably a fur coat," said Jane. "She was on her own for the furniture and rugs. That's why they're el schlocko."

"Interesting but not what I had in mind," said Owen.

"Which was?"

"That three of the couples here are married but the wives don't have the same last name as their husbands."

Jane hadn't thought about it before but Owen was right. Natalie Sher covered Seventh Avenue for *Women's Wear Daily*. Her husband, Timothy Coleman, was a real estate lawyer. Helene Ockent was an assistant producer on the *Today* show. Her husband, Steve Heller, produced TV commercials. Marsha Jerome, the hostess, designed model rooms at Bloomingdale's. Her ex was named Barry Schwartz.

"And what about *your* wife? Does she use her name? Or yours?" asked Jane, looking up at Owen from her vantage point at floor level.

"I don't have a wife."

Jane moved over a bit so that Owen Casals could share the cushion with her.

On their first date, Owen followed the courting ritual he had found, through vast experience, to be foolproof: an esoteric movie followed by an offbeat restaurant. Women, Owen had learned, interpreted the choice of a foreign-language film and a restaurant serving exotic cuisine as signs of taste and discernment in a man. Not to mention sophistication and sensitivity in a lover.

The flattering compliment to taste and intelligence rarely failed. An appeal to the intellect, Owen had discovered, led straight to bed. The brain was, after all, the most powerful sexual organ of all. Owen took Jane to see *Last Year at Marienbad* and, afterward, to El Faro on Horatio Street in the West Village.

"Have the mariscada with garlic sauce," he suggested. "It's a specialty."

"If I have garlic you won't want to get close to me," Jane said.

"I'm having the shrimp with garlic," Owen replied.

"So we'll neutralize each other," said Jane.

"Neutrality wasn't what I had in mind."

Later, when Jane saw Owen's penis in all its erect glory, she could barely believe her eyes.

"Holy shit! Is that for real?"

"Kiss it and find out for yourself," said Owen.

"It won't turn into a frog?"

"A prince like this?"

Not only was it the size of a Louisville Slugger but, even more miraculously, Jane learned that Owen knew exactly how to use it. He knew how and when to put it in, when to move it around, and when to pull it back a bit. He knew when to go fast and when to go slow, when to put it in inch by inch, and when to go full throttle forward and jam it in all the way.

"Oh, God, stop!" Jane begged, writhing and almost weeping in ecstasy.

"You don't really mean that," Owen said with a tender smile and a hot little movement of the hips.

"Yes, I do. I mean, no I don't. Oh, God, I don't know what I mean," Jane gasped.

The next day as soon as she got home to the Perry Street walk-up that she shared with Wilma Elbaum, Jane shared the news of her amazing discovery.

"No kidding! It's as big as a Coke bottle," she told Wilma.

"That's not possible. Gene was hung but even he was only the size of a tube of toothpaste. Economy, of course."

"Jojo was zip compared with Owen's," said Jane. "I mean it."

"Really?"

"Yeah, really."

"Did it hurt?"

"Are you kidding?"

"Like a zucchini," she told Natalie Sher and Helene Ockent, who came over later for pizza and red wine.

"Jesus," said Natalie. "Tim's is the size of a thimble. Half the time I need a flashlight to find it."

"Steve is hung like a horse," said Helene. "It's huge."

"Exactly how big is huge?" asked Wilma in the spirit of scientific inquiry. She was now interning at University Hospital and, although she saw plenty of penises, they were mostly limp. You could never tell from a limp one how big it would get when erect.

"It's not that long but it's really thick. Sort of like a can of tomato paste," said Helene.

"Contadina?" said Natalie.

"Progresso."

"Owen's is long *and* thick," said Jane. "Like a banana but a lot thicker. And, let me tell you, he knows how to use it, too."

"That's important," said Natalie. "A lot of them have big ones but they barely know where to stick it. You practically have to draw them a road map."

"Not to mention the ones whose hard-ons are sort of mushy," said Jane. "You know how they sort of try to wedge it in but it always keeps slipping out? I hate that."

"Who doesn't?" said Helene. "Steve's a good fuck. Now. In the beginning, though, he was strictly wham-bam. I had to tell him that speed was *not* of the essence."

"Owen doesn't have *that* problem, either," said Jane. "He's the perfect fuck. I don't have one criticism."

"No kidding?" said Wilma. Jane was a connoisseur and her standards were uncompromising.

"No kidding. Four stars."

"Yeah, but can he read?" asked Natalie.

"Doesn't even move his lips," said Jane.

Everyone laughed.

"What do you think guys talk about when women aren't around?" asked Wilma later when she and Jane were cleaning up.

"Boobs and baseball."

Owen and Jane saw each other six times in the next four and a half weeks. They actually spent part of the time talking.

"I've been published, too," said Jane, when Owen told her that *Esquire* had published two of his short stories. "But not in anything as commercial as *Esquire*. Have you ever heard of the *Hawthorn Review*? It's very literary."

"Despite the fact that I work for *Newsflash*, I'm not a moron," said Owen. "I have a feeling I read your story. *Bonjour, Santa*, wasn't it?"

Jane nodded proudly.

"You have a fresh voice," Owen said. "Of course, the plot is awfully derivative."

"Derivative? Who are you? Leo Tolstoy?"

"Maybe derivative is the wrong word. Perhaps I should have said that you remind me of an American Françoise Sagan."

"I wish the *New Yorker* thought so. They keep rejecting my stories," said Jane.

"What do you care about the *New Yorker*? They're for the Darien commuters anyway," said Owen.

"That's what Glen says," said Jane.

"Glen?"

"Glen Sinclair. He's a one-man book factory. I do research for him. That's how I support myself. Until I get famous, of course."

"He's a Hank Greene client, isn't he?" asked Owen.

Jane nodded.

"So am I. Hank's great."

"That's what Glen says. I took a manuscript over to his office once. He looks like a used-car salesman. What's his story anyway?"

21
LINCKY

1963:

Roche Labs markets a new
tranquilizer, Valium.

HANK Greene wasn't like anyone else Lincky Desmond had
ever known. He wasn't like anyone else, period.

From Lincky's point of view, Hank Greene had the wrong
background, wore the wrong clothes, and lived at the wrong
address. He wasn't suave and handsome the way Lincky's
boyfriends had always been. He wasn't attentive and adoring
like Peter. He wasn't Brooks Brothers and Ivy League. He
wasn't Protestant and WASP-y. He wasn't athletic or well
coordinated. He wasn't rich and he wasn't powerful and he
wasn't chairman of the board of anything, including the literary agency that bore his name but was too small and insignifi-
cant even to have a board.

He had none of the social graces. He apparently did not
know the words "hello" or "goodbye" and, as far as Lincky
could tell, "thank you" was an expression relegated to a dead
language. A dialect of some cuneiform language, perhaps, for
which the Rosetta Stone had yet to be found. Hank treated his

secretaries like dirt. He fired them regularly and exploded when they didn't show up the next day.

"Where the fuck is Brian?" he screamed when the gay secretary he had fired the day before failed to arrive for work one morning.

"You fired him," Ralph said. He did not remind Hank that he had also called Brian an uptight little faggot during his tirade.

"That's no reason for not showing up!" yelled Hank, cursing because there was no one to answer his phone.

As far as Lincky could see, Hank Greene didn't even eat. His code for lunch was to bark "food" at whoever was unlucky enough to be near his office when he got hungry. "Food," everyone who worked for him knew, meant three packs of Parliaments and two cartons of black coffee.

Hank did not seem to know that Lincky was alive. He walked past her desk as if she weren't there. He frequently did not reply to her comments in staff meetings. When it came to Lincky Desmond, Hank seemed to be deaf, dumb, and blind.

"He makes me feel invisible," she told Peter.

"No wonder people can't stand him. Hank Greene doesn't say good morning, good night, or good work! I don't think he thinks about anything except what deal he's working on, how much money he can get for his authors and which new clients he might be able to sign up," Lincky told Peter one March evening over one of her special, super-duper, ready-in-an-hour gourmet dinners.

"Then why do you care so much what he thinks about you?" Peter asked. "Ralph likes your work. You say you're learning a lot, which is the primary reason you wanted to work for him. So what if Hank Greene doesn't seem to know you're alive? The editor-in-chief of *Women's World* didn't pay any attention to you either."

"There were sixty-three people working at *Women's World*. The Henry Greene Agency has five employees: Ralph, me, the bookkeeper, the receptionist, and Hank's secretary-of-the-week," said Lincky. "It's a small office. It would be nice if Hank acted as if I were alive."

Peter shrugged.

"An office is an office," he said. "Not a social club."

"It's also not supposed to be Siberia," said Lincky. "Hank completely ignores me."

"Maybe that's good," said Peter. "Considering his reputation."

The time clock Lincky had heard about really existed. It hung in the corridor that led from the small reception area to the back offices. Hank Greene's employees were required to punch in and punch out.

"Hank hired people who were used to publishing hours. They came in at quarter to ten. Left for a two-hour lunch and disappeared at five to go to a cocktail party," Ralph told Lincky. "Hank says that his clients can't get the service they're paying for unless people are working full time."

"People want to work here, they can punch in like workers everywhere else," growled Hank, skipping the fancy explanations.

Lincky found out that Hank Greene really had fired someone, a junior agent, on December 24 the previous year.

"Christmas Eve?" Lincky asked Hank.

"Bet your ass! I found out that he had given a twofer. That's grounds for immediate dismissal. Clients do not come to Hank Greene to be horse traded," said Hank, still angry.

"What's a twofer?" Lincky asked Ralph.

"Sometimes agents who represent two authors published by the same house will make a package deal with the publisher. The agent will take a smaller price for one author in exchange for a larger price for another," said Ralph.

"Don't the clients find out?"

"Almost never. How can they? The agent is their only source of information. The agent calls and tells each author what a greal deal he got. He's smart enough never to take less than for a previous book so the authors are happy and the agent gets a bigger commission plus he makes points with the more important writer."

"That's disgusting," said Lincky. "No wonder Hank fired him."

Ralph shrugged.

"Maybe. On the other hand, it's just possible that Hank was in the mood to fire someone. After all, it *was* Christmas Eve."

"You must be a lot happier now that you've left *Women's World*," Coral Weinstein told Lincky over a hamburger lunch at P. J. Clarke's. Coral's hair was currently jet black, her lipstick pale, and her eyeliner exaggerated à la Elizabeth Taylor in *Cleopatra*.

"I am. Ralph is just as nice as Hank is difficult so things even out," said Lincky. Then she told Coral why she had invited her to lunch. "Ever since I got out of college and started working, I began wearing makeup every day. I'm a complete amateur with cosmetics and I thought wouldn't it be great if there were an expert to tell me what to wear and how to wear it. Have you ever thought of writing a how-to makeup book?"

Coral shook her head. "Daphne du Maurier I'm not."

"You don't have to be Daphne du Maurier to write the kind of book I'm thinking about," said Lincky.

Coral reconsidered. "At Revlon, we used to provide the sales reps with manuals showing women how to use the products. One of my jobs was writing those booklets. It wasn't great art. Just how to put on your lipstick so it doesn't smear, how to apply mascara so it doesn't clump. I guess it could be expanded into a book."

"If you could write a proposal, maybe Hank could sell it for you," said Lincky.

"Could you help me with the outline?" asked Coral. "A book credit would be good for my career."

By the time Lincky had worked for Hank for almost five months, she had yet to hear a single syllable from him that wasn't strictly business. One day in mid-May, at ten past six in the evening when the office was almost empty, Hank Greene stopped by Lincky's desk.

"Where's Ralph?"

"He just left," said Lincky.

Hank grunted and turned to leave. Abruptly, he spun around and faced Lincky.

"Did you know that my real name is Greenberg?" he demanded.

"Like the baseball player?" Lincky replied. Like everyone who worked for Hank, Lincky knew that being Jewish was one of Hank's major hang-ups. As far as Lincky was concerned, Hank Greene's Jewishness was not the problem. Hank Greene was the problem.

"Yeah. Hank Greenberg," Hank replied. "What the hell do you know about Hank Greenberg?"

"That he hit a lifetime .313 and led the American league in home runs and RBI's in 1946," said Lincky, rattling off the stats she recalled from childhood.

"He had trouble with left-handed pitching," said Hank.

"I didn't know that," said Lincky. "When did you get rid of the 'berg'?"

"When I was trying to get a job on Wall Street. The little snot who interviewed me told me point blank that there were no jobs at Cromwell, Scott and van Heusen for Jewboys," said Hank. "I changed my name that same week. I went to a lawyer and did it legally. I dropped the 'berg' and added an *e*."

"Why the *e*?"

"I thought it was classy," Hank said.

Then he turned away, ending the conversation as abruptly as he'd initiated it.

In early June, Hank Greene sold Coral Weinstein's outline for a how-to book on makeup to Raintree Books. He accepted a five thousand dollar advance against standard royalties. Ted Spandorff thought the deal was complete. He was wrong.

"We're keeping first serial," said Hank. First serial rights represented material from books that appeared in magazines prepublication. Raintree had a long-standing policy of acquiring those rights for its magazine division.

"We always get first serial," said Ted. "It's part of what we're buying."

"Not this time," said Hank.

Hank sold three separate chapters of Coral's book to three different magazines. The chapter on makeup for the office went to *Mademoiselle*. The one on party makeup went to *Vogue*, and the charts on how to choose color went to *Woman's Day*. The total price for all three was six thousand dollars.

"Hank more than doubled my advance before the first copy has even been printed!" Coral told Lincky.

"I would never have written the book without Lincky," Coral told Hank. "It was her idea. *And* she helped me put together the outline."

"Is that true?" Hank asked Ralph that same afternoon.

Ralph nodded.

"Lincky mentioned the idea to me one day and I told her to run it past Coral."

"No shit," said Hank.

"Check it out with Coral if you don't believe me."

The next morning, Lincky found a check for one hundred dollars on her desk. It was signed by Hank Greene.

"What's this for?" she asked.

"Coral told me the beauty book was your idea. So far, the agency has made eleven hundred dollars in commission. I figure you should get part of it."

"Thank you," said Lincky, astounded to see a side of Hank Greene that actually seemed nice.

"What's that 'thank you' crap? I'm not your daddy and you're not my little Lincky. You earned it. Act like it."

"Okay," said Lincky. "Next time, I'll tell you it's not enough."

"What 'next time'?" Hank said and stalked away.

Even though Lincky was independently rich, that hundred dollars meant more to her than any money she had ever earned or inherited. It was special money that meant that she and her work were special.

During the three weeks that followed, Hank Greene returned to his stance of indifference toward Lincky. He behaved as if their conversation about baseball and Jewboys had never taken place. He acted as if he had never given Lincky a share in the commission for Coral's book.

"Sometimes I even doubt it happened myself," Lincky told Ralph. "Do you think he remembers?"

"Hank never forgets anything."

The dog days of August had begun. The office had emptied and early one evening, Lincky was standing alone in the corridor waiting for the elevator when Hank appeared. As usual, he was in an assault mode.

"*You* don't think I'm classy, do you?"

Shifting slightly from one foot to the other, Lincky hesitated. She didn't know what to say. If she told Hank that she thought he was classy, she'd be lying. If she told the truth, she might find herself out of a job.

"You can tell me the truth. I won't fire you," Hank said. "You think I'm classy or not?"

"Not exactly."

"Why not? What do I do wrong?" Hank asked. Just then the elevator came. Hank elbowed Lincky aside and got in before her.

"Among other things, what you did just now," Lincky said, following him into the elevator.

"Oh! You mean not letting you go ahead of me?" he asked. To his credit, he flushed slightly.

"That was nothing," Lincky said. "It was almost knocking me down first."

Hank and Lincky stood next to each other in awkward silence, carefully not touching, as the elevator descended. When its doors opened to the lobby, Hank Greene stood back deferentially and allowed Lincky to leave first.

"I'm sorry I almost knocked you over. I won't push ahead of you again, either," Hank said.

Lincky didn't know what to say. "Sorry"? Had she actually heard Hank Greene say "Sorry"?

Hank interpreted Lincky's silence as disapproval.

"What do you want from me? I *said* I'm sorry!" Hank growled, as he and Lincky crossed the granite lobby.

"For almost knocking me over or for pushing ahead of me?" Lincky asked.

Even Hank had to laugh. Then, without another word, he walked away. In a moment, his scurrying, awkwardly clothed figure was lost in the after-work throngs crowding Third Avenue. As Lincky looked after him, she was surprised to realize that, for a moment, Hank Greene had actually seemed attractive.

22
LINCKY

1 9 6 3 :

The times they are a-changin' . . .

—Bob Dylan

LINCKY and Peter had been married for over two years and Lincky tried hard to keep the honeymoon mood alive. She always looked her best for Peter and continued to put him first. She devoted herself to him and told him that he was her mother, her father, her lover, her husband, her best friend, her everything. Without him, she said, she would die. She automatically smoothed over the small conflicts that had begun to come between them ever since she had left *Women's World* and began working for Hank Greene.

"I've been home an hour already. Do you have to work late every night?" Peter asked one evening when Lincky didn't let herself into their apartment until almost quarter to seven.

"I'm always home in time to make you dinner."

"Not always."

"Okay," said Lincky, "Almost always."

* * *

Peter had said they were twins and so Lincky had thought that Peter was a male version of herself. Lincky was determined to stand out and succeed. She wanted to be proud of herself. She wanted her parents to be proud of her. She assumed that Peter felt the same way. She had no way of anticipating the attrition of ambition and confidence that resulted from Peter's secure but uncomfortable perch at Desmond & Desmond. Although Uncle Harry kept promising to make Peter a partner in the firm, Uncle Harry never quite delivered on the promise. In the late summer of 1963, Bo Skinner, Peter's college roommate, made partner in his law firm.

"Aren't you jealous?" Lincky asked when Peter told her the news. Uncle Harry was still refusing to put Peter's name on the letterhead.

Peter denied it. "Jealous of what? The chance to work my nuts off?"

Peter proved his point two weeks later when a former colleague who had moved from Desmond & Desmond to Pryce, Wardroon asked Peter to join him.

"I've been given the job of starting a mutual fund. It will be a hell of a lot of work but the payoff will be sensational," Eric Leighton told Peter, offering him a job as his associate.

Peter turned Eric down. "I'm happy where I am," Peter said.

"Uncle Harry would kill me if I leave. My father would have a stroke," he told Lincky.

"Aren't mutual funds the coming thing?" asked Lincky. "Wouldn't it be a terrific opportunity?"

"Probably," said Peter. "Eric already has an ulcer. It'll only get worse as the pressure gets greater. I'm not interested in getting an ulcer of my own."

"Who says you'd have to get an ulcer? Plenty of people have important jobs who don't have ulcers." Lincky was thinking of Hank who always said that he didn't get ulcers, he *gave* them.

Peter wouldn't change his mind. "I'm staying where I am. If I hang in enough, the whole shebang will be mine."

"I thought you wanted to get away from your uncle," said Lincky.

"I do but I don't."

Lincky sympathized with Peter's dilemma, although she wished he would either confront Uncle Harry and insist on being named partner or leave Desmond & Desmond and make his own way in the world. Most of the time, Lincky kept her feelings about Peter's detached attitude toward his work to herself. She kept telling herself that the situation would eventually resolve itself. She just wished she weren't so annoyed with Peter's passivity.

Lincky was no Pollyanna. She was certain that her parents must have had problems, too. She wished she could ask her mother how they had worked them out. Instead, with no one to ask, Lincky ignored her feelings and told herself what she told everyone else: that she and Peter were just as happy as her parents had been.

"Every year gets better," she told Alvin Hayes, barely aware that she wasn't telling the truth.

The only overt conflict in the marriage occurred when Peter expected Lincky to adopt the same attitude toward *her* work that he had toward his. Coral Weinstein delivered the manuscript of *The Beauty Book* to Hank in early September.

"Since the book was your idea, why don't you take over the in-house editing?" Hank said, giving Lincky the manuscript late one Thursday afternoon. It was the first time Hank had given Lincky an assignment of her own. Until now, she had worked under Ralph's close supervision. Lincky understood the vote of confidence for what it was.

"I'd love to," said Lincky, her fingers itching to turn the pages.

"Get me a report by Monday. If it's ready to go, I want to get it over to Ted Spandorff that afternoon."

"The Philadelphia Institute is showing a collection of Palladio's drawings. This is the last weekend. Let's drive to Philly, have dinner at Bookbinder's and spend Saturday at the exhibit," Peter suggested to Lincky that same evening.

"I can't. Coral delivered her manuscript this morning. Hank's asked me to work on it," Lincky said. "He wants the internal report and editorial letter, if we need one, on Monday morning. I'll have to work this weekend."

"Come on, Lincky! Hank Greene pays you to work Monday through Friday. You don't owe him weekends."

"He didn't owe me one hundred dollars either," Lincky said.

"You're not coming with me?"

"How can I?"

"I guess I'll have to go alone."

"It's the timing," said Lincky. "Any other weekend and there'd be no problem."

"But it's *this* weekend," Peter said.

The next morning Peter left the apartment with an overnight bag.

"Aren't you coming home before you leave?" Lincky asked.

"I'm leaving right after lunch. I'll go to Philadelphia straight from the office," he said. Peter was always anxious to leave the office, always searching for a reason to get out early.

"But the market doesn't close until three," Lincky said.

"The market will survive without me. So will Desmond & Desmond."

"Kiss?" asked Lincky as Peter was about to leave.

Underneath Lincky's sympathy and affection roiled a growing sense of disappointment. She wanted to look up to Peter. She needed him to be as successful as her father had been. It was important to her to admire him. The fact that she didn't upset her. That she sometimes even agreed with Uncle Harry made her feel disloyal.

"Peter's too young to give up," Lincky told Coral Weinstein. "If anyone treated me the way Uncle Harry treats Peter, I'd find another job. In fact, I did."

"You're not Peter. Charlie Lamb wasn't your uncle and *Women's World* wasn't the family store."

Lincky blushed. "You're right. I guess I'm too hard on Peter."

Still, Lincky wished that Peter would *do* something about his problems with his Uncle Harry. She wished he would confront his uncle openly about the partnership that he was promising but then sadistically withholding. Instead, he expressed his unhappiness by cutting out early whenever possible and pretending that he didn't give a damn.

Lincky wished she didn't keep comparing Peter to Hank. Hank was aggressive and ambitious. The impression he gave of being in perpetual motion radiated an exciting kinetic energy. Hank was the smartest, most dynamic man Lincky had ever met. He seemed to be one thousand percent alive at all times. Lincky wished Peter had more of Hank's fire and ferocity.

"Hank wouldn't put up with Uncle Harry's shilly-shallying for ten seconds. He'd ask him point blank if he was going to be named partner or not. If the answer was no, Hank would walk out and make partner somewhere else. Or even start his own company," Lincky told Peter as the unresolved partnership situation dragged on.

"Do you really expect me to act like Hank Greene? Are you crazy?" Peter replied.

Just as Lincky was disturbed by Peter's passivity, Peter was upset that every time he brought up the subject of children, Lincky procrastinated.

"Later," she would say. "I want to work for a little while longer."

"But you were so anxious to have a family," Peter would reply.

"I know. I didn't say never. Just later."

23
LINCKY

1 9 6 3 :

I want to hold your hand . . .

—The Beatles' first American hit

IN early October 1963 Lincky, Hank, and Ralph went to a cocktail party given by the Hearst Corporation to mark the recent overhaul of *Cosmopolitan* magazine. Once an extremely popular journal of light fiction, *Cosmo* had fallen on bad times and management had sent out for a resuscitation squad. The new editor was Helen Gurley Brown, who had become famous the year before as the author of *Sex and the Single Girl*.

Before the Sixties became The Sixties, the title itself with the implication that unmarried women actually Did It was a shocking notion. Mrs. Brown's assignment was to bring the quasi-moribund *Cosmo* back to life. She was succeeding and the celebration was to applaud her progress.

There were a number of models present at the party who had appeared either on *Cosmo*'s cover or in its fashion pages. Tall, aloof and extremely beautiful, their very existence catapulted Hank into a particularly belligerent mood.

"I hate beautiful women!" Hank muttered to everyone and no one as he and Lincky and Ralph left the party.

"You mean the models? That's only because they're taller than you and ignore you besides," said Ralph, who liked to annoy Hank with the truth whenever possible.

"I hate you, too!" Hank said, ignoring Ralph and turning on Lincky.

"I didn't know you thought I was beautiful," Lincky said, wondering fleetingly if Hank had had too much to drink.

"Who says I think you're beautiful?" Hank snapped.

"I'm out of here," said Ralph suddenly, hailing a passing taxi as if it were the last flight out of Casablanca. "I'll see you tomorrow."

"You'd never give me the time of day, would you?" Hank asked as he and Lincky, now alone, walked from the Plaza Hotel where the party had been held toward the corner of Fifth Avenue and 58th Street.

"I give you *all* my time, every day," Lincky said.

"I don't mean in the office."

"What do you mean?"

"Do I have to draw you a picture?"

Hank lit a Parliament, a brand Lincky knew he considered classy. Increasing his speed, he began to walk away from her. Hank was walking very quickly now, almost racing, and Lincky struggled to keep up with him.

"Are you asking me for a date?" Lincky asked, catching up with him.

"Shit, no! I'm not asking you for a date! I'm asking you to go to bed with me!" Hank replied.

Lincky looked at him as if he'd fallen out of a tree.

"The flowers! The perfume! The poetry! The promises! You really believe in sweeping a woman off her feet, don't you?"

"You want flowers?" asked Hank, sounding confused.

"Isn't it a bit late?"

"Well? Are you saying yes or no?"

| 143 |

"I'm married," replied Lincky.

"So?"

"You're married, too."

"So?"

Lincky was momentarily struck speechless. Hank Greene had just asked her to go to bed with him and so far, they had barely exchanged a civilized word, never laughed at the same joke, never shared a meal, never so much as grazed hands. He was really too much, thought Lincky.

By now, Hank and Lincky had stopped walking. They stood in the middle of the sidewalk on Fifth Avenue facing each other in an attitude better suited to pugilists than potential lovers. Holding their turf, they blocked the passage of other pedestrians. New Yorkers, accustomed to witnessing major emotional scenes being conducted in public, simply walked around them.

"What if I don't?" Lincky asked. She wondered whether sex was part of the job.

"If you don't, nothing. It's a free country," said Hank. "Going to bed with me is not a condition of keeping your job."

"And what if I do?" Lincky asked, barely believing the words coming from her own mouth.

Hank shrugged.

"We'd have to see."

Still not touching, Hank and Lincky headed downtown. Each was lost in thought. Hank was so amazed that Lincky had considered going to bed with him that he actually tried to think of a way to back out. Lincky was temporarily numb.

"I don't believe this," she said, as they walked up the front steps into the St. Regis hotel.

"I don't either," said Hank, taking Lincky's arm and guiding her to the check-in desk.

Ten minutes later Hank and Lincky found themselves in a large double room. The white-and-gilt furniture, curved and carved, was in the Grand Bordello style that passes for elegant among hotel decorators. Tiered, billowing curtains and thick carpeting gave the room the overripe feel of a luxurious cocoon. Dirty doings were definitely in the air.

"Looks like a whorehouse," commented Hank, glancing at the peach silk lampshades and the apricot-colored curtains.

Then, not allowing Lincky time to respond, he reached for her and pulled her to him. He kissed her on the mouth and, before she could react or even utter a syllable, opened her mouth with his tongue. He tasted of cigarettes and heat and, as he deepened the kiss, he pushed Lincky back toward the bed. With one hand he raised her sweater and fondled her breasts almost roughly. The fire of his hands ignited her nipples. Numbly, she remembered Peter and told herself that she should resist. Instead, she began to writhe out of her pantyhose. Even before they were entirely off, Hank pushed her hand away and pinned her down. Sweating and panting, he entered her. She was wet and slippery. He was feverish and insistent. They clung to each other and rocked fiercely back and forth, forcing themselves closer, raising the pitch of excitement higher and higher. Lincky screamed as she came. Hank groaned and collapsed on top of her. They rested that way until their breathing had returned to normal.

"Surprised you!" Hank gloated. "You thought Hank Greene would be a selfish creep, didn't you?"

"You do seem to go out of your way to give that impression," Lincky said as she peeled off the other leg of her pantyhose. Now that sex was over, Lincky and Hank lay in bed, naked and holding hands. She felt surprisingly comfortable with him.

"It's just my basic defensiveness," Hank said as he lit a post-coital Parliament. "Basically, I feel everyone is better than I am."

"*Is* everyone better than you are?" Lincky asked. She was fascinated by Hank's revelation.

"You'd feel that way, too, if your father was low man on the totem pole because his name ended in 'berg.' You don't know what it's like to be on the outside looking in. I'm perpetually pissed-off against the whole world," said Hank. Then he shrugged. "Probably there's a diamond underneath the rough exterior."

"Then why don't you get rid of the rough exterior?" Lincky asked, thinking that without the rough exterior Hank Greene would be able to conquer the world.

"I would if I could," Hank replied. "I don't know how."

"It's not that hard," Lincky said.

" 'It's not that hard' *if* you grow up with all the advantages," Hank mocked, his usual contentiousness resurfacing. "It's damn hard if you were always second best."

"Was your life really such a struggle?" Lincky asked.

"I won't bore you with tales of my lousy childhood, if you won't bore me with yours," snapped Hank. He smashed out the cigarette and began to dress. "It's getting late. It's time for me to send you home to your hubby."

"I wish you wouldn't say 'hubby,' " said Lincky, chilled by the expression.

"What do you want me to call him? 'Mr. Desmond'?" asked Hank. His tone exuded contempt and Lincky felt annihilated. She didn't know what to say and so she said nothing. Hank seemed pleased with the assassination and they dressed silently. The moments of magic were over. The time-out to their mutual hostility and suspicion had ended.

24
LINCKY

1 9 6 3 :

The start of something big—Julia
Child debuts on a TV cooking series
called *The French Chef*.

LINCKY went to bed with Hank Greene for the second time
two days later. They met at lunchtime at the Commodore
Hotel, big, commercial and anonymous. On fire with memory
and anticipation, Hank and Lincky ravished each other in an
act that bordered on mutual rape. Dripping with sweat, they
slid on each other's skin, grabbing at each other, tearing at
each other. Sex was pent-up hunger, a ravenous appetite born
of memory and savagely suppressed emotion. Never had
Lincky opened her legs so wide, never had she abandoned
herself so recklessly. She had never experienced such intense
and explosive orgasms. Needs and desires that Lincky thought
had died with her parents were stirred in the act of making
love with Hank Greene. In Hank Greene's arms, Lincky became a woman who knew nothing of isolation.

"I can't stand this!" she said.

"Yes," said Hank.

"Are you always this hot?" he asked, amazed at Lincky's feverish eroticism.

"No. I don't understand it," said Lincky. She was shaken by the ferocity of her appetites and her utter lack of inhibition. She had always enjoyed sex. She had never before craved it and she had never before been overwhelmed by it. She was staggered by the intensity of her reaction. It seemed to Lincky that she had found an unexpected and potentially even dangerous stranger dwelling within herself.

"I guess your husband can't take care of you," Hank commented, electing himself victor in a secret, two-way competition.

"I wish you wouldn't bring Peter into this. I don't talk about your wife," Lincky said, warning Hank off. She resented Hank's casual dismissal of Peter and his offhanded encroachment into her personal life. Lincky was willing—more than willing—to go to bed with Hank Greene. She did not intend, even conversationally, to allow him into her life. Lincky hung a DO NOT ENTER sign across her emotions. Because she would have obeyed such an injunction, she assumed that Hank Greene would, too.

"Ever since the St. Regis, I'm walking around with a hard-on all the time," Hank said, ignoring Lincky's attempt at dissuasion. "That hasn't happened since I was eighteen."

"How old are you now?"

"Thirty-four."

"A dozen years older than I am," said Lincky.

"You're only twenty-two? You seem older."

"People have always thought I'm older than I really am," said Lincky.

One week later, Hank and Lincky met at the Waldorf, the perfect place for Manhattan adulterers with its honeycomb of entrances and exits on Park, Lexington, 48th, and 49th. As if starved, Hank and Lincky consumed each other and were consumed by each other. Sexual fire burned away the boundaries of self as Lincky abandoned herself to orgasm after orgasm and Hank fought to dominate and satisfy her. Lincky's skin was flushed and her hair was plastered to her forehead.

"Are you all right?" Hank asked.

"Fine," said Lincky. She attempted a smile. "Never better."

Afterward, Hank lit a cigarette and Lincky wrapped herself in a sheet.

"You," he said, touching her nipple through the sheet, "are like royalty."

"I am?"

Hank refused to elaborate.

"What do you do on weekends?" Hank asked in one of his lightning changes of mood.

"Go out to dinner. Go to the theater. See friends," Lincky replied, answering as evasively as possible. What she and Peter did was none of Hank Greene's business. Her body was available to Hank. Her marriage was out of bounds.

" 'Go out to dinner. Go to the theater. See friends,' " mocked Hank. "Sounds boring."

"Well, it isn't," replied Lincky, even as she realized that Hank was right. It *was* boring.

Peter preferred to patronize the same three or four restaurants where he was well known and well treated. He went only to Broadway plays and only if he could get seats in the fifth to tenth row center. "Their" friends were really Peter's friends, people he knew from the office or college and with whom he felt comfortable. The husbands talked about the stock market and sports. The wives talked about their children. No one ever spoke to Lincky about her work or whether she liked it.

"When are you going to have a little one?" asked June Leighton, Eric's wife.

"Later. Right now I'm very interested in my job," replied Lincky.

"A marriage isn't complete without children," said June, who had three.

"Anything in the oven?" asked Bo Skinner.

"What a revolting expression," said Lincky.

"You don't know how to treat a woman," said Bo, addressing Peter as if Lincky hadn't spoken. " 'Pregnant and barefoot in the kitchen.' That's my motto."

Lincky looked over at Bo's wife, Beth, who was seven months pregnant. She looked down at the tablecloth and said nothing.

On October 25, Hank and Lincky met at the Plaza. Three days after that, they rendezvoused at the Barclay. Lincky seemed able to handle the sexual part of adultery with little conflict. She convinced herself that she felt neither particularly guilty nor ashamed. She was fanatically discreet and determined not to hurt Peter in any way. As far as Lincky was concerned, the scarlet A had gone the way of crinolines and push-up bras. Her relationship with Hank Greene was about sex. Period. A great fuck was a great fuck and that was all.

Totally unanticipated by Lincky, it was the emotional aspect of her relationship with Hank Greene that began almost immediately to get out of control. The things Hank said and the questions he asked made Lincky think about her life and her marriage in ways she never had before. Hank's comments about an exhibition of modern art, an off-Broadway play, or a foreign movie made Lincky realize that there was a whole world she knew little about. They also made Lincky realize that under Hank's crude façade, he was suspiciously cultivated, well educated, and even sensitive.

Hank's negative observations about Peter's lack of energy, both sexual and professional, upset Lincky terribly. He had an uncanny way of seeming to sense Lincky's most secret doubts about her husband. Hank's comments touched troubling aspects of Lincky's own most private feelings about her marriage, feelings that she would have preferred to leave untouched and unexamined.

"I suppose you'll work for a few more years. Then what

will you do?" asked Hank. "Have kids? Buy a house? Move to the suburbs? That kind of crap?"

"What most people consider a normal life isn't necessarily crap," replied Lincky.

"It's crap if that's all there is. It wouldn't be enough for you. You need more. You could get somewhere if you ever got serious."

"Don't you think I'm serious? Don't you think I work hard?"

"Oh, you work hard," said Hank unenthusiastically. "You also always leave in time to get dinner for your hubby."

"Is that so awful?" asked Lincky. After all, she *was* married. She *did* have responsibilities outside the office.

"It's amateur night," said Hank.

"If I worked harder, what would happen to my marriage?" Hank looked at her.

"That's your problem," he said.

When Lincky tried to turn the tables and deflect Hank's attention away from her and Peter and toward himself, Hank became evasive. When Lincky asked him what he did on weekends, Hank replied with one word.

"Work," he said, telling Lincky nothing—and everything.

When she asked him to tell her how he had started his business, Hank wasted no words.

"I rented an office, got a telephone, and struggled," he replied.

When she asked him to tell her about his wife, Hank was equally opaque.

"Sarah does her thing. I do mine," he said.

"What's Sarah's thing?" Lincky knew that Hank and his wife had had one child, a boy, who had died of jaundice in infancy. Since then, they had not been able to have other children.

"Dogs. She breeds and shows them."

"What kind of dogs?"

"German shepherds," said Hank. "What else?"

By early November, Lincky and Hank, magnetized by an out-of-control sexual attraction, were meeting several times a week.

"Am I the only girl you see?" she asked Hank. "Or are there others?" Lincky wanted to know.

"What do you think I am? Superman?"

Assaulted by raging sexual and emotional appetites she had never before experienced, Lincky began to fear that Hank had told Ralph Weiss about their affair and that Ralph had told Peter.

"Why would I tell Ralph? Why would I tell anyone?" asked Hank.

"I don't know. No reason," said Lincky, not understanding her dread. "I guess I'm just getting paranoid."

She began to think, without evidence, that people in the office had guessed about her affair with Hank and were talking about her behind her back.

"Your secretary was talking to the receptionist in the ladies' room. They stopped the minute I came in. I'm sure they were talking about us. Do you think they guessed?"

"They haven't guessed," said Hank. "They all think you're an ice princess."

"They do?" Before Hank could reply, Lincky answered her own question. "They do. Everyone does."

"I don't," said Hank.

Lincky began to have elaborate fantasies that she would divorce Peter and Hank would divorce Sarah and that she and Hank would marry.

"Marry? You and me? That would be a disaster," said Hank.

"Why?" asked Lincky.

"I have a lousy disposition and you're too uptight. We'd drive each other crazy."

Lincky's emotions, under vigilant control since her parents' deaths, floated closer and closer to the surface. She tried unsuccessfully not to compare Peter and Hank. Peter did what was expected of him. Hank carved out his own place in the world. Peter was dutiful. Hank was rebellious. Peter was subdued. Hank throbbed with energy. Peter never fought back. Hank never took no for an answer.

Lincky wondered what her parents would think of Hank. She imagined that, as people who had started their own business, they would approve of Hank and the agency he was building. She thought that they would admire his iconoclasm and respect his intelligence.

Lincky still loved Peter but it was Hank who brought her to life. She felt confused and torn between the two men, alternately depressed and elated. She lurched from optimism to pessimism. She felt on top of the world and then blanketed by despair. She questioned the very meaning of life in a way she hadn't since adolescence. She felt frayed and worn out and sometimes her emotional exhaustion erupted into unruly fits of temper.

"Are you getting your period?" asked Peter, mystified when Lincky flew into a screaming rage over breaking a 59-cent Pyrex measuring cup.

At other times, she drifted into woolgathering daydreams.

"I said hello and you didn't even look up," said Becky Reese, who ran into Lincky at Lord & Taylor's Clinique counter and telephoned her later to ask why she had been so distracted.

Lincky's sexual appetites continued to intensify.

"Who do you think I am? Casanova?" said Peter, when Lincky wanted sex twice in one night.

"Where'd you learn that?" he asked when Lincky kissed him in a place where Hank had once kissed her.

"In a book," said Lincky, making a mental note never to do it again. When had sex with Peter become so routine? Lincky tried to remember but couldn't.

At the same time that her relationship with Hank tantalized Lincky with the possibility of new and exciting worlds, her continued association with him was threatening the world she already knew. Lincky increasingly feared that she was becoming obsessed with Hank. She dreaded becoming sexually dependent on him and she wondered despairingly what she was doing, why she was doing it, and what she would have to do to stop.

She had a husband she loved, a marriage she valued, and a job that was increasingly absorbing. She had an almost perfect life and yet she was risking them all for a few hours in bed with a difficult and demanding boss, a mysterious and mercurial man who undermined her confidence, attacked her marriage, and sneered at her privileged background. Assaulted by emotions she could neither understand nor control, Lincky did something she had never done before. She confided in someone.

"I don't understand what I'm doing or why I'm doing it," she told Coral Weinstein. "I'm risking everything for a man who attacks my husband, tells me I don't work hard enough and refuses even to talk about marriage. All I know is that when I'm with Hank, I never want to leave him. It's completely irrational."

"Suicidal is what you mean," Coral said. "If you keep it up, you'll lose everything. Your job. Your husband. Your boyfriend. Believe me, Lincky, because I've been there. I know what I'm talking about."

Lincky nodded. "I know you're right," she said. "I have to stop. I have to put Hank Greene out of my mind and out of my life."

25
LINCKY

A week in November . . .

LINCKY promised herself that she would never see Hank Greene in private again. She began to keep that promise when Hank asked her to meet him on the third Saturday afternoon of November.

"You name the place," he said.

"I'm not going to name a place because I'm not going to meet you," Lincky replied firmly. "Weekends are completely out of the question."

"What's the matter? Hubby set a curfew for weekends, too?"

"Don't be ridiculous. Of course not." Lincky said, defending herself—and Peter—against the attack.

"Then what are you scared of?" Hank asked. He was like an armored tank, Lincky thought. He never gave up. He never retreated. He never showed wounds.

"Nothing," said Lincky. "I'm not afraid of anything."

"Bullshit!" said Hank. Even though they were in the office

and people could see them through Hank's open door, he moved close to Lincky. She could smell his soap and feel the heat his body exuded. "You're scared of me. You're scared of your husband and you're scared of yourself."

Unnerved, Lincky wordlessly moved back a step. Hank Greene didn't act like any man Lincky had ever met and she didn't react to him like any man she had ever met.

"So what's the answer?" Hank demanded. "Yes or no?"

Lincky hesitated. Hank answered the question himself.

"The answer is yes. Now, pick a place," he ordered.

Her large turquoise eyes flickered anxiously. "I can't."

"You can and you will," said Hank, boring in on a silent, stricken Lincky.

"No," said Lincky, stumbling as she tried to take another step back.

"I said yes. *You* pick the place," he insisted. He moved toward her. His eyes seemed radioactive. He dominated her with his will and his intensity. If he had ripped her clothes off right there in front of the whole office, she would not have been able to resist.

"The Commodore?" she replied. "Okay?"

That Saturday, Lincky told Peter that she was having lunch with Charlie Lamb. Her emotions lacerated her. Desire collided with fear. Anticipation with self-accusation. Arousal with terror. She scurried furtively through the lobby of the Commodore, afraid that she would run into someone she and Peter knew. She carried a shopping bag filled with brie, a loaf of French bread and a bottle of Brouilly. If she and Hank shared a picnic, Lincky thought, she wouldn't feel like such a liar. If she and Hank shared a picnic, she *would* be having lunch.

With a sick, excited feeling in the pit of her stomach, Lincky arrived at the room Hank had reserved.

"What took you so long?" Hank asked as he opened the door to her. He was naked. He turned the sheet down in welcome. Lincky dropped the shopping bag into a chair and turned toward him, her lips parted, her heart racing.

The picnic languished ignored in its shopping bag. Without a word, Hank began to undress her. His hands scorched her naked flesh. His mouth was avid and demanding. He pushed her down on the bed, ravishing her with hands, mouth, and tongue. He was insistent yet mindful of exciting her, igniting her, evoking a response from her.

Even as Lincky's body responded, her mind held back. The knowledge that she had broken her promise to herself never to see Hank again taunted at her. The fact that she had lied to Peter seemed far worse than the physical act of adultery.

While her mouth and hands pursued their own ravenous quests, Lincky's mind spit out warnings and condemnations. Hank Greene didn't care about her. He didn't give a damn about her thoughts, her feelings, her hopes, her future. He didn't care about anything except sex. He had not even said hello. He had not asked her how she was. He had taken one look at her, asked her what had taken her so long and turned down the sheet. You: on your back. Hank Greene was interested in fucking her. Period.

They kissed hungrily, their legs entwined. Their bodies moved in volcanic harmonies. As she felt herself sink further into the rhythms of sex, Lincky made a deliberate effort to resist. She fixed her gaze at the cracked paint on the Commodore's ceiling. The fissure paralleled the void in her own life and Coral's word suddenly ran through Lincky's mind: suicide.

Pinned beneath Hank Greene, his mouth on hers, his cock in her cunt, Lincky asked herself, What am I doing here? What, she asked herself, am I doing with my life? Do I really hate myself this much? Why do I seem determined to ruin my marriage and my job? What's wrong with me? What do I have to do to stop? *Can* I stop? Am I obsessed? Am I addicted? Am I trapped, bereft of will, robbed of choice?

A surge of panic ran through Lincky. At the thought that she was nothing better than a prisoner, an animal, the panic transformed itself into an instinctive, self-preserving impulse to flight. Run! Get out! Escape! Now!

Abruptly, literally leaving Hank in midthrust, Lincky

shifted her body and with a quick jerky movement rolled away out from under him.

"What!" he demanded. He was stunned, outraged by Lincky's sudden withdrawal. His penis shivered with the exposure, engorged and purple, wet with their excitement.

"What am I doing here?" Lincky said, the question she had silently asked herself bursting from her lips. She got out of bed, wanting to be far away from Hank.

"You can't go out at night. That's why we decided to meet at lunchtime. *You* suggested the Commodore," Hank reminded her, using the facts like a club. His penis still erect, he lunged across the bed and grabbed for her. As Lincky twisted away from his reaching hands, she saw herself from afar, a stranger in a 50-point tabloid headline. A liar and a cheating wife. A naked woman alone in a hotel room with a man she didn't much like and certainly didn't love.

"I'm not like this! This isn't me!" she exclaimed as she began to gather her clothes from the floor where she had flung them.

"Then just who the hell is it?" Hank demanded. His voice was harsh, his face dark. "Betty Grable? Ed Sullivan?"

"I thought an affair would be exciting. Fun. It's not. It's awful," Lincky said. Her hair was disheveled, her makeup smeared. She was halfway between tears and fury. Holding her clothes across her body, Lincky ran into the bathroom and slammed the door behind her. Hank followed her and banged on the door with his fist.

"You wanted it as much as I did," Hank shouted. He pounded at the door and tried to push it open but Lincky snapped the lock shut.

"You bullied me!" she replied, her words half muffled by the closed door.

"Some bully! My back is bleeding from your nails!" he said, relentlessly shoving reality at her through the locked door.

She decided not to reply. No matter what she said, Hank would have an answer. He wouldn't stop. He wouldn't go away. He was hammering at the door, ordering her to open it. If she didn't escape, he would overwhelm her. If she didn't get back to Peter, she would be ruined, annihilated.

Lincky dressed swiftly and patched her makeup. She slipped out of the bathroom and ran to the door. With a last glance at Hank, Lincky told him what she had just told herself.

"Never again, Hank. I mean it," she said.

Before he could reply, Lincky fled from the room.

Lincky spent the weekend cringing at every ring of the telephone and recoiling at the sound of the doorbell, afraid that it would be Hank. Lincky knew that she had acted unforgivably on Saturday and, fearing Hank Greene's temper, she dreaded that he would arrive on her doorstep. Lincky could imagine the wild tantrum and the ugly accusations. Not only would he publicly humiliate her but he would make sure to do it in front of Peter.

"You're as nervous as a cat," Peter said on Sunday night. Lincky had spent the day cleaning the bookshelves and the books, dismantling the kitchen cabinets and rearranging their contents, scrubbing the bathroom, and reorganizing her closet. Now she sat in front of the television set, flicking from channel to channel, getting up and sitting down, picking up a magazine and flinging it aside.

"Nervous? Me? Of course not," said Lincky. Her mouth was dry and her heart pounded.

On Monday the 18th, Lincky walked through the small reception area of the Hank Greene Agency on the way to her desk. Her knees shook and the palms of her hands were slick with sweat at the prospect of encountering Hank. She had gotten out of the weekend alive. She did not know how she would survive the coming week. Lincky expected the worst and feared the unimaginable.

To Lincky's unspeakable relief, she did not even see Hank that Monday. He had meetings outside the office all morning and he spent the afternoon in his office with an author, the door shut.

At the regular Tuesday morning staff meeting, Lincky reported on Glen Sinclair's outline for a new diet book. Hank accepted her presentation without comment. He did not look at her nor did he call her on the interoffice telephone. Lincky alternated between moments of relief and panic. Perhaps he, like she, simply needed time to get used to the new distance between them. Or perhaps there would be a delayed reaction. Lincky waited for the bomb—if there was one—to explode.

On Wednesday the 20th, just after lunch, Lincky spoke briefly to Hank about Kathleen van Doren's progress on her new novel.

"She said that it's going slowly but she'll make her deadline," Lincky said.

Hank did not reply. He acted as if he hadn't heard her, although Lincky knew that he had.

Late on Thursday afternoon, Hank threw a manuscript on Lincky's desk and asked her to read it overnight.

"Have the report on my desk first thing tomorrow," he said and walked away without another word.

Hank's words, so ordinary and even banal, splintered the wall of Lincky's anxiety. Could it be that everything was finally back to normal? Was it possible that there was no bomb? Was the fear of a delayed reaction only in her mind? Lincky allowed herself to think so.

It was Thursday. Although tense and distanced, she and Hank had made it almost through the week.

Only Friday was left. If they could endure Friday, then everything would be fine. TGIF, Lincky thought, invoking the old office prayer, as she arrived at her desk the next morning.

Friday, November 22, would be the last day in what had been the worst week in her life. If she could survive Friday, she thought, everything would be all right.

III

NOVEMBER 22–24, 1963

REACTIONS IN THE WORLD
PRESS:

Terrible history has been made in Dallas, and the
magnitude of our city's sorrow can only be measured
against the enormity of the deed. The bullet that felled
our President was molded in an unstable world. . . . But
to our great sorrow, it found its mark here.

—*Dallas Times-Herald*

He has been murderously cut off in the prime of life and
power; the Nation has suffered another day of infamy
which the American people will never forget.

—*The New York Times*

He was the one authentic hero of the post-war world.

—*The Sunday Times*, London

26
JANE

NOVEMBER 22, 1963
12:38 CST:

Case 24740, white male suffering
from gunshot wounds . . .

—Admittal record, Parkland Hospital

WHEN Owen Casals invited Jane Gresch to go to Dallas with him while he covered the presidential trip, Jane accepted. Neither of them gave even a passing thought to politics or presidents or the rift in the Democratic party in Texas. What they thought about was fucking their brains out in Texas hotels on Owen's *Newsflash* expense account.

"It's a long way to go to get laid," Glen Sinclair said, giving Jane the extra time off. "Zucchini or no zucchini."

The instant the official at the Trade Mart announced that the president had been shot, Jane and Owen ran downstairs. The press bus would take everyone to Parkland Hospital. When they reached the curb, Jane tried to force her way onto the bus along with the rest of the press corps.

"Don't! Wait!" Owen shouted. He grabbed Jane by the arm and prevented her from boarding the bus.

"Why? Don't you want to go to Parkland?" asked Jane, instinctively shoving forward along with everyone else.

Owen's reply was drowned out by the shouting, frenzied press corps. His tight grip stopped Jane from moving and when the bus was finally packed with reporters, Owen and Jane stood alone on the deserted curb for a moment.

"Now!" yelled Owen.

He pushed Jane forward up the stairs and onto the bus just as its big doors began to close. Leaping to the steps, Owen scrambled on board after her, barely making it.

This time, the press bus sped. It careened around corners and ran red lights, heading along the still-cleared motorcade route for Parkland Hospital. The press bus was a metal hive of speculation and controlled panic. Someone thought he remembered hearing something that could have been firecrackers. Or a motorcycle backfiring. Or gunshots. How many had there been? Three? Five? No one could say for certain. Had the noise been heard before the bus went under the underpass? Or just after? No one was quite sure.

"Shot? Does that mean an attempt?" asked the Associated Press stringer.

"Was he wounded?" someone else shouted.

"Who? Kennedy or Connally?" came a voice from the back. John Connally, governor of Texas, was in the same limousine as the president, sitting just in front of him.

Everyone talked at once. Reporters were at war with themselves, with each other. They fought to suppress their personal reactions as they focused on the job at hand. Each man dealt with fear. Fear that the president might have been hit. Or worse. Fear that the shooting might not be over. Fear that the press bus might be the next target. Fear that someone else would get the story first, faster, or better. Hangovers were forgotten as adrenalin pumped through excited veins.

Owen, jammed against the door of the bus, did not participate in the fevered speculation. Instead, he peeled several twenty-dollar bills out of his wallet and put them into his jacket pocket along with a handful of dimes. Then he told Jane what to do.

"I'm calling New York the minute we get to Parkland. I need an open phone line. I want you to find out exactly where they've taken the president. Remember everything you see. I can't be in two places at once," Owen told Jane. As always, Owen Casals was determined to be first, to be best, to be the most successful.

When the bus skidded to a halt in front of the hospital, Jane realized why Owen had refused to board the bus along with everyone else. The last on, Owen was first off.

He bolted for the telephones banked along the ground-floor corridor of the hospital. The White House Signal Corps had already commandeered all of them. Using an old police reporter's trick, Owen ran up to the second floor. Near an almost deserted waiting room for friends and family of patients, he found an unoccupied pay phone. He dialed *Newsflash* in New York.

"Hold this line open," he told a nearby orderly, giving him a twenty-dollar bill and a handful of dimes. "There's another twenty when I get back."

The rest of the press corps crowded off the bus and into the pandemonium of Parkland. As journalists, police, and hospital workers rushed past, Jane noticed that the president's car, license plate GG300, its transparent bubbletop now up, was standing at the Emergency entrance. Its back door was still open, evidence, Jane realized, of the panic with which the limousine had been evacuated. A bucket of pinkish water stood on the sidewalk and a trail of blood led into the Emergency entrance. Not touching anything, Jane observed the mute, tragic scene and peered into the back seat of the car.

Looking for Owen, Jane ran in to the hospital's main floor. She saw Owen just as he ran down the stairs.

"The Emergency Room!" Jane shouted. "The president's in the Emergency Room! A trail of blood leads right to it!"

Together, Jane and Owen ran toward the Emergency Room.

"Jackie's bouquet of red roses is still in the back of the president's limousine. It's spattered with blood and there's a bucket of bloody water still standing on the sidewalk," Jane told Owen as they ran.

"Are you sure about the roses? How do you know about them?"

"I saw them myself. They left the door open, they got out of the car so fast. I looked into the back seat."

Jane and Owen joined the mob of press milling around outside the Emergency Room. They were waiting for a word, an indication, a sign. It came with the arrival of two priests.

Owen ran back upstairs to the open phone on the second floor and was first to report to New York that two priests had arrived at Parkland to administer the last rites to Case 24740.

27
ELLY

AUGUST 28, 1963:

"I have a dream . . ."

—Martin Luther King, Jr., at the
Lincoln Memorial

VINCE McCullough had gone to Washington as an assistant press secretary, but in the summer of 1963 he learned that in Washington politics ruled everything—even the White House. On the same week that Elly moved to Washington, Vince's boss told him that he was going to have to replace him.

"I'm sorry, Vince. I hate like hell to do this to you but Rick Warner has contacts in California up the yazoo."

California, Vince did not have to be told, controlled thirty-two electoral votes and getting the Kennedy message out to Californians would help hold those votes in the next election.

Telling Vince how indispensable he had been, his boss arranged for a job for Vince with a high-powered firm of lobbyists representing the Detroit automobile industry.

"Come with me. The salary's practically double," Vince told Elly. "Besides, it's a terrific office. Lots of single guys."

"You'd be lobbying for the Big Three?" asked Elly. She could just imagine what her labor-lawyer father would say if she told him she was working for a company that represented the corporate interests of Ford, General Motors, and Chrysler.

"It's got power, prestige, and perks," said Vince.

Like her father, Elly was not impressed by the Three P's. Not when a fourth P was involved: principle.

"I came to Washington to work in the White House," Elly said.

"The new guy is bringing in his own people," Vince said.

"Maybe they can find a place for me."

"Are you for real?"

Elly decided to stay on in Washington anyway. Even though Ethel had given Owen her D.C. number, he had not—at least so far—used it. Elly had no desire to return to New York. Everything about the city—the Village, the ethnic restaurants, the art movie houses, the nightly parties, the electric buzz of interesting people doing interesting things—reminded Elly of Owen. She had come to Washington thinking that perhaps a new city, a new job, and new people might help her forget Owen Casals.

Living on the savings she had accumulated while working at Parmenides, Elly rented a studio apartment in what turned out to be the only slum in Georgetown and began to look for a job. She spent weekends in jeans and a work shirt drowning her double disappointment in work and in love by throwing herself into the fight for civil rights. She marched and demonstrated and was among the two hundred thousand who massed around the Lincoln Memorial to hear Martin Luther King's "I Have a Dream" speech.

Elly's family didn't understand why she stayed in Washington.

"You gave up a good job here in New York," Louise Cullen said.

"Good?" replied Elly, remembering that her boss, Adrian Holland, seemed barely able to remember her name and had not made the slightest effort to stop her from leaving Parmenides. "I did an assistant's job for a secretary's salary."

"Come back home, baby," her father said, taking the phone from her mother. "I miss our Sunday talks."

"I do, too," said Elly, remembering how she and her father

walked through the streets of the Village, stopping at Sutter's bakery for coffee and Danish, all the while discussing the state of the world.

"Washington is the miserable single-woman capital of the world," said Margaret. "Why do you want to stay there and add to the glut?"

"I feel more in the middle of things here. This week I applied for a job with the Peace Corps. Maybe I'll be able to make a difference in this world, after all."

Elly found a job at the Pappagallo Boutique in Georgetown. The pay was minimal but Pappagallo paid a commission for every sale and Elly, it turned out, could sell anything. She sold more shoes than any salesperson that had ever worked at the boutique.

"I come in to get a pair of basic black shoes and I walk out with sandals, ballet slippers, and a pair of silver evening shoes," one of the customers told Janice Kellen, the owner. "Plus, of course, the basic blacks and browns, too."

By November 22, Elly was still selling shoes and waiting. Waiting on customers. Waiting to find out if, maybe, the Peace Corps had a place for her. Waiting to see if Owen would ever call. Waiting to find out what she wanted to do with the rest of her life.

With the news of President Kennedy's death, Elly ran from the Pappagallo Boutique. There was one and only one person she wanted to talk to. Girls never called men but this was different. When Elly got home, she called Owen's 13th Street apartment but there was no answer. When she tried to call the offices of *Newsflash* magazine, she got a busy. She learned from television that phone circuits throughout the country were tied up. Sometimes unable even to get a dial tone on the beleaguered switchboards of the nation's capital, Elly switched on her television set and watched Walter Cronkite weep as he informed the nation that its president was dead.

28
ELLY

ALL weekend long, like millions of other Americans, Elly sat transfixed in front of her television set. She saw Air Force One, bearing the body of the murdered president, set down at Andrews Air Force Base. She watched as the casket was placed in an ambulance and as Jacqueline Kennedy, still wearing the bloodstained pink suit she had worn in Dallas, accompanied her husband's body. She saw the flag-draped coffin being carried into the White House by a military escort, Mrs. Kennedy erectly walking behind.

The next day, Saturday, was gray and rainy. Elly watched the scenes no one would ever forget. She watched the long procession of dignitaries filing into the White House to offer condolences. As the signals flashed to Paris and London and Berlin and Tokyo, she watched people from around the world mourn the fallen American president. She watched as, in Dallas, wreaths were placed on the spot where Kennedy had been shot and she stayed up until late in the night as a military honor guard and two priests kept vigil at the President's flag-draped coffin in the East Room of the White House.

Sunday dawned sunny and chilly and Elly continued to sit in front of her television set. She watched as the president left the White House for the last time, his casket lifted to a horse-drawn caisson for the somber procession to the Capitol. The sound of muffled drums haunted her and the silence of the crowd along Pennsylvania Avenue was profound. She also watched as Lee Harvey Oswald, the president's alleged assassin, was shot at point-blank range as Dallas police transferred him from the city prison to the county jail.

Throughout the eulogies, the funeral and second murder, Elly kept watching for a glimpse of Owen. She wondered where he was. She wondered if he had gone to Dallas to cover the assassination or if he was right there in Washington covering the state funeral. The telephone at his apartment did not answer. *Newflash*'s switchboard was usually busy. When Elly did get through, she was put on hold and apparently forgotten.

Wherever Owen was and whatever he was doing, Elly told herself sadly, she was sure that Owen was not thinking of her.

Then, early on Sunday evening, her telephone rang.

29
LINCKY

"America wept tonight not alone for its dead young President, but for itself. . . . Somehow the worst prevailed over the best. . . . Some strain of madness and violence had destroyed the highest symbol of law and order."

—James Reston on the Kennedy assassination

"THE president is dead. That is a confirmed report."

The portable radio Lincky had turned on in Hank Greene's office repeated the stark bulletin over and over. Sitting alone at Hank's desk in the manuscript-cluttered office, Lincky began to weep.

President Kennedy's death reverberated with the memory of her parents' death. He was young. So were they. He was in the prime of life. So were they. He had everything to live for. So had they. Lincky wept for the country, for the president, for his wife and children and the big, close-knit Kennedy family. Finally, she shed tears for herself. She cried for her parents and her orphaned self, for Peter and for Hank. She cried for what was and for what might have been.

Lost in tears, Lincky did not hear Hank enter his office.

"What are you doing in here?" he asked in the first nonessential words he had addressed to Lincky since the previous Saturday afternoon at the Commodore. He looked volcanically angry and tightly controlled, a man who could not forget or forgive what Lincky had done to him.

"President Kennedy has been shot. He's dead," Lincky said. She looked up at Hank and wiped the tears off her face as she flicked off the radio. "Isn't it terrible?"

"Terrible," he said. "I asked what you're doing in here. Sitting in my chair."

"I'm sorry." She got up, stumbling in her haste.

"Why aren't you working?" Hank asked. "Don't you have anything to do?"

"It's hard to think about work at a time like this."

"Then you shouldn't be working here," Hank said. He reclaimed his chair and lit a cigarette from the butt of the one he held.

"Not work here?" she asked. Her job was the most exciting and rewarding part of her life. "You said I could be really good."

"That was then. This is now," he said. He picked up a telephone and began to dial.

"Are you firing me?"

"No, Mrs. Desmond, I'm promoting you. Pick up your check in Accounting on the way out. I don't want to see you in here again."

Physically trembling, Lincky left Hank's office. She felt numb, stripped of her senses. She was overwhelmed by a sense of abandonment that was fundamental in the extreme, a deprivation that stirred firmly buried memories of the other great loss in her life: the loss of her parents. Lincky could not even begin to put boundaries on what was lost or the extent of its enormity. She felt diminished in every way and sensed that some parts of her life were gone entirely.

As she wobbled out of Hank's office, Lincky dimly heard Hank talking to a paperback publisher about an instant book on the assassination.

"Owen Casals is in Dallas for *Newflash*," Hank was saying in his intense way. Hunched over the phone, cigarette smoldering, all business. Lincky, her problems and the possibilities her very existence raised for Hank Greene, apparently no longer existed for him. She marveled at the way he had shut her out so quickly, a surgeon striding from the table, leaving it to others to sew up the bleeding patient. "He can provide a manuscript by Sunday night. You can have copies on the newsstands Tuesday."

30
LINCKY

By 1 P.M. Dallas time 68 percent of
all adults in the United States knew
of the shooting. . . . Before the end
of the afternoon, when 99.8 percent
had learned that the elected
president had been murdered, the
country was in the grip of an
extraordinary emotional upheaval.
An entire nation had been savaged.

—William Manchester, *The Death of
a President*

LINCKY walked up Third Avenue in a city as silent and
shocked as she was. She moved as if she were a shadowy ghost
in a surrealistic dream of tears and silence. Her eyes did not
see. Her memory had gone blank. Her emotions had been
snuffed out.

It was two-thirty when Lincky got home. She washed her
face and brushed her teeth and put on her nightgown. She
wanted to sleep. If she had had sleeping pills, she would have
taken one but she did not permit them in the apartment. Hank
had been right. She *was* afraid of herself. She was dangerous.
To others and to herself.

As she turned down the covers to get into bed, she heard
Peter call from the foyer.

"Lincky? Are you here?" he asked, seeing Lincky's purse
on the table in the foyer. Peter had taken a subway up from
Wall Street, stopped at Lincky's office and been told by the
ashen-faced, weeping receptionist that Lincky had gone home.

Peter had followed her there, arriving at the apartment several minutes after she did.

When he got no answer, he called again.

"Lincky?"

There was no answer. She wasn't in the living room. Peter walked past the kitchen and into the bedroom.

"Are you all right?" Peter asked. He had never before seen Lincky in bed in the middle of the day.

"I'm fine," she said in a barely audible voice, although she didn't look fine. There were dark circles under Lincky's eyes and a drawn look of exhaustion on her face. Peter himself had wept at the news that the president had been murdered. He had seen people all over the city weeping openly but Lincky seemed to be somewhere beyond tears.

She took a black sleep mask from the night table and put it over her eyes. She did not want to see Peter. She did not want Peter to see her.

"I'll put on the television," Peter said, thinking that Lincky looked drained and pale, almost bloodless. He assumed that she was shocked, as everyone was, by the stunning news from Dallas.

Peter switched on the television set. Every station had cut away to the news of the president's assassination. Peter sat down on the edge of the bed next to Lincky and took her hand. It was icy.

"I'm fine," said Lincky.

Then she began to weep. The tears, having nowhere to go, clotted behind the sleep mask, pooled in and around her eyes and Lincky felt that she would drown in them.

"What's the matter?" asked Peter.

"Nothing," Lincky said, raising the sleep mask slightly to allow the tears to escape. She drew herself into a tight fetal ball, wanting to be impervious to touch or feeling or memory. When Peter reached out to comfort her, Lincky again flinched from his touch.

"Leave me alone," she said, barely audible. "Please."

Lincky did not leave her bed for the entire weekend. She did not wash her face or brush her teeth or eat a single mouthful of food. She huddled silently under the covers, hidden behind the sleep mask, tears now and then flowing down her face.

"What's the matter? Can't I help? Can't I do something?" Peter kept asking. Peter and Lincky, like Elly, like so many millions of Americans, had kept the television set on the entire weekend. The somber music, the muffled drumbeats from the president's funeral in Washington sounded in the background.

"No. There's nothing you can do," said Lincky.

On Monday morning Lincky was still in bed. The black circles under her eyes had deepened. She had lost so much weight that she looked like a wraith. Peter was frightened. Nothing he said or did caused her to respond. Work, he thought, always energized her.

"Aren't you going to go to the office?" he asked when she did not get up and get dressed.

"No," she replied, in the hollow voice that Peter had begun to dread.

"You always go to work," Peter said, remembering the times that Lincky had ignored bad colds and miserable viruses to drag herself into the office.

"Not anymore," she replied. "I've been fired."

"Fired? You?" Peter could hardly believe her. Lincky fired? It seemed inconceivable. But why hadn't she said something? Why hadn't she told him?

"He fired me," Lincky said and turned away from him.

On Wednesday, Peter called Lincky's doctor. He told him that Lincky had once tried to commit suicide and he said that he was concerned about her mental state. He was afraid that Lincky might be having a nervous breakdown. He described Lincky's behavior since Friday, her failure to eat or speak or dress.

"I don't know about a nervous breakdown," said the doctor. "But it sounds like she should see someone."

Peter carefully made a note of the name and telephone number of the psychotherapist Lincky's internist recommended: Eliot Landauer.

"What good can talking do?" Lincky said in her toneless, uninflected voice. She had forgotten how to talk. Except for her conversations with Hank, she hadn't truly spoken since her parents' accident.

"You have to try," said Peter. "Otherwise you'll just stay here and die."

31
JANE

"I am absolutely sure he never knew what hit him."

—Chief surgeon, Parkland Hospital

JANE and Owen spent the rest of the assassination weekend together. On Saturday, along with a *Newsflash* photographer, they visited the residence of the alleged presidential assassin at 2515 West Fifth Street and interviewed Lee Harvey Oswald's Russian wife, Marina. On Sunday at 12:21, they were in the basement of the Dallas police station when Jack Ruby, a Dallas nightclub owner, shot Oswald in front of live television cameras.

As always on a breaking story, Owen's adrenalin kicked in. Running down rumors, interviewing witnesses and badgering local police contacts while staying in twenty-four-hour phone contact with his New York office, Owen subsisted for the next three days on Camels, bourbon, and black coffee. He dictated constant updates to his New York office while consulting constantly with Jane about facts, memories, impressions.

"Was Marina wearing a dress or a skirt and blouse?" he asked Jane.

"Did you notice what books were in Oswald's book-shelves?"

"Would you call the neighborhood middle class or lower middle class?"

"Was the brim of Ruby's hat turned up or down? Could you see his face or was it in shadow?"

"Did Oswald see the gun? Did he say anything? Do you think he knew what was going to happen?"

Owen's colleagues praised him and said they wished they could be like him. His editors said that only Owen could perform so consistently under extreme stress. Owen's work on the Kennedy assassination and its aftermath, his peers all agreed, was a model of the reporter's art and craft.

"No one could do it except you," said Owen's boss, Ray Jessup.

"Good job!" said Chet Huntley, in a congratulatory phone call.

"Come on board," said Hubert Dessanges of *Week* magazine, *Newsflash*'s biggest competitor, offering Owen a fat raise.

"Aren't you impressed?" Owen asked Jane early that Sunday evening after she had read the cables loaded with praise and congratulations from *Newsflash*'s New York honchos. She handed the stack of papers back to him without a word.

"Sure," said Jane.

"Would it kill you to say so?"

"You didn't do it alone," Jane said. "I was there. I helped."

"So?"

"So did I get a cable of thanks from the managing editor? Did I get a 'good job!' from old Chet? Was I offered a plummy job?"

"You're just a girl," said Owen.

"So what does that make me? Chopped liver?"

"You're not a reporter. You tagged along."

"Yeah. And gave you the lead. 'A bucket of crimson water and a bouquet of blood-stained roses . . .' " said Jane, quoting the beginning of Owen's *Newsflash* story. "You wouldn't have had that without me."

"Great lead!" said Owen.

Jane was silent.

"Haven't I thanked you? I meant to."

"Well, you didn't."

"I didn't? I'm sorry. I really am."

Jane shrugged.

"All you think about is yourself. How much space you're going to get. How many times your story got picked up. Who quoted you. What Senator So-and-so and Congressman Blah-di-blah said about you. What about me? Wasn't I here? Didn't I help?"

"You helped. I already said thank you."

"And what about other people? Don't you give a damn about Mrs. Kennedy and the children? Or about what's going to happen to the country now?"

"Don't hand me your pious moralizing," said Owen.

"Why not?"

"Because I don't deserve it."

"And I don't deserve being used and then ignored," said Jane. "I also don't deserve being treated like a sex doll."

"Who used you and then ignored you? Who treated you like a sex doll?"

"You did. You act like I'm invisible unless you want to get laid or find out who said what or what happened next. Then you remember I'm alive."

"You didn't have to come along," said Owen.

"You invited me. Or don't you remember?"

"I remember," said Owen.

"You sound like you're sorry you asked me."

"You're making me feel that way."

"All you care about are your byline and how many inches you'll get in the special assassination edition."

"What's wrong with that? My byline and the number of inches I get are my goddamn living," Owen said.

"Your byline and the number of inches you get are bullshit!" retorted Jane.

It was, as she intended it to be, her curtain line.

Before Owen could open his mouth to reply, Jane threw her overnight things into her bag and slammed out of the room. She got a taxi in front of the hotel and headed for the airport and a flight home.

She thought that she'd probably never see Owen Casals again and she told herself that that was just fine with her. There was room for only one egomaniac in any given relationship and, if there had to be one, that egomaniac, Jane told herself, was going to be her. She, too, had witnessed the assassination. She, too, was a writer. She, too, had seen something the world would be interested in reading about.

" 'Only a girl!' " she quoted to Wilma that Sunday night just as soon as she got home. "What kind of shit is that?"

32
ELLY

"I do solemnly swear that I will
faithfully execute the office of
President of the United States, and
will to the best of my ability,
preserve, protect, and defend the
Constitution of the United States. So
help me God."

—Lyndon Baines Johnson

IT was Owen. At a time when people all over the country were having trouble placing telephone calls, Owen had gotten through. He was, Elly thought, extraordinary. Owen Casals could do things other people couldn't do.

"Ethel gave me your number and I've been carrying it around all summer," he told Elly. Jane had just walked out on him and he thought that if she hadn't, he would have. She was a major pain in the butt and he was glad he'd never have to see her again. "I almost called you a thousand times and I don't really know why I didn't. But at a time of crisis like this, you were the person I most wanted to talk to."

"I've been thinking about you all weekend," Elly said. "I called you in New York and at *Newsflash*. Where are you?"

"In Dallas," he said. "I was there when it happened."

"How awful."

"It was," Owen said. "What are you going to do now?"

"I don't know," said Elly.

"Why don't you come back to New York? There's a new Thai place on Mott Street. Galaxy-class gae ying."

IV

MODERN MEN/OWEN CASALS

I only know that what is moral is what you feel good after and what is immoral is what you feel bad after.

—Ernest Hemingway, *Death in the Afternoon*

33
OWEN

Byline . . .

HEMINGWAY was the man who had invented macho. Owen Casals was, in the eyes of many, the man who perfected it. He had Edward R. Murrow's charisma, Hemingway's sense of morality, Bogart's flinty integrity, and John F. Kennedy's grace under pressure. He was an idealist in cynic's clothing, a romantic who was most comfortable denying his emotions. Owen's conscious personality was organized around competence and control. He was a man's man and a woman's man. He had the respect of his peers to prove the first and two wives and legions of lovers to prove the second.

Born in 1931, Owen Casals grew up in a blue-collar neighborhood in Cincinnati. He was the only son of a police reporter and a housewife mother with a genuine but unfocused love of culture. Owen, on the receiving end of admiring attention from his mother, father, and two younger sisters viewed himself in the flattering, larger than life-sized mirror they held up.

"For as long as I can remember, I knew I was destined for big things," he said.

From his very earliest years, Owen was single-minded, industrious, disciplined, achievement oriented, capable of enormous concentration. Not surprisingly, Owen did very well in school, particularly in English. Athletically inclined although not outstandingly gifted, he was a hard worker during batting practice and infield drills, and he became an indispensable utility infielder and pinch hitter on his high school baseball team.

After school, Owen hung around the police station, his father's beat, soaking up cop stories, cop slang, cop lore and cop mind-set. It was at the Sixth Precinct, on his twelfth birthday, that Owen had his first beer, a local brand called Deutsch's. Even the hardened, seen-it-all flatfoots were impressed at how enthusiastically Owen took to the brew.

"Shit, Vic, in a week the kid'll drink you under the table," Kenny "Suds" Tudor teased Owen's father.

Victor Casals had a reputation, well documented and well deserved, as a man who could hold his booze. Owen, who idolized his father more than anyone on earth, did not take Suds's compliment lightly.

By the time he was fourteen, Owen worked after school and summers at his father's paper, the Cincinnati *Dispatch*. He rose rapidly from copy boy and general gofer to cub reporter covering church sales, Lion's Club meetings, and Garden Club activities. He earned his first byline when he was fifteen and his first front-page story just after he turned sixteen.

He was on his way to work late one afternoon at the peak of rush hour when he saw a Ford pickup run a red light and plow into a bus. The driver of the truck was killed and seven people on the bus were injured. Owen phoned the story in from a phone booth, the way he'd seen his father do dozens of times. When the *Dispatch* offered Owen a scholarship to college and a job afterward, Owen turned down the scholarship.

"I'll take the job, though," he said.

He was too impatient for success and recognition to waste four years with academic irrelevancies at college.

In 1951–1952, Owen discharged his military service in Korea, the war that wasn't called a war. It was referred to as "a conflict" or as a United Nations "police action." Although cease-fire negotiations were started in Panmunjom in 1951, fighting continued in places called Pork Chop Hill and Heartbreak Ridge. Acting as a junior assistant to the military press attaché in Seoul, Owen fed journalists facts, figures, maps, casualty statistics, and the latest line from headquarters.

Most of the things Owen saw and heard while in Korea did not fit neatly into the rigid who-what-when-where-why formula of the traditional newspaper story. They were filed nowhere except in Owen's memory. Owen would live with those memories for almost a decade until, inspired by Jane Gresch, he would realize how to use the material that accident and the U.S. army had thrust upon him.

Returning from Korea, Owen went back to Cincinnati and the job that was waiting for him at the *Dispatch*.

"I was hungry, horny, and ambitious," he said. "I was waiting to conquer the world."

34
OWEN

Wild Turkey . . .

WHEN Owen was twenty-one, he married the *Dispatch*'s society editor. Four years older than Owen, Marge Heller seemed considerably younger. Her life had been sheltered, Owen's had been the opposite. Marge's work centered on parties, engagement announcements, and weddings. Owen covered City Hall and reported on municipal budgets, bungles, and scandals.

"High life and low life. That's us," Owen told Marge.

Because Marge's father was a rich local businessman, Owen felt that in marrying her, he was marrying up and out of the blue-collar background he'd never really felt part of. Because Marge was a newspaperwoman, Owen thought she'd be like the other reporters he knew: sophisticated, unsentimental, hard working.

When their daughter, Emily, was born, Marge quit her job with relief to become a full-time mother. Her decision was a death sentence to the marriage. Owen lost all interest in her sexually, intellectually, and emotionally. He rationalized his indifference by telling himself that instead of being like his father, Marge had turned out to be exactly like his mother: fuzzy-minded, dependent, and prone to easily hurt feelings followed by long periods of sulking silence. Owen got divorced for the first time when he was twenty-four, leaving Emily in the custody of her mother.

"It was mutual," he told their friends on the paper.

"Owen is impossible," Marge told everyone.

Owen's divorce coincided with a job offer from the Chicago *Herald*, a coincidence Owen considered highly serendipitous. Moving from Cincinnati to Chicago was like moving from the minor leagues to the majors. The municipal budgets were bigger and so were the bungles.

What influenced Owen even more was the post-Capone, post-Prohibition atmosphere that still lingered. Chicago was an open town where anything went—as long as Mayor Daley approved. In 1956, a series of stories about cops' lives on and off the beat won Owen a George Polk Memorial Award, a cash bonus from the *Herald*, and three job offers.

"I wasn't merely conquering the world," he said. "I had it by the nuts."

From Chicago, Owen went to Seattle, to Baltimore, back to Chicago, on to Denver, and then East to Boston. He began to become known in his trade as a gun for hire.

In Baltimore, Owen got married for the second time. He met his second wife in Baltimore's excellent covered market. He was covering a story on mob influence among produce truckers and Trudy Steaves was shopping for broccoli.

"It looks nice and fresh," she said to Owen, holding up a bunch.

"So do you," he said.

Trudy was a good cook, a great lay, and dying to get out of marriage to a man fifteen years her senior who thought that getting it up once every two weeks was plenty. Trudy and

Owen got married at City Hall on the same day her divorce became final.

"Let's celebrate," said Trudy, as they left City Hall.

"Great idea," said Owen. "Let's go home and fuck."

"But we just got married," said Trudy, who had been thinking more along the lines of an expensive restaurant and a fancy nightclub.

Trudy and Owen separated one year from the day they were married.

"I'm amazed it lasted that long," Owen told friends at the paper.

"We really tried hard," said Trudy.

Six weeks later, Trudy informed Owen that she was pregnant.

"So now what?" asked Owen, wondering if Trudy was trying to get him back.

"Now nothing," said Trudy. "Except that I'm going to have the kid."

"You're going to have to do it without me."

"That's okay. I was planning to."

By the time his second daughter was born, Owen was back in Chicago.

In Denver Owen got fired for the first and only time in his life. Like every reporter who considered himself a real pro in those days, Owen kept a bottle in the bottom drawer of his desk. It was hardly the only one secreted on the premises of the Denver *Courier*.

It was, however, the one that broke one night when a flooring crew moved desks in order to reinstall poorly laid floors. The *Courier* building was almost brand new and boasted every modern convenience: air conditioning, electric typewriters, and multiline telephones with hold buttons. Instead of windows that opened and let in fresh air from the outdoors, ventilation was accomplished by machines that recycled the existing air.

The fumes from Owen's bottle of Wild Turkey circulated and recirculated throughout the building for the next six weeks. The story became a classic among Denver's newspaper people. Management told Owen to find another job.

Owen went to Boston where, now having to support two ex-wives and two children, he supplemented his *Herald* salary by writing and selling an occasional short story, because this did not conflict with his duties for the paper and his one-day-a-week teaching job at Bennington College. The pay from Owen's combined activities was generous and so was the supply of attractive young women. It was at this time that Owen first met Elly McGrath. Occupied with other romances, he barely noticed her and he promptly forgot her as soon as the school year was over.

Even when he met Elly again at the party at the Gotham Book Mart in 1961 and took her to dinner and to bed, Owen did not take their brief interlude seriously. For one thing, his work for *Newsflash* was extremely demanding and required a great deal of travel. For another, although Elly was sweet and extremely pretty, she was very young, not only in years but also in attitude.

"You're just too innocent and too inexperienced for me," he told her.

When Elly confessed that she loved him, Owen panicked. He'd been married twice, divorced twice. He was not looking forward to a third at-bat.

Elly, he sensed, would be a responsibility and Owen was not ready at that time in his life to take on additional responsibility. Jane Gresch, by contrast, who openly said that she had no interest in marriage or babies, seemed like the perfect woman.

And she was. Until Dallas.

35
OWEN

Ten inches . . .

JANE picked the exact wrong moment to tell Owen that he was less than perfect. In his state of exhaustion, Owen had no patience with Jane's comments about Mrs. Kennedy, the Kennedy family, the country, and how much he owed Jane Gresch. Her final crack about his interest in his byline and the number of inches he got infuriated him.

He had been wrong about Jane. She was no different from other women, Owen thought. She was exactly like the rest of them. Sniping. Critical. Judgmental. Impossible to please.

When Jane stormed out of the hotel room, Owen found himself overcome with a sudden, nostalgic longing for Elly. Elly wouldn't have criticized. Elly would have admired. Elly wouldn't have carped. Elly would have praised. Elly wouldn't have judged. Elly would have understood.

Elly knew how to love. Jane knew how to make a nuisance of herself.

Even before Jane's taxi deposited her at the airport, Owen picked up the telephone and called Elly. When he hung up after talking to Elly, Owen felt much better.

"Elly always has a good effect on me," he told Ray Jessup. "Elly always makes me feel better."

The fight with Jane, Owen realized after he had calmed down, had probably been his fault as much as hers. It had most likely been more a matter of frayed nerves and almost terminal exhaustion than anything else. For days, Owen had lived on nicotine, caffeine, candy bars, booze, and no sleep. He regretted his angry words and short temper.

He remembered how helpful Jane had been in the hours and days following the presidential assassination. Jane had functioned as another pair of sharp eyes and a provider of keen observations.

Owen had added Jane's comments about the mood in the press bus to his story about the moment of the murder. He had used her descriptions of the bloodied roses and the bucket of pinkish water standing on the curb in his *Newsflash* lead. He had mentioned the open door of the Presidential limousine in his reports of the scene outside the Emergency entrance at Parkland. He planned to incorporate her impressions of the stunned reactions of the lunch guests who had come to hear President Kennedy speak at the Trade Mart into the instant paperback Hank had sold.

Jane's comments and observations had been sharp and provocative all weekend long. As Owen phoned in the shocking news of Lee Harvey Oswald's murder, the sound of gunfire echoed in his ears. When Jane commented that gunfire was the sound of the twentieth century, the memories of the sound of gunfire on another continent that Owen had carried with him for over a decade suddenly came back to him.

"I remember once we were close to the banks of the Yalu River. There were half a dozen of us. We thought we were alone when suddenly there were eight enemy soldiers to our left. They were armed and they looked mean. We didn't know they were there. We didn't know where they had come from," he told Jane, recalling a terrifying episode he had forgotten for years.

When Owen reported on Dallas nightclub owner Jack Ruby's furtive life on the fringes, Jane observed that there was more drama in shadows than in sunlight. At her words, memories of nighttime battles in Korea turned effortlessly into scenes in Owen's mind.

"Our orders were to hold the goddamn hill. Every night the casualties were worse. We held it for ten nights. We couldn't tell the rain from the blood. Then the order came down: retreat," said Owen.

As he made love to Jane that last day in Dallas, a title for the novel he had been wanting to write for years suddenly came to Owen.

"*The 39th Parallel*," he said. "What do you think of it?"

"Great," said Jane. "Now let's get back to where we were. I sort of liked that thing you were doing with your toes."

On his own, Owen had been a superior journalist. With Jane by his side, he became inspired. Owen knew that the quality of his work in Dallas had risen to new heights. Jane's eyes and Jane's ears and Jane's special way of perceiving things had helped Owen transcend himself. When Ray Jessup told him that his work was better than ever, Owen accepted the compliment.

"I hope I've learned something after all these years," he said with macho modesty.

Jane was special and Owen didn't want her to go away mad. She was an exciting companion, a spectacular lover, and one of the few women whose company didn't leave him drained but, instead, energized him.

Having regained his perspective, Owen picked up the telephone again later that Sunday night. He dialed the number of a twenty-four-hour florist on Lexington Avenue. As the public address system at the Dallas–Fort Worth airport announced the first call for boarding Jane's New York flight,

Owen ordered a dozen red tulips. He carefully dictated Jane's Perry Street address.

As Jane showed her ticket and walked through the boarding gate—no security searches and no baggage X-rays in those days—Owen dictated the message he wanted to appear on the card:

Byline: Owen Casals
Ten inches

36
OWEN

Chinatown . . .

"THERE'S a Szechuan place on Chatham Square. Dynamite shrimp with pepper sauce," Owen told Jane on the phone when he got back to New York from Dallas several days later.

"I like the one on Bayard Street better," replied Jane.

Bed, as usual, turned out to be even hotter than the hottest sauces Szechuan cooks could come up with.

Bed with Jane was something Owen always felt good after.

So was bed with Elly.

V

THE AGE OF AQUARIUS/ 1964–1968

I started having a dream in the '60's. In the dream I am fighting with someone. They are trying to kill me or kill someone I love. I'm fighting with all my strength. But I just can't hurt them. They just smile. It must be a classic dream of powerlessness and rage.

—Gloria Steinem, *She's Nobody's Baby*

37
ELLY

1 9 6 4 :

Declared: the war on poverty
Debuted: the touch-tone telephone
Probed: the moon and Mars by the
    Ranger 7 rocket and the Mariner 4
Protested: university control over
    student political activities in a
    series of sit-ins at the University of
    California, Berkeley

WHEN Elly returned to New York, the art supply salesman had moved in with Ethel. There was no space for Elly in the West 57th Street apartment. Elly's parents told her that her old room was hers for as long as she wanted.

"We missed you!" Elly's father said, welcoming her with a hug. At forty-nine, Brian McGrath was at the height of his powers. His reputation as a labor lawyer was established and the McCarthyism of the Fifties that had often cast him in a outsider's role was now history. Brian's physique had enlarged at the same time his reputation had and Elly was surprised at how heavy her father had become. He carried his weight mostly in his midsection, around the waist and abdomen. His girth made him seem old and for the first time Elly realized that one day she would lose him. Her father's vulnerability gave Elly one more reason to be glad that she had decided to come back home.

"We're so glad to have you back," Elly's mother said. Four years younger than her husband, Louise Cullen looked thirty-five rather than forty-five. She was still as slim as a girl and she was, Elly noticed, wearing her skirts fashionably above the knee and her sweaters poor-boy tight. If fashion was Elly's enemy, it was, as it had been for as long as Elly could remember, her mother's ally.

"You came back at just the right minute. There's a cute new guy in the office. I've already told him about you and he's interested," said Margaret.

"Owen called," said Elly.

Margaret rolled her eyes. "Oh, God. Here we go again."

"Washington was a big disappointment. Nothing worked out the way I hoped," Elly admitted to her parents. "I'll get a job here."

"What kind of job? Perhaps I could help," Elly's mother said.

"I thought I'd try to get my old one back," Elly said, indirectly turning down her mother's offer of help. Elly felt that she was returning home from Washington in complete defeat. She had not helped change the world. She had never set foot in the White House. She had not found a new boyfriend. Only Owen's phone call gave her the slighest reason for hope. Elly was twenty-three now and independence—if only the illusion of independence—was important to her. She wanted to get a job on her own terms, even if it wasn't a terribly good one.

"No more shoes!" she vowed to her father, when they were alone. "I'll call Adrian Holland. Maybe I can go back to work at Parmenides."

"Sorry, Elly, but you've been replaced," said Adrian.

"So I see," replied Elly. On her way into Adrian's office, Elly had seen the long-haired, bright-eyed girl sitting at her former desk. A straight-A student, no doubt, a graduate of one of the better schools, doing her own job and probably at least half of Adrian Holland's, too. Elly was experienced enough in the ways of bosses and secretaries by now to know that some things never changed.

"Do you know of anyone who might have a job for me?" she asked.

Adrian was silent. A connoisseur of many things, including trivial cruelty, he let Elly hang in suspense for a long moment.

"There's a new paperback line called North Star Books. It's a mass market operation but they're doing pretty well," Adrian said finally. The thought of the hopeless vulgarity of mass market paperback publishing permitted Adrian a bit of condescending generosity to a rival.

"The owner, Gordon Geiger, is an acquaintance of mine. He needs a secretary." Adrian continued. "I'll call him for you."

What Adrian left out was that he and Gordon Geiger were two rich boys making good. Adrian had chosen the high road, Gordon, the low road. The twain often met at the bar at the Yale Club. Adrian secretly envied the money Gordon seemed likely to make. Gordon envied the Tiffany aura Gordon had created around Parmenides.

Unlike Parmenides' wood-paneled and antique-filled offices, which were located in a handsome brownstone just off Gramercy Park, North Star's offices were three dingy rooms over a kosher deli in the diamond district. They were reached via a rickety freight elevator whose operator sidelined as the neighborhood bookie.

North Star, in existence for just over eight months, published four books a month: a western, a war novel, a mystery, and an action adventure. All were directed toward the undiscriminating male reader eager for blood, lust, and violent action.

"Comic books without the pictures," Gordon admitted freely.

Gordon Geiger, in contradiction to the run-down surroundings in which he operated, was modishly dressed and handsome in a heavy-set pugnacious way. Also in contradiction to the lowbrow books he published, Gordon himself was intelligent and well educated. He had founded North Star with an inheritance from his maternal grandmother, turning to paperback publishing as a business he considered to have an almost unlimited future.

Elly's appointment with Gordon was at three o'clock on the Wednesday afternoon following the assassination. At three thirty, after an interview that consisted mainly of chat about Adrian Holland's foibles and pretensions and a number of questions about Elly's work experience, Gordon offered her the job.

"Type, answer the phone, try to drum up a little publicity," said Gordon describing Elly's duties.

"The salary is seventy-five bucks a week. Starting next week if you can."

Elly smiled and nodded.

"Thank you," she replied, thinking that working for North Star, while hardly intellectually rewarding, might turn out to be fun.

Elly's reunion with Owen was passionate. He brought her roses and champagne and covered her with kisses.

"It's been too long!" he said. "Way too long! It's great to see you. I have a million things to tell you. I want to hear all about you, too. I want to know everything that's happened to you," he said, embracing her.

Then he stood back a pace while his pale gray eyes swept her from head to toe.

"And you're even prettier than I remember," he commented. "Spun-gold hair. Body by Modigliani."

Elly instinctively touched her abundant wavy hair and smiled. It was the first time anyone had ever complimented her string-bean shape and Elly thought that she might faint from pleasure.

"Now, about that gae ying . . ." Owen said, taking Elly's arm possessively and heading her toward the door.

"Holding you is so good," Owen murmured later when they were in bed. "So good." He ran his hands up and down the length of Elly's back, delighting in her elegant bones and the velvety texture of her skin.

His voice was husky and tender and Elly felt warmed by his closeness. She traced the outline of Owen's lips with her forefinger. Owen moved his head slightly and took Elly's exploring finger into his mouth. Gently, he began to suck it.

Elly stroked his thick, dark hair with her other hand and began to caress his lean, rangy body. Moving down, she took his penis in her mouth, marveling at its size and strength.

"Don't stop," Owen said.

"I wasn't planning to."

"Don't go away again. We're too good together," Owen said the next morning over coffee. Elly noticed that he did not tell her to leave right away. He did not say that he had to go to work. Elly sensed that things had changed since she'd seen Owen last. Perhaps the assassination made him more aware of the people who really mattered to him. Perhaps absence simply *did* make the heart grow fonder.

"I won't if you don't want me to," replied Elly, her eyes shimmering with emotion.

"I don't want you to," Owen said, uttering words that Elly engraved on her memory.

38
OWEN

DECEMBER 1963:

Idlewild is renamed John F. Kennedy
International Airport.

WHEN Owen got back into his frenetic *Newsflash* routine, he found that although memories of Korea and ideas for *The 39th Parallel* continued to cascade into his mind, he had no time to write. His job absorbed all his time and energy. In early December Owen went to his boss.

"I worked my ass off in Dallas. I think I earned some time," he told Ray Jessup. "How about a six-month leave of absence?"

"A six-month leave of absence? Old farts get leaves of absence. Not young hotshots who might be up for the Pulitzer," Ray said.

"Pulitzer?"

"I didn't want to say anything but the boys upstairs are impressed. They think your work on the assassination is worth at least a nomination, if not the prize itself. They're talking about pushing you with the committee," said Ray. "They won't push you for shit if you're off on a leave playing with yourself. If you want to write a novel, do it on your own time."

Owen repeated Ray's dialogue to Jane.

" 'My own time'?" he said, sarcastically quoting Ray's phrase. In the past week, Owen had been to Boston, New Orleans, and Washington for *Newsflash* covering postassassination stories. "What time?"

"So quit your job. That way you could write full-time," Jane said, putting into words the wild idea Owen had been toying with.

"Do you have enough money to live without a job?" asked Elly, showing her practical side when Owen told her that he was thinking of leaving *Newsflash* in order to write his book.

Owen nodded. "The *Eyewitness* money is coming at the perfect moment," said Owen, referring to the deal Hank Greene had made for the instant paperback on the Kennedy assassination. Owen had begun the manuscript in Dallas and finished it in New York. The book, an expansion and elaboration of the stories Owen had already filed for *Newsflash* along with a series of eyewitness reports based on his and Jane's memories of that weekend in Dallas, was already on the stands and selling out everywhere.

"But are you sure you really want to quit your job? It's a big decision," Elly said. She wanted Owen to be happy but she didn't want him to do anything he hadn't thought through carefully.

"I'm *not* sure," Owen said, looking uncomfortable.

Indecisiveness was uncharacteristic of Owen. Indecisiveness did not marry well with his in-control, in-command self-image. Owen loved being a journalistic star. The perks and status that came along with a *Newsflash* byline inflated the egos of many men far less secure and self-confident than Owen Casals. Ray's hints about a possible Pulitzer nomination had also been very strong bait. On the other hand, Owen also had an image of himself as Hemingway's heir.

For a week, Owen wobbled this way and that. He tried to balance security against risk, a known future against an unknown one, a regular salary against the indefinite paydays of a first novelist. He tried to weigh what he would certainly give up against what he might possibly gain. He tried to calculate certainty against uncertainty and found no satisfactory formula.

"This isn't arithmetic, this is your life," Jane pointed out. "If you really want to write a novel, you have to make a commitment."

"If you have to leave *Newsflash* to find the time to write your novel, then that's what you have to do," said Elly.

Owen finally told himself that thirty-three was now-or-never time. He remembered his own father's bitterness about the way journalism had finally used up his youth and energy and decided that he did not want to end up like his father. Buttressed by the success of *Eyewitness* and encouraged by Jane and Elly, Owen told Ray that his mind was made up.

"It may be reckless of me, but I'm determined to write this novel. I'm afraid that if I don't do it now, I'll never do it," he told Ray. "I plan to resign from *Newsflash* as of January first, 1964."

Ray shook his head. "No second chances. Management is very firm about that," he told Owen, warning him that any decision Owen made would be final and irrevocable. The enlightened, benevolently paternalistic management of *Newsflash* did not take rejection lightly. "*Newsflash* never rehires people who leave."

"I know," said Owen. "My mind is made up."

Owen shook hands with Ray and his colleagues at *Newsflash* and got appropriately drunk at the stag farewell party. The next day, Owen was surprised at how anxious he felt about the decision he had reached. Had he made the right decision?

Could he really make the switch from reporter to novelist? Had he gone out on a limb that was going to be cut off behind him? Questions that Owen could not answer buzzed around unsettlingly in the back of his mind.

Owen ascribed his doubts to his monumental hangover. He did not, of course, reveal them to others, feeling as he did that talking about emotions was a waste of time at best, self-indulgent at worst. Instead, he blotted out his troubling anxieties by throwing himself into a complicated, time- and energy-consuming private life.

In December, the last hectic month that Owen Casals worked at *Newsflash*, he continued to date both Jane and Elly. Like many Americans in the weeks following the assassination, Owen felt an unusually intense need to reach out for emotional connections. Owen's decision to leave the status and security of *Newsflash* also made him hungrier than usual for affection and appreciation, stimulation and competition. What work had always supplied, Jane and Elly now contributed.

"You make me feel so good," he told Elly.

"You always get me to do my best," he told Jane.

Owen excused his absences from Elly by citing his final *Newsflash* deadlines. His assignments centered on follow-up assassination stories—the formation of the Warren Commission to investigate the murder and the conspiracy theories that were already gaining popularity. These important reportorial assignments, Owen said truthfully, entailed research trips to Washington, to Dallas, to Kennedy's home state of Massachusetts, and to New Orleans and Mexico City where Lee Harvey Oswald had lived.

He explained his absences from Jane the same way.

Owen spent Christmas Eve with Jane, Christmas Day with Elly. He gave Elly a specially bound, lovingly autographed copy of *Eyewitness*, which she cherished, along with a bottle of Joy perfume.

"It's the most expensive in the world and you're worth every penny," he told Elly as he presented it to her.

Elly wore the opulent scent constantly. Its rich jasmine fragrance made her feel loved and valued and cherished. Its timeless crystal bottle seemed to promise eternity.

He gave Jane an elegant new Olivetti typewriter.

"To replace your old Smith-Corona," he told her, referring to the beat-up typewriter Jane had been carting around since college. Then, referring to Jane's notoriously terrible typing, he added: "Not that it's going to help with the typos."

Owen celebrated New Year's Eve with Elly, New Year's Day with Jane. He took Elly to a romantic old inn in Vermont for a brief, snowy, Currier & Ives weekend at the beginning of January.

"Beginning the new year with you means a lot to me," he told Elly.

"It does to me, too. It means everything," replied Elly.

The next weekend, he took Jane to Montego Bay for a brief, sunny midwinter break.

"The round hill I like best is the left one," he told Jane, caressing her left breast.

"What's wrong with the right one?" she asked.

39
JANE

Zip codes, the Ford Mustang, freeze-
dried coffee, the Kennedy half
dollar, Dynel, Pop-Tarts

AS the new year started and America's new president vowed a
"war on poverty," Owen began his career as a novelist. Accustomed to the instant feedback of working with *Newsflash*'s
editors, Owen showed Jane the early drafts of *The 39th Parallel*.

Owen liked Jane's idea that he use short sentences to
convey the rat-a-tat-tat urgency of combat scenes and longer
sentences to underscore the thoughtfulness of more pensive
moments. When Jane proposed that he include Negro characters, Owen accepted that suggestion too. On the other hand,
he angrily rejected her idea about including scenes with the
women in his characters' lives.

"This is a combat novel," Owen reminded her. His good
looks turned to stone when he felt unfairly criticized.

"They've still got cocks," Jane said.

Owen thought over Jane's comment and eventually decided to include his characters' memories of the women they
had loved and left behind.

"You were right about using the women," Owen told Jane later.

"Of course I was right," Jane said absently, dragging a comb through her hopelessly frizzy hair. "Men without women are a drag."

Owen also showed Elly his chapters. Her reactions were consistently positive.

"I cried when I read the scene about the hill of rain and blood that the army finally made them abandon," she told Owen. "Your descriptions are brilliant and I can't wait for the world to find out what I already know about you."

"Amos, the black sergeant who doesn't know why he's fighting Orientals, is a memorable character," she said. "You're a wonderful writer and I'm proud to know you."

What Elly really wanted to talk about was how she felt about Owen and how Owen felt about her.

"I never forgot what you said about not leaving you," she said. "I never will."

"Did you really mean it when you said that starting the new year with me meant a lot to you?" she asked.

In January, as Owen made the transition from well-known journalist to first novelist, Owen found that Jane inspired him while Elly made him feel slightly squeezed.

Owen continued to see both Jane and Elly although gradually he began to spend somewhat less time with Elly and more with Jane. When he and Jane weren't discussing *The 39th Parallel*, they were screwing. Owen liked to suck strawberry ice cream out of Jane's mouth and then kiss her until her cold mouth turned hot from his tongue. He liked to paint his name on her stomach with chocolate sauce and then lick it off, causing her to go wild as he circled nearer and nearer her immensely sensitive navel. He liked her to keep her panties on during sex so that he could feel the wet nylon before he pushed the fabric crotch to one side and entered her. He never ran out of ideas or energy. Neither did she.

Jane adored oral sex.

"Sixty-nine is my favorite number," she told Wilma.

She also said that the best day of her life was the day she learned that sperm was high in protein and low in calories.

"Not only is it good for you, it's not even fattening!"

She liked to unzip Owen's fly with her teeth and fish his penis out with her tongue. She also liked to go down on him in movie theaters and dimly lit restaurants.

"I'm afraid we'll get caught," said Owen, trying to dissuade Jane from going down on him in a taxicab that was stuck in a traffic jam on Second Avenue.

"You sure don't act it," she said.

It wasn't only fancy sex that appealed to Owen.

"I like plain vanilla, too," he said and proved it to Jane by fucking her hard and fast in missionary position.

"So do I," replied Jane and proved it by getting him excited all over again. They also liked it standing up, sitting down, and back to front doggy style—in the kitchen, in the living room and on the fire escape, on the beach, in the grass, and in the back seat of parked cars.

They spent a weekend in Puerto Rico and on the night flight back from San Juan, Jane and Owen joined the Mile High club. They Did It in the back row of Economy under a blue Pan Am blanket. The stewardess, sitting nearby in the pull-down seat, had observed amorous couples a hundred times before. She yawned and hoped she'd make her London connection.

"I love you," Owen whispered as Jane pulled him on top of her.

"I love you," Jane replied. To her surprise, the sky didn't fall. The plane didn't crash either.

"I love you," she said again, just to get the hang of it. Not so bad, she thought, as he lowered his face toward hers and began to kiss her. In fact, pretty damn good.

"When are you two getting married?" asked Wilma.

"Don't be bourgeois," said Jane.

"When are you coming down off Cloud Nine?" Glen asked.

"Never!" Jane told her boss with an airy wave of her hand.

L-O-V-E, however, did not end the fighting and bickering, almost all of it triggered by Jane's reactions to *The 39th Parallel.* What had once been lovers' tiffs rose in volume and intensity.

"What the fuck do you know about a night raid along the shores of the Yalu River?" Owen shouted after Jane had told him that a scene needed rewriting.

"A scene where someone I don't care about gets shot in the throat is a yawn," replied Jane.

"I'm not going to rewrite it!" Owen yelled back. It was ten o'clock at night. He was exhausted.

"So *don't* rewrite it!" snarled Jane, slamming out the door. "And in the future don't ask me for my opinion if you don't want to listen to it!"

When Jane got home, her telephone was ringing.

"I was tired," Owen said, as a way of apologizing.

"So was I," Jane admitted.

As usual, they made up their fight with a fuck.

"If we were married you wouldn't slam out the door," Owen told Jane later. They were in each other's arms, temporarily sexed out.

"We're not married," Jane reminded him.

"We could change that," Owen said.

"I don't know," replied Jane dubiously. "All we seem to do is fuck and fight. It hardly seems like the basis for a mature relationship, never mind marriage."

"It sounds like the basis for a hell of a lot of fun to me," said Owen.

"And what about your other girlfriend?" asked Jane. "What are you going to tell her?"

"What other girlfriend?"

"The one you see when you don't see me," said Jane.

"She's not important," said Owen.

"Don't hand me that crap," said Jane.

"How do you know about her anyway?"

"I see the notes she leaves in your mailbox. I found some American Express receipts for dinners on nights I wasn't with you. There were some blond hairs in the bathtub plus a tube of pink lipstick in the medicine chest in a shade that I wouldn't be caught dead in," said Jane.

"What are you? The CIA?"

"I'm watching out for my own interests," said Jane.

"We can get married and live together and love together. For always and all the time. Forever and ever and ever," Owen said. He went on and on, day after day, week after week. He used all the words that Elly used: love, always, forever. Words that, when he heard them, made Owen feel trapped. Words that, when he said them, made him feel powerful.

"You're not saying no anymore," Owen noticed at the beginning of February. "That means you must be thinking about saying yes."

Owen was right. He was getting to Jane. His pleas and promises reminded Jane that life did not have to be an uphill bohemian struggle. Happiness could come in familiar packages, too, couldn't it? Why couldn't she have the comfort of a conventional kind of life along with the excitement of an unconventional kind of man?

Owen was divine, he was sexy, he was a writer, he was madly in love with her and she was madly in love with him. Jane thought Owen Casals was the smartest, hippest, most sophisticated person she'd ever met. He'd been everywhere, seen everything, done everything. She felt that if she married Owen, her life would take on new, thrilling dimensions. She felt that if she married Owen, her writing would break loose of the inhibitions that were standing between her and worldwide fame. Just as she inspired him, he would inspire her.

Jane added up all the reasons Owen had given for marriage. Owen was a writer. She was a writer. Or, at least, one day she'd be a writer. He was from the Middle West. She was from the Middle West. He was a sex maniac. So was she. They liked the same movies, restaurants, and books. Not to mention the fact that he was one of the handsomest men she'd seen outside the movies *and* he had a cock that even Catherine the Great would drool over. They were, she thought, when you stopped to think about it, perfect for each other.

Even their fights were fun and the sex that followed them was celestial. The thought of a future with Owen Casals and unlimited great sex was only one of the lures that Jane began to consider that February. A permanent life, a permanent address, a permanent husband, she thought, had their attractions.

"Let's do it," Jane said. She and Owen were having Chinese take-out at his apartment.

"Do what?"

"Get married," said Jane in her sexy alto voice.

"For real?" asked Owen.

"For real," Jane replied.

Owen threw his chopsticks up in the air and before they had come down, he was wrestling Jane to the floor. They made love, finished the sesame noodles, made love again, consumed the moo goo gai pan, and made love for the third time, leaving the shrimp fried rice to get cold. Marriage? Jane and Owen both agreed it only made good things better.

40
JANE

JANUARY 1964:

In response to the surgeon general's report linking cigarettes to lung cancer and other diseases, the Federal Trade Commission is proposing a mandatory warning message on cigarette packs and an end to advertisements that feature endorsements by athletes.

THE next day Jane told Owen that her parents were anxious to meet him. He didn't reply. Instead, he lit a cigarette and looked out the window.

"They'll be so impressed," she said, telling Owen that *Newsflash* had been on the Gresch coffee table for almost as long as Jane could remember. "Let's go home so you can meet them in person."

"Home? You mean St. Louis?" Owen had spent his entire adult life fleeing the Midwest. The thought of returning filled him with depressing memories of the drab blue-collar neighborhood he had grown up in.

"Of course St. Louis. Where else?" said Jane.

"To meet your parents? Jesus Christ!" Owen said, remembering all the pain-in-the-ass responsibilities involving families and in-laws that marriage inevitably brought along with it. He had forgotten all about *that* part of marriage, the part that made him feel trapped and confined, the part that made him feel he'd given up his freedom and gotten nothing in return. "What next? Monogrammed towels?"

"What's wrong with monogrammed towels?" Jane asked. She liked monogrammed towels. She was looking forward to them. Monogrammed sheets, too.

"If you don't know, I'm not going to tell you," Owen replied in a stony tone of voice.

Jane looked at Owen as if she'd never seen him before. What, she wondered, was his problem?

And that was just the beginning.

When Jane asked Owen where he thought they ought to live after they got married, Owen replied that they'd live in his 13th Street apartment. Of course.

"Where else?" he asked, mystified by the question. He loved his apartment. Its high ceilings and tall windows were very European and the Village neighborhood in which it was located was convenient and friendly. There were good, inexpensive restaurants, several art film movie houses, a number of smoky jazz clubs and excellent libraries, all within walking distance. Owen pointed out that the controlled rent was a bargain and that the back windows overlooked a garden.

"Somewhere bigger," Jane replied, saying that the apartment was too small for two wardrobes, two typewriters, and two writers. She loved the Village but she expected a bit of comfort, too.

"I can't afford anything bigger," Owen said, biting off the words.

"I'll help with the rent," Jane said.

"The hell you will!" Owen snapped.

Jane wanted Owen to share their new happiness with others. He wasn't interested. He did not want to see Glen for drinks.

"I like Glen but don't have anything to talk to him about," he said, not admitting that without his *Newsflash* ID and stream of inside gossip, he felt handicapped.

He did not want to attend Marsha Freeman's dinner parties either.

"I met you at one of Marsha's parties. You *used* to go," Jane said.

"I wasn't involved with anyone then. I went because I was interested in meeting someone." To Owen, parties were strictly for making business contacts or meeting women. Socializing, as such, bored him.

"So now that you've met someone, you've turned into a hermit?" asked Jane.

"I've turned into a novelist," retorted Owen in his unyielding, steely tone of voice. "When I can find time to write," he added snidely.

He also did not want to double date with Wilma and her cardiologist boyfriend.

"We don't need other people," Owen told Jane.

"Maybe you don't. *I* do."

"We have each other," Owen countered instantly. "Or aren't I enough for you?"

When Jane read about the surgeon general's report in the newspaper she suggested that Owen stop smoking.

"What's with you? We're not even married and already you're trying to change me," he said, telling Jane that she was as bad as both his wives. He then lit a cigarette in defiance.

Jane was mystified by Owen's sudden about-face. He had been after her for almost a month, begging and pleading with her to marry him. He had sworn eternal love and adoration. He had told her that he couldn't live without her, that she meant everything to him, that she was the woman he'd been waiting for his entire life.

Once Jane had accepted the proposal, however, everything seemed to have changed. In less than a month, Owen had turned from impassioned lover into reluctant husband-to-be. Their fights no longer ended with a good fuck. Their fights now ended with two people going to bed mad.

Owen no longer showed her the new chapters of his book. There weren't any to show, he said. He complained that he was blocked.

"It's your fault. You're too critical," he said. "You've made me so self-conscious I can't write."

Owen no longer had a parade of exotic restaurants for them to try. Gone were the delights of Kyoto, Andalusia, Provence, and Lebanon. Owen now seemed content with the Chinese joint on the corner of Sixth Avenue and 13th Street.

"It's good and it's close," he said when Jane complained that they'd been there three nights in a row.

"I'm bored with spring rolls and broccoli chicken."

"So order something else."

Owen began to have regrets about quitting his job. He muttered about having let himself get pussy-whipped.

"I gave up the possibility of a Pulitzer for a novel that's not going anywhere," he said gloomily.

Owen now blamed Jane not only for being blocked but for talking him into quitting *Newsflash*. It had been her idea, he reminded her. An idea that now seemed not so wonderful. Owen was all too aware of the things he missed: the recognition, the perks, the stimulation, the competition, the steady paycheck. Now he feared he wouldn't have a book either.

"You talked me into quitting," he said. "I should have taken Ray's advice and written my book in my spare time."

"What spare time?" asked Jane, furious at being unilaterally elected the guilty party.

Worst of all was the fact that Owen was no longer a Houdini of the mattress. Plain vanilla, night after night, suddenly seemed perfectly acceptable to him. When Jane complained about their bland sex life, Owen got angry.

"I'm not a sex machine!" he said, telling Jane that it might be a good idea if she went to her own apartment to sleep that night.

* * *

Sex the next night was as explosive as ever.

"I thought you'd forgotten how," sighed Jane in a combination of ecstasy and relief. Owen was back to his old tricks.

"Forget? With inspiration like you?"

When Jane left for work the next morning, Owen sent her off with a deep, passionate kiss. Everything was back to normal. Owen had probably just been suffering from a temporary attack of male bridal jitters. Everything, Jane thought, would be just fine.

When Owen did not call her the next day, Jane made a thousand excuses for him. He had started writing again. He was in the shower. He had gone to the post office. He was having a drink with someone. Finally, she called him just before she left work. When a woman answered, Jane hung up.

Furious, Jane went straight to Owen's apartment on 13th Street. When Jane knocked on his door, Owen opened it.

"Who answered that phone?" Jane demanded.

"I don't own you and you don't own me," Owen replied.

Jane could see a tall, slim blonde standing just behind him.

"You're the one with the pink lipstick," Jane said. "I suppose you fill in on the nights I'm not around."

She turned around and slammed the door so hard that the dog on the floor below began to howl.

Jane went home and considered various forms of revenge.

"I'll kill the son of a bitch!" she told Wilma.

"It wouldn't be worth the jail sentence," Wilma said.

"I'll sneak into his apartment and burn his goddamn manuscript," Jane swore.

"And how are you going to do that? You don't even have a set of keys," Wilma reminded her.

"I'm going to tell his girlfriend that's he's been fucking me blind nights he doesn't see her," said Jane.

"And what's that going to prove? That he's a rat and a two-timer?" asked Wilma. "She probably already knows that."

"So what am I going to do?" fumed Jane.

"Get rich and famous," said Wilma.

"Yeah. Rich and famous," mused Jane. "That would really burn his ass, wouldn't it?"

41
ELLY

MARCH 1964:

Refusing to get involved, neighbors
passively watch as Kitty Genovese is
murdered in Queens. The event
makes headlines across the nation.

LOUISE Cullen, despite her chic Sassoon haircut, and up-to-
the-minute wardrobe, was vehemently opposed when, in early
March, Elly told her that she and Owen Casals were going to
live together. Louise feared that Elly would wake up an April
Fool.

"Live together? And not get married?" Louise asked with
a sharp intake of breath.

"Not right away," Elly said. Owen had told her that since
he had no job and nothing except his hopes for *The 39th Parallel*
he couldn't really offer marriage. On the other hand, he said,
he loved her and wanted to live with her. "We're going to live
together and find out if we're compatible. If we are, we'll get
married later."

"And why, pray tell, should he marry you 'later'?" Louise
asked.

"Because I love him and he loves me!"

"If he loved you, he'd marry you," said Louise. "He's just taking advantage of you."

Elly's father was equally opposed.

"Owen is a playboy. He's almost ten years older than you are. He's been married twice and divorced twice. He gave up an excellent job for what? To write a book?" Brian said. Brian McGrath remembered the Depression. He could not understand how anyone could have quit a job like Owen's at *Newsflash*. "Suppose he never finishes this book? Then what?"

"He'll finish it," said Elly. "Owen's very talented."

"Talent means nothing. Determination and discipline are what counts. Even if he does finish it, who says that it will ever be published? Most writers starve."

"Owen's different."

"What makes him different? A few articles in a news magazine and a quickie paperback? That's a far cry from writing and publishing a book and making a living at it," Brian said. "If Owen respected you, he'd get a job and write his book in his spare time. Then when he was established, he'd marry you."

"He *does* respect me. He loves me," insisted Elly.

"Then why doesn't he marry you?" her father asked.

"He thinks we should live together for a while to see if we're really compatible," said Elly. "Is that so terrible?"

"It's ridiculous and even if you don't know any better, Owen should. You'll never really know if you're compatible until you get married," Brian McGrath said. "Playing house doesn't have the slightest thing to do with the problems and adjustments of marriage."

"I don't see why not. After all, what difference does a piece of paper make?" said Elly.

She was determined to move in with Owen no matter what her parents thought or said or did. Her parents were old, Elly told Ethel. What did they know or care about love?

In mid-March, Elly moved her clothes, books, and records from her parents' apartment to Owen's.

"You're making a big mistake. He's using you. He's going to break your heart," Louise told Elly as she finished packing.

Her father helped Elly carry her suitcases and cartons downstairs.

"You still have time to change your mind," Brian told Elly as they stood on the sidewalk in front of the building Elly had grown up in. "Please don't move in with him. He's too old for you. He's too sophisticated."

"I've made up my mind," said Elly as she hailed a taxi. She was unable to look at her father. "I love Owen and I'm going to live with him. I know what I'm doing!"

Although Elly had defied her parents to move in with Owen, their warnings had their impact. What if Owen were just using her? What if he never finished his novel? What if he met someone else? Or suppose he started seeing that other girl again, the one with the frizzy hair? Even though he swore to Elly that she wasn't important and that he would never see her again, Elly wasn't sure whether or not she could really trust Owen. She was weeping by the time she got to 13th Street.

"What's the matter?" asked Owen, after he had taken her belongings from the taxi to his apartment. "Why are you crying?"

"I'm not crying," Elly said, forcing a smile. "These are just tears of joy."

From the first week that they lived together, Owen and Elly traded traditional roles. Owen worked at home while Elly went to the office. She had begun her new job at North Star Books in January 1964, taking on publicity and promotion assignments in addition to her secretarial chores. On weekends, she participated in civil rights rallies in Greenwich Village, Harlem, and Central Park. Nevertheless, from the day Elly first moved in with Owen and wedged her clothes into a corner of his closet, it was Owen and their new life together that consumed most of Elly's time and attention. She was determined that she and Owen would be the happiest couple anyone had ever known.

"I'm going to prove to Mom and Dad that they were wrong about Owen," she told Margaret. "Owen's wonderful. I know that he'll make me very happy."

"I hope so," said Margaret. "I just wish I thought it would be easy for you."

Elly provided the domestic stability and constant praise that permitted Owen to begin writing again. Without the energy-sapping arguments and sexual distractions Jane had triggered, Owen was able to work on *The 39th Parallel* from early in the morning, even before Elly left for the office, until late in the evening when she put dinner down in front of him.

Owen worked Saturdays and Sundays, unwilling even to take time off for a movie or an evening with friends. Elly, unlike Jane, did not complain.

"All women should be like you," Owen told Elly. "You really know how to treat a man."

During the spring of 1964, while the Old Guard and the avant-garde continued to clash over everything from the length of hair to the definition of obscenity in the Lenny Bruce trial to fears of violence during the Rolling Stones' first United States tour, Owen worked on his novel with single-minded concentration. He finished the manuscript one Sunday in June.

When Elly got home from a civil rights demonstration in Central Park, Owen greeted her with a chilled bottle of champagne.

"It's finished!" he said, looking tired but happy and showing her the stack of neatly typed pages.

The next day, Owen brought the manuscript to Hank Greene.

"Here it is," Owen told his agent.

"Oh, boy!" said Hank, practically licking his chops. "I've been looking forward to this!"

"I hope you won't be disappointed," said Owen.

"Cut the fake modesty," said Hank, riffling the manuscript pages. "We can go literary or we can go commercial," he said, laying out the basic choice open to authors and agents at that time.

"What about Parmenides?" asked Owen. "Their reputation is the best."

"I'll give Adrian Holland a call," said Hank. "I'll get back to you."

"Parmenides is taking it. They've agreed to pay ten thousand dollars," Owen told Elly several weeks later. He looked slightly stunned. Ten thousand dollars for a first novel was an enormous advance in 1964 when the usual price for a first novel was fifteen hundred dollars or, if the agent really got tough and the book was outstanding, twenty-five hundred.

"That's absolutely wonderful!" said Elly, thinking that she couldn't wait to tell her parents.

Elly knew of course that Parmenides was one of the country's top prestige publishers. Adrian Holland prided himself on the literary quality of the books he published. Being published by Parmenides automatically meant intellectual respect and serious critical attention. Between the sizable advance and the literary clout that Parmenides had to offer its authors, Elly knew that Owen's book would not be published in obscurity.

"Ten thousand dollars is a lot of money for a first novel. Ten thousand dollars means that the publisher is really serious," she told Owen, her blue eyes shimmering with excitement and already wondering how she could use that exciting piece of information. "I know one of the editors at *Publishers Weekly*. Maybe he'll run an item."

Elly thought that Owen was absolutely wonderful. She thought that *The 39th Parallel* was absolutely wonderful. The part of her job doing publicity gave her a voice with which to make sure that the world thought so, too.

42
ELLY

OCTOBER 1964:

"We are not about to send American
boys nine or ten thousand miles
away for home to do what Asian
boys ought to be doing for
themselves."

—President Lyndon B. Johnson

THE year between September 1964, when Owen signed the
contract for *The 39th Parallel*, and September 1965, when the
book was published, was the year of hair. Hair as symbol, hair
as emblem, hair as political statement—hair as Great Divide
between the establishment and the young triggered a domestic
war. Meanwhile, despite the promises of President Johnson, a
foreign war raged in Vietnam.

On the cutting edge of hip, tie-dyes and beads, denim and
fringe were quickly replacing the gray flannel suit and all the
conservative, establishment attitudes it represented. Youth was
pushing aside age. No one over the age of thirty was to be
trusted. Incense and Eastern religions promising transcen-
dence now seemed more appealing than the white-steepled
churches of the Puritan forefathers with their austere tenets of
discipline and self-restraint. Rock had replaced the romantic
ballad and the peace sign was the sign of the times.

The signs for Owen and Elly also seemed to be positive

and Owen's daring decision to quit *Newsflash* seemed to have turned out to be a wise one.

Ray Jessup took Owen out to a congratulatory lunch at 21.

"I always said you had a big pair of *cojones*," Ray said. "I never doubted you'd come through."

"I certainly can't complain about the way Owen treats you," Louise told Elly. "And he's very nice to us and to your sister, too."

"Maybe I was wrong when I said a writer couldn't make a solid living," said Brian, impressed by the ten thousand dollar advance. "Owen does seem to be different."

Thrilled by the item *Publishers Weekly* ran about *The 39th Parallel* and knowing how much Adrian Holland disdained publicity, Elly appointed herself Owen's unofficial publicist. She clipped the PW item announcing the impressive ten thousand dollar advance and sent it to the "literati" columnist of *Variety* and the New York editor of the *Hollywood Reporter*. Both responded with telephone calls and items of their own.

When the Wordsmith Book Club, intrigued by the PW item, asked for first look, Elly wrote an item about early book-club interest in the new novel about Korea by the former *Newsflash* star reporter and sent it off to the *Daily News*.

When Parmenides set a substantial first printing, Elly called a journalist friend of Owen's now at the *New York Times* who saw to it that the *Times* book page ran an article about the exciting things that were beginning to happen to a first novel called *The 39th Parallel*.

Publicity was creating interest in the novel and interest was creating excitement. Lion Books, one of the big paperback houses, weighed in with a hundred thousand dollar floor bid for the paperback rights. It was a huge amount of money and Elly immediately called her contacts at *Publishers Weekly*, the *New York Times*, and *Variety* with the exciting news. Her only disappointment was that *The 39th Parallel* was now way beyond North Star's budget.

Lincky Desmond, who had come to work as North Star's editor in the spring of 1964, was anxious to get North Star into the big time.

"Unfortunately, Owen's too expensive for us," Lincky told Elly. "But if I have my way, next time around we'll be right there in the bidding!"

"We won't sell the paperback rights until after hardcover publication," Adrian told Owen when initial advance orders from bookstores prompted him to raise the first printing to an impressive twenty-five thousand copies. Adrian explained that the decision whether to sell paperback rights before or after hardcover publication was a difficult one.

"If the book does well in hardcover and makes the best-seller list, the paperback price could be astronomical," he told Owen. "On the other hand, if the book's sales are disappointing, the price would reflect that disappointment. It's a tricky decision. Do we sell promise or performance, sizzle or substance?"

"Let's go for the sizzle," said Hank. "Let's hold the auction right now while we've got the publicity."

Adrian disagreed.

"The decision is mine and I think we should wait. We'll get much more money later on," he said, overruling the agent.

"We'll sell paperback rights just as soon as *Parallel* makes the list," Adrian told Owen.

Hank Greene called Owen to say that several Hollywood movie producers, alerted by the constant stream of publicity, were already lining up for the privilege of paying a fortune for the screen rights.

"I'm playing them off against each other," he told Owen. "I want to squeeze every dollar I can."

Sensing a major publishing success in the offing, Adrian Holland treated Owen with deference. He wanted to know about Owen's next book.

"Do you have something in mind yet?" Adrian asked Owen over an expensive, expansive lunch. Knowing that Owen Casals would be important to Parmenides' future, Adrian had abandoned his usual Gramercy Park haunts and taken Owen uptown to La Côte Basque. It was a case of publishing's finely calibrated Restaurant Index operating at maximum pitch.

"I've been thinking about a coming-of-age book," said Owen, ready for his publisher's question. "I see it as a go-go generation combination of *Catcher in the Rye* and *Lord of the Flies*. It'll be my own boyhood but I'll set it in the present tense. I want to call it *Precincts of Childhood*."

"Great title!" said Adrian, nodding enthusiastically. He stopped just short of kissing Owen's hand. Adrian listened attentively as Owen told him raunchy, exciting, and colorful cop stories recalled from the childhood days he had spent hanging around Cincinnati's Sixth Precinct. The stories, combined with Owen's lean, masculine writing style, would make an excellent second novel, Adrian thought.

"I'll call Hank," Adrian said when Owen had finished explaining the plot and characters he envisioned for *Precincts of Childhood*. "We'll get started on a contract right away."

"I don't want to sign a contract right now. I want to write the book first," Owen said. One gamble had paid off. Owen was ready to take on another. He knew perfectly well that Adrian would pay more for a completed manuscript than he would for an outline.

Adrian was deflated. Even his brush-cut grayish hair seemed to go momentarily limp.

"Well, Owen, whatever you want," he said soothingly, knowing that he had no choice. Adrian knew, as Owen did, that buying a completed manuscript from a bestselling author was going to cost him a fortune. A fortune, Adrian consoled himself, that would be well worth it.

"Let me make the deal for *Precincts* now," Hank told Owen later that day. "Adrian called. He's all turned on. He'll go for twenty-five grand. It's a damn good offer."

"I'd rather wait until the manuscript is finished," said Owen. "Who knows? Maybe it'll be worth even more."

"Maybe," said Hank. "But if Adrian has your new book under contract, he'll have even more motivation to push this one."

"I'd still rather wait," said Owen.

"You're taking a big chance," said Hank.

"That's what I'm known for," said Owen. "Hell, look at the chance I took when I quit *Newsflash*."

"You're the boss. Whatever you say," said Hank. "But you really ought to think about selling *Precincts* now. I can get you a hell of a good deal."

As the autumn of 1965 and the publication date of *The 39th Parallel* drew closer and closer, the signs seemed to get more and more positive. Adrian ultimately raised the size of the first printing to a staggering fifty thousand copies and committed for a full-page ad in the *New York Times Book Review*. Hank Greene sold the film rights to Gold Ribbon Studios.

"They paid fifty thousand dollars outright," Hank told Owen. "At first they wanted an option. I told them they already had an option: Either buy it outright or lose it."

Anticipating the big sums that *The 39th Parallel* now seemed certain to command, Hank advised Owen to get an accountant to do some tax planning.

"You also ought to think about how you want to invest your money," Hank told Owen, mentioning stocks, bonds, and real estate as various possibilities.

The optimism was contagious and Owen found himself bursting with energy and creativity. He now had no need of Jane, of his *Newsflash* environment, of outside stimulation.

Every day, brimming over with ideas, Owen was at work early in the morning. As Elly left for the office, she could hear the staccato bursts from Owen's typewriter.

"*Precincts of Childhood*," he told Elly, "is going to be even better."

The 39th Parallel was published as scheduled, and the reviews were superlative. The *New York Times* called the book "harrowing and realistic" and its author "a singular and unforgettable voice." The *Atlantic* called it "the definitive novel of the Korean experience." *Harper's* called it "a punch in the stomach . . . never to be forgotten." The *Saturday Review* hailed the arrival of "a new and major talent destined to be heard from again and again."

"I couldn't have written them myself. I wouldn't have dared," said Owen buoyantly. Usually very contained, he seemed almost drunk with joy. He took Elly out to a different, expensive restaurant every night and used the movie money to buy the 13th Street brownstone they lived in.

"I could have," replied Elly smugly. In her opinion, no matter how much praise Owen received, it could never be enough. Shuttling between her job at North Star and the civil rights and antiwar demonstrations she still took part in, Elly told her parents that she had never been happier.

"Owen and I are proof that you don't need to get married to live happily ever after," she said, thinking that her own gamble seemed to be paying off, too. Owen's other girlfriend, the one with the frizzy hair, had disappeared. Owen never mentioned her. It seemed clear to Elly that Owen had been telling her the truth when he had said that she wasn't important and that he loved Elly and only Elly.

43
JANE

PUBLISHED IN 1965:

Unsafe at Any Speed, by Ralph Nader, the book that marked the beginning of consumerism

MANHATTAN Jane looked different from St. Louis Jane. In trying to find herself, Jane had performed transformation magic.

After almost four years in Manhattan, Jane dressed in big-city colors of black, gray, and beige spiked now and then with shots of psychedelic orange and acid green. Her big ass and fat thighs took partial cover under the A-line dresses and fishnet pantyhose that were right in the height of style. Jane set her hair on rollers the size of soda cans and used flat beer as a setting lotion. On crisp, dry days, her hair looked as good as it had ever looked. With the slightest bit of humidity, though, it reverted to its usual unruliness. Still, on perfect, clear, sunny days, even Jane's usually despised hair pleased her.

Manhattan Jane talked differently from St. Louis Jane. She sprinkled "fuck" through her conversations so casually that she no longer even heard herself say it anymore. She used drugs only occasionally, although she spoke knowingly about grass and acid. She talked about feeling high and getting turned on as if she were one of Ken Kesey's Merry Pranksters. She went on about good vibes and expanded consciousness as if she were a disciple of Timothy Leary.

She threw around terms like "masochist" and "sadist" like a psychiatrist and vintages like Montrachet and St. Emilion like a wine connoisseur. She could talk about royalties and sub rights like a literary agent and about dimension, perspective, and optics like an East Village painter. She was on comfortable speaking terms with words she had never heard of in St. Louis. Words like *panache* and *cachet*, *kvetch* and *mensch*, *nada* and *gracias*. Instead of saying goodbye, Jane had taken to saying *ciao*.

On the surface, Jane's transformation from new-girl-in-town to Manhattan Woman was a success. Jane no longer experimented in green and purple ink with the spelling of her name. Still, part of her feared that she might be destined to be plain Jane.

In all the years that Jane had been in New York, not one of her stories had been accepted for publication and, even worse, in the months since her affair with Owen Casals had so traumatically blown up, Jane had not been able to complete another one. There had been starts, of course. False starts. Begun with high hopes. Abandoned almost immediately thereafter.

There were opening sentences jotted in notebooks, phrases scrawled on cocktail napkins and stuffed into a manila file labeled Story Ideas. There were fragments of overheard conversations scribbled on envelopes and plot twists penciled on the backs of telephone messages. There were half-completed character sketches abandoned in various notebooks and partially worked-out outlines left in midsentence.

Doggedly, Jane sent out an essay she'd written about her view of the Kennedy assassination, submitting it to every magazine from *Reader's Digest* to *Saturday Review* to *Glamour*. Time after time, it reappeared, like a mangy mutt returning home, in her mailbox. Even though a few people found nice things to say about it, no one wanted to publish it.

As the rejections piled up, even the number of false starts began to diminish. Jane had never felt remotely as guilty about her early sexual experiments with Gene Schuble as she now did about her apparent inability to write.

She blamed all her miseries on Owen Casals.

"Owen Casals did me in and now I'm blocked. It's *his* fault," she told Glen miserably when, as he did now and then, her boss asked Jane what she'd been working on.

"I fell in love with a bastard. I'm still recovering," she told Wilma when Wilma wanted to know why Jane wasn't at her new Olivetti.

"I'm working on a big project for Glen. I haven't been able to spend any time on my own work," she told her parents defensively when they asked her how her writing was going.

Everyone who knew Jane, and Jane most of all, had been waiting for her to publish something. A story. An article. A novel. *Something.* No one, except Jane, knew that nothing was forthcoming.

When *The 39th Parallel* was published, Jane went crazy. Crazy with envy, crazy with jealousy, crazy with misery. Not only had Owen Casals ruined her creativity, *he* was wallowing in fame and attention.

Jane read Owen's reviews and she felt sick. When critics praised the crisp, short sentences that made the combat scenes jump to life, Jane screamed to Wilma that, goddamnit, the short sentences had been *her* idea.

When civil rights groups singled out the sympathetic treatment of Negro troops in *The 39th Parallel,* Jane told Glen that she wanted to ask them who the hell they thought had gotten the brainstorm of including black characters?

Jane even wrote a letter to the *Times Book Review* spelling out her contributions to Owen Casals' masterpiece. She never received an answer. Not even a printed form letter.

"I should have thrown my letter off the Empire State

Building!" she bitched, telling everyone within earshot that *her* contributions to *The 39th Parallel* had been utterly ignored.

Jane had contributed to Owen's success and no one knew it. Her name wasn't on the book or anywhere in it. She was like a Soviet nonperson. Owen, that egomaniacal shithead, hadn't even written an acknowledgment mentioning her ideas and contributions. Jane thought about suing him but realized that she didn't have the money to hire a lawyer. She told everyone who would listen that *she* deserved some of the success but, quite soon, Jane's friends got bored with her complaints and people who didn't know her made it clear they didn't believe her.

Whenever Jane saw stacks of *The 39th Parallel* in bookstores she burned with fury. Why weren't they stacks of *her* book? Why wasn't *she* being featured at the cash registers? Why wasn't *her* book in bookstore windows? When she saw Owen's photo on the back cover—he looked handsome and lean and sophisticated and romantic in military khakis holding a cigarette and squinting against the sun—she didn't know whether to kill him or kill herself. Or both.

It just wasn't fair, Jane thought. Owen was successful because he was a man. Men went to war and then they wrote books about it and everyone told them they were geniuses. If she'd gone to war, she'd have written a masterpiece, too.

Furiously, Jane remembered what Professor Engler had told her about needing experience. Well, the goddamn problem was that the kind of experience she had no one cared about. Finding a cheap Village apartment through friends? Learning how to survive in New York without a conventional nine-to-five job? Trying to be a writer when not one single person was interested in publishing her? Who gave a damn? No one. Half the time, not even Jane herself.

Jane thought of calling Owen a million times but didn't. A million times, she thought of going to see him but didn't. What would she say? Give me money? Money wasn't the point. Give me credit? The book was already out. What would she do? What could she accomplish? Other than utterly humiliate herself?

Owen's blazing, public triumph contrasted sickeningly with Jane's lack of achievement and Jane fell into a state of morose depression punctuated by titanic rages. It was Owen's fault that she was alone. Owen's fault that she was blocked. Owen's fault that she was fat and miserable. He was a liar, a cheater, a user, a double-crosser, a hit-and-run lover, a heartless monster.

"You're burning yourself out with anger. It's not going to help you or hurt Owen," Glen told Jane, worried about her inability to put Owen Casals and their affair behind her. He had spent hours acting as an unpaid shrink, listening to Jane's recital of unhappiness and confusion in the wake of her breakup with Owen.

"Well, what should I do?" asked Jane.

"Don't get mad. Get even," Glen recommended, quoting old Joe Kennedy's celebrated remark.

"How?" asked Jane. She felt like a nonentity. A disgusting, unlovable, fat nonentity. How could a nonentity get even? What weapons did fate hand out to nonentities?

"Write about it," Glen said, as if it were the most obvious solution in the world.

"And admit I got ditched?" Jane asked. Her ego was already demolished. The thought of going public with her pathetic story and telling the world that she had gotten dumped made her ill. "Who'd want to read that?"

"Only a million other women who got ditched," replied Glen.

Jane could not believe it. She could not even begin to write it. She was still too close to the emotional catastrophe that had befallen her. Instead, she turned to Hershey's (with and without almonds) for solace and indulged herself in bitter fantasies about how absolutely perfect, wonderful, and incredibly satisfying Owen's entire life had to be.

Elly, on the other hand, was uneasily wondering what had gone wrong.

44
ELLY

Fertility drugs, body stockings, the
30-minute evening news show, draft
card burnings, the credibility gap,
the phrase Flower Power by Allen
Ginsberg at a Berkeley antiwar rally

STRAWS in the wind drift slowly. They come to earth silently, weightlessly, as if without impact. Portents become significant only in retrospect. Hindsight not foresight tests twenty-twenty. Even looking back, Elly could not remember exactly when the first chill premonitions about *The 39th Parallel* entered her mind. Was it when she found out about the book club? When the paperback auction fizzled? Or when it became clear that *The 39th Parallel* would not hit the bestseller list?

The first letdown came in the autumn of 1965 even as Jane tortured herself with fantasies of Owen's success.

Elly found out about the book club not from Owen but from Lincky Desmond.

"I'm sorry that Wordsmith didn't make *The 39th Parallel* a main selection," Lincky told Elly as the weekly promotion meeting at North Star broke up. Wordsmith was the biggest, most powerful book club. A Wordsmith Main Selection not only sold hundreds of copies through the mail, it always resulted in tens of thousands of additional sales in bookstores.

"I didn't know the decision had already been made," Elly said. Her heart sank. Owen had said nothing.

"The selection committee met on Friday," said Lincky. "I had lunch with a Wordsmith editor who told me that the committee members felt that the club's readers wouldn't be responsive to the Korean War background. I really feel bad because the book is so good. I hope Owen isn't too upset."

"Owen's never mentioned it," said Elly. "Is it possible he doesn't know?"

Lincky, of course, had no way of knowing.

When Elly brought up the subject of the Wordsmith decision that evening, Owen told her that he already knew.

"I didn't say anything," he explained, "because it's no big deal. The clubs aren't the end of the world. Besides, a lot of times alternates outsell main selections."

Elly could tell from Owen's tone of voice that he was in no mood for a major discussion of why the book hadn't been made a main selection despite Adrian's and Owen's expectations. Elly silently crossed her fingers hoping that *The 39th Parallel* would be one of the alternates that outsold the main selection.

Was it then, Elly asked herself later, that she first suspected that *The 39th Parallel* wasn't going to be the sure thing everyone kept predicting it would be?

Or was it the telephone call from Adrian Holland one evening at 6:15 to tell Owen that none of the other paperback houses had come through with a competing offer for the reprint rights? *The 39th Parallel*, Adrian said, had gone to Lion for the original floor bid of a hundred thousand dollars. Adrian tried to sound upbeat but, even listening to Owen's end of the conversation, Elly heard the clear note of disappointment run through the congratulations and positive words.

"What the hell? A hundred grand's still a fortune," said Owen, shrugging and turning to Elly as he hung up. "Lion will push the paperback like crazy. They got lucky is all. They got a bargain. That's what Adrian said and Adrian's right."

"A hundred thousand dollars *is* a fortune!" said Elly, meeting Owen's façade of confidence with one of her own. "And, for a first book, it's almost unheard of. In fact, it's probably a record. Adrian ought to publicize that fact."

"Let's let Adrian worry about what to publicize," said Owen, sounding irritated.

Owen had become very touchy whenever Elly mentioned possible publicity angles for *The 39th Parallel*. Like Adrian, Owen considered book hype cheap and vulgar, especially when the book concerned was one of obvious high quality. Owen had not been at all happy with the *Variety* and *Daily News* items and had asked Elly to stop interfering with the publication plans.

"Now, tell me, where would you like to go to dinner? A hundred thousand dollars calls for a real celebration!"

Failure was mostly an attitude, Elly reminded herself when, despite the rapturous reviews and Parmenides' best efforts, *The 39th Parallel* failed to make any of the bestseller lists. Failure could be a learning experience, she told herself staunchly through the paperback publication in the fall of 1966. Although Lion Books tried hard with a silver-foil cover, counter display units that featured the critics' raves, and a six-city publicity tour of which Owen loathed every moment, the scuttlebutt in the trade was that the book just wasn't moving.

Most people, including Adrian, ascribed the lack of sales to the growing antiwar mood in the country. The massive Vietcong New Year's Tet offensive reversed what little progress American troops had made in Vietnam. Every day the headlines and evening television newscasts were filled with stories of draft card burnings, of young men fleeing to Canada, and of public opinion polls that showed that one half of all Americans thought that United States involvement in Vietnam was a mistake.

Millions, including Elly herself, were demonstrating

against the war. People greeted each other with the peace sign and wore buttons that said "Hell No, We Won't Go." Flower Power and antiwar sentiment were on the rise. People did not want to read about war. Any war. They did not care how brilliant the writing was, how compassionate the view of infantrymen was, how realistic the combat scenes and descriptions of battle were. War was unpopular. Any war. Every war. Battlefield heroics had gone out of fashion and *The 39th Parallel*, about the Korean war, was considered to be an unfortunate victim of poor timing.

"Some publicity stressing the personal stories of the characters might counteract the perception that it's a war book," Elly told Owen. "It might help sales."

"I told you I'm not interested in publicity," said Owen. "Now just shut up about it."

Owen insisted that he regarded *The 39th Parallel* as a success. He reminded everyone that all he had wanted was to write a good book.

"The reviews were everything I could have hoped for *and*, between the movie sale and the book rights, I earned plenty of money, too," Owen said. "Not many first novelists have that kind of success."

Owen was right, Elly thought. He was hard at work on *Precincts of Childhood* and, because he was excited about it, so was Elly. However, when Owen decided to try to make a deal with Parmenides based on an outline and several completed chapters, Adrian decided not to make an offer.

"Beware of 'literary' publishers," Hank told Owen. "They claim they're aesthetic. Wrong. They're eunuchs. No balls."

"Once burned, I guess," Owen said grimly. "Adrian screwed up on the paperback auction. You were right, Hank, he should have sold those rights pre-pub. He would have gotten a lot more money and the reprinter would have had a much bigger stake in putting the book over."

"It happens all the time. Agents make twenty sales a

month, publishers make twenty sales a year, but still they won't take advice from the agent. But everything passes. Listen to Hank Greene: combined hard-soft deals are going to be the wave of the future."

When Hank sold *Precincts of Childhood* to Ted Spandorff of Raintree Books, he was able to get Owen a five thousand dollar advance.

"Ted's a cheap bastard and it was the best I could get," Hank told Owen.

"You were right about that, too," said Owen. "I should have let you sell *Precincts* to Adrian while he was still so high on the prospects for *Parallel*."

When Owen missed the first deadline for delivering the manuscript, Elly refused to get upset. She told herself that she would be silly to worry.

"Writers often miss deadlines," she told Lincky.

Lincky nodded knowingly, sympathetically.

"Inspiration doesn't run on timetables," Lincky pointed out, telling Elly about all the overdue manuscripts North Star and every other publisher carried in inventory.

Elly remembered Lincky's comment and used it when Owen missed the second deadline. Missing a deadline, after all, wasn't the end of the world. Missing a deadline, when it came to books, was sometimes part of the lengthy and difficult process.

Elly was determined to look at the bright side. Whenever Elly felt herself getting upset about finances or the way Owen sometimes drank too much and had gradually stopped seeing old friends like Ray Jessup, she sternly told herself that all disappointments should be so terrible.

After all, Owen wasn't upset and his reaction was the one that mattered. Wasn't it? Meanwhile, without saying anything to Owen, Elly began using her salary to help cover household expenses. The money Owen had earned, even in the mid-Sixties, only went so far and they needed the money Elly earned to live on.

45
LINCKY

1964:

Over 250 million paperback books
are sold.

WEEP, weep. Cry, cry. Starting in January 1964, Lincky had
three appointments a week with Dr. Eliot Landauer. He
seemed to be about thirty, Lincky thought, young enough to
understand what she was going through, old enough to have
experience. He was dark haired, small-featured but had dispro-
portionately large ears. He seemed quite handsome from some
angles, blandly unmemorable from others.

For a while, Lincky thought she was in love with him and
wanted to marry him. He seemed to her to be the kind of man
who would take good care of her. She did not know, of course,
that Eliot Landauer's own marriage was in trouble and that
although he could help other people solve their problems, he
was currently having his own personal difficulties.

Promptly at 12:10 on Tuesday, Wednesday, and Friday, she
entered his dimly lit, beige office and flung herself onto his

couch. She wept as she confronted the grief and guilt she had kept bottled up since September 1961.

"I'm a murderer and an adulteress," she said. "I killed my parents and betrayed my husband."

"Murder? Wasn't it an accident?" asked Dr. Landauer. He had a calm, reassuring voice.

"Engine failure," said Lincky. "But I still feel guilty. And angry, too. My parents were all I had. How could they have left me all alone? How could they have done that to me?"

Eliot Landauer patiently led Lincky through the thickets of her confusion until her focus shifted from the irrational to the rational, from the past to the present, from her marriage to her affair.

"I love my husband but I wish he were happier. He hates his job but he feels he can't leave," said Lincky. "He says that if we have a baby he'll forget about his problems at the office but I want to work for a few more years. I *think*. I'm not even sure of *that* anymore. Thanks to Hank Greene. He was like Svengali. I felt as if I were hypnotized," Lincky said, describing Hank Greene as a man she didn't exactly love but couldn't resist.

"Hypnotized?" asked Dr. Landauer. "Could you go into that a bit more?"

"Hank made me feel that I wasn't alone anymore," Lincky said. "Ever since my parents died, I've been numb. Hank was rude. He was abusive and insulting but he got closer to me than anyone except my mother and father. I couldn't stay away from him even though I knew that if I kept seeing him it would probably destroy my marriage."

"Are you still seeing him?"

"No."

"How did the relationship end?" asked Doctor Landauer.

"Hank fired me," said Lincky. She burst into tears. "Hank Greene is the worst thing that ever happened to me."

"The worst?" asked Eliot Landauer when her sobbing had subsided.

"The worst!" said Lincky immediately. Then she paused for a moment. "The best?"

Eliot Landauer was quiet.

Lincky was confused. She wasn't sure of anything anymore. Her life was a mixed-up mess and she was a mixed-up mess. No wonder Hank had fired her. No wonder she was spending a fortune on a shrink instead of looking for a new job or using the time to do the grocery shopping the way Peter wanted. No wonder Hank had accused her of being a spoiled rich girl. No wonder Peter complained that she was more ambitious than most men. Lincky begged Eliot Landauer to tell her who she was and what she wanted, something he refused to do.

"That's your job," he told her, placing the burden for her life squarely on her. "All I can do is help."

"All I want is everything," Lincky told Dr. Landauer. "I want to be an ideal wife, spotless housekeeper, ultimate gourmet cook, hostess with the mostest. I also wanted to be the best editor, the number-one manuscript reader and the all-around office favorite. Miss Sills in the sixth grade told me I couldn't be smart *and* pretty. I guess she was right. I guess you just can't do two things well," said Lincky.

"I think you're smart and pretty," Eliot Landauer said.

"You do?" asked Lincky. "That's what my parents said."

Still, Lincky sounded unconvinced. "I wish I could be a wife and a winner. I guess it's impossible," she said.

"You said 'impossible.' I didn't," said Eliot Landauer. More than anything, he wanted a wife who was a winner. It was the basis for the conflict in his own marriage. "Do you really think it's impossible?"

"I *know* it's impossible!" said Lincky. "At *Women's World* only two of the editors were women. One, the beauty editor, is divorced. The other, the assistant to the head of the test kitchen, has never married. At the Hank Greene Agency, the only other woman in a nonsecretarial job is a bookkeeper who's going to quit just as soon as she and her fiancé get married."

Working women on television like Marlo Thomas on *That Girl* were single and lived alone, Lincky pointed out. Married women like Lucille Ball on *I Love Lucy* devoted their time and energy to their husbands and children.

"No one does both. Not on television and not in real life," said Lincky. "Who am I to be different?"

"Who says you have to be like everyone else?" asked Dr. Landauer.

"Name one woman who worked and was happily married!" said Lincky.

"Your mother," replied Eliot Landauer.

Lincky turned around and smiled at him.

"My God! How could I have forgotten!"

Although there was as yet no feminist movement as Lincky wept her way through the early months of 1964, the earliest stirrings of women's liberation were just becoming apparent. Women were observing the successes of blacks and were just beginning to feel that if blacks could assert and claim their rights, so could they. There were so many restrictions women were just beginning to become aware of: legal, economic, professional, sexual, reproductive, athletic, intellectual. Too many doors had been closed to women for too long, too many paths sealed off.

With Eliot Landauer's sympathetic but realistic help, Lincky began to examine and gradually shed the myths with which she and most women of her generation had grown up. She began to feel more in control of herself and her feelings. She decided that she didn't want to have a baby—yet. She decided that she was still interested in being an editor.

"I've started to get serious about looking for a job," she told Dr. Landauer in February. "I have interviews scheduled at Raintree Books, at Parmenides Press, and at North Star."

"I do have an opening for an assistant," Ted Spandorff told Lincky, stroking the mustache that grew more luxuriant year by year. "But between your work for Charlie Lamb and your experience at the Hank Greene Agency, I'm afraid you're overqualified."

What Ted told his managing editor was that he wouldn't have Lincky Desmond on the premises.

"Pushy," he said. "She'd be after my job in six weeks."

What Lincky told Dr. Landauer was: "Overqualified? He's probably afraid of me."

"We would definitely like to have you," said Adrian Holland. "Your experience and your energy would be big assets. We could give you a job as editor. The salary would be eighty dollars a week."

"That's less than I earned at Hank Greene's by the time I left," Lincky pointed out.

Adrian formed his round, cherubic face into a smile.

"We're only publishers, Lincky. We're not nearly as rich as agents."

"So far, zero for two," Lincky told Dr. Landauer. "I hope Gordon Geiger is going to break my streak of bad luck."

46
LINCKY

Hell No! We Won't Go!
LSD Not LBJ!
Make Love, Not War!
Turn On, Tune In, Drop Out!
God Is Dead!

—Slogans of the Sixties

IN March 1964, Lincky got the job and the title she wanted from Gordon Geiger: Editor. It was a job Gordon himself had initially performed during the first few months of North Star's existence. Success, Gordon told Lincky during their interview, had put him out of a job.

"I can't be sales director, production manager, publicity man, *and* editor," Gordon told Lincky when he hired her, explaining that, although North Star was still a tiny company with only eight employees, sales had been rising each month and the future seemed bright.

"We're in the right business at the right time. We've made a good start. Your job is to build on that base."

Lincky smiled and accepted the assignment. She had put her personal crisis behind her. She was ready to deal with the challenges of the world of work.

Gordon promised not to stand in her way.

"I'm much too busy to second-guess my editor. Basically,

you're going to be on your own," he told Lincky, although he said that he of course expected her to inform him of all her decisions. "I don't want you to go off half-cocked," he said, as if under Lincky's svelte good looks lurked a wild-eyed dingbat.

Not only did Gordon Geiger have his own excellent impression of Lincky to go on, he had checked her references with Charlie Lamb and Hank Greene.

"Best secretary I ever had. Hard working and smart as a whip," said Charlie, adding that she was slightly pushy, a negative that Gordon interpreted as a positive.

Hank Greene said nothing about personal feelings and confirmed Charlie Lamb's words.

"She's smart. She works hard. She's headed somewhere," he said, adding that the Hank Greene Agency missed her.

"Then why did you fire her?" asked Gordon.

"You know me," replied Hank. "I've fired half the vice presidents in publishing."

When Hank read in *Publishers Weekly* that Lincky had gotten the editorial job at North Star, he sent her a note of congratulations. Lincky wondered if he expected a reply. She thought about what to do for days and finally decided not to send him a response.

"Why ask for trouble?" she told Coral.

North Star was a young, with-it company and Gordon liked the idea of having a young, with-it editor to reinforce that image. The fact that Lincky was female also made North Star different and Gordon liked being different. The fact that Lincky was female meant that Gordon didn't have to pay as much in salary as he would have had to pay a male editor. He liked that, too.

While Gordon Geiger occupied himself with the sales, distribution, and financial aspects of his business, Lincky found herself free to make editorial decisions almost without interference. Gordon Geiger turned out to be as good as his promise and Lincky turned out to be as good as her references.

Looking north of the border, Lincky noticed how well the Canadian-published romance novels sold both in Canada and in the United States. In her first editorial move, Lincky decided to add one romance novel a month to the North Star list of *mucho* macho spy adventures, hard-boiled mysteries, and combat novels that Lincky referred to as "true romances for men."

"Some for the boys, one for the girls," she told Gordon.

Lincky knew from working at the Hank Greene Agency that romance novels could be bought for as little as $750, making them inexpensive additions to a publisher's list. In addition, Lincky cited booksellers' surveys showing that a majority of book buyers and readers were women.

Gordon was impressed by Lincky's clear thinking, businesslike approach, and nose for profit.

"It's time North Star diversified," he said.

The romance novels were immediate money makers and Lincky had the satisfaction of seeing other paperback houses, much larger than North Star, follow her lead. The successful departure gave Lincky the courage to branch out further.

"We should add some popular psychology to North Star's list," Lincky told Gordon in 1965 when *Games People Play* hit the bestseller lists. Recalling how helpful her sessions with Eliot Landauer had been, Lincky felt that many people who could not afford a private therapist might be helped by books. She persuaded Gordon to add occasional titles on personal growth to North Star's list even though, up until then, North Star had published fiction exclusively.

"Next thing, we'll need to hire a house shrink," Gordon joked, when the self-help books sometimes outsold even the fiction, and the rapid growth of North Star's sales occasionally created production and distribution snags that threatened to drive him nuts.

Lincky also got ideas from the movies, television and other books. Spies and spying were everywhere and wildly popular. They ranged from the serious John Le Carré novel, *The Spy Who*

Came In From the Cold to the jazzy, sexy, and adventure-packed James Bond films, *Goldfinger* and *From Russia With Love*. Lincky studied *The Ipcress File*, both the Len Deighton novel and the Michael Caine movie; *Get Smart* with Don Adams and Barbara Feldon; *I Spy* with Robert Culp and Bill Cosby; *Mission: Impossible* with Barbara Bain and Martin Landau. They were all great successes, yet each was different and distinct. Except for one thing: the heroes were all men.

Lincky thought the time had come for a change.

"What about an adventure series with a female heroine?" Lincky asked Gordon in 1966.

Thrillers and spy stories were perennial sellers, Lincky pointed out. A thriller with a female protagonist ought to sell, too, she reasoned. After getting Gordon's okay, Lincky went to Glen Sinclair with her idea.

"The title would be *Supermodel/Superspy*, she told him. "The heroine is a Twiggy-like fashion model who's also a daredevil international spy."

"I love it," said Glen. "How much sex do you want?"

"Enough to keep the readers interested but not enough to get us thrown into jail," laughed Lincky.

The fact that Glen was a Hank Greene client bothered Lincky but Glen was the perfect writer for the job and Lincky was determined to be professional. She had been at North Star for two years and so far had managed to avoid Hank Greene and the Hank Greene Agency. The time to put her personal feelings aside had come and, taking a deep breath, Lincky dialled Hank's number to negotiate the deal with Glen.

"This is Lincky Des—" she began.

"I know who it is," Hank said. "What do you want?"

"To make a deal with Glen Sinclair."

"What are you offering?"

"Five thousand dollars with eight and ten percent royalties."

"Forget it. Glen gets seventy-five hundred from Castle Books."

"Seventy-five hundred," Lincky said.

"And a straight ten percent on the royalties," said Hank.

"All right," said Lincky. "But no step-up to twelve and a half after a hundred thousand copies."

"I don't like it," said Hank.

"Tough," said Lincky. "That's the offer. The concept and the character are both mine. If you won't take the deal, I'll find another writer."

"Okay," said Hank. "Seventy-five hundred, half on signing, half on delivery. A straight ten percent royalty. Right?"

"Right," said Lincky.

There was a moment of silence.

"How are you?" she asked.

"Fine," he snapped and slammed down the phone.

The pop art covers suggested by Lincky were standouts on paperback racks. The books themselves were written in a sassy, sexy style. The *Supermodel/Superspy* series became North Star's biggest seller ever and the television rights were bought by Gold Ribbon films.

"They paid twenty-five thousand dollars with escalators to a hundred," Hank told his client.

"Wow!" said Glen. "I think I'm going to marry Lincky."

Hank grunted and hung up.

Although, as editor of North Star Books, Lincky did business with Hank, it was always over the telephone. Lincky made a point of deliberately not going to places where she might run into Hank Greene and, when she saw him at publishing parties, she nodded coolly and immediately found someone across the room with whom she had to speak.

"Out of sight is out of mind," Lincky told Coral Weinstein, explaining her attempts to avoid Hank Greene. Then she added with a rueful smile, "Most of the time."

"You've got the golden touch," Gordon Geiger told Lincky as he watched the North Star list grow from four books a month to six to eight in the two years since he'd hired Lincky. However, when it came to hiring another editor to help Lincky deal with the success she had helped create, Gordon did not consult Lincky.

"His name is Erwin Elder. He'll be an editor, just like you." Gordon told Lincky when she asked what the new editor's title would be.

"I've been here longer," Lincky said. "Don't you think my title should be bigger?" Lincky wanted to be called editor in chief.

"He's more experienced than you," replied Gordon, thinking that Lincky's reputation of being somewhat pushy was deserved. She was good but she needed to be kept in her place. "Erwin's been in publishing for a dozen years."

Lincky was uneasy about the intruder but Gordon calmed her down with a raise and told Lincky that he didn't want any office politics at North Star.

"We all work together here," he said, echoing a long-ago Charlie Lamb piety. "Besides, you and Erwin are in charge of different areas."

Erwin Elder was a science fiction specialist, a man as weird as the books he published. Small, roly-poly, pipe-smoking, Erwin Elder was entirely bald. He made up for the lack of hair on his head with the hair on his face: he wore a humongous beard that puffed out on both sides of his face and hung to almost midchest level. He had met all three of his wives at science fiction conventions and his claim to fame was discovering and publishing the bestselling Zap Man series for his previous employer. He sat in his office all day long reading manuscripts and drinking gin martinis out of a Thermos.

"Doesn't he ever talk?" Lincky asked Elly when Erwin had worked at North Star for four months and attended editorial, sales, and print-order meetings without speaking more than three or four words in a voice so soft that he could barely be heard.

"Not that I know of," Elly replied, as put off as Lincky was by the spooky, silent editor.

Lincky found publishing a fascinating business with a fascinating cast of characters. It was a combination of the crass and the commercial, the intellectual and the intelligent, the creative and the practical.

Through her work, Lincky found a network of friends with common interests. She worked well with Elly McGrath and was personally very fond of her.

"We both had working mothers. They were unusual for their times," Lincky pointed out.

She bought the paperback rights to Coral Weinstein's beauty book and suggested that Coral write a book on personal style.

"Not the latest look from Paris," said Lincky, "but how any woman on any budget can develop a personal look."

She also asked Becky Reese, who was still slaving away at *Women's World*, for a cookbook.

"Recipes that are fast but good," said Lincky, thinking of how she was always on the lookout for quick dinners she could whip up after work. "Everyone always wants to save time."

Everything Lincky touched sold well. Her writers liked to work with her, and Gordon, although not effusive, clearly appreciated her contributions to North Star's continuing growth. Lincky had found another place in the world beside the magic circle where she truly fit in. Hank Greene had been right. If she were really serious about her work, she could become someone. Somewhere in the mid-Sixties, Lincky decided that she wanted more than just a good job. She resolved to have a career.

47
LINCKY

1 9 6 6 :

> We seek to confront with concrete
> action the conditions which now
> prevent women from enjoying
> equality of opportunity and freedom
> of choice, which is their right as
> individual Americans and as human
> beings.
>
> —Manifesto, National
> Organization for
> Women

BY the time she had been married for four years, Lincky's life increasingly revolved around her job. She regularly stayed late in the office at night. She left for work early in the morning. When she wasn't at the office, she was having business lunches, attending meetings with agents or authors, or dropping in on publishing parties in the habit she had formed back when she had worked for Charlie Lamb. She spent hours visiting bookstores to see how books were being displayed, talking to clerks to find out whether or not people liked the newest bestsellers and to note for herself which books were shunted aside to the back shelves, which were on prominent display right next to the cash registers, and which were being featured in the windows.

When Lincky was on the phone at night after dinner she didn't talk about recipes and clothes like other women. She talked industry gossip: book deals, which author might be ready to leave which publisher, which editor was moving to another house, and who had overpaid for which over-hyped manuscript.

"Don't you ever get tired of publishing?" asked Peter. After a day of watching the tape, he was bored to death with AT&T and IBM. Didn't Lincky feel the same way?

"Not at all. Every book is new. Every author is individual. Every manuscript is different from every other manuscript," Lincky said, trying to explain the addictive nature of the novelty that was built into the business of publishing books.

"All you do is work, though. Don't you ever want to spend the afternoon shopping?"

"Shopping?" Lincky was incredulous. She grudgingly went to Saks twice a year to stock up and then forgot about clothes for another six months. "Why would I want to shop when I can stay in the office and make a deal or come home and read a new manuscript?"

"Other women like to shop," Peter said quietly.

"I'm not other women," Lincky replied.

Peter nodded. By now, he knew that all too well. There were many times when he wished that weren't the case. There was something in Lincky's life that was now just as important as he was. That something was work and it stimulated and satisfied her in a way that he couldn't. Sensing that he couldn't win or even compete, Peter began to feel as frustrated and resentful at home as he did in the office.

"Are you married to me or to that manuscript?" he asked Lincky one Saturday morning in September 1966. Peter had tickets to the U.S. Open and he wanted Lincky to join him in Forest Hills to watch John Newcombe, Billie Jean King, Rod Laver, and Arthur Ashe. Lincky, absorbed in her work, had decided to spend the day at home, finishing an editing job.

"I'm married to you," Lincky had replied clamly, knowing that a fight was brewing and wanting to avoid it. "But the manuscript is due at the typesetter on Monday."

Peter didn't give a damn about the manuscript. Ever since

they'd met, he and Lincky had gone to the tennis matches together every year. Why wouldn't she go with him this year? Wasn't he as much fun as her manuscript?

Peter went to Forest Hills by himself, feeling lonely, rejected, and angry. Halfway through the sixth game of the first set he picked up a blond, blue-eyed Smith graduate in the center stands and took her to the nearby Forest Hills Inn for lunch and sex.

It was the first time Peter had ever been unfaithful to Lincky and he despised himself for it. He loved Lincky and fidelity mattered to him. The sex had been only fair and Peter felt miserable and guilty afterwards. He understood that he had picked up the girl—exactly the kind of girl he had once sworn never to marry—as a way of getting back at Lincky for refusing to attend the tennis matches with him. The understanding did not make Peter feel better. Instead, it made him resent Lincky even more.

Sometimes it seemed to Peter that Lincky preferred everything and everyone to him: her job, her manuscripts, her friends in publishing. Although he loved Lincky and tried hard to be fair to her and her interests, Peter was beginning to feel like the odd man out. The Smithie in the stands was followed by others, girls Peter had sex with, girls he didn't like nearly as much as he liked Lincky, girls he knew weren't as interesting, as pretty, or as nice as Lincky was. He didn't know what he was doing and he couldn't stop doing it.

"Sometimes I almost wish you were having an affair with Gordon," said a resentful Peter when Lincky came home late from the office several months later. That way Peter might not feel so guilty about his own affairs. "If you were screwing Gordon, you'd make a point of spending less time with him so I wouldn't get suspicious. At least you'd get home at a reasonable hour."

"I'm sorry," Lincky apologized, guiltily remembering the time she had been having an affair. Thank God Peter had never found out. "It was unavoidable. There was an auction. Paperback rights for the new Phyllis Whitney—"

"Spare me the details. I'm hungry and I want to eat," Peter groaned, holding up his hand and cutting Lincky off. He was bored now with Lincky's daily activities at the office. The days when he had been fascinated by the *Women's World* gossip had long since gone. Didn't Lincky know he didn't care about her goddamn auction? Didn't she know that he wanted her attention? Didn't she know that a wife should put her husband first?

"We'll order up," said Lincky.

"I didn't get married to order up," said Peter.

"If we had a kid we'd have a normal life," muttered Peter as they sat down to lemon chicken and sweet and sour spareribs. He remembered when Lincky had cooked gourmet dinners and they had sipped fine wines. Now it was Chinese food, Tab, and tea.

Lincky pretended she hadn't heard Peter's comment. The subject of children was becoming another in a whole list of touchy subjects.

Peter who had once adored everything about Lincky now found much to criticize. He pointed out that she didn't seem as enthusiastic about entertaining his friends from Yale and Wall Street as she had in the early days of their marriage. He accused her of no longer enjoying quiet evenings at home. He spoke about his increasing sense of getting older, not younger, and of his acute awareness of time passing. By the middle of 1966, Peter had turned thirty. He spoke more and more often and more and more longingly about having children.

"We're the only people our age who don't have children," he told Lincky, sounding what had become a familiar theme as they drove back from Connecticut from a Sunday visit to Bo Skinner and his wife. Although Peter's tone was quiet and pensive, Lincky heard his words as the accusation they in fact were. Not having children was, according to Peter, entirely Lincky's doing.

"I don't want to end up like Beth," said Lincky. Beth Skinner had given up an assistant production job in television to care for her two toddlers. While Peter and Bo shot baskets out on the driveway, Lincky stayed in the kitchen, helping Beth prepare lunch. Beth had complained to Lincky that she missed her big West Side apartment and the daily stimulation of having a show to put on. "She said that being around people under two feet tall all day long is turning her brain to mush."

"That wouldn't happen to you," said Peter.

But Lincky wasn't so sure. If it had happened to Beth Skinner, why wouldn't it happen to her? Who was she to be different? Why should she and she alone escape the pitfalls of motherhood?

Lincky had always been proud of her decisiveness. The way she shopped was a perfect example. Lincky often shocked salespeople with the swiftness of her decision. She had chosen her wedding gown in ten minutes. She chose the carpeting for her apartment in five and her fur coat in two.

Lincky had always been proud that not only were her decisions easy to arrive at but that she had always been pleased with their outcome. Her wedding gown had shown off her tiny waist to advantage and made her complexion seem opalescently creamy. The neutral gray of the carpeting had gone with everything she had subsequently bought for the apartment and her fur, a soft, fluffy lynx, made her feel like a movie star every time she put it on.

So why, Lincky asked herself over and over in 1968 as her marriage went into its sixth year, was she still unable to decide how she felt about having a baby? Uncharacteristically, Lincky did not know what she wanted or how she felt. She was torn down the middle. Half of her wanted a baby. Half of her didn't. Half of her thought she and Peter would spend the rest of their lives together. Half of her wondered.

While Lincky's ambivalence about her personal life continued, her dreams and ambitions for North Star were becoming even more clear-cut and unambiguous. Pop paperbacks were fun to create and fun to publish but there was a serious side to Lincky, too, a side that pressed more and more for expression.

"I think we ought to start a hardcover line," she told Gordon. "Better authors would come to North Star. We wouldn't have to compete against other paperback houses for reprint rights to hardcover bestsellers. More and more these days, agents are selling combined hard- and softcover rights," she said.

"Not so fast. We don't have a hardcover sales force. Or a warehose. And we don't have collections clout. I've heard horror stories about small publishers being the last to get paid by bookstores."

"Gordon, I've thought of all that."

"And?"

"We get a major hardcover house to distribute us for a commission. They've got the sales reps and the warehousing, and they're too big for the stores to stiff."

"Lincky, be realistic. What main-line house would take us on when we haven't got any books yet?"

"I've already got three to say they would. Our track record with the bestselling paperback originals looks good to them. I haven't committed anything, Gordon. You're the boss. You're the one who signs. I told them that."

Gordon gazed at her. He was impressed.

"You really think this would work?"

"Yes. Within five years you'll have clout of your own. Then we go independent, hire our own reps and get our own warehousing. It's the way for us to go."

It did not escape Gordon that the "you" had changed to "we." He didn't love it but he liked it. The pushy Lincky Desmond might just push North Star into the big time.

"I'll want to see some numbers," he said.

"Of course," said Lincky.

48
JANE

Guru, hang-up, narc, kicky, shades,
peacenik, cool, ballsy

1967 is the year people mean when they talk about the Sixties.
It was the year of the long, hot summer. Black Power coexisted
with Flower Power. It was the year of feelin' groovy, of marijuana, minis, and microminis, of Hare Krishna, Twiggy, the
Love Generation and the Monterey Pop Festival. Patriotism was
considered mindless flag waving at best, warmongering at
worst. God was dead. Religion had become irrelevant and
churches grew emptier, their parishioners gone to find salvation elsewhere.

Capitalism had become a dirty word, and business, big
and small, was loathed as part of an increasingly untrustwor-
thy and contemptible establishment. Monogamy was thought
to be hopelessly old fashioned and sexual experimentation was
the cry of the times, the wilder the better. Soberness of all
kinds was out. Euphoria of all kinds was in. Drugs, once the
indulgence of the bohemian avant-garde, went public for the
first time as a cloud of marijuana hung over college campuses

| 261 |

and a vast menu of consciousness expanders from LSD to mescaline to peyote became widely available.

1967 was the year Jane started lying about her age. She studied herself in magnifying mirrors and bright lights and noticed the beginnings of crow's feet around her eyes. She saw the faint tracery of the brackets between nose and mouth that were prominent in her father's family and began making notes of the names of the plastic surgeons whose advice was so copiously and uncritically quoted in women's magazines. Twenty-seven seemed ancient. Twenty-seven seemed over the hill. Twenty-seven would have to go.

Just as Jane had once changed her name, she now changed her age. Just as she had once fooled around with colors of ink, she now fooled around with years. Twenty-five, she told most people. Twenty-four was what she told men she wanted to go to bed with. She figured they'd be so blinded by passion that they wouldn't notice the lines or the lie.

She shortened her skirts until they were ten inches above her pudgy knees. In the vernacular of the times, she was proud to let it all hang out. Influenced by a consciousness-raising group's rage against the male chauvinist idealization of the child-woman, she stopped wearing a bra, ceased shaving her legs and armpits and let her impossible frizzy hair grow until it hung (actually it drooped) almost to her shoulders.

"My hair is longer than my skirts," Jane liked to announce proudly, aggressively proclaiming her liberation, knowing that the more shocking she was, the more attention she'd get. As the ads advised, if you've got it, flaunt it. It was advice that Jane had no difficulty taking to heart.

In 1967 Jane sold her first pieces of writing. Without a steady man in her life, Jane found time to write. Just as Jane had become bolder, so did her writing. She no longer wrote painfully perfect short stories à la Colette or examinations of ennui à la Sagan. Her determination was stoked by her wish to get even with Owen. Her confidence was buttressed by the early glimmerings of the women's liberation movement and her ambition was fuelled by her own long-standing determination to be Someone. Deciding to stop fooling around and go for broke Jane boldly cast aside her inhibitions. In a cool and ballsy way, Jane, who had always instinctively known how to get attention, began to write about her hang-ups.

"Write about what you know," Glen told Jane, repeating himself.

Jane and Glen were in his kitchen in the spring of 1967, taking a break from editing his latest manuscript. As she poured saccharine into her coffee, Jane blurted out exactly what had been on her mind.

"What I know is that I'm too goddamn fat and that even though I pretend not to, I feel like a fool in a miniskirt. Thunder thighs! I hate 'em!" Jane said. She was feeling blimplike and miserable. None of Glen's diets worked. None of anyone's diets worked. Right now, Jane was depressed by the failure of yet another diet, the currently popular *Doctor's Quick Weight Loss Diet*, which counseled high protein and six glasses of water a day. If anyone lost any weight, Jane thought sourly, it wasn't from the diet but from running to the john every twenty minutes.

"So write about thighs," suggested Glen.

"Who gives a shit about thighs?" Jane asked. Thighs were a long way from Colette's sensuous silk sheets and Sagan's worldly ennui. Writing to Jane was still all the things she'd been taught—serious, formal, elegant.

"Only every woman I've ever met," answered Glen, the voice of authority.

Jane thought about thighs. She also thought about something she didn't like to think about: the fact that since *Bonjour, Santa* had been published almost seven years before, she had not seen one word she'd written in print. She thought about the praise and attention Owen had received and imagined that he was hard at work on another book that would make him even more famous and successful. Then she thought about thighs some more and suddenly remembered dancing on the table with her skirt raised high over her head.

Thighs had brought her some attention then. Thighs might bring her attention now. Jane thought about thighs some more and decided *why not?* What did she have to lose? Her anonymity?

Jane, who had learned from Glen how to research anything and everything, researched thighs. She went to the library and found an anthropological monograph on body size from the earliest *Homo sapiens* until the present day as well as an art history text on artists' concepts of the human body from Michelangelo through Rubens up to Modigliani. She spent three weeks interviewing women about their thighs and three weeks after that writing about what she had read, heard, and observed. She revealed every humiliating thought she or every other woman had ever had about her thighs.

She wrote about how every single time she went to bed with a new man for the first time, she feared that he would take one look at her thighs and reject her. She wrote that she had learned that her fear was hardly unique—that almost every woman she had spoken to had had the same self-demeaning fear. She wrote about the thousands of leg lifts she had done—in vain—and the hundreds of diets she had tried—in vain—to reduce her big, fat, ugly, horrible, repulsive thighs.

Jane titled her piece "Thighs and Whispers" and sent it to Barry Goldsmith, the articles editor at *Downtown*, a hip Greenwich Village weekly. Barry ran Jane's article with no editing. The reaction was instant. *Downtown* had never received so many letters in response to a single article and Barry invited Jane to lunch and asked her to write another article. The subject was up to her.

"Help! I need an idea!" Jane said to Wilma.

"Remember what you said when I asked you what men talked about when women weren't around?" replied Wilma. "Write about that. It's a natural to follow thighs."

Jane had to think for a moment.

"Perfecto! Besides, what the hell do I know about baseball?" she replied with a grin.

"You need an agent," Glen told Jane when she had finished her second article. "Why don't you go talk to Hank? He'll work hard for you. Let me call him and tell him a bit about you."

"I'm Jane Gresch," Jane told Hank, walking into his office and introducing herself.

" 'Boobs'?" replied Hank. It was Jane's title for her second article.

"Right," said Jane. *Downtown* wants to publish it. Glen said maybe you'd handle the deal for me."

Hank nodded. "I'll handle more than just the deal. What you write sells papers. I want you to have the cover. Plus, of course, more money," said Hank. "I'll talk to Barry Goldsmith and I'll get back to you."

Two months after "Thighs and Whispers" appeared, *Downtown* had an attention-grabbing cover story: "Boobs." Too big, too small, too pendulous—women had as many hang-ups about breasts as they had about thighs. Hair came next. Too straight, too curly. Too fine, too coarse. Dry, brittle hair. Oily, greasy hair. Split ends and cowlicks. Washing it, setting it, never-being-able-to-do-a-thing-with-it, hating the way it was unmanageable when first washed and immediately lank thereafter, how it got frizzy in humid weather and filled with static in cold weather—how hair was, if Jane were going to tell the God's honest truth, more important than Vietnam, civil rights, and the atomic bomb.

Jane had finally learned to write about what she knew. She wrote about fat, wide, high, low, and fallen asses in an article titled "Butts" and about hooked, ski-jump, big, small, and Roman noses in a piece called "Beaks." With each article, Hank got Jane more money and her name in bigger, more prominent type.

The world, at last, was paying attention and plenty of it. Everyone who could read, it seemed, was reading Jane's *Downtown* articles. They were quoted, talked about, and Xeroxed.

"You're writing what everyone else is only thinking," Hank told Jane, explaining the flurry of attention.

Jane adored every single moment of her mini-celebrity-hood. She loved her busy phone, the invitations from people she didn't know that came in the mail, the sense of being lionized, listened to, admired and courted. She loved the fact that she finally felt she was breaking free of the past.

"Whole days go by when I feel like a real writer!" she confessed to Wilma.

"Good," said Wilma. "But don't quit your day job."

Jane nodded. "No way. I know the difference between steady salary and selling a freelance piece here and there."

In the aftermath of her attention-getting *Downtown* articles, Jane was invited to speak at consciousness-raising groups from Boston to Washington, at a journalism seminar in Philadelphia, on a local television talk show, and at a coed dorm in Rhode Island. People often knew who she was at parties and Jane was rewarded with the sudden jolt of interest people gave off when they realized she was Someone. The president of a beauty products company (he looked and talked as if he'd recently gotten out of the slammer) asked if she'd endorse his line of shampoos and setting lotions. No fee would be involved, he said, just all the shampoo she could use. Ditto an advertising agency that had a bra manufacturer's products to unload.

With a rapturous sense of high integrity and unimpeachable principles, Jane turned them both down.

"Shampoo? Bras? Who do they think I am? Miss America?" she told Wilma.

Editors (male) at two different book publishers invited Jane to fancy lunches and asked her if she had a book in mind. Of course she did, she told them confidently.

"I just don't want to give away any of the details yet," she said mysteriously.

Jane told Hank the truth about her ideas for a book.

"Zip, zero, zilch," she told her agent. "Articles are one thing. They're short. I can research them so I don't have to make too much up. Filling up a whole book is something else. I don't know what to write about."

"What interests you the most?" Hank asked Jane, sounding the old theme song.

"Fucking," replied Jane. Candor had brought her attention and Jane now embraced candor like a convert embracing a crucifix.

"So write a book about fucking," he said.

"The best fuck I ever had turned out to be a ratfink shithead," said Jane. She was referring to Owen Casals, although she did not, of course, mention his name.

"Sounds good to me," said Hank. "Just change it enough so he can't sue."

49
JANE

1 9 6 8 :

Feminists picket the Miss America
Contest and deposit girdles and bras
in trash cans. The report that
demonstrators burned bras was
widely promulgated although it was,
in fact, untrue.

"I'M the body-parts guru," Jane said self-deprecatingly with a
laugh when Eliot Landauer congratulated her on her recent
celebrity. They were at Glen Sinclair's annual Christmas party
as 1967 was fast forwarding to an end. Glen, who occasionally
wrote self-help books, used Eliot Landauer as a consultant.
Eliot Landauer was cute, Jane thought, but too short—that is,
shorter than she was.

Jane did a double take when Eliot invited her to have
dinner with him the next Saturday night. No one had invited
Jane to dinner since she'd broken up with Owen Casals. Most
men these days thought they were coming on like Rhett Butler
when they suggested sharing a joint.

"You're the only man I know who still wears a suit!" Jane
said in response to Eliot's invitation.

"Does my suit make me unacceptable?" Eliot asked.

"No," she said, thinking about how soft and inviting

| 268 |

Eliot's shiny walnut-colored hair looked. Jane had to restrain herself from reaching out and touching it.

"If you like, I'll leave my suit at home. I can wear tie-dyes and jeans," Eliot offered. Jane herself was wearing an off-the-shoulder embroidered peasant blouse, a purple miniskirt, fishnet tights, and multicolored patchwork leather and suede boots. She wore at least one ring on every finger and several long necklaces made of feathers and Day-Glo enameled spools. The ensemble was topped off with a fringed and sequined paisley thrift-shop shawl.

"Don't," Jane said with a laugh. "I'd never admit it because it would ruin my image but the fact is I sort of like the suit. It makes you look like a grownup."

Eliot took Jane to the Fonda del Sol in the Time-Life building for dinner. He did not wear tie-dyes and jeans as he had threatened, but a sport jacket with a shirt and tie. He looked casual but well put together and Jane began to revise her earlier opinion that he was bland looking. She also realized, contrary to her initial reaction, that Eliot Landauer was actually an inch or two taller than she was. She'd been afraid that she towered over him.

"I come on like such a freak. What made you ask me out?" Jane wanted to know.

"I wanted to find out what was underneath the façade," Eliot replied.

"What makes you think it's a façade?"

"Anyone who writes as sensitively as you do is more than a man-hating exhibitionist. I always try to look beneath the surface," said Eliot.

"Is that what you learned in shrink school?" asked Jane.

Eliot smiled. "Among other things."

When dinner was over, Eliot asked Jane if she'd like to go to the Blue Note to listen to some jazz.

"Chet Atkins is playing," said Eliot.

"I never heard of him," said Jane. "I don't know anything about jazz."

"You might like it."

"I'm willing to try," said Jane, who was more into acid rock.

What Jane thought but didn't say, as the taxi took them downtown, was that being with Eliot Landauer made her feel like a grownup, too. What surprised her was that part of her actually liked the feeling. It was probably the good side of being twenty-seven although, of course, Jane would never admit that out loud.

Instead, Jane being Jane, she distracted herself by studying Eliot and wondering if his hair got messed up when he fucked.

"Aren't you going to kiss me good night?" Jane asked when Eliot dropped her off in front of the Perry Street apartment that she now lived in alone. Wilma, who had graduated from med school and was now in practice as a dermatologist, had married her cardiologist and was living on Morningside Drive near Columbia.

"I wasn't planning to. I thought we'd get to know each other better," said Eliot.

"Guys usually expect to fuck on the first date," Jane said.

"Is that what you expect?" Eliot asked.

"Sure. Why not?"

"Let's be different. Let's take our time," said Eliot.

He touched her lightly on the cheek and disappeared toward Sixth Avenue.

Eliot took Jane to a Knicks game when the 76'ers were in town.

"Everyone, even you, should see Wilt Chamberlain once in her life," he told her.

He also took her to a Ray Charles concert.

"Sexy, right?" Jane asked.

"Sexy and soulful," replied Eliot.

Eliot produced tickets to *The Birthday Party*.

"Every writer needs to know Pinter's work," he told Jane.

"You mean what you leave out is as important as what you put in?"

"Exactly."

Eliot introduced Jane to the pleasures of wine, teaching her the difference between Burgundy and Bordeaux, between the Côtes du Rhône and the Côtes de Bourg.

"It's better than a joint once you get used to it," said Jane.

"And legal as well," added Eliot.

With her usual big mouth, Jane had once publicly declared courtship obsolete. Now that Eliot was on the giving end and she was on the receiving end, Jane changed her mind. She loved being taken to nice restaurants—and having the man pick up the check. She adored receiving roses—especially when an affectionate note came along with them. She enjoyed wearing perfume—particularly when Eliot had carefully chosen it especially for her.

"When I'm with you I feel feminine," a surprised Jane told Eliot, using a word she had once condemned in print as a curse word, calling it the "real F-word."

"You *are* feminine even though you go out of your way to deny it," said Eliot. "Underneath your wise-ass exterior, you're vulnerable. There's something about you that makes me want to take care of you."

Sex with Eliot was, Jane thought, the best sex she had ever had in her life. Owen had been hung but so was Eliot. Owen had been athletic but so was Eliot. The difference was that Eliot was emotional and passionate in a way that Owen had never been. Owen was like a fucking machine. Eliot was loving and tender. Eliot *talked* while he made love.

"I want you to tell me what you like and don't like," he told Jane, caressing her gently. "Do you like me to touch you here? Or here?"

"Both," said Jane.

"But which do you like better?"

"You'll have to do them both again," said Jane. "So I can compare."

"Has anyone ever told you how beautiful your skin is? It's so velvety," Eliot said.

"You have lovely breasts. Full and lush," he told her.

"Your mouth was made for kissing. It tastes like oranges," he said.

When she was in bed with Eliot, Jane forgot all about her hopeless hair and fat thighs. Eliot made her feel beautiful and desirable.

"You never talk about what Eliot's like in the sack," Wilma told Jane.

"His hair gets messed up," said Jane.

"I mean what he's got and what he does with it," said Wilma.

"That's private," said Jane, who had always avidly dissected her lover's anatomy and technique in the most minute detail.

"Does that mean it's serious?" asked Wilma.

"Who knows? What's serious these days?" replied Jane.

"How do you feel about marriage?" Eliot asked Jane after they'd been seeing each other for almost a year.

"Marriage is a repressive bourgeois institution for the enslavement and exploitation of women," replied Jane.

"So what does that make me? A male chauvinist pig?"

"Sure," said Jane. "Aren't all men?"

50
LINCKY

HER marriage ended not with a bang but with a whimper.

Lincky's downstairs neighbor called her at the office in the late autumn of 1967 to tell Lincky that water was leaking through the ceiling of her kitchen. The super wondered if it might be coming from the Desmonds' apartment. Lincky excused herself from a scheduling meeting and got into a taxi.

She let herself into her apartment and went straight into the kitchen, entering it from the door that led off the foyer. The faucet was off, Lincky could see. Whatever was leaking into the downstairs apartment obviously wasn't coming from her kitchen. As Lincky turned to leave the kitchen, she thought she heard a noise from the back of the apartment.

"Who's there?" she called.

"Me."

"Peter?" For a moment, Lincky felt relieved. At least it wasn't a burglar. "What are you doing home?"

Peter came down the hall from the bedroom, tying a

bathrobe around him. Under it, Lincky could see that he was naked. Behind him, Lincky suddenly saw in the shadowy hall, was someone else, a girl.

The girl, who was also naked, screamed. She turned around and fled back toward the bedroom.

Peter stood still for a moment, staring at Lincky. He seemed paralyzed, a man trapped in a nightmare.

"It doesn't mean anything," Peter told Lincky in a strangled voice, finally regaining his ability to move and coming into the kitchen. He waved vaguely toward the bedroom. His handsome features seemed crumpled and dirty white, like slept-in sheets.

Lincky swallowed.

"Yes, it does," she said when she could find her voice. She thought that what it meant was that now both she and Peter had broken their marriage vows. Where had the hopes gone? Where the promises?

"What are you going to do?" Peter asked, as if the decision were entirely Lincky's. He looked shattered. He reached out and tried to touch Lincky's arm but she pulled away.

"I don't know," she said.

Lincky tried to meet Peter's eyes but found that he couldn't look at her. Feeling unutterably embarrassed, Lincky turned toward the sink and, suddenly parched, filled a glass with tap water and drank.

"Do you want some?" she asked Peter.

Peter nodded. His mouth was dry. He could think of nothing to say.

As Lincky and Peter stood silently in the kitchen sharing a glass of lukewarm tap water, they heard Peter's girl let herself out the front door. The rattle of the knob sounded, and the closing of the door in its frame shot loudly through the abnormally quiet apartment. Lincky and Peter stared at each other wordlessly.

"Some lousy date," Lincky finally said, raggedly attempting a smile. "Don't you even put them into a taxi?"

"Don't leave me," said Peter, his clean-cut good looks shadowed with brand-new lines of pain. "Please."

Lincky didn't know what to say. At the office she could deal with anything. In her personal life, she felt helpless.

Two months later, Lincky and Peter agreed to a divorce and Lincky moved out. She rented the small but pleasant top floor of a brownstone on East 74th Street just off Park Avenue. On moving day, Peter rented a van and helped Lincky move the cartons of books, suitcases of clothes, and potted plants she was so fond of to her new apartment. He stayed and helped Lincky unpack. Together, they put the books into bookshelves, hung up Lincky's clothes, and arranged the plants. They were finally finished at nine thirty.

"I'm exhausted," said Lincky, her nose smudged, her thick butterscotch hair hidden under a scarf. "I'm going to order up Chinese. Do you want some?" she asked. Offering Peter dinner was the least she could do after all the help he had given her.

"If you get lemon chicken, I do," replied Peter.

They ate at the chic, new table Lincky had just bought at Lucidity and, since the dishes weren't unpacked yet, ate with chopsticks right out of the cartons. Peter, who had once despised ordered-up food, now seemed to think of it as an adventure. When they had finished eating, Peter got up and kissed Lincky good night on the cheek.

"Do you want me to come back tomorrow?" he asked. "I'll help you unpack the dishes and the kitchen stuff."

"I'd love you to," Lincky said, hesitantly, unsure of how people who had agreed to a divorce should act with each other. She was also acutely aware that while they were living together Peter would set foot in the kitchen only under extreme duress.

"I'll take you out to a nice lunch when we're done," Peter promised, leaving Lincky to spend her first night in her new apartment alone. By unspoken mutual agreement, sex was no longer part of their relationship.

Now that their marriage was over, Peter and Lincky learned that they made better friends than husband and wife. Peter was much less rigid and demanding as a friend than a husband and Lincky was much less resentful and critical. From the moment of their divorce, Peter called Lincky two or three times a week and on Sundays they often met for lunch and a movie.

"Peter and I have a friendly divorce," Lincky told people who didn't understand their unconventional relationship. "When my lawyer told me I should ask for alimony, I told him that I don't need Peter's money. I finally fired him. I knew that Peter would be part of my life a lot longer than the lawyer."

Unlike Jane who interpreted the rebellions of the late Sixties as a license to indulge and experiment, Lincky was not attracted by or interested in free love, free sex, or free anything else. For almost a year, Lincky refused all invitations from men.

"I just got divorced. I'm too hurt to smile and make small talk," she told Coral. "Besides, I doubt that I'll ever get married again."

"What about Hank? You once thought about being married to him."

" 'That was then. This is now.' " Lincky quoted from the still bitter memory.

The only people Lincky had even heard of who got married in 1968 were, to everyone's surprise including their own, Elly McGrath and Owen Casals.

51
ELLY

1 9 6 8 :

Elected: Richard M. Nixon
Married: Jacqueline Kennedy and
Aristotle Onassis
Declared candidacy: Robert F.
Kennedy

ELLY, like almost every other woman of her generation, knew a great deal about birth control. In the course of her twenty-seven years, she had tried the rhythm method, the pill, the diaphragm, the Coca-Cola douche, and Lady Luck. Most of Elly's knowledge had come from conversations with other women. Those conversations had been, at different times and in different places, anxious, tearful, raunchy, hilarious. None of her information had been learned from the men with whom Elly had made love. *Their* interest in birth control, if any, had been limited to a quick question before penetration: "You're okay, right?"

Nor had very much of Elly's information come from doctors. The elderly family doctor in Bennington who fitted her with her first diaphragm informed her that the effectiveness of the diaphragm depended on good technique. He then expounded on good technique at elaborate and confusing length. He was sincere, patient, concerned, and long-winded. He had plump hands with short, stubby fingers and Elly was profoundly ashamed that those short, red fingers had explored her insides and knew the deepest secrets of her body. It was not the doctor's fault but Elly could hardly bear to be in the same room with him.

"It is essential that the rim of the diaphragm be fitted securely between the cervix and the pelvic bone. This is important so that the diaphragm will not become dislodged during intercourse," he said in his pedantic way, showing Elly a diagram in a medical book that in no way resembled Elly's own understanding of her genitalia. Elly, too embarrassed at eighteen to speak, never mind ask exactly where the cervix and pelvic bone *were*, could barely wait for the doctor to finish before fleeing from his office.

Shy about touching her own body, Elly had struggled with the slippery diaphragm throughout college. Because her sex life at that time was so sporadic, she never became adept at its insertion. Her diaphragm, which should have been a source of protection, became instead a focus of anxiety and embarrassment. Elly never knew whether or not to put it in her purse when she went out on a date. If she did, would a boy think she was easy? If she didn't but later decided that she wanted to have sex, then she would have to make a spur of the moment decision. Should she go home horny and maybe never see the boy again or take a chance on becoming pregnant?

When Elly did use her diaphragm, she could never figure out how to be suave about interrupting her lovemaking to disappear into the bathroom. What was she supposed to say to the boy? "Just a moment?" or "Can you wait a minute?" And at that point in the proceedings was it best to disappear? After the first kiss? Wasn't that too soon? Suppose things didn't progress further? The diaphragm was such a nuisance to use that putting it in and then not making love was just too much trouble. Should she excuse herself when he began fondling her breasts? Then she risked breaking the spell. When he got further down? By then, it might be too late.

Between her erratic love life and her discomfort with the mechanics, Elly's diaphragm languished in its case far more often than it got properly lubricated and inserted between cervix and pubic bone. Good technique turned out to be an excellent theory, rarely implemented. Finally, over the Thanksgiving weekend of Elly's junior year at Bennington, the rubber dome finally dried out and died of disuse and old age.

Elly's understanding (imperfect) of the rhythm method had come from the reading of various sex manuals and late-night conversations in the dorm. Like most of her friends, Elly referred to it as Vatican roulette and, just to make extra sure, crossed her fingers and douched with Coca-Cola every time she slept with a boy even though it was only the week before or the week after her period.

The problem with the rhythm method was that the Catholic church considered only a woman's biological rhythms. It did not take into account holidays, weekends, proms, and other times when sexual opportunity might be greater. The fact that Elly never became pregnant while depending on the rhythm method had more to do, she was sure, with sheer, random chance than any inherent reliability of the method backed by the church in Rome.

As soon as the Pill was introduced in 1960, Elly, along with many of her friends, rushed to the nearest doctor for a prescripton. Salvation, finally, had arrived. Conscientiously swallowing the small white pill every morning, Elly for the first time in her life gained weight. It should have been a joyous occasion indeed: breasts plus worry-free sex. That was not, alas, to be the case.

Elly's breasts grew so large that she eventually overflowed even a B cup. They also grew sensitive and sore. Elly could not touch them nor could she bear for a boy to touch them. Furthermore, not only did Elly's breasts grow, so did her belly, her ass, her thighs, and her face. She felt big and bulky and awkward and from her moon face to her swollen feet, she thought she resembled an oversized, two-legged balloon.

Just as bad as the physical reactions to the pill was the fact that Elly now felt miserably premenstrual thirty days a month: weepy, jumpy, crabby. Now that Elly was free to have sex anytime she wanted, she found that not only wasn't she in the mood but that her hypersensitivity and bad temper were so off-putting that boys were more than happy to stay far away from her. After almost a year of unhappy and celibate blimphood, Elly abandoned the pill.

She returned, reluctant but resigned, to the diaphragm at the time she began her affair with Owen. The second time around, Elly found the diaphragm much more of an ally. Now less inhibited about touching her own body, Elly found the diaphragm easier to insert. Having a stable relationship also helped. Usually knowing in advance when she and Owen would have sex, Elly felt no compunction about putting in her diaphragm every time she saw Owen.

When they began to live together, Elly inserted it every night before she went to bed just as routinely as she brushed her teeth. She never went so far as to fall in love with her diaphragm but, as the years passed, it lost its associations of guilt, embarrassment, and anxiety and Elly gradually became quite adept at popping it in and out.

"The biggest problem with the diaphragm," Elly told Lincky over ordered-up sandwiches one lunch hour while they were both working at North Star, "is spontaneity. Owen likes sex at any time of day or night."

"Such a problem," said Lincky enviously, thinking of Peter's Swiss-railway approach to sex.

Owen Casals not only liked to make love at any time of day or night, he also liked what he called fast and dirty sex. He said that it reminded him of high school, the time in his life when, walking around with a twenty-four-hour-a-day hard-on, he felt sexiest of all. To recapture that fast and dirty feeling, Owen liked to indulge in sex without foreplay and without warning at odd times and in odd places. Elly, turned on by the randiness and illicitness of it all, liked it just as much as Owen.

Standing up in the kitchen after breakfast or before dinner was a favorite. So was the front seat of a car, any car, in full daylight with people passing nearby. Owen and Elly had also enjoyed quickies in elevators, hotel corridors, the ladies' room in the American Airline terminal at LaGuardia, and once in the temporarily abandoned office shack of a Kinney car lot in the East 50s.

The diaphragm, of course, was never a part of Elly and Owen's fast and dirty sex. The diaphragm was too mature, too deliberate, too matter-of-fact. When Elly learned she was pregnant in March 1968 she realized that conception must have occurred during one of their fast and dirty adventures.

Nothing could have pleased Elly more. Nothing, she imagined, would please Owen more. Now, she thought, Owen would finally agree to marry her.

"You're sure?" Owen asked, sounding disappointed when Elly told him that she was expecting. He did his best to try to share Elly's excitement and succeeded only in partially hiding the fact that he hoped the child would be a boy. Owen did not say anything about marriage, and Elly, once again unwillingly defying convention, decided to go ahead and have the baby anyway.

Owen wasn't thinking of the baby several weeks later when he told Elly not to get involved with Ernest Jones. He was thinking of Elly. He knew how idealistic she was and how innocent she could be.

"I don't want you to be used," Owen told Elly, warning her that Ernest Jones was no longer the idealistic young man she had once known. Ernest Jones, Owen said, had become dangerous.

52
ELLY

MAY 1967:

"There is no need to go to Vietnam
and shoot somebody who a honky
says is your enemy. We're going to
shoot the cops who are shooting our
black brothers in the back."

—Stokely Carmichael

SUMMER 1967:

"Violence is as American as apple
pie."

—H. Rap Brown, after ghetto riots

LIKE many of the people Elly had gone to school with—like Elly herself—Ernest Jones had changed. Tall, broad shouldered, and more physically powerful than Elly remembered, Ernest had stopped working for his father and was devoting his life to the fight for civil rights.

In 1968, he was working for a Black Panther weekly called *Uhuru*, the African word for freedom. Orphaned by his politics, Ernest had no permanent address. He camped out, sleeping on a sofa in *Uhuru*'s shabby storefront office on East 136th Street, only a few blocks from where he'd grown up. Ernest's hair had grown into a halolike Afro and his once smoothly shaven face was now densely bearded. He wore a dashiki printed in earth tones of green, brown, and khaki with jeans and work boots and spoke fervently, messianically, of black separatism.

Elly ran into Ernest Jones for the first time since high school at a weekend civil rights demonstration in Washington Square Park in 1966. Bringing each other up to date on their lives since high school, Elly told Ernest about Owen and about her job at North Star. Ernest told Elly that he had decided against the dry cleaning business and was devoting his time and energy to the struggle for civil rights.

He knew that he could never be H. Rap Brown or Eldridge Cleaver, Ernest admitted, but he also knew that not to fight against racial injustice would be to waste the one life he had been given. Although Ernest accused Elly of selling out with her straight job and straight life, he smiled as he spoke.

'I'm glad you're happy," he told her affectionately, his olive-amber eyes brimming with warmth and energy. "I am too. I believe in the cause, I believe in the struggle," he said intensely. Then he paused for a moment. "My parents aren't speaking to me anymore. They don't approve."

"I'm sorry. I liked your parents," Elly said, recalling Hazel and William Jones and remembering the high hopes and dreams they had had for their only son. She wondered how they felt. She wondered how they bore the hurt.

"I'm a man with a cause. Also a man without a family," said Ernest without self-pity. Elly felt sorry for him. A family was a high price to pay for freedom, she thought.

"Maybe you'd like to have dinner with us," Elly said, wanting Ernest to feel included somewhere. "I'd like you to meet Owen. You'd like him."

"I doubt it," Ernest said curtly, ending the conversation suddenly, leaving Elly to wonder whether his animosity was against white people in general or a result of some residual personal resentment against her.

Elly did not hear from Ernest after that brief encounter and after three weeks, then three months, had passed without a word from him, she thought that she never would. Elly was therefore surprised when Ernest called her at her office in June 1967 and told her that there was going to be a sit-in on the escalators of the Pan Am building.

"We want to show that we can stop the white establishment in its tracks," explained Ernest. "Can you join us?"

Elly didn't really want to. She was busy at the office, busy with her personal life. Owen had warned her about the violent rhetoric so many black leaders were turning to. Still, Elly believed in racial equality and she also felt a guilty and sentimental obligation to Ernest—who after all, was not H. Rap Brown. Feeling that it was the right thing to do, Elly agreed to attend.

The escalator sit-in turned out to be a sparsely attended non-event and over the next several months, Ernest called Elly every now and then to ask her to participate in one kind of protest or another. Sometimes, depending on her mood and her schedule, Elly would agree to take part. Other times, she would beg off. Owen was opposed to any involvement with Ernest at all.

"His politics are too far out. The Black Panthers are not only against whites, they're against most moderate black leaders too. They're preaching violence and killing," Owen told Elly. "Someday, someone's going to get hurt. I don't want that someone to be you. It's not like college when you and other well-meaning Ivy Leaguers marched with grateful blacks for voting rights."

"I've known Ernest since I was in high school," Elly replied, defending Ernest and his political struggles and stung by Owen's put-down of her heartfelt efforts. "He's always been against violence."

In May 1968 Ernest called and asked Elly to join in a march to protest Southern racist George Wallace's entrance into the presidential race. Elly was two months pregnant at the time and she hesitated. She found pregnancy surprisingly fatiguing and, although she continued to go to the office, she looked forward to the weekends as a time to rest.

"It's phony liberals like you who let the pigs get away with murder. You want to help the niggers but you don't want to get your lily-white hands dirty," Ernest said, his disgust with Elly palpable even over the telephone.

"I'm pregnant. What if things get violent?" Elly asked, cut by Ernest's accusation. Although Elly always argued vehemently on behalf of Ernest, Owen's warnings had made an impression. He had recently pointed out to Elly that there had been riots in Chicago, Baltimore, Washington, and Cincinnati following the assassination of Dr. King.

"This is New York. Not Cincinnati. Lindsay doesn't want any race riots here," Ernest said, dismissing Elly's concerns. Then his voice turned softer, entirely reasonable. "Elly, please. I know that sometimes the rhetoric goes overboard but the plain fact is we need white support if we're going to have any credibility at all. Everyone's so busy demonstrating against the war in Vietnam, they're forgetting about civil rights. I know how busy you are but your presence would mean a lot to us. It would also mean a lot to me personally, Elly."

Promising Ernest that she would be there, Elly told herself that she would not give him another reason to feel that deep down all whites were fundamentally racist. After all, Elly reminded herself, some people were devoting their entire lives to racial equality. She was devoting only a Saturday afternoon.

53
ELLY

"I want it said even if I die in the struggle that 'He died to make me free.' "

—Martin Luther King, Jr.

THE demonstration was called for three o'clock on Centre Street in downtown Manhattan, right in front of police headquarters. Elly was surprised that there were at most fifty demonstrators, almost all of them black and almost all of them her age or even older. Where were the kids? Elly wondered. Where were the idealistic and committed young people who had once made up a large part of the civil rights movement? She thought for a moment and then she realized where they were. They were preoccupied with Vietnam.

As Elly walked the length of the barricades looking for Ernest, she also noticed that no television crews were there to cover the protest. It made her sad when she remembered college demonstrations and the march on Washington only a few years before at which more than half the demonstrators had been white and very young and the press had sent squadrons of reporters.

No wonder blacks were becoming more militant, Elly

thought, still searching the sparse turnout and looking for Ernest. Blacks seemed to be making up in anger and intensity what they had lost in numbers. Realizing that the civil rights movement now had two struggles—against racism *and* indifference—Elly was doubly glad she had told Ernest that she would be there to show her support.

"Elly! Elly! Come over here!"

It was Ernest, motioning Elly to join him. He was standing next to the yellow-and-black-striped wooden crowd control barricades that had been placed by the police to keep the protesters safely across the street from headquarters. Elly quickly made her way toward Ernest through the knots of would-be protesters and the few passersby who had stopped to watch.

"Right up front, right here!" Ernest told Elly, taking her by the arm and showing her where to stand. On the other side of the barricade was three feet of empty sidewalk extending to the curb. In the street itself stood a line of uniformed policemen, most of them white. Silent and wary, they stared at the demonstrators.

"Don't go away. I'll be back in a minute. When the protest actually starts, I'll be right behind you," Ernie told Elly. He introduced her to the woman next to her and disappeared.

Jean Garry was a tall, large-boned woman with olive skin and deep blue eyes who taught history at City College. She wore dangling copper earrings and her long, reddish hair streamed down her back. She nodded in response to Ernest's introduction and jokingly told Elly that what she really taught was Civil Insurrection 101.

"They always want white faces up front," Jean said, telling Elly that she had contributed occasional articles on African history to *Uhuru*.

Elly smiled. Looking around, she realized that other than Ernest and Jean Garry, she did not know one single person present. It was, Elly thought, a sad and pathetic little demonstration, a protest no one cared about that wouldn't get noticed, a protest that wouldn't make one bit of difference to anyone anywhere.

The speaker, Claud Jackson, invoked the legacy of white violence against black, the lynchings and murders inside the law and out. He quoted Huey Newton, H. Rap Brown and Stokeley Carmichael and eventually generated an emotional response in the small crowd. People began to chant softly.

"*Uhuru*! *Uhuru*! Freedom! Freedom!"

Looking straight into the alternately mean and frightened eyes of the policemen who stood on the other side of the barricades, nervous hands on nightsticks, Elly felt a surge of primitive hatred toward the power and indifference of authority and joined in.

"Pig! Pig!" the demonstrators shouted.

"Pig motherfuckers!" Claud Jackson yelled, shaking his fist at the police and inciting the crowd to even more provocative shouts.

The curses of the demonstrators swelled and rose in volume. Hands at the end of blue uniform sleeves that moments before had nervously hovered near nightsticks, now grasped them firmly. The police took a step forward, nightsticks raised threateningly. The crowd responded.

"Honky pigs! Pig motherfuckers!"

"Stay back!" said a voice through a police bullhorn. "Stay back!"

The crowd was defiant. Its shouts continued. The curses turned more violent and abusive. Elly felt the demonstrators behind her stir and surge forward. Caught between the protesters and the heavy wooden barricades, Elly struggled to remain on her feet. She suddenly felt herself being shoved forward from behind.

"Don't push!" she screamed, afraid that she would fall. She put her hands against the barricade to brace herself. She felt it totter. It almost fell over; then, miraculously, it righted itself. Elly stumbled and scrambled for balance.

"Don't push!" Elly shouted as loud as she could but she

realized that no one could hear her over the noise of the bullhorns and the screaming of the protesters. "Don't push!"

As the demonstrators surged forward once again, Elly felt a sudden, violent shove in the middle of her back. Panicked and off balance, she glanced behind her and caught a sudden glimpse of green and brown and khaki. Ernest Jones's dashiki-clad arm propelled her full force into the barricade, causing her to knock it down and pushing her squarely into a blue uni-formed mountain of a man who kicked her savagely between the legs. Then, using a nightstick, he struck her viciously against the breasts.

Screaming in shock and pain, Elly fell. She was trapped between the police who stood on one side of the barricades and the protesters who surged toward the police from behind her. Sprawled on the ground as the demonstrators behind her pressed forward and the police stepped up to meet them, Elly screamed and screamed but no one heard. Lying on the pave-ment, trampled by the stamping feet of protesters and police above her, Elly cradled her arms over her stomach and curled into a fetal position, instinctively protecting the baby within.

Just before Elly lost consciousness, she saw a bright stream of blood gush from Jean Garry's ear as her copper earring was ripped through the flesh of the lobe. The next thing Elly remembered was waking up in a hospital room. She knew before anyone said a word that she had lost her baby.

The sad and pathetic little demonstration, the Saturday afternoon protest no one cared about, the protest that wouldn't make one bit of difference to anyone anywhere made all the difference in the world to Elly. Ernest Jones had given up his family for his ideals and now, so too had Elly.

Jean Garry visited Elly in the hospital.

"I'm sorry about your baby," she said sympathetically. Her left ear was clumsily bandaged and her left eye was blackened. "I didn't realize that you were pregnant. If I were pregnant, I would never have had the courage to do what you did."

"What courage? All I did was stand up for what I believed in," replied Elly.

"Don't you know? Don't you get it?" asked Jean. She looked dubious, suspicious, almost as if she thought Elly was purposely playing dumb.

"Get what?" asked Elly.

"They use whites. Most of all, they use white women," Jean said matter-of-factly. "It's deliberate. They do it on purpose. They put us up front because they know that cops hate white women who associate with black men. It gets the cops crazy. They think we're nigger lovers and they don't feel any compunction in beating the shit out of us.

"The cops feel we deserve the beating and the blacks get the advantage of not being the ones to initiate the violence," Jean continued. "If they can get the cops to attack first, the blacks can retaliate with justification. That way if a cop is hurt or killed by a black, they can get away with it in court by being able to prove that the cops started it and they were only acting in self-defense."

As Jean spoke, Elly saw the green and brown and khaki-clad arm that shoved her forward into the barricade. Ernest had pushed her. Owen was right. She had been used. Elly looked at Jean wordlessly, tears of betrayal forming in her lovely blue eyes. Elly shriveled inwardly at the second death in thirty-six hours, the death of innocence.

"If you know this, then why do you demonstrate?" Elly asked.

"Because I think racism is abhorrent," said Jean. With a resigned and sad expression in her deep blue eyes, she added: "I'm an idealist without illusions."

When Elly asked her doctor if she would be able to have children in the future, he told her that he didn't-know-wasn't-sure-couldn't-say-for-certain.

Elly never heard from Ernest Jones. He did not call her. He did not visit her in the hospital. He had used her, Elly realized.

She had become a pawn to him, a pawn to be played and then discarded.

All that saved Elly's life and sanity was Owen. In times of crisis, he was unsurpassable. A macho man, a man's man, Owen lived by certain codes. He felt that women were to be protected and cared for. He comforted Elly. He fought for her. He made her feel loved and cherished. He gave her a reason to go on.

54
ELLY

MARCH 1968:

"To not permit the presidency to become involved in the partisan divisions that are developing . . . I shall not seek, and I will not accept, the nomination of my party for another term as your president."

—Lyndon B. Johnson

MURDERED:

April 4, 1968:
Martin Luther King, Jr., Memphis
June 5, 1968:
Robert F. Kennedy, Los Angeles

ELLY thought that Owen would be angry at her for not listening to his warnings about Ernest. She had risked not only herself but she had risked—and lost—their child. She feared that Owen would remind her of his warnings. She feared that he would leave her.

When Owen received the telephone call from St. Vincent's Hospital telling him that Elly had been brought to the Emergency Room, he ran to the hospital through the streets of Greenwich Village. By the time he arrived, the baby had been lost and Elly, suffering from shock and the loss of blood, was in serious condition. She could barely turn her head toward him when he was finally permitted to see her.

"You're not mad at me?" she whispered, beginning to weep at the sight of him.

"No, I'm not mad at you. I love you," said Owen, embracing her as best he could. For the first time that he could remember, tears welled up in his eyes. He had lost a baby he thought he didn't care about. He realized that there was a chance he might lose Elly. The thought of being without her came almost as a physical blow.

"What happened?" he asked. "Who did this to you?"

"Ernest," she said and told Owen what had happened.

When Owen left St. Vincent's, he went uptown to *Uhuru*'s storefront office on East 136th Street.

"Which one is Ernest Jones?" he asked. Two men sat on the sprung sofa. One was drinking Coke. The other was doing a crossword puzzle.

"Him," one of them answered, pointing to a third man.

Ernest was taking a pot of coffee off a hot plate when Owen went up to him.

"You know what you did, don't you?" Owen asked.

"No. Who the hell are you?"

"I'm Owen," Owen said. "I'm the father of the baby Elly McGrath was going to have. Was. Past tense."

"Don't look at me," said Ernest. He looked over toward the two blacks who watched the scene silently.

"You deliberately pushed Elly into the line of the struggle," said Owen. "I have a witness and you have a choice. I can either take you to court for inciting to riot or I can beat the shit out of you right here and now."

"I'm not scared of the court," said Ernest. He curled his fists and stepped toward Owen.

"Then you'd better be scared of me," said Owen.

Ernest took a swing at Owen, who ducked. Crouching and moving in low, Owen hit Ernest in the gut and, as he doubled forward, caught him with an uppercut to the chin. Ernest staggered backward and came toward Owen with a knife. Owen wrestled the knife from him. As Ernest stumbled off-balance, Owen decked him with a vicious left to the jaw and a fast right to the ribs. He fell against the table that held the hot plate. It tipped over, drenching Ernest with scalding coffee.

"Honky motherfucker!" screamed Ernest, writhing on the floor as Owen turned to leave.

The two blacks sat riveted to the sofa. One of them rose and went for Owen, his fists curled.

"You want to walk out of here upright or you want me to kick your balls into your throat?" asked Owen, crouching into an attack stance.

Without a word, the black changed direction and headed for the door.

Owen turned to the second black. "You in the mood to dance?"

"Not me."

Owen then turned to Ernest. "If you ever call Elly again or try to get in touch with her, I'm going to kill you," he said. "And you won't die because you're fighting for your people's rights, you'll die because you're a fucking coward who hid behind a woman's skirts."

"Will you marry me?" Owen asked on the evening he brought Elly home from the hospital after her miscarriage.

"Yes," said Elly softly. Owen was still Elly's hero, the man she thought she didn't quite deserve, the man who would boldly face her enemies and defend her from them.

"Even though I'm not a rich and famous author?" he asked, referring for the first time to his professional disappointments. *Precincts of Childhood* had been even less successful than *The 39th Parallel*.

"It's you I love. Whether you're rich or not, famous or not, doesn't matter to me," said Elly.

"I'm going to call Hubert Dessanges," Owen said, referring to the editor of *Week*. "I'm going to see if his offer of a job is still good."

Elly smiled. "Of course it will be good. You're the best, aren't you?"

"So they used to tell me," he said.

The fox trot, white gloves, good manners, respect for one's elders, debutantes and debutante parties, bras, girdles, garter belts, and crinolines weren't the only extinct species of 1968. So was the Mendelssohn and orange-blossom wedding with the bride wearing white as a sign of virginity. Free love seemed to be replacing love and marriage. Young people were living together openly and dispensing entirely with the legal, religious, and ceremonial aspects of a relationship. What had been shocking and daring in 1964 when Owen and Elly had first decided to live together was now commonplace.

Weddings, when they *did* occur, had gone hippie. Barefoot brides with flowers in their long, ironed hair wore flowing granny dresses (often to camouflage their pregnancies), while their grooms wore stovepipe pants and embroidered Indian shirts. The wedding march had been replaced by sitar music, the traditional vows to love, honor, and obey by readings from Kahil Gibran's *The Prophet*. Traditional churches and catering halls had been replaced by hilltops at dawn and beaches at sunset, the lavish spreads of roast beef, lobster, and champagne by alfalfa sprouts, stone-ground breads, and organic apple juice.

Elly and Owen, in a mutually serious and even somber mood, wanted neither the traditional wedding extravaganza nor the updated hippie version. They felt grown up and dignified, and they wanted—and got—a wedding to reflect that mood.

Elly McGrath and Owen Casals were married on Saturday, June 1, 1968, in the living room of the lower Fifth Avenue apartment in which Elly had grown up. The fireplace was banked with flowers and the ceremony was conducted by Herbert Englund, a judge of the state supreme court who had known Elly's father for three decades. After a champagne reception at home for close friends and family, Elly and Owen drove to Wood's Hole, Massachusetts, and took the ferry from there to Nantucket Island for a week-long honeymoon in a rented beach cottage. They were fast asleep at one o'clock in the morning on June 6 of that week when the telephone rang. It was Brian McGrath.

"Bobby Kennedy has been shot," her father told Elly.

Holding her hand over the mouthpiece of the phone, Elly told Owen what her father had said.

"The Sixties are over," Owen said, his journalist's mind capsulizing the consequences of the second Kennedy assassination. It was an epitaph that Elly would never forget, one that would have been widely quoted if Owen were still working for *Newsflash*.

After Elly hung up, she and Owen got out of bed and switched on the black and white television set, which got only grainy reception on the island in the middle of the Atlantic. Silently holding hands, they listened to the updates from the Ambassador Hotel in Los Angeles.

Elly could not help but remember the assassination of another Kennedy brother. John F. Kennedy had been murdered at a time when she was selling shoes, living miserably alone in a strange city, thinking that she had been cut off from family, friends, and lover. She smiled sadly at the memory.

"What are you smiling at?" Owen asked.

"At the me I used to be," replied Elly, remembering her younger self wistfully.

"Was she different from the you of today?"

"Oh, yes," said Elly sincerely. "Then I was just Elly McGrath. Now I'm Elly Casals."

Even though Elly was a civil rights advocate, an antiwar protester, and a feminist, it still mattered most of all to her that she had a husband. At a time when women were refusing to take their husband's surname, Elly proudly called herself Elly Casals. At a time when women were beginning to demand to be called Ms., Elly insisted on being called Mrs. Casals. She felt a secret thrill every time she wrote a check or signed a letter with her new name.

"I'm a modern woman," she told her sister. "With traditional values."

VI
MODERN MEN/ELIOT LANDAUER

Physician, heal thyself.

—Luke 4:23

55
ELIOT

1 9 5 2 :

Elizabeth II becomes Queen of
   England.
Eisenhower defeats Stevenson for
   presidency of United States.
United States ends occupation of
   Japan.
Jonas Salk tests polio vaccine at the
   University of Pittsburgh.

ELIOT Landauer was different things to different people. He was one thing to his patients, another to his family, friends, and colleagues, a third to himself.

To his patients, he appeared wise and compassionate. They sought his advice and his good opinion. They brought him flowers and books they thought he might enjoy. They were, for the most part, a mirror that cast back a becoming and largely positive image. Of all those who knew him, Eliot Landauer's patients saw him the way he most wanted to see himself.

To his family, Eliot was proof that in democratic, classless America, anyone with brains, talent, and the capacity for hard work could rise in the world. He had grown up in Hempstead, Long Island, in a white house in a middle class neighborhood that his father could only just afford.

Eliot's grandfather had lived in an Essex Street tenement, working in a kosher butcher shop during the week and praying in *shul* on Saturdays. His grandmother had cooked and cleaned and never learned English. His parents, both born in America, had made the short but significant move to Long Island where Eliot's father, a pharmacist, worked in a local drug store and his mother, her sights set firmly upward, always spent more than the family could afford, particularly on her first and favorite child, Eliot.

To his friends and colleagues, Eliot was, at various times in his life, a sissy, a highbrow, a snob, a conciliator, a fashion plate, a good listener, a financial wizard. To himself, Eliot was, he knew, unusually ambitious. He dreamed of money, success, and recognition. Instead, he spent his childhood as an outcast. Eliot was fat and uncoordinated. The boys teased him and the girls ignored him. Only Eliot's teachers seemed to see a glimmer of promise. Looking at his outstanding academic record, they thought he'd go on to become a lawyer or a doctor.

In the summer between high school and college, Eliot, with the help of his social studies teacher, got a job at a local law office. There was good money in law and Eliot wanted a taste of a potential career. Eliot soon realized that law was not for him. He loathed the dry-as-dust law books with their cases and citations, the routine typing and filing of deeds and wills, the emotionless courtroom rituals of suits and countersuits. Exciting courtroom confrontations, he soon learned, existed solely on television and in the movies.

The only good thing that happened that summer was that Eliot went on a self-prescribed diet of hard boiled eggs, shrimp cocktails, and iced tea and lost forty pounds. The rejection of law as a career and the loss of weight were the first steps in what would become Eliot's ongoing quest to improve his life and himself.

Eliot entered Long Island University in the fall of 1952 with a new self-image and a determination to put the taunts and ignominy of Hempstead High behind him. Knowing that a career in law was definitely not for him, he signed up for a premed course with the idea of becoming a plastic surgeon or a dermatologist. Both specialties were lucrative, both offered patients immediate relief, and neither involved the depressing aspects of having to work with seriously ill and/or dying patients.

Eliot continued his splendid academic performance at college and it seemed certain that he would become an M.D., the first professional in the Landauer family. In the second half of his junior year, Eliot took an ill-regarded but required course in psychology that was called a "gut" by students and sneered at by the hard-science professors. Eliot, however, quickly found himself fascinated. He did not think the course a gut; nor did he sneer.

Psychology explained himself and others to Eliot. Psychology with its unjudgmental view of the personality logically and coherently explained the dynamics of interpersonal relationships. Psychology held out to Eliot a real hope for understanding and improvement. It changed Eliot's life and led him to a career.

56
ELIOT

PUBLISHED in 1955:

The Life and Work of Sigmund Freud,
Ernest Jones

THE sensitivity that had once earned Eliot the taunts of his schoolmates suddenly became an invaluable asset. A former liability had turned into an advantage. Eliot's painful memories of his childhood as an outcast were now transmuted into an unusual ability to be compassionate to people in emotional difficulties.

The central mystery of Eliot's childhood—his parents' stormy, ill-matched marriage with its constant battles over money—became less mysterious when looked at from a psychologist's point of view. Money was not what was being argued over, Eliot found out. It was power, in fact, that was really at issue—power cloaked in terms of dollars and cents, wall-to-wall carpeting, this year's model car.

The professor who taught the course, Samuel Wallenberg, a clinical psychologist, told Eliot that the future of medicine would increasingly be in the mental health area. Mental health, Samuel Wallenberg said, had crucial influence over an individual's emotional and physical well-being. Eliot, knowing how much his study of psychology had already helped him, could only agree. Additionally impressed by the recently published biography of Sigmund Freud, which he read cover to cover, Eliot decided to change majors in 1955.

"Learning to monitor blood chemistry and set a broken leg isn't nearly as interesting as finding out how the mind works," he told Dr. Wallenberg.

"I'm going to drop out of premed. I've decided that I want to become a psychologist," he told his parents, explaining that he felt that medical school, with its narrow focus on biology and physiology, was irrelevant to his real interests.

"You could have been a surgeon. You could have been somebody," said his father, seeing three years of expensive schooling going down the drain.

Bernard Landauer had willingly made the financial sacrifices involved in preparing Eliot for medical school. He did not feel the same way about paying for an education in something that had no medicines, no pharmacopeia, no surgical techniques, no final cures in its arsenal, and he angrily withdrew his financial support.

"You want to be a head shrinker, you can pay the tuition yourself," said Eliot's disapproving father. Bernard Landauer had the same respect for psychologists that he had for astrologers, psychics, and believers in UFOs: none.

Eliot's mother was more open minded. "Can I still tell my friends that you're a doctor?" she asked anxiously. All Helen Landauer cared about was that Eliot do well, be happy, and make her proud of him.

"When I get my Ph.D., I'll be a doctor," Eliot told his mother. Reassured, she began an ongoing and semisuccessful struggle to get her husband to change his mind.

"Stop *hocking* me," Bernard told his wife. "I'll pay. But only so much."

Bernard eventually agreed to pay the basic tuition for

Eliot's continuing studies. Eliot got a summer job in a local stock brokerage office, an area he found far more simpatico than law, to help pay for the rest of his schooling. He graduated from LIU with his master's degree in clinical psychology in 1958 at the age of twenty-four.

Eliot applied for and got a job as a psychologist with Nassau County's Board of Education's health and social services department working with school psychologists and guidance counselors. He also married Anna Cornelius, one of the girls at Huntington High who had snubbed him, now a first grade teacher in Roslyn.

"I always knew you'd be a success," Anna told Eliot.

"Even when I was fat and unathletic?" Eliot asked.

"Even then."

Along with his work for the county, Eliot went into private practice. He shared a Mineola office with an LIU classmate who had become a pediatrician. Eliot's first patients were troubled children and their families, usually referred to him by school psychologists or his office partner.

Those early patients were followed by a broader spectrum of people. There were housewifes who suffered from depression, employees who had trouble getting along with their bosses, couples who had marital problems, businessmen suffering from burn-out, and adolescents going through various family, social, or academic crises.

Eliot's income and local reputation grew quickly and by the early Sixties his private practice was thriving and he had risen close to the top of his department, with the title of assistant director. Believing in psychology not only for his patients but for himself as well, Eliot obeyed the biblical injunction to physicians and spent a year and a half in the early Sixties in psychoanalysis.

Eliot chose a well-reputed analyst, Martha Schneider, who had an office on 81st Street and Central Park West. Twice a week, Eliot made the trip into Manhattan. On his analyst's couch, Eliot explored himself—his attitudes and values. It was, he thought, the most valuable year and a half of his life.

In the course of his therapy, it became clear to Eliot that despite his ambition he had an unconscious tendency to hold himself back. He realized that in Long Island his opportunities would always be limited. Manhattan was clearly more lucrative, challenging and intellectually stimulating. Manhattan had also always been frightening and Eliot had always shunned it.

"I'm afraid of the city," he told his analyst. "I'm afraid I'll get lost here."

"Have you ever gotten lost?" asked Dr. Schneider.

"No," said Eliot. "Not even on the subway."

With encouragement from Anna and from his mentor, Samuel Wallenberg, Eliot planned his escape from the suburbs the way his father had once planned his escape from Essex Street. Both men took advantage of an America whose streets were lined not with gold but with opportunity. In 1961, Eliot sublet a share in an office on West 72nd Street already rented by two other psychologists, both slightly senior to Eliot and both former students of Samuel Wallenberg.

"Some of my patients from Long Island are going to follow me," Eliot told Anna, his confidence growing. "The other psychologists in my office have promised to give me referrals and so has Dr. Wallenberg."

57
ELIOT

1 9 6 3 – 1 9 6 5 :

New words and usages:
Beatlemania, fake out, groupie,
vibes, no way, computerize

MANHATTAN was made for Eliot Landauer and Eliot Landauer was made for Manhattan. It was in Manhattan that Eliot drew the first truly free breaths of air in his life. Everything in Manhattan was bigger, better, more interesting: the work, the patients, the fees. By late 1963, Eliot and Anna were living in a small but comfortable apartment on West End Avenue. Eliot immediately began to explore the manifold opportunities offered by the city.

"I've joined the staff of the Mid-Manhattan Center for Psychotherapy," he told Anna. "Dr. Wallenberg sponsored me and I was accepted on the first try.

"*Tom Jones* opened this week. Let's go on Saturday," he suggested. Now that he lived in Manhattan, Eliot made a point of seeing every first-run movie.

"Dave Brubeck is playing this weekend. I don't want to miss him," said Eliot. A jazz nut since college, Elliot liked to attend performances of his favorites. Now that he lived in New York, it was easy.

While Eliot thrived on the energized air of Manhattan, Anna felt overwhelmed and out of place. Eliot took Anna shopping at Saks and Bergdorf's but she never acquired the knack of big-city dressing. He urged her to read the *New Yorker* and the *Times* Arts and Leisure section on Sunday so she could join in the conversation at social events but she said she felt like a phony. Anna was intimidated by Eliot's associates and their wives, who were often psychologists themselves.

"They act like I'm not there," said Anna.

"You have to be more outgoing," said Eliot, who noticed that Anna sometimes sat through entire evenings without saying a word.

Eliot, once the outcast, became the pace setter. Anna, once the most popular girl in her class, became invisible. The tables had turned and the price was the marriage.

In the early spring of 1964, just after Lincky Desmond first walked into Eliot's office, Anna had moved back to Roslyn alone and she and Eliot were living apart in the first of what would turn out to be several trial separations.

Because of his profession, Eliot Landauer had made a career of studying people, including women. He knew women, he hoped, inside and out. He also liked them and, in general, found them much more sympathetic than men. Women, Eliot thought, were more flexible, more open to change, more resilient, more realistic.

Despite the problems in his marriage, Eliot believed very strongly in love and the possibility of a happy marriage—if not with Anna, then with someone else. Because he had learned so much about people and how they succeeded and failed in their personal relationships, Eliot thought that with the right woman—a woman who shared his interests, who possessed character, intelligence, warmth, and a capacity to love—he would be able to enjoy a truly happy marriage.

Meanwhile, he worked hard and, although his patients seemed to do quite well in therapy, Eliot always felt that he should be doing more. In his own opinion, his greatest failing was that he never helped his patients quite enough. He always had the uneasy feeling that he could and should have done more—should have had more profound insights, more compassionate responses, more immediately helpful interpretations. To overcome his feelings of professional inadequacy, Eliot returned to his former analyst.

"Stop beating up on yourself," Martha Schneider told him when Eliot complained of his wish to do more and his fear that he wasn't doing enough. "You can't be God. No one can be God."

In his head, Eliot knew that Dr. Schneider was right. In his heart, Eliot felt that if he wasn't God, he was a failure. Eliot could control his head. He could not always control his heart. Most of the time, though, Eliot had, as he should have, a reasonably good opinion of himself and his professional abilities.

By 1965 Eliot Landauer had gotten his Ph.D. in clinical psychology and had worked as a therapist for almost half a decade. In the course of those years, he had met many women he was glad he hadn't married.

There were women who were intelligent but too neurotic. There were women who were beautiful but filled with anger. Some who were outwardly charming but prone to crippling depressions, some who were seductive but self-obsessed. Others who were professionally successful but privately prone to passivity and whininess and secretly looking for a daddy to take care of them.

Eliot wondered into which category, if any, Lincky Desmond would fall. He wondered if she would be the exception. He wondered if she would be the woman he had been looking for.

Although he had a strict policy, never broken, against

seeing patients socially, Eliot knew that he was not superhuman. He had decided that if the right woman walked into his consulting room, he would refer her to another doctor and attempt to continue the relationship on a social basis. He was disappointed to learn that Lincky was already married.

Eliot could see right away that Lincky Desmond was attractive, intelligent, verbal, and young. She would be able to understand the concepts of psychotherapy and work well with them. She was most certainly the ideal kind of patient to take full advantage of the benefits therapy had to offer. The fact that she was attractive and charming made the prospect of spending several hours a week with her appealing. Furthermore, despite her tears, she seemed to be fundamentally in control of herself. She would not be the kind of patient who would telephone at all hours of the day and night with demands, tears, crises, and suicide threats.

In addition, and although Eliot Landauer knew that it might sound mercenary, she clearly would be able to pay the bills. Therapists, like everyone else, had to pay the rent, buy food, and clothe themselves. Finances, unfortunately, were almost always a factor in taking on a new patient, although Eliot often wished that money never had to enter into his professional relationships. Therapy, Eliot thought, should really be available to everyone; this was one of the reasons he worked at reduced fees for several hours a week at the Mid-Manhattan Center.

Undoubtedly because of his parents' continual conflicts over money as he was growing up, talk of money had always made Eliot acutely uncomfortable.

"Perhaps it's because money is so important to you," Martha Schneider said.

"It *is* important to me," replied Eliot. "And I wish it weren't."

"Why not?"

"Because I feel guilty about wanting to earn a lot."

"Why do you feel guilty about wanting to earn money? You don't steal it, do you?"

"No," said Eliot.

"Don't you think you deserve to earn it?"

"Of course," said Eliot. "I know that I work hard."

Eliot spent many sessions with Dr. Schneider talking about money. The sessions were not wasted because one of the most important benefits Eliot felt he received from his own therapy was the ability to think rationally about money and to handle it without undue shame or guilt.

"If I ever get rich, I feel that I'll be able to enjoy it," he told Martha Schneider. "Thanks to you."

VII

INTO THE SEVENTIES

"[This is the time of] hedonism . . . narcissism . . . the cult of the self."

> —Christopher Lasch, *New York Review of Books*

"It's the Me-Decade."

> —Tom Wolfe, *New York* magazine

58
JANE

MONEY AND MARRIAGE IN 1969:

> Jackie and Ari Onassis reportedly
> spend $20 million in their first year
> as man and wife.

> Richard Burton buys the Cartier
> diamond for Elizabeth Taylor for a
> price in excess of $1 million.

WHEN Eliot met Jane in late 1967, he and Anna had separated again, this time for good. Eliot was a free man and he was ready to fall in love again. In the years he had lived and practiced in New York, Eliot had met many accomplished, interesting women. They had good jobs, stimulating ideas, and open-minded attitudes. Anna, unfortunately, suffered in comparison.

"I feel disloyal saying it, but Anna just hasn't kept up," Eliot told Dr. Schneider.

"When I get married again, I'd like to marry someone who's more on my level," he added. "I'd like a wife who's a winner."

Just as Eliot had felt a prickle of possible sexual attraction to Lincky the first moment he saw her, Jane Gresch felt precisely the opposite when she initially met Eliot Landauer. The first thought that crossed Jane's mind when she met him at

Glen Sinclair's Christmas party was that she wasn't attracted to him. Was not and could never be. Never, never, never. The man was a midget. He made Jane, who was five feet ten and perpetually twenty pounds overweight, feel like an elephant— a giant, a big, klutzy giant.

The ridiculous image of dancing with Eliot Landauer, her boobs practically stuck in his face, crossed Jane's mind in a mini-fraction of a second. My God, she would suffocate him! Not only ridiculous but ludicrous. The Amazon and the ant. Jane and Eliot? Ha ha. Not in a thousand million years, Jane told herself as a feeling of relief came over her.

Those thoughts passed through Jane's mind virtually simultaneously, so quickly that they barely registered. Jane would, of course, not remember them, and even at the time what she was primarily aware of was her enormous sense of relief and relaxation. She would not even wonder until much, much later, why she had felt such relief.

What, she would ask herself then, had she been so afraid of? Had she really, at that early date, somehow foreseen that one day she *would* overwhelm him?

Eliot Landauer had grown to like Lincky Desmond very much indeed during the course of their work together but, attractive as she was, Eliot had eventually decided that she was not the woman for him. Lincky was too cool, too self-contained. Eliot wanted someone warmer, more uninhibited, more emotionally available.

Someone like Jane Gresch.

Eliot was attracted to her bright hazel eyes, voluptuous figure, smoky voice, outspoken opinions, and burgeoning celebrity. The moment someone pointed her out at Glen Sinclair's Christmas party, Eliot decided to introduce himself. Jane Gresch exuded vitality and Eliot had a lust for life.

When, almost one year later, Jane told him that marriage was a repressive bourgeois institution for the enslavement of women, Eliot told Jane that she was full of shit.

"You're too bright to parrot the party line," he told her. "Why don't you try to think for yourself?"

"My mother spent her life doing dishes," Jane replied.

"You're not your mother and I'm not your father," said Eliot. "If we got married, do you really think I'd chain you to the kitchen?"

"No," said Jane. "I'm a lousy cook and you're a gourmet."

"Be serious," said Eliot.

"You mean I could keep on writing?" asked Jane.

"I'd insist on it," said Eliot. "You're very talented. I wouldn't stand by and let you waste that talent. Besides, it's time you wrote that novel you've been talking about."

"Yeah, that," said Jane. Her "novel," much talked about, yet still unwritten, had become a source of embarrassment.

"If we got married, you could quit your job. You could afford to write full time," said Eliot. "You're already well known in New York. When you publish a novel, you'll be even more successful, more famous."

"I'd definitely like that," said Jane. "Are you sure I'm not making a bargain with the devil?"

"Do I look like Satan?"

"No."

"Then give me one good reason why we shouldn't get married," Eliot said.

Jane thought a moment.

"I'd have to give up my name," she said finally.

"Says who?"

"You mean I could still be Jane Gresch?"

"Of course," said Eliot.

"Ms. Gresch?" asked Jane, wanting confirmation.

"Ms. Gresch," replied Eliot.

The decision took an instant. Its reverberations would echo through the years.

"No one gets engaged anymore," said Jane, turning Eliot down when he wanted to take her to Tiffany's to buy her an engagement ring.

"It's a nice custom," said Eliot. When he had married Anna, he had been too poor to afford a ring. He wanted to do things right this time around.

"I was engaged once," said Jane. "It was the pits."

"It was the wrong guy," Eliot said. "*That* was the problem."

"I don't want a ring," said Jane, hewing to her feminist principles. "They're a symbol of male domination and the position of women as chattel."

"Spare me the lecture," said Eliot. "If I wanted to marry Gloria Steinem, I'd propose to her."

Eliot and Jane got married in June 1969 in the River Suite of the Sutton Place Hotel. The wedding was a combination of the traditional and the contemporary. Eliot's and Jane's families attended along with friends and professional associates. Jane wore white—a white pants suit. When it came time for Eliot to place a ring on Jane's finger, he produced a circle of diamonds and emeralds set in platinum.

"You wouldn't let me get you an engagement ring so I did the next best thing," he told her after the ceremony.

"It's beautiful," said Jane. "I've never had a decent piece of jewelry before."

"I hope it doesn't compromise your principles," said Eliot.

"I guess I'll just have to suffer," sighed Jane theatrically.

"It's a nice custom," said Eliot, "whom he had married
Anne, he had been too poor to afford a ring. He wanted to do

59
JANE

JULY 1969:

"Houston, Tranquility Base here.
The eagle has landed. . . . I'm at the
foot of the ladder. I'm going to step
off the LM now. That's one small
step for man, one giant step for
mankind."

—Neil Armstrong, landing on the moon

ELIOT and Jane felt happily exempt from the battles that were
raging in kitchens and bedrooms across the country. From the
moment they agreed to get married, they had decided that
theirs would be a modern marriage, a marriage between equals.
Jane, because she considered herself a feminist. Eliot, because
he did not want to duplicate the problems and inequities that
had torpedoed his first marriage.

Jane and Eliot decided that marriage meant sharing and
that they would share everything: money, housework, friends.
Right after their wedding, Eliot changed all his bank accounts
into joint accounts and Jane made a schedule for dividing the
cooking, cleaning, and laundry chores.

"It's not really fair to you," Jane told Eliot, thinking that
she was getting more than she was giving. "You earn a lot
more money than I do."

At the time Eliot was charging private patients fifty dollars
an hour. His consulting work for the Nassau County board of

education paid him fourteen thousand dollars a year. Between the two, Eliot was earning more than fifty thousand dollars a year while Jane, who had quit her job with Glen Sinclair to devote herself fulltime to her writing, was earning nothing.

"I feel like a kept woman," said Jane unhappily, wondering if she were compromising her feminist principles by letting her husband support her.

"Only temporarily. You'll catch up to me soon enough," predicted Eliot, unperturbed by the inequity. He pointed out that nowadays women could make just as much as men, citing the incomes of Barbara Walters, Billie Jean King, Lauren Hutton, and Barbra Streisand. "You'll earn even more than that when you write your novel. I have a lot of confidence in you."

Eliot kept his end of the bargain when it came to housework. Unlike many other husbands, he did not shirk, complain, or undermine the agreement by leaving the kitchen a mess after cooking, mixing colored with white in the laundry, or "forgetting" when it was his turn to make the bed.

He went to the supermarket without complaint. He cooked simple but appetizing meals several nights a week, uncomplainingly took his weekly turn in the basement laundry of the West 74th Street apartment building they lived in and was unfailingly pleasant to Jane's friends. A neat freak, Eliot even straightened out the clothes that Jane left strewn around the bedroom. He folded and put away the sweaters abandoned on a chair. He put the bras and panties scattered on the floor into the laundry basket. He hung up the dresses flung on the bed.

"I have *the* perfect husband," Jane kept saying, hardly able to believe her good luck. Eliot was so good, so reasonable, so responsible. She, by comparison, was so bad. Messy, disorganized, overly emotional, impulsive, and erratic. She was a dreadful cook, often forgot to enter the checks she had written into the checkbook, and tended to be moody and weepy for the entire week before her period.

"I don't know how he puts up with me," Jane told Wilma.

"He's a shrink," replied Wilma. "It's his job."

Jane also realized that she had been wrong when she had thought that she was taller than Eliot. At five feet eleven, he was, she knew, a full inch taller than she was. Nevertheless, to preserve the height differential, Jane felt that she had to wear flats. Being Jane, she turned the one flaw in her new paradise into a reason for celebration. She gave a reverse bridal shower during which she gave away all her high heel shoes to her friends. Away with the Ferragamos, the Charles Jourdans, the Margaret Jerrolds!

"Banished forever!" Jane said giddily, thinking that, finally, she was coming back down to earth in more ways than one.

Eliot Landauer seemed to be the one man in a million who loved women for all the right reasons. He loved Jane for her sense of humor, her outspokenness, her joie de vivre. Fat thighs, she realized deliriously, were not the fatal barrier to true love and eternal happiness she had once imagined. Of course, she reminded herself, she had been very young then. Very young and, as Eliot would say with his understanding and tolerant smile, awfully immature.

Most of all perhaps, the thing Jane loved best about Eliot was that she could tell him anything. By the time they were married for a year, there was not one single thing about her feelings, her dreams, her past, and her hopes for the future that Jane hadn't told her husband. Eliot always said something to make her feel better. Eliot always understood. Even about Owen's big cock.

"Size isn't everything," Eliot said with the confidence that only a man who was hung himself could afford.

Jane liked to tell all her friends that every woman should marry a therapist.

"There's nothing like having a shrink in the house," she told her friends, glorying in her new happiness. Her husband was her analyst, her lover, her best friend. What could possibly go wrong?

60
JANE

1 9 7 1 :

Eliminating the patriarchal and racist
base of the existing social system
requires a revolution, not a reform.

—*Ms*. magazine, first issue

THE only real troubles Jane had in the early years of her
marriage were her troubles with herself. Her marriage to Eliot
permitted Jane to pursue the dream she'd had ever since
girlhood about being a famous novelist. She spent the first year
of her new marriage arranging a life that would leave her free
to work. She replenished her wardrobe, organized a linen
closet, bought rugs and sofas and, once she and Eliot got over
the novelty of doing their own housework, hired a cleaning
woman. She made out grocery lists, gave dinner parties, and
carried a fistful of credit cards. She was, she joked, laughing at
her transformation from free spirit into hausfrau, the very
model of a middle-class matron with, of course, a liberated
Seventies spin.

By the time she'd been married a year, Jane had what she
had yearned for for years: no financial worries and plenty of
time for her own creative work. As a surprise birthday present,
Eliot furnished a corner of the living room as an office with a

good-looking desk, a comfortable leather chair, and even a businesslike file cabinet.

"Now you have no excuses not to be brilliant," Eliot told her, wanting to make everything as easy as possible for her.

"You mean put up or shut up?" Jane teased, hugging him. She was delighted with Eliot's thoughtful gift but unprepared for the sudden anxiety it evoked in her.

In the first three years of her marriage, Jane started three different novels. In one way or another, each was about sex, the subject that Jane had told Hank Greene interested her most.

The first was literary, Jane's attempt to write the Colette-like novel she had dreamed of ever since college. Because she and Eliot had gone to Quebec and Nova Scotia for their honeymoon, Jane decided to write about the sexual awakening of a young French-Canadian girl. Set in a small fishing village near Cape Breton Island, the novel had a main character called Evangeline named after Longfellow's heroine. Jane wrote forty pages and gave up when she realized that there was no plot and that she, herself, did not give a damn about what happened to her characters.

"I must have been nuts. I don't know one French-Canadian person, male or female, and I know less than nothing about life in a fishing village," Jane told Eliot, relieved when she finally stopped torturing herself.

The second attempted novel was a thinly disguised autobiographical novel about Jane's own adolescence. The emphasis was on Jane's discoveries about sex, a *Portnoy's Complaint* for women, Jane thought. Jane abandoned it after almost a hundred pages when she decided that memories of finger fucking on her parents' sofa were not only juvenile but embarrassing.

"Besides," she told Wilma, "I don't feel like getting sued by Gene Schuble."

The third novel, begun in a conscious effort to get away from the artsy-fartsy trap Jane felt she had set for herself in attempting to write her more literary novels, was an outright attempt to write a Harold Robbins kind of blockbuster about a woman who grabbed for sex, money, and power as greedily as a man. Jane jettisoned it when she found herself constantly blocked, literally unable to imagine a woman as bold and dominating as Robbins's larger-than-life ultramacho heroes.

"It's my fault," Jane told Eliot. "There's no reason women can't be just as selfish and insensitive as men. It's just that I can't seem to write about them."

Three tries, three flops. In 1972, Jane added up the dismal bottom line. Was writing novels like baseball? Three strikes and you're out? Jane tried very hard not to believe it. Hadn't her novella been published? Hadn't she made suggestions that had helped Owen Casals, suggestions that even critics applauded? Hadn't she written a number of articles for *Downtown* that people had responded to? False starts were part of the creative process, Jane said. False starts weren't fatal. False starts could lead to the real McCoy.

That was what Jane said in public. In private, Jane began to wonder how many false starts a writer was allowed before the writer herself was considered false.

"When do I stop being promising and start being a no-talent faker?" she asked Eliot.

"Never," he replied. "A lack of talent is not your problem. What you need is the right idea."

"That's exactly the problem," Jane said, complaining that she had no ideas, no plot, no characters. I'm tapped out," she said. "Tapped out and bummed out."

"Write something you know about," said Eliot.

"That's what everyone always says," replied Jane, remembering that she had had almost the identical exchanges with both Glen and Hank. "I can't think of anything I know one thing about. Even the food at my dinner parties is lousy."

"Think of something that affected you deeply. Think of something that really engaged your emotions," Eliot advised, reminding Jane that all the ideas that had worked best for her, ideas for articles about thighs and breasts, were connected to her very deepest feelings.

"I've tried. I can't," said Jane.

"Try again," said Eliot. "Don't give up."

61
JANE

SEX ON THE BRAIN IN THE
SEVENTIES:

Movies:
Last Tango in Paris
Deep Throat
Carnal Knowledge

Books:
*Everything You Always Wanted to Know
   About Sex But Were Afraid to Ask*
The Joy of Sex
The Sensuous Man
The Sensuous Woman

JANE tried. She began a fourth book, a historical novel set in the years between the First and Second World War. She bought a shelfful of reference books and read them all, making careful notes of historical events and period detail. Deciding to duplicate the deliberate way Glen Sinclair plotted his novels, Jane began a long outline. She detested every moment of writing the nuts and bolts of plot and incident without dialogue and scenes.

"Glen kept strict business hours. He worked from nine till five-thirty every day," Jane told Eliot. "If I last from ten until ten-fifteen, I'm lucky."

By the time they had been married for almost three years, Eliot was getting concerned about Jane's chronic depression about her failure to write. He continued to be sympathetic and supportive but Jane's complaints about how blocked she was and what a fraud she was had become oppressive. Eliot was doing well professionally. He hadn't divorced Anna to marry another woman who felt frustrated and out of place. He wanted a wife whose accomplishments he could be proud of.

"Your depression is depressing me," he told Jane. "What happened to the live wire I married? What had happened to the woman who was going to out-Sagan Sagan?"

"I don't have any ideas," said Jane.

"You have dozens," said Eliot.

"Name one."

"Mr. Ten Inches," Eliot said. "Mr. Ten Inches" was the nickname Jane have given Owen. Whenever she had a few glasses of wine, she recounted the tale of her ill-fated affair. Her memories were as clear as if the events had happened yesterday. Her fury, resentment, bitterness, jealousy, and outrage seemed newly minted. Ditto the X-rated details and raunchy humor that accompanied them.

"Write about my romance with Owen?" she asked gloomily. She and Hank had discussed the idea years before. The idea of a book had ultimately intimidated her. Instead, she had begun an article called "Dumped." Begun more than once, as a matter of fact, and never finished. "I tried. I flopped. I never finished it."

"That was an article; I'm suggesting fiction. It's a great literary tradition, isn't it, using some fierce personal experience as the basis for a novel?"

"I'll think about it," Jane said without much enthusiasm.

"What the hell, you've already done the research," said Eliot.

"That's true."

When Jane woke up the next morning, scenes and snatches of dialogue were already beginning to run through her mind. Eliot left for his office at quarter to eight and Jane found that she couldn't stay away from her desk.

"My God, I started writing at eight thirty this morning," she told Eliot when he got home that evening and found her still at her desk. "I stopped for some yogurt and a cup of coffee at lunchtime and that was it. I went right back to work. The day flew past!"

Jane, who had always liked to sleep late, now couldn't wait to get up in the morning and get to her desk. Remembering Hank's advice about not getting sued, Jane changed jobs, addresses, families, backgrounds. She named her heroine Francine Cord. The hero was named Evan Rhinelander. Francine was Jane. Evan was Owen. Even though the facts were changed, the emotions remained the same—and they sizzled. Jane let loose. Payback time had finally come.

"I made him a total goniff!" she told Eliot, describing her account of how Evan stole ideas from Francine and passed them off as his own.

"I gave him a huge cock. I also gave him a huge ego to go along with it!" she told Helene.

"When I get done with this, no woman is ever going to put up with any shit from an emotional fascist like Owen again!" she told Wilma.

"Even male chauvinist pigs are going to hate Evan!" Jane said, describing what a two-timer and a liar Evan was. "Women are going to want to lynch him. Strawberry ice cream or no strawberry ice cream!"

Jane was also surprised at how physically and mentally exhausted she felt after a day at her desk.

"I'm drained. My eyes are glazed and my back is killing me," she told Glen.

"Join the club," said her former boss, giving her the name of a good masseur.

Every night when Eliot got home, there would be more pages added to the growing stack of manuscript on Jane's desk. Over a drink, he would read what she had written that day and usually he would tell her that it was wonderful.

"I can't wait to see what happens tomorrow," he would say.

Occasionally, he would have a criticism. "Owen is *too* selfish," he said. "You have to show something nice about him. The reader needs to understand why Francine is in love with him in the first place."

"You're right," Jane replied. "I'll put in the snappy restaurants he took me to, and the nice presents. When I think about it, I see that he was exciting-by-association. He was always where the action is. And he always had groovy gossip."

"I can't wait to finish. Writing this is the hardest thing I've ever done," Jane told Eliot.

" 'This?' " asked Eliot. "Don't you have a title yet?"

"So far, nothing that I like," said Jane.

"I thought of a title. *Fucked-Up*," Jane told Eliot several weeks later.

Eliot shook his head. "No way."

"*Fucking Miserable? Fucked Over? Fucked Again?*" suggested Jane.

"You can't use 'fuck' in a title," Eliot said. "Not even you."

As Eliot spoke, an idea flashed into Jane's mind. An inspiration that was pure Jane, one thousand percent Jane. She looked at Eliot and smiled.

"Wanna bet?"

62
LINCKY

"This is not a bedroom war. This is a
political movement."

—Betty Friedan

Don't cook dinner tonight—starve a
rat.

—Feminist slogan

JANE'S inspiration would change many lives—Jane's and
Eliot's, Owen's and Elly's, and, not least, Hank's and Lincky's.

Lincky's first serious romance after her 1968 divorce from
Peter took place in 1970. Alan Goldmark was the East Coast
vice president of a movie company. Alan combined flash with
substance. He was sandy haired and teddy-bear cuddly, energetic and dynamic, clearly headed for a top studio job. Alan,
thirty-eight, had been too busy with his career to marry.

"Plus I never met the right woman," he told Lincky.
"You're different."

He told Lincky over and over that he loved her.

"You're absolutely perfect for me in every way. You're the
only woman in my life. Present and future," he told her.

He talked about marriage, carefully planning all the details
of their life together.

"We'll have a New York apartment, a house in L.A., and a
place in the Hamptons. You'll run North Star. I want to end up

with my own production company. We'll have a couple of kids. We'll be happy, Lincky, really happy," he said.

Although Alan continued to talk about marriage, he never quite got around to proposing.

"Marriage is a big step. I admit it: I'm nervous as hell. I can okay a twenty million dollar production budget without flicking an eyelash. That's just money. Marriage is different. Marriage is *life*," he told Lincky. "I think I just need time to really get used to the idea. I'm getting there, don't worry."

On the night that Lincky thought Alan was going to propose, he drank a glass of champagne and took a Valium. Then he made a confession that left her reeling.

"You know my friend James? Well, he's more than just a friend. I love you but I want to live with him," Alan said.

Lincky's next affair was with an advertising executive named Edgar Sanderton. He was three years older than Lincky and creative director of one of Madison Avenue's hottest shops. Clios lined his office and competing agencies lined up to offer him bigger and better jobs, more outrageous salaries, and even more lavish perks. Like Lincky, Ed had been married and divorced.

"My divorce almost killed me," he told Lincky. "I think of myself as a stable, solid guy. When my marriage broke up, I realized I'd been fooling myself."

Ed had been in analysis since the collapse of his marriage four years earlier. He blamed himself for the divorce and wanted to get to the bottom of the conflicts that had driven his wife away. He was determined not to make the same mistakes twice. Ed would make no decision without consulting his shrink, Martin Brazill.

"Let me run it past Marty," Ed would say, whether the subject was where to spend the weekend, what to get Lincky for her birthday, or whether they should live together. His dependence on his therapist was driving Lincky crazy.

"With Peter there were other women. Alan preferred another man. Now I'm competing with mental health," Lincky told Coral.

After a year of steady dating, Lincky delivered an ultimatum.

"We're both in our thirties. We seem to be compatible. We share the same tastes and ambitions. I want to know if we have a future together."

"Let me run it past Marty," Ed said.

Lincky shook her head.

"If I wanted a ménage à trois I'd have stayed married to Peter."

"It's important to me to be clear," Ed said.

"And it's important to me to be number one with someone I love."

Lincky met men who were turned on by her job and power and she met men who were turned off by them. She met men who were recovering from their divorces, men who weren't sure whether or not they wanted to get involved, men who wanted sex but no commitment, men who wanted emotional involvement but no sex. Manhattan seemed filled with men who had been burned by women and were out to get their revenge.

Lincky had almost given up on men when she met Josh Butterfield, an investment banker, in January 1972. He was tall and rangy, a Clint Eastwood lookalike in a pin-striped suit with the eyes of a lone plains drifter, a perpetual tan, and perfect white teeth. He was successful, heterosexual, and unambivalent about commitment. He was separated from his wife, Deirdre—a no-talent phony posing as an artist, he said—and was in the process of getting a divorce.

"I'm a marrier," he told Lincky on their fourth date. "If you're not willing to get serious, let's stop everything right here."

"As soon as I'm free, we'll get married," he told Lincky. "You're one in a million. I'm not going to let you get away."

* * *

Meanwhile, Lincky's professional life continued to be one success after another. The expansion into hardcover had been solidly profitable and North Star's paperback line now competed equally with Dell and Bantam.

"Now your personal life has to catch up. When are you and Josh going to set the date?" Elly asked in the spring of 1973.

"As soon as his divorce is final," replied Lincky.

"That's the world's longest-playing divorce," said Elly.

"His wife has been fighting it every inch of the way. She's holding him up for money and no matter how much he agrees to pay, she decides it's not enough," said Lincky, reporting Deirdre Butterfield's latest financial demands.

"Are you sure he's worth waiting for?" asked Elly. She knew that Josh's divorce was upsetting him. She could see for herself that it was also taking its toll on Lincky. She seemed drawn and unhappy.

"Absolutely. Josh has all of Peter's attributes and none of his drawbacks. He's perfect for me," said Lincky. "Besides, I've put all this time and emotion into the relationship, I'm not going to give up now."

In early June, Lincky called Josh's office to make arrangements for the coming weekend. His new secretary sounded surprised. She told Lincky that Mr. Butterfield would be out of town for the weekend.

"Mrs. Butterfield is having an exhibit in Washington. He's going down to attend the opening," she told Lincky.

"Mrs. Butterfield?" repeated Lincky. "*Deirdre* Butterfield?"

When Lincky called Josh at home that evening, he answered the telephone on the first ring. It was as if he knew in advance who was calling and why.

"I'll meet you at Melon's," he told Lincky before she could say a word. "We'll have a drink."

When Lincky arrived at Melon's, Josh was seated at one of the corner tables in the back. His usual scotch on the rocks sat on the checkered tablecloth in front of him. It looked untouched. He wore a shetland sweater and a trapped expression. He avoided Lincky's eyes and barely glanced at her when she sat down.

"You ask the questions, I'll answer," he said, his lone-plains-drifter eyes darting everywhere except at her.

" 'Mrs. Butterfield'? *'Deirdre* Butterfield'?" Lincky asked, repeating her stunned words to Josh's secretary earlier that day. "I thought you hated her. You said she was a money-grubbing bitch, a no-talent phony. You said you never wanted to see her again."

"I meant it. That's how I felt." He shrugged helplessly.

"Then what happened?"

"Then we got divorced."

"Divorced! You and Deirdre got divorced! When? You never told me you got divorced. You kept telling me that the divorce was being held up."

Josh looked absolutely miserable. Even his tan looked unhappy.

"I feel like a complete shit. I was lying. I didn't want to let you go."

"So you were seeing Deirdre all along?" Lincky asked. She wanted every revolting detail. Time and place. Chapter and verse.

"Not all along."

"Then since when?"

"Since a few weeks ago. After all, she was my wife. We had been through a lot together."

*"Ex-*wife," Lincky corrected him. "Deirdre was your *ex-*wife."

"Ex-wife," conceded Josh.

"But only for a while?" asked Lincky, suddenly getting the picture. She forced herself not to punch him in the mouth right then and there in front of all the attractive East Siders eating cheeseburgers and spinach salads. "Right?"

Josh nodded.

"When did you remarry her?"

"A month ago."

"And how long were you two lovebirds divorced?"

"Six weeks. Then we ran into each other on Park Avenue. Things sort of took off from there."

"But at the same time you kept telling me how much you hated her and how you couldn't wait to be free and how you were dying to marry me?"

Josh looked defeated. "I didn't know what else to do."

"And what about the future? Did you plan to keep on seeing me as if nothing had happened?"

"Sort of," said Josh. "Why not? We really get along."

"But not as well as you and Deirdre?"

"It's different with her and you."

"I bet," said Lincky.

"I knew you'd find out," said Josh. His tone was one of utter resignation.

Lincky smiled bitterly.

There was nothing left for her to say. She picked up Josh's drink and poured it slowly over his head. He made no attempt to stop her. His soaked hair streamed down his forehead and ice cubes landed on his shoulders and lap. When the glass was empty, Lincky put it back on the table. She threw a napkin at Josh, got up, and slowly walked out.

"Sometimes I feel there's a gypsy curse on me," Lincky told Coral, recounting the story.

"It's not you. It's men. They're all crazy," replied Coral.

Lincky tried not to think so.

VIII

MODERN MEN / HANK GREENE

"Life is too short to live with a bad deal."

—David Geffen, talent agent and
recording executive

63
HANK

New York! New York!
It's a wonderful town!

—from "New York, New York" by
Leonard Bernstein, Betty
Comden, and Adolph Green

IN the decade since the assassination of John F. Kennedy, Hank
Greene had upgraded his business and, he hoped, himself. He
had, not so accidentally, done it to prove that Lincoln Desmond
had been wrong to walk out on him.

When Lincky had left him at the Commodore, she had
struck at the heart of Hank's worst anxiety: that he wasn't good
enough, that he didn't measure up, that he didn't fit in. Hank
had devoted the next ten years of his life to an effort to
convince the world—and himself—that that fear was un-
founded.

Hank went into a year-long depression after his breakup
with Lincky. He was furious at her for walking out on him,
angry at himself for firing her in retaliation. For a while, he
stayed mired in a black pit of rage and resentment. He didn't
think he could ever forgive her or himself. By the time black
lightened to gray, Hank had rethought his life. In a personal
five-year plan, he divorced his wife, sold his house in the

suburbs, moved to the city, and methodically proceeded to change his agency, his life and himself.

Starting immediately after the end of his affair with Lincky, Hank worked on improving his client list.

"I don't want to take on any more romance writers unless they're so good they deserve to be on the bestseller list," he told Ralph Weiss. "*And* I want to upgrade the ones we already represent."

"Catherine Newell has sold three million copies of her Regency romances," Hank told Ted Spandorff, speaking of one of his longtime clients. "It's time she got out of paperback originals and into hardcover. She writes a book a year and her newest is her best. I want a two-book deal for her with guarantees of major publicity and promotion."

"We'll sell her as a woman who writes for women," replied Ted after he had read the manuscript.

"That's okay as far as it goes," said Hank. "But I want a more concrete proposal from you. I want details: size of printing, promotion and publicity plans, advertising strategy. If you come up with something solid, we've got a deal."

"I'll get my people on it," Ted promised.

Raintree Press not only did a good job selling Catherine Newell's Regencies in hardcover but, at Hank's suggestion, Catherine Newell began to set her novels in the twentieth century.

"Not contemporary, mind you, but up until the beginning of World War Two. Stay out of the trenches. Focus on the home front, the man-woman problems, the styles, the fashions, the cultural climate, and social attitudes. You'll keep your historical fans and you'll draw a whole new audience besides," Hank told his client. "It'll take you out of the categories and into the mainstream. Ralph will help you with the editing. I'm going to get Raintree to up your advances and alter your image."

Hank also saw possibilities for improvement for Glen Sinclair. He advised him to drop the diet and self-help books and concentrate his energies.

"You write too fast," he told Glen, advising him to raise his sights. "You're writing five or six books a year and it shows. Slow down. Focus on the action thrillers. You've got the touch. You come up with damn good plots and your characters live and breathe. If you write longer, more solidly researched books, I'll be able to get you more money and better deals."

"Why not?" replied Glen. Consciously patterning himself on a combination of Ian Fleming and Robert Ludlum, Glen began to write spy thrillers with sophisticated international backgrounds and paranoid scenarios. Glen's books went from softcover to hardcover, from oblivion to the bestseller list. His price per book went from five thousand to twenty-five thousand to fifty thousand in three years.

"Next time around, I'm going to break the six-figure barrier for you," Hank told his client.

At the same time that Hank worked on improving his agency, he also tried to compensate for his impoverished personal life. Afraid that no woman would love him, Hank had married the first one who seemed to respond to him. His marriage to Sarah had been a mismatch from the beginning. Hank knew he had made a mistake and, in the early years of his marriage, he often dreamed of being single. He regretted the women he hadn't known, the romances he hadn't had, the adventures he had missed. When he and Lincky broke up, Hank tried to make up for lost time.

"I chased every secretary, every receptionist, everything that breathed, but I wasn't happy," he told Glen.

Women had changed by the time Hank was divorced and nothing had prepared him for the change. Some wanted commitment, which made Hank nervous. Others didn't, which made him even more nervous. Sex, once a no-no, had become easily available and, to Hank's surprise, somewhat less exciting now that women no longer had to be assiduously chased and courted.

"Now they say 'yes' before I even get a chance to ask," he complained to Ralph. "What fun is that?"

Women were now demanding quality orgasms and were not shy about pointing out their lovers' sexual deficiencies, real or imagined.

"Jesus Christ, one of them even told me to hurry up. She said that I wasted too much time in foreplay," he told Glen. "I thought women *liked* foreplay!"

Even when Hank did meet someone he was attracted to, he compared her with Lincky. Sooner or later, Lincky inevitably won. Lincky was brighter. Lincky was more sensitive. Lincky knew more about publishing. Lincky had a better sense of humor. Lincky knew how to tease him and how to challenge him. Lincky was prettier, sexier, nicer, more fun to be with. Instead of being out on the town most nights, Hank found to his surprise that by 1970, he preferred to have a quiet dinner and go home and work.

Hank's sober life and focus on work paid off. The agency's client list and profits increased steadily, and in 1972 Hank moved his office from Third Avenue to Madison, from the fourth floor to the fifteenth. He stopped eating sandwiches at his desk for lunch and began circulating at restaurants frequented by publishing people, such as the Italian Pavilion and Brussels. He increased his contacts and expanded the number of publishers he regularly did business with. He paid attention to his clothes and grooming and made an effort to clean up his language.

"Have you noticed? I even stopped screaming in the office," he said to Ralph, pointing out that Judy Valentine, his current secretary, had been working for him for seven months, an all-time Hank Greene record.

With each success, Hank's sights rose even higher.

"I want the Hank Greene Agency to be a combination of

Tiffany's and IBM. I want to blow every other agent on the map out of the water," he told Ralph in the spring of 1973. "What I need is the breakthrough book. The Number One, super-duper, drop-dead, get-out-of-my-way, kick-ass bestseller. The book that will knock their socks off. The book that will make Hank Greene king of the hill."

"And how are you going to find a book like that?" asked Ralph. Hank's clients were solid producers and steady earners. Still, not one of them was a superstar. None had broken the million dollar per book barrier.

"By waiting and watching. By plotting and planning and conniving. By never giving up and never giving in," said Hank. "It's going to come my way. I can sense it. I can almost taste it."

"You really mean that, don't you?"

"You can take it to the bank."

IX

SUCCESS AND ANGER / 1973–1975

64
LINCKY

1973: WATERGATE

"People have got to know whether
or not their President is a crook.
Well, I'm not a crook."

—Richard M. Nixon

"I was hoping you fellows wouldn't
ask me about that."

—White House aide Alexander
Butterfield to the Ervin committee
about the White House taping system

"GODDAMN motherfucking cocksucking son of a bitch!"
screamed Hank, turning purple and slamming down the
phone.

"Is something the matter?" asked Ralph.

Hank was beyond words. He choked on his own fury.

"Morons!" he finally sputtered. He got up, picked up a
manuscript, put it under his arm, and stalked out of his office.

"*What* was that!" Judy Valentine asked Ralph. She had
never heard such language from Hank.

"*The F Factor* just got turned down again," said Ralph,
who had figured out the reason for Hank's conniption. *The F
Factor*, Jane Gresch's novel, had become Hank's holy grail.

"Where is he going?"

Ralph shrugged.

"Probably to murder the guy who turned it down."

Sex sold. Fancy fucking and emotional violence were money in the bank. The minute Hank read Jane's novel, *The F Factor*, he knew he had hit the jackpot. *The F Factor* was It. The big, surefire, can't-miss, go-for-broke book he had been waiting for. Number One on the list. A million bucks in the bank. Movie sale. Book clubs. Foreign rights bonanza. Hank rubbed his hands together and licked his chops. He sat back and waited for the publishers to line up, begging to buy the publication rights at any price.

Instead, Hank had made eleven submissions and gotten eleven turndowns. That morning on the telephone, he had received number twelve.

It did not make Hank Greene happy.

Like a bullet shot out of a .357 Magnum, Hank Greene barreled over to North Star's offices. Hank hadn't really seen Lincky face to face in ten years. Whenever he ran into her at a party, she looked in the other direction. She acted like she was too high and mighty for him. He was sick and tired of being treated like dirt. He didn't care what she said or did, it was time they stopped crapping around and at least did some business together.

Hank screeched to a halt in front of the receptionist and demanded to know where Lincky Desmond's office was. As soon as the woman raised her hand to point, Hank took off again. He barged past Lincky's secretary, hurled himself into Lincky's office and planted himself into her visitor's chair. He banged a manuscript down on her desk.

"*This*," he said, "is what you've been waiting for. It will put North Star on the map in hardcover. It will make you look like a genius and it will make Gordon richer than he ever dreamed. Now, how much are you going to pay me for it?"

Lincky stared at Hank. She hadn't really looked at him for years. He looked different, better. Partly it was the clothes and haircut. It was also his expression: the scowl had relaxed, the perpetually burrowed brow had softened. However, the intensity of the heat he generated was the same. It was still there, burning as fiercely as ever. Lincky could almost feel it from across the desk.

"How many turndowns have you had?" she asked.

"What the hell kind of question is that?" Hank replied. He allowed himself to take a good look at her. Royalty, hell. She made queens look dumpy and frumpy.

"A good one. I know perfectly well that you wouldn't come to North Star unless you were having plenty of trouble."

"Twelve," admitted Hank.

"What am I, unlucky thirteen?"

"What you are is smart," he said. "The rest of them are idiots."

Lincky looked at the manuscript and then at Hank.

"Let me read it."

As soon as she read *The F Factor*, Lincky knew that Hank was right. A first novel, *The F Factor* was unlike anything Lincky had ever read. Once she started it, she was unable to put it down. Once she finished it, she was unable to put it out of her mind.

The F Factor was a love story—and a hate story. It told of a sizzling love affair between a Manhattan research librarian and a glamorous, two-timing television correspondent that ended cruelly and without warning at the very brink of marriage. Evan Rhinelander, the Hemingway-style hero, was priapic and egotistical. Francine Cord, the heroine, was imaginative, uninhibited sexpot. Francine gave Evan the inspiration and ideas for his bestselling novel and then lost out to an uncritically adoring and traditionally submissive rival.

The novel was about the overriding and obsessive power of sexual passion—written from a woman's point of view. It was vicious, hilarious, and incandescently obscene.

"You're right about Jane Gresch and *The F Factor*," Lincky told Hank over the telephone when she had finished reading the manuscript.

"I knew you'd see it my way," replied Hank.

"We'll offer an advance of ten thousand dollars," Lincky said. It was a modest amount of money. Lincky held the phone away from her ear and waited for one of Hank's volcanic outbursts.

"That offer sucks. *The F Factor* is worth a million dollars. You know it and I know it," Hank said, surprising her with his matter-of-fact tone. "But you and I also know that the whole town has turned it down. They're too dumb or too scared or maybe both. I'm going to sell it to you for ten grand but I'm going to nail you for advertising and promotion guarantees."

"That's fair enough," said Lincky. "The book—and the author—are perfect for a big campaign. I've met Jane through Glen Sinclair. She's perfect for the talk shows."

Hank and Lincky agreed on a twenty-five thousand dollar ad budget and bestseller list guarantees of ten thousand dollars a week for ten weeks.

"That's the best deal you've ever made," Hank told Lincky when they had finished the negotiation.

"Are you still rating my job performance?" replied Lincky.

"Naturally," Hank said. "Once a Hank Greene employee, always a Hank Greene employee."

"Even after you fired me?"

"Fired? What does a little thing like being fired mean between friends?"

"Are we friends?" asked Lincky.

"I'm available if you are," said Hank. "Isn't it time we buried the hatchet?"

"This is going to be our lead book for the summer. It's going to be the biggest book we've ever published," Lincky told Elly, giving her the manuscript of *The F Factor*. "I have no doubt that with any luck at all it's going to make the list. Maybe even number one. After you read it, let's discuss the promotion and publicity angles."

65
ELLY

1974:

The good: Stevie Wonder, Hank
Aaron, Jimmy Connors, Billie Jean
King
The bad: Inflation, gas shortages,
Watergate
The inevitable: Richard Nixon, facing
impeachment, resigns from office,
the first American President to
do so.

ELLY read the manuscript of *The F Factor* with a queasy sense of déjà vu. Could there really be more than one glamorous journalist-turned-novelist with impressive equipment and technique running around the city? Was the character of Evan Rhinelander based on Owen Casals? Elly wasn't exactly sure, only ninety-five percent certain. Innocent until proven guilty, she reminded herself, and gave Owen the benefit of the doubt.

"Do you know a writer named Jane Gresch?" she asked Owen.

"The feminist fruitcake who wrote 'Boobs' and 'Butts' for *Downtown*?" asked Owen. "I've met her."

"Enough to fuck her?"

"What is this? The Inquisition?" he replied, telling Elly all she needed to know.

"She's written a book about you. And your cock," said Elly.

"No way!" said Owen.

"All ten inches," said Elly.

At North Star, Elly did what her mother had done throughout her career in retailing: she showed an instinctive talent for sales and merchandising. Just as her mother knew how to sell a new silhouette, Elly knew how to sell a new book. In Washington, Elly had turned in outstanding sales records at Pappagallo. She created the same bottom-line magic for North Star. Elly and Lincky had worked together on project after project.

At the height of discomania, Lincky published a dance-craze book that Elly promoted with dance contests that made local television news and entertainment shows.

"Every time there's another contest, we go back for another printing," Lincky told Elly. "You've turned a nothing book we paid very little for into a real winner."

When Elly and Lincky learned that North Star's resident astrologer had originally started out as a psychologist, Lincky hit the editorial angle and Elly created a publicity gold mine. Lincky guided the astrologer into writing a series of books on Astroanalysis and Elly found that selling talk-show bookers a Star Shrink made the author a natural for television.

"We even got Merv Griffin," said Elly. "And the local CBS station is talking about a three-times-a-week slot on their nine A.M. show."

When a romance novel writer turned out to be a Methodist minister as well as an author, Elly persuaded him to perform a wedding at the North Star booth at the annual convention of the Paperback & Magazine Dealers of America. The lucky newlyweds—he drove a truck for a paperback wholesaler and she worked in a Chicago chain store—won a wedding trip paid for by North Star. Both the national print media and network television covered the wedding and billed it as a triumph of real-life love, romance, and marriage. As a result, the author, the author's books, and North Star got priceless free coverage.

"You can sell anything," Lincky told Elly.

"Except myself," replied Elly.

When Lincky bought *The F Factor*, she and Elly worked together once again. Lincky was Jane's editor. Elly handled the publicity.

"*The F Factor* is funny but you can make it funnier. It's sad, but you can make it sadder. It's sexy, but you can make it sexier," Lincky told Jane at a three-hour editoral lunch. "I feel you held yourself back a little while you were writing."

"I wanted to get it published," said Jane, laughing at the fact that her idea of holding back was most editors' idea of going too far.

"You're outrageous," said Lincky. "Now be more outrageous. Put in the things you left out. I know there must be at least a few."

Jane remembered that her mouth wasn't the only place Owen liked to put strawberry ice cream.

"No problem," said Jane. She took the manuscript home and spent one solid month of twelve-hour days responding to all of Lincky's marginal comments, sharpening the story line as Lincky had suggested and, of course, being as outrageous as possible.

When Jane returned the revised manuscript, Lincky was delighted with the changes.

"But I'm not, repeat *not*, going to let Gordon read the revisions," said Lincky. "He'll have a stroke."

By the time *The F Factor* was published, Elly had resolved her conflicts about working with a woman who had once been a rival. Owen had convinced her that his affair with Jane had been over for a decade. She was an old flame.

"Yesterday's news," said Owen. "Hell, I even forgot she was alive."

"She's definitely alive," Elly told Owen. "And my job is to help sell her book."

"Sexy trash," said Owen dismissively. "No one's going to read it."

"Sexy trash sells," said Elly. "Although I don't happen to think that the book is trash. Jane is a good writer."

When Lincky introduced her to Jane Gresch, Elly was prepared, both personally and professionally.

"We've met. About ten years ago. In Owen Casals' apartment on Thirteenth Street," said Elly.

"You're the one with the pink lipstick, aren't you?" asked Jane, remembering the tall, thin woman. "Did you ever see that sleazeball creep again?"

"I married him," said Elly.

Even Jane was taken aback for a moment.

"So now what?" she asked, sure that her hopes for a dazzling publicity push were down the drain.

"So now I'm going to make you into a star," said Elly.

Jane looked at Elly to make sure she wasn't kidding. Then she nodded, impressed by Elly's professionalism.

"Does Owen know he's the model for Evan Rhinelander?"

"Of course," said Elly. "I told him."

"Doesn't he care? Isn't he worried that when the book is published everyone will find out what a shithead he was?"

"No. Owen thinks that anything women do is unimportant. 'No one's going to read it,' he told me."

"I have a feeling Owen's in for a bit of surprise," said Lincky mildly.

North Star published *The F Factor* in the spring of 1974. The ad, written by Lincky herself, featured a list of F-words: Fun. Female. Feminist. Freedom. Friends. Frankness. Fabulous. The headline read: "WHICH WORD IS THE F WORD?" The tag line was: "Read *The F Factor* and decide for yourself."

"Great ad!" said Hank.

"Great book," replied Lincky. "It's going to bring North Star into the major leagues."

"Still the baseball fan?" teased Hank.

"Not since Hank Greenberg retired," replied Lincky.

"You mean there's hope for me?"

"Hope for what?" asked Lincky.

"Dinner?"

Lincky hesitated. Just because she and Hank were able to be in the same room together without murdering each other didn't mean that Lincky wanted to get any closer to him. On the other hand, the energy, brains, and imagination that had attracted her years before still fascinated her. Dinner couldn't hurt, she told herself. As long as it was dinner on her terms.

"I'll make a deal with you, Hank. If *The F Factor* hits the bestseller list, I'll take you to dinner. *You* pick the place. It'll be my treat."

"When it hits the list," replied Hank. "*When.*"

The F Factor started to sell when the first ads appeared but what really broke the ice was a rave review of *The F Factor* in *Downtown* by Bartlett Crispen, America's grand old man of smut. The review and the ensuing publicity bonanza were masterminded and engineered by Elly.

Bartlett Crispen was notorious as much for the sexually blunt books he had written in English and published in France during the Forties and Fifties as for the landmark Supreme Court case of the early Sixties that bore his name. The lawsuit came about when an American paperback house published Crispen's hitherto banned books in the United States, making them available in bookstores, airports, and drugstores throughout the country.

Bartlett, who had never received so much as a traffic ticket, found himself embroiled in an obscenity action that eventually reached all the way to the Supreme Court. In what would be a historic decision, the Court struck down all existing state laws on pornography, and the F-word (in its printed form at least) was declared legally kosher.

At eighty-six, Bartlett had more or less lost his marbles and was not allowed out except with an attendant. He seemed to think he was still married to his first wife and living in

Kansas City working as a ticket seller for the Nickelodeon. Wafty as Bartlett was on most occasions, when it came to the written (filthy) word, his mind magically cleared and he became as sharp as he'd been thirty years before.

Barry Goldsmith, the articles editor at *Downtown*, had come of age reading Bartlett's d.b.'s and had once written a column about his adolescent masturbation habits inspired by smuggled-from-Europe copies of Bartlett's notorious novels. Elly remembered the column when she ran into Barry on the 42nd Street shuttle.

"We've just published a book by a woman who writes about sex the way Bartlett Crispen did," Elly told Barry, wondering, as she always did, why the shuttle smelled the way it did. A revolting yet compelling combination of sugar, sweat, and filth nowhere else experienced.

"No kidding! Sounds hot!" Barry said, suddenly flooded with fond memories of himself at seventeen whacking off morning, noon, night, and whenever possible in between. *Those* were what people meant when they talked about the good old days, Barry thought. Screw the nickel Coke and the 10-cent subway ride. "Send me a copy. If I like it, I'll ask Bartlett to review it."

Elly was right, thought Barry, when he skimmed *The F Factor*. Jane Gresch wrote about cock the way she'd written about tits and thighs: a woman obsessed.

Barry sent his hero Bartlett a copy of the book with a request for a review. *Downtown* was always looking for ideas that combined elevated literary sensibility with sexual outrageousness. *The F Factor* seemed to be ideal.

66

JANE AND
ELLY AND
LINCKY

DIED IN 1974:

Jack Benny, Duke Ellington, Chet
Huntley, Walter Lippmann, Ed
Sullivan, Jacqueline Susann, Earl
Warren

IN his review of *The F Factor*, Bartlett, who most people thought
was dead, praised Jane's novel as being a book that he wished
he had written himself.

"The author uses four letter words like Heifetz uses the
violin," Bartlett raved in the review he sent in two weeks later.
He also praised the fact that Jane wrote about sex from a
woman's point of view, saying that, although he himself had
written extensively about sex and the sex act, he had always
wondered—but never quite known—exactly how women felt
about eroticism and what they said about men when men
weren't around to hear. Now, he wrote, having read *The F
Factor*, he knew.

What Bartlett had learned, he went on to say, was that as many orgasms were due to thespian talent as to biology. Not all male members, he had discovered from the pages of *The F Factor*, were inevitably the size and hardness of baseball bats. Some were disappointingly small, limp, or thin. Women, he had found out, had fantasies of being sandwiched between two lovers. Women, Bartlett found much to his delight and amazement, dreamed of hot and horny interludes with total strangers. They imagined having sex with Robert Redford or Montgomery Clift even as they moaned and told their boyfriends and husbands that the earth had moved. Women liked romance. They also liked to get down and dirty.

The F Factor was a revelation, Bartlett wrote. He declared himself rejuvenated.

Downtown ran the review on the front page and Bartlett's comments, liberally sprinkled with four-, five-, and ten-letter words, were what broke the dam. *The F Factor* went from invisible to notorious overnight.

Customers stormed into bookstores wanting to buy *The F Factor*. Elly's office was deluged with requests for review copies, and reviews—good and bad but never neutral—began to appear in newspapers in Boston, New York, Dallas, Miami, Chicago, and Los Angeles. With each controversial review, copies of *The F Factor*, only a few days before destined for return to North Star, began to sell.

"I never thought it would happen," said Gordon.

"I always knew it would," said Lincky.

Elly, knowing that publicity created publicity, arranged for Jane, now being hailed as the standard bearer for liberated modern women, to pose for a photograph with Bartlett. The photo, showing Bartlett's ancient claw draped suspiciously near Jane's left breast, was picked up by newspapers across the country. On the strength of the increasing publicity, Lincky ordered a second printing, increased the ad budget, and told Elly to book a national publicity tour for Jane.

"Boston, Chicago, San Francisco, and Los Angeles," Lincky told Elly, naming the cities to be included on the tour after she had consulted the sales sheets to see where sales of *The F Factor* were strongest.

Talk show producers called Elly, begging to have the outspoken, salty-tongued Jane as a guest. Jane's appearances on local New York shows further stimulated sales and Lincky ordered a third printing. *The F Factor* appeared on the bottom of the *New York Times* bestseller list in the first week of July and its appearance on the list stimulated sales even further. Stacks of *The F Factor* that had once languished in the rear of stores were now moved to the front, and copies were put into bookstore windows. The bandwagon was rolling.

All the things that were supposed to have happened to Owen were happening to Jane.

Not entirely to Lincky's surprise, Gordon Geiger began to talk about how he had spotted *The F Factor* from the very beginning.

"There was never about doubt *The F Factor* at North Star," he told Ted Spandorff. "The minute it came into the house, we knew it was going to be a big winner."

In private, he was more realistic.

"You twisted my arm but you were right," he told Lincky. "There'll be a big bonus for you at the end of the year."

"I'd also like to be named editor in chief," Lincky said.

"I'll think about it," said Gordon. "I don't want to hurt Erwin's feelings."

"What feelings? He spends his days in a gin-and-Valium coma," said Lincky. "You'll have to wake him up to give him the news."

Other admirers of *The F Factor* now began to come out of the closet. Younger women further down the ladder in publishing came up to Lincky at parties and publishing conferences to tell her how much they had loved *The F Factor*.

"I'm so glad *someone* had the courage to publish it," said Cindy Hoffman of Parmenides Press. "I wanted to buy it but Adrian absolutely refused."

"Gordon refused at first, too. He said it was pornography," Lincky said. "I practically had to threaten to quit before he'd let me make an offer."

"I begged Ted to publish it," Rhoda Black of Raintree Press told Lincky. "He said he wouldn't dream of it. He said that no one would care about Francine Cord's orgasms."

"He didn't think anyone would care about Evan Rhinelander's cock?"

Fan mail for Jane poured into North Star's offices. Flattering quotes about *The F Factor* from famous writers appeared in magazines and newspapers. Women's groups all over the country wanted Jane to lecture and a few of the more adventurous Women's Study college courses even assigned the book as required reading. Cash began to flow into North Star and agents who had never dealt with North Star started to call.

"Melanie Cornell has just delivered a new book," Archibald Duzen told Lincky. Archibald Duzen was a powerful agency head who had never before deigned to sell to North Star. Melanie Cornell was a tits-and-glitz author whose novels were solid midlist bestsellers. "Her publisher is balking at my terms. How'd you like to have a shot at it? Based on what you did for *The F Factor*, I think North Star could mount the kind of campaign Melanie needs in order to get to number one."

Hank Greene did not forget the deal he and Lincky had made. He called her up as soon as the *Times* bestseller list came into his office with *The F Factor* in the number seven slot.

"You owe me a dinner," he reminded Lincky.

"A deal's a deal," said Lincky. "Have you picked a restaurant?"

"Yes," said Hank. "Maxim's."

"Maxim's is in Paris!"

"I know."

"Look, Hank. I said I'd buy you dinner and I will. I'm not going to fly you to Paris, too."

"Who said anything about your taking me to Paris? You buy the dinner. I've got two tickets to Paris."

"I am not going to go to Paris with you."

"Didn't you just tell me that a deal's a deal?"

"Yes."

"And didn't you tell me to pick the restaurant?"

"Yes."

"Well, I've picked Maxim's. Now, are you going to welsh or not?"

Hank stayed at the Plaza Athenée on the Right Bank. Lincky stayed at the Lenox on the Left Bank. She occupied Room 54, a compact beamed-and-whitewashed balconied duplex overlooking the Rue de l'Université. Although she and Hank slept apart, they spent the weekend together. They dined at Maxim's, browsed in the bookstalls along the Seine, had iced vodka and beluga at Caviar Kaspia on the Madeleine, shopped for Hank at Charvet in the Place Vendôme and for Lincky at the Sonia Rykiel boutique in the Rue de Grenelle. They bought bread at Poilane, cheese at Androuet, and wine at Fauchon for a picnic in the Luxembourg gardens.

"I brought a picnic for us once," said Lincky, spreading some *reblochon* on a chunk of bread. "What happened to it?"

"At first I was going to smash the bottle I was so mad," said Hank, sipping the Gigondas Lincky had chosen. "Then I decided it would be a waste of wine. I decided to get drunk instead. I opened the bottle and began to drink. I didn't know wine could taste so good. I was used to rotgut. I realized that you must have picked it out specially. I remembered that your family was in the wine business. It made me even more miserable. It made me *really* realize what I had lost when I drove you away."

Lincky looked surprised. Hank was saying that their breakup had been his fault.

"Do you really think what I did was your fault? I've always blamed myself. My behavior was inexcusable."

"Neither of us covered ourselves with glory, that's for sure," said Hank. "I was right about you: you were scared. What I didn't realize was that I was scared, too. I was terrified of you. I thought you were some kind of aristocrat far above me. I resented you for making me feel inferior. So I acted like a crude sex maniac to cover up my own sense of inadequacy. I was young and dumb."

"So was I," said Lincky.

They were both silent for a moment.

"I've changed," said Hank.

"That's obvious," said Lincky.

"I don't mean just the decent clothes and better manners. I've changed inside. Even though I still have plenty of hang-ups about my childhood, I'm not the insecure jerk I used to be," he said. "I've never forgotten the impact you had on me. You're one of the reasons I did the overhaul on myself."

"I feel flattered," said Lincky. "I never thought I made the slightest dent on you."

"Only like a twenty megaton weapon," said Hank.

They cleaned up their picnic and Hank dropped Lincky off at the Lenox.

"I'll see you later," he said, referring to the plans they had made earlier to have dinner at L'Ami Louis. They both wanted to try the famous roast chicken and *pommes allumettes*.

Lincky hesitated.

"Would you like to see my suite?" she asked. She seemed almost shy. "It must be one of the most charming hotel rooms in all of Paris."

"Are you sure?" asked Hank, understanding the invitation.

"I'm sure for now. For Paris," she said, putting boundaries on her desire.

They made love under the skylight and, several hours later, ate Antoine Magnin's fine dinner with excellent appetite.

67
ELLY

TOP MOVIE GROSSERS IN 1974:

The Towering Inferno
Earthquake
The Exorcist

IN the years since the publication of *The 39th Parallel*, Owen's dreams had not died, only gone underground. *Precincts of Childhood* had been a severe disappointment. Raintree had done a feeble job and books seemed to have gone straight from the bindery to the remainder tables. A return to journalism, despite Owen's initial confidence, was impossible. Hubert Dessanges had not been willing to hire an ex-*Newsflash* star whose contacts had dried up and whose byline had been forgotten.

"News moves fast. I'm afraid you haven't kept up," Hubert told Owen.

"Reporting is a young man's job," Ray Jessup told Owen when Owen hit a dead end in his job search. "Face it. You're almost forty. You're not a kid anymore."

With Hank Greene's encouragement, Owen eventually discovered a talent for commercially viable hostility. He was writing television scripts for various cop shows and hard-boiled paperback mysteries under a variety of pseudonyms. Unlike

Glen Sinclair, Owen did not thrive in the embrace of anonymity.

"I hate writing this shit," he told Elly.

"So write something better."

"I did," Owen said. "Look where it got me. Nowhere."

At first Owen refused to read *The F Factor*, telling Elly that everything he heard about it made it sound like unmitigated trash. He had finally picked it up the week that it first reached number one on the bestseller list. It was ten years after Elly had defied her parents and moved in with Owen. Six years had passed since Elly had lost her baby in the demonstration on Centre Street. Four since Elly and Owen had had a son, Brian, named after Elly's father, two since their daughter, Angela, had been born.

It was almost a decade since *The 39th Parallel* had been published and eight years had evaporated since *Precincts* had failed. It had been a very long time since Owen had felt good about himself.

The F Factor was about to make him feel worse than ever.

The F Factor was the story of Owen's affair with Jane Gresch—told from Jane's point of view. She wrote about their sex life, her contributions to his work, their battles, their breakup. She accused him of stealing her ideas and passing them off as his own. Practically all she had changed, as far as Owen could see, was their names and their professions. *The F Factor* wasn't a novel. It was autobiography masquerading as fiction. And semipornographic fiction at that, in Owen's opinion, the rantings and ravings of a man-hating ballbreaker.

Jane had exposed their most intimate moments, portrayed him as an unfeeling sexual athlete, a macho egomaniacal pseudo-Hemingway dependent on his girlfriend's creative energy and, finally, in the worst blow of all, as a washed-up has-been. He couldn't even sue unless he wanted to admit to the world that his ex-girlfriend thought he was a thief and a nobody. Suing would only give Jane and her book *more* publicity.

Owen's bitterness and frustration erupted when Lincky sold the paperback rights of *The F Factor* for two million dollars, breaking the record Doubleday had set earlier that year when it had sold *Jaws* for $1.85 million.

"*The F Factor* is beneath discussion. It's an absolute piece of crap," he told Elly, when she came home with the news about the paperback sale.

"That's not what a lot of critics think. It's not what a million readers think," said Elly. "And it's not what I think. I thought it was terrific."

"You should be embarrassed to be associated with it," said Owen. Usually tightly wound, Owen seemed almost on the verge of losing control. His hand shook as he lit a cigarette.

"Embarrassed? I'm proud. Jane's book happens to be an important one," replied Elly.

"Proud to publicize your husband's affair?" Owen asked.

"Publicizing books and authors—including Jane Gresch—is my job!" Elly said, her own frustration finally erupting. "I tried to do the same for you but you wouldn't let me!"

"So now it's my fault?" Owen asked. The scars surrounding *The 39th Parallel*, never completely confronted, had still not healed.

"Jane's cooperative! Jane works her ass off! *You* were too pure and holy for publicity. *You* said it was vulgar. *You* hated your publicity tour! *You* told me to back off!" Elly replied.

"We were fucking each other blind. I used to shuttle between the two of you," Owen said.

"Now you're having an affair with someone else, aren't you? That secretary on the show?" asked Elly after a moment. She suddenly understood the reason behind Owen's recent absences and the unconvincing excuses that he used to explain them.

"That's right. I *am* having an affair," said Owen. "Haven't you heard of open marriage?"

"Of course I've heard of open marriage but I never discussed it with you, much less agreed to one," Elly said.

Elly hated to admit it but Jane had nailed Owen. Evan Rhinelander, the hero of *The F Factor*, was exactly like Owen: proud, macho, emotionally remote, sexually obsessed. And a two-timer.

"You were right about Owen," Elly told her sister. "He's my perfect neurotic type. Why do I always seem to pick men who make me suffer? What's the matter with me?"

"If you're not miserable, you don't think it's love," replied Margaret. She wished she could do something to help with the pain.

Elly wasn't the only one who suffered. Owen suffered, too. The tables had turned. The situation was reversed. Now it was Owen who raged over publicity, reviews, and bestseller lists. Now it was Owen who felt sick and crazy with envy. This time, Owen was on the outside looking in.

Jane was on the inside looking out. The views were very different.

68

JANE

1 9 7 5 :

Elton John signs $8 million recording
contract.
Stevie Wonder gets $13 million.
Free agent relief pitcher Catfish
Hunter signs record $2.85 million
contract with New York Yankee
owner George Steinbrenner.

BEWARE of answered prayers, said Saint Teresa. Be careful of
what you want because you might get it, warns the cynic.

"I want to be famous," Jane had said ever since she could
remember.

"I want you to be famous," Eliot had said since the earliest
months of their marriage. "I want a wife who's a winner."

The pandemonium and the clamorous success surrounding the publication of *The F Factor* made Jane more famous than
she had ever dreamed and Eliot had ever hoped. Jane was
ready to be admired. Eliot looked forward to moving in worlds
that had once seemed beyond his reach. Both imagined that all
their problems would disappear Neither was prepared for the
reality of sudden fame.

Jane's half share of the two million dollars that Lincky got
for the paperback rights to *The F Factor* made Jane into an
overnight millionaire.

"A million dollars?" said Jane when Lincky telephoned her with the news. Jane didn't believe her at first. "For me?"

"For you," said Lincky.

"You're sure?"

"I'm sure."

"Jesus Christ!" said Jane. She wasn't exactly sure how she felt. Scared more than anything, although that didn't make any sense.

"Jesus Christ is right. It's a new record," said Lincky. "Enjoy!"

"A million dollars!" Jane told Eliot, calling him as soon as she hung up with Lincky. She still didn't believe it. The reality of an almost instant million dollars still hadn't sunk in.

"That's wonderful! Congratulations!" said Eliot. There was obvious excitement in his usually calm voice. He had always wanted to be rich. Now, between his earnings and Jane's, they were.

"Now what?" said Jane. She had a feeling that the rug had been pulled out from under her.

"Now enjoy it."

"That's what Lincky said. Does that mean I can buy a mink coat?" asked Jane. One of the few material luxuries Jane had ever coveted was a fur coat.

"Sure," said Eliot. "It means you can buy three."

"One will be enough," said Jane. Then she added, "For openers."

If she was going to be a millionaire, she might as well act like one.

The million dollars was only the beginning.

As the publishing success of *The F Factor* continued, the value of other rights increased. Lincky agreed to license a special Main Selection with the Wordsmith Book Club, which had originally turned down *The F Factor*.

"They'll do a special mailing just for *The F Factor*," Lincky told Hank, informing him of the deal she had negotiated.

"They've advanced two hundred and fifty thousand dollars. They think they can sell a quarter of a million hardcover copies. At least."

Conducting an auction between four major film studios, Hank sold the movie rights to *The F Factor* for a million dollars.

"Another million? What is this? My standard fee?" asked Jane when Hank told her the news.

"Don't get greedy," said Hank. "Foreign rights will only add up to half a million."

"Half a million?" repeated Jane. "What a comedown!"

In six months, Jane made more money than her father had in an entire lifetime. Although she wasn't in Elton John's or Stevie Wonder's league, she could play in Catfish Hunter's. Compared with what she was accustomed to, Jane's finances were somewhere up there in the stratosphere and Jane was giddy from the altitude.

She went on a wild spending spree, buying thousands of dollars worth of clothes and accessories at Saks and Bloomingdale's. She bought her brother a new car and treated her parents to a European vacation. She took groups of friends— and casual acquaintances—to lavish restaurant dinners, charging everything to her American Express card.

"It's fine to enjoy your money but you're going overboard," said Eliot when Jane almost passed out at a twelve thousand dollar American Express bill.

At Jane's request, Eliot put her on a generous but sensible budget.

"I don't know what I'd do without you," she told him.

The only problem Jane had ever had with money was when there had not been enough and she had sweated the rent. Now, it seemed, there was almost too much money. Thoughts about money and conversations about money seemed to be taking over Jane's life. She zoned out when Eliot,

Hank, or the accountant Eliot hired tried to explain the reasoning behind various tax strategies and financial decisions.

"If we push off part of the income to January, you'll have use of the money for another sixteen months since taxes aren't due until April," Hank told Jane in September 1974, asking her permission to request North Star to hold back certain payments until the following year.

"Can you explain that in English?" Jane asked.

"That was English," Hank said.

"You're in the fifty percent bracket. Twelve percent triple tax-free bonds are worth over twenty percent in real yield to you," Eliot explained, telling Jane that he had invested a quarter of a million dollars in New York State dormitory bonds.

"Are you sure?" asked Jane. She didn't have a clue what he was talking about.

"Of course I'm sure," replied Eliot. "Don't you remember? I used to work at a brokerage company."

"If you prepay New York State taxes, you'll be able to write the amount off your federal return," said the accountant, asking Jane to sign the State return and write a check for one hundred twenty thousand dollars to submit with it.

"And I won't go to jail?" asked Jane. Everything the accountant told her sounded vaguely dishonest.

"No. I'm not in business to send my clients to jail," replied the accountant.

Jane's hand shook almost uncontrollably as she signed her name and tore the check out of her checkbook.

"I've never written a check that big," she told Eliot, feeling slightly sick. She remembered the Perry Street apartment for which she and Wilma had paid $98 a month.

Jane didn't comprehend the mind-boggling complexity of the tax forms, investment agreements, and other financial documents she seemed to be forever signing. In her more paranoid moments, she was sure that no one else did either.

"Are you sure I'll get paid?" she asked Hank when he and Lincky negotiated a three-year payment schedule for Jane.

"Of course. I get ten percent," said Hank. "You don't think I'm going to let myself get screwed out of that, do you? For me to get paid, I have to make sure that you get paid."

"Income averaging? I never heard of it," Jane told the accountant when he suggested it.

"It's a well-known technique for saving taxes," replied the accountant, who had given up trying to explain her finances to Jane and now worked with Eliot instead. "Is your husband there?"

"I hate money! I used to pay forty-nine dollars for my share of the rent, ten for the phone, and eight to Con Ed. I used to understand money!" Jane panicked as she leafed through her dense, number-studded Internal Revenue return.

"You used to be poor," Eliot reminded her, trying to introduce a bit of perspective, trying, God forbid, to make her laugh. Money seemed to have destroyed Jane's sense of humor.

Jane didn't—or couldn't—react.

"I used to be happy! Life used to be simple! Now I have depreciation and tax shelters to worry about! I have accountants and tax lawyers and investment advisors to cope with! I used to have the landlord and the fag who cut my hair once a month to worry about. Period. I liked it better the old way!" Jane said, as if Eliot hadn't spoken. Tears intermingled with rage.

She even hated the mink coat she'd bought for herself.

"You never wear it. Is something the matter with it?" Eliot asked. He had been looking forward to escorting his elegantly dressed wife to nice restaurants and stylish parties. Instead, Jane continued to drape herself in her thrift shop shawls and long, flowing capes.

"It's an old lady's style. Whenever I put it on, I feel like I'm wearing my mother's coat," she told Eliot.

"You picked it out," Eliot said.

"Don't remind me. It was so fucking expensive, I got conservative," said Jane. "Since when did you ever see me in conservative clothes?"

"Have it restyled," said Eliot.

"What?" said Jane. "And throw good money after bad?"

The coat hung in her closet and Jane felt guilty every time she opened the door and got a glimpse of it.

69
JANE

1975:

FORD TO NY: DROP DEAD

—*Daily News* headline on president's
response to New York City's fiscal
crisis

MOVING was Eliot's idea. It was Eliot who called the brokers—
Eliot who looked at a score of apartments, Eliot who found the
one he told Jane they should buy: a spacious seven-room
terraced penthouse on Riverside Drive. There was plenty of
space: for a baby, even though Jane wasn't pregnant and wasn't
even thinking about it, and for a live-in maid, if they wanted
one.

"And," Eliot added, pointing out the advantages, "plenty
of space for a full-scale office for you."

Everyone agreed that Eliot and Jane were making a big
mistake. They paid the then ridiculous sum of fifty thousand
dollars for the apartment. Everyone told them that they were
overpaying. Everyone told them that they had been had. The
tax lawyer told Jane and Eliot that they should move to Connecticut.

"If you live in Connecticut, you'll save the New York City

income tax and the unincorporated business tax, not to mention New York State taxes," he said.

The accountant said that the city was on a steep downhill slope. Crime was rampant, the city's economy was shot, New York was filthy, ungovernable, and fit only for those who couldn't afford to live elsewhere.

"A lot of my writer clients have moved to Connecticut," he told Jane and Eliot.

"My practice and my colleagues are here and so are our friends. I don't want to move to Connecticut and commute," said Eliot.

"I don't want to move to Connecticut either. I hate grass and trees. They're boring. Why should I be bored just to save money?" said Jane, agreeing with Eliot. She had gotten the idea for *The F Factor* because of the people she had met and the things she had done while living in the city. New York City had become inextricably connected with her creative life and Jane did not want to leave it.

The accountants and tax lawyers exchanged glances that said that Eliot and Jane were foolish spendthrifts. Easy come, easy go seemed to be their disapproving, unspoken message. Eliot disagreed.

"Letting money dictate your life is letting the tail wag the dog," he told Jane, saying that he thought the apartment would not only be a nice place to live but, since New York real estate was at an all-time low, an excellent investment as well.

Jane, in one of her more rational moods, thought that, as usual, Eliot made the most sense. The rest of the time Jane alternated between listening to "everyone" and listening to Eliot.

"It's a fucking fortune! We're not that rich!" Jane said when it came time to sign the contract for the new apartment. "The accountant said we're overpaying."

"The accountant lives in Nassau County," said Eliot. "He hasn't kept up with Manhattan prices."

"My parents paid ten thousand dollars for the house I

grew up in!" Jane told Eliot. "A whole house! And we're spending fifty thousand for an apartment!"

"We can back out if you want," said Eliot.

"You're sure we can afford it?" asked Jane.

"I'm sure. You've just earned almost three million dollars and I'm not exactly a deadbeat."

"Suppose I never earn another dime?" Jane asked. "Suppose I can't keep up the payments?"

"Do you want me to sign the contract alone?" asked Eliot.

"Then you'd be responsible for the payments?"

"Yes," he said. "The apartment would be mine. I'd be entirely responsible for it."

"You don't mind, do you?" asked Jane, thinking that she was sticking Eliot with an unfair part of the financial burden.

"Of course not," said Eliot. "Not when I see how upset you are about the payments."

Since the apartment, although architecturally gracious, was old and run-down, Jane and Eliot spent another fifty thousand dollars to rewire, air-condition, and renovate it. Eliot hired the architect and selected the contractor.

"Six thousand dollars for painting?" asked Jane, looking at the estimates.

"It's a big apartment," said Eliot. "The walls are in bad shape and need extensive spackling and plastering. It's a competitive bid and the painters have an excellent reputation."

"I sure as hell hope so," said Jane, who remembered brown bag lunches and taking the bus instead of a taxi just a year ago.

Jane couldn't seem to get used to the radical change in her finances. She worried about bankruptcy, debtor's prison and other financial catastrophes. Over and over, Eliot did the simple arithmetic that proved that they could easily afford the apartment and the renovations and still have plenty of money left over.

After all, he reminded Jane, his practice was well established and more successful with each passing year. She, meanwhile, had earned literally a small fortune. Money, Eliot said, was the least of their problems.

Jane didn't feel any better when it came time to move into the new apartment. The large apartment, with its fantastic views of the Hudson River, its formal marble lobby with its huge crystal chandeliers and Oriental rugs, its imposing uniformed doormen and elevator men seemed light years away from her Perry Street walk-up. It was also a big jump upward from the comfortable but unpretentious apartment on West 74th Street that she had shared with Eliot ever since the first days of their marriage.

"I feel like an impostor," Jane confessed to Eliot when they moved into their new and freshly decorated apartment. She was intimidated by the place in which she now lived and felt as if she were an interloper who didn't really belong there. "Me? Jane Gresch? In a penthouse?"

"Why should you feel like an impostor?" replied Eliot. "After all, you were the one who earned a good part of the money that allowed us to move here."

"I did?" asked Jane in genuine surprise.

Jane's work was real to her. And so was the pleasure she derived from it. However, the money *The F Factor* had earned still wasn't real to Jane. It was just a bunch of huge numbers that scared her almost to death.

Thanks to his sessions with Martha Schneider, Eliot had no problem adjusting to his new status in life. Nor did he have a problem dealing with the decorator, the maid, the doormen, and the super. When the paperback edition of *The F Factor* headed straight for the number one slot on the bestseller lists, Eliot had no trouble deciding that a beach house on East Hampton's Lily Pond Lane was next in order.

"We can afford it," he told Jane.

"We can?" she asked.

70
JANE

1 9 7 5 :

A total woman caters to her man's
special quirks, whether it be in
salads, sex or sports.

—Marabel Morgan,
The Total Woman

MONEY, high finance, and a dizzying change in lifestyle were
the tangible byproducts of Jane's success. A feeling of emotional dislocation was its psychological byproduct. Just as there
were many times when Jane felt she didn't really belong in a
penthouse, there were also many times—money completely
aside—when she felt she didn't really deserve the success that
The F Factor had brought her.

"I turned my romance with Owen into a novel that a lot of
people responded to. What if it's just a fluke? What if I just
lucked out?" she asked Eliot.

"What makes you so convinced it was just luck? Don't you
think talent had anything to do with your success?" he asked.

"Yeah. I guess I'm talented," said Jane. "But I was lucky,
too. And what if luck, like lightning, doesn't strike twice?"

Jane dreaded the prospect of being a flash-in-the-pan.
Although she sometimes joked about it, in her deepest heart
of hearts, she feared that she would become another of Ameri-

ca's here-today, gone-tomorrow, instant, instantly disposable celebrities.

"I'll be the answer to a trivia question of the Eighties," she told Eliot.

Jane fretted constantly about her ability. At the precise time when her talent was being dramatically confirmed by the outside world, Jane found herself prey to devastating episodes of almost crippling insecurity.

"I'm famous. Most of the reviews of *The F Factor* were better than just good. I've been called original, exceptional, even brilliant," she told Eliot in one of her calmer moments, turning to him for help in trying to understand her paradoxical, incomprehensible reactions. "Why am I so depressed? Unhappy and afraid?"

"Probably because your life is much more complicated now than it used to be," he said, reminding Jane of her repeatedly stated nostalgia for the simpler times of a cheap Village apartment and a secure job with an appreciative and generous boss. "I have a feeling that you're also afraid you won't be able to write another book as successful as *The F Factor*."

Unexpected tears came to Jane's eyes as Eliot's words hit home. Eliot seemed to be confirming Jane's own worst fear.

"I am afraid," Jane said. "Terrified. What do I do about it?"

"Give yourself a chance to get used to your success," said Eliot. "One day you won't feel so overwhelmed by your finances. One day you'll get an idea for a new book. The nice thing is that you don't have to rush into anything. You can afford to wait."

"I can?" asked Jane. She had become almost like a child who needed to have everything explained.

Before Eliot could reply, Jane threw her arms around him and covered his face with kisses.

"I love you!" Jane exclaimed. "You always know what I should do. You always know just what to say. You always know how to make me feel better!"

Eliot Landauer smiled. It was a smile of mixed emotions. He was good at taking care of people. It was the basis of his profession. He was afraid that it was also becoming the basis of his marriage. Instead of being able to relax at home, Eliot found that he had to support and care for Jane the way he supported and cared for his patients. He told himself that the situation was temporary and that Jane would soon adjust.

Despite Eliot's reassurances, Jane was persistently haunted by fears of being a one-book writer. She felt that she should be writing a second book but she couldn't decide what it should be about.

"I can't get an idea," she told Eliot in late 1975. "I'm a blank."

"Be patient," said Eliot. "Don't be so hard on yourself."

"You gave me the idea for *The F Factor*. Can't you think of something else?" asked Jane.

"That was only after you'd been blocked for a long time. I'm a psychologist. Not a writer."

When Eliot failed to come up with an idea that Jane liked, she got angry.

"You don't give a damn if I ever write another book or not!"

After the first adoring rush of critical me-too's following Bartlett Crispen's *Downtown* review, came the inevitable backlash. The outside world began to confirm Jane's own worst fears about herself at a time when she was at her most defenseless. For everyone who had loved *The F Factor*, someone else now seemed to loathe it. Penelope Astrachan, an American novelist high up in literary circles, reviewed *The F Factor* for the Sunday *Times* and called it "trivial and ditsy." The *Chicago Tribune* reviewer called it "vulgar, junky, a book for people who never read."

"Penelope Astrachan is brilliant. Her opinion matters," Jane told Lincky, calling her editor in tears when she saw the review.

"It's one person's opinion," said Lincky. "Besides, Penelope Astrachan has written half a dozen books and not one of them has ever been on the bestseller list. Hasn't it occurred to you that she might be jealous?"

Lincky's words helped but only for a moment.

" 'Vulgar, junky'?" Jane quoted to Eliot. "The *Chicago Tribune* is a powerful newspaper. People are going to believe that *The F Factor* is junk."

"Do you believe it's junk?" asked Eliot.

"Sometimes," said Jane, bursting into tears.

Other times Jane's ego soared skyward with the evidence of her new importance. Raintree advertised a novel as "in the tradition of *The F Factor*."

"Lincky told me that I created a new voice for women. She was right," Jane said, showing Eliot the ad.

Publishers now sent Jane galleys for forthcoming books. They solicited quotes from her for use in their advertising and promotion.

"My name really means something. Anything Jane Gresch endorses is going to sell," she said.

Eliot wanted to enjoy their success and money. Jane often seemed to want to hide. Eliot wanted to expand their horizons. Jane tried to keep their lives the same. Eliot looked forward to attending the parties society hostesses now invited them to. Jane refused.

"I didn't know you were such a social climber," she said, insisting that Eliot refuse an invitation from a Park Avenue socialite.

Eliot suggested spending two weeks at posh La Samanna in the Caribbean where Samuel Wallenberg went every year. Jane didn't want to go.

"I wouldn't have anything to say to the rich phonies who go there," she said.

Eliot used their money for more than material indulgence.

He donated a generous sum to the Mid-Manhattan Center for Psychotherapy.

"It's an excellent cause and it's tax deductible. Plus, a donation will help me get on the board," he said.

"Then you'll have even more boring meetings to go to," said Jane.

"I don't find them boring," replied Eliot.

Adding to Jane's upset was her mail. Like Gaul, it was divided into three parts. Most of the letters were from grateful women who wrote page after page of intimate personal confessions. They, too, had been emotionally devastated by men. These readers wrote to say that Jane had written their story and they expressed their gratitude to her for putting their feelings into words. They asked her for advice in handling their heartbreak.

"I wish I could help them," she said. Although she didn't have to, Jane felt obligated to write a personal answer to every letter. She spent hours reading her mail and thoughtfully composing replies.

"Time," she told Eliot resentfully, "that I should spend planning and writing a new book."

Another chunk of mail came from people in small towns, mostly in the South and Midwest, who found *The F Factor* indecent, revolting, disgusting, filthy, nauseating, and otherwise unspeakable. Their language tended to be more obscene than *The F Factor* at its most outrageous.

"And they call *me* a pornographer!" Jane said, appalled but also frightened.

The third section of mail was by far the smallest but also the most disturbing. It came on all kinds of paper from the cheapest dimestore tablets to the most expensive bond. Sometimes signed, usually not, always explicit, the letters, invariably written by men, contained pages of bizarre, repellent, and sometimes violent sexual fantasies, often personally directed at Jane herself. Those letters made Jane feel as if *The F Factor* had somehow opened a cesspool whose diseased contents were now being directed at her.

Jane also received obscene telephone calls. She changed her phone number, but was eventually forced to get an unlisted number. In desperation, Jane finally asked Eliot to screen her mail and phone calls for her.

"I want to see only the intelligent letters. Please just throw the rest away," she wept after she noticed an unkempt, sinister-looking man hanging around across the street from their apartment building.

Success built Jane up and tore her down at the same time. The passions of strangers threatened to engulf her, then receded, leaving her feeling more vulnerable than before.

"I thought you'd be hot stuff. You're just a fat, sloppy broad," said the handsome blond entertainment editor of the local six o'clock news ten seconds before his interview with Jane.

"I just adore trash! Do you think I'd like your book?" burbled a neighbor in Jane's building as they went up in the elevator together.

"Are you really a good fuck or do you just talk a good game?" asked a total stranger who stopped Jane on 57th Street because he recognized her from a television interview.

Once again, Jane was dancing on the table holding up her skirts. People were looking but this time not all of them were laughing. Jane was crushed by the criticism and had no experience in being treated like public property. With nowhere else to turn, she focused her insecurities, anger, and confusion on her husband.

"You want to run my life!" she said, bursting into tears when Eliot suggested that Jane set aside time each day to think about an idea for a new book.

"I'm not interested in running your life," replied Eliot. He reminded Jane that she had been talking about how worried she was that she'd never get another idea. "I'm just trying to help."

"Help? That's not help!" she said, almost shouting. "It's an excuse to tell me what to do and when to do it!"

When Eliot suggested that Jane take some freelance magazine assignments as a way to start writing again, she refused.

"Why should I waste my time on articles?"

"I thought writing something short might help," said Eliot.

"I don't need help!" flared Jane. "I'm sick of being helped!"

Jane had come to loathe being understood so well. She felt she had no privacy. She no longer saw Eliot as a lover, husband, and savior. She began to see him as an invader. She felt that even her mind was no longer hers.

Jane began to accuse Eliot of being interested in her only for her money.

"The big apartment and the fancy house in East Hampton are all you care about!" she said, reminding Eliot that moving had been his decision and telling him that she had just gone along with the idea. "You couldn't afford any of this without me!"

"You couldn't afford it either, without the stocks I bought for you that have gone up and the bonds that are paying regular dividends," Eliot replied.

"All you care about is money. You don't love me. You love my money!" insisted Jane.

"I love you. I like money," replied Eliot. "What's wrong with liking money? Particularly when I handle it and you only want to ignore it? Without me, you'd have gone through your money in a year and not even known what happened to it!"

Their sex life reflected the other conflicts in their lives. Sometimes Jane would want sex three times a day. Sometimes three weeks would go by without a kiss. Eliot found that emotional exhaustion combined with Jane's erratic moods left him with little libido.

"I guess you expect me to be a Total Woman," Jane said angrily when Eliot had trouble sustaining an erection.

"I just want you to be the Jane I married," he replied.

"I'm sorry," she said later. "I know I'm impossible sometimes. I guess I'm a Total Asshole."

"You said it, I didn't," replied Eliot.

Eliot had thought that money would make him happy. He had thought that having a wife who was a winner would enhance his life. Instead, he felt increasingly disappointed and disillusioned. He was good at helping people yet his attempts to help his wife were greeted with rage and contempt. Eliot realized that he had fallen into a trap: in his relationship with Jane, he was a failure both as a husband and as a psychologist. In an attempt to rescue himself and his marriage, Eliot returned to his former analyst, Martha Schneider.

"Nothing I do is right any more," Eliot told her. "I'm a psychologist and my own wife is driving me crazy."

"Andy Warhol said that everyone would be famous for fifteen minutes," he told Dr. Schneider. "I hope that Jane's fifteen minutes are going to be over soon."

71
ELIOT

TITLES OF THE MID-SEVENTIES:

I'm O.K., You're O.K.
How To Be Your Own Best Friend
Your Erroneous Zones
Looking Out For #1

JANE'S fifteen minutes lasted through the end of 1975 and into 1976. She was alternately depressed and arrogant, dependent and resentful of that dependence. Even though he had learned to laugh when people called him "Mr. Gresch," Eliot increasingly resented being cast in the role of shrink, weeping post, accountant, lawyer, switchboard operator, and mailroom boy.

"I want to be your husband again," he told Jane.

"What's stopping you?"

"You are. I'm tired of taking care of you," Eliot said in mid-1975 as the second year of Jane's celebrity began. "It's time you grew up and started taking care of yourself. You're smart enough to get what you want. You're smart enough to deal with it."

"You wanted a famous wife," replied Jane. "Now you've got one. So what if famous isn't perfect?"

When Eliot advised Jane to see a therapist, she refused, saying that she wasn't crazy, just successful.

"You're the one who needs the shrink. Not me!" Jane said, referring to Eliot's sessions with Dr. Schneider.

When Eliot suggested that Jane hire a secretary to help her with mail, business chores, and errands, she also refused.

"I can't afford a secretary!" she said, upset by a two thousand dollar bill that had just come in from the accountant. Jane could remember a time not so long ago when she could live for months on two thousand dollars.

Eliot's own interests and accomplishments were ignored in the tidal wave of Jane's success. The money and fame resulting from *The F Factor* engulfed their lives. Almost every conversation seemed to be about Jane, her career, *The F Factor*, its foreign sales, the movie, the interview requests.

The fact that Eliot was appointed to the governor's commission on public schooling went unremarked by Jane. Eliot's selection as the associate director of the Mid-Manhattan Center for Psychotherapy went uncelebrated.

"Sometimes I feel invisible," he told his analyst.

He told his wife the same thing.

"The report our commission wrote on the need for psychological counseling at the grade school level has been adopted by the state assembly," Eliot told Jane in early 1976, proud of his success.

"The University of Michigan is having a seminar on changing women's roles since World War II and they want me to speak. Do you think I should go?" replied Jane, showing Eliot the invitation. "It would mean canceling my lecture at the New School."

"And you wonder why I have the feeling you don't even hear me," Eliot said, ignoring the piece of paper Jane thrust at him.

Although he was a student of human behavior and emotion in his professional life, in his personal life Eliot was only human.

"You're getting to be an incredible prima donna. You

believe your own press clippings," he told Jane when she summarily refused delivery of a new Mercedes because it arrived three days later than promised.

He accused Jane of being a bottomless pit of demands and a monster of self-interest. A newspaper photograph that she thought made her look fat sent Jane into a hysterical tirade that lasted for almost three days.

"I'm going to sue!" she threatened. "How dare they? I'm a celebrity!" she raged.

"You're an egomaniac! All you think about is yourself and your precious public image," Eliot said.

"My precious image is important!" yelled Jane, still incensed at the unflattering picture. "What the hell do you think pays the bills around here?"

Jane continued to accuse Eliot of loving her money more than he loved her.

"If it weren't for my money, you'd leave me," she told him.

"If I leave you, money won't have anything to do with it," he replied, "even though I'm getting tired of being your unpaid financial vice-president and getting nothing in return but complaints and accusations that I'm cheating you."

"I know I go off half-cocked sometimes. I don't really mean it when I say things like that," Jane said. "You know that, don't you?"

"Most of the time I know it," said Eliot. "It still hurts."

Jane accused Eliot of being materialistic and parasitic and, worst of all, of not being creative. She told him that he was emotionally detached, a robot posing as a man, all head and no heart. She criticized his calm and rational approach toward life.

"I wonder what your patients would say if they knew what an icy bastard you are," Jane said whenever she felt that Eliot wasn't sufficiently sympathetic to her problems.

Jane detested Martha Schneider, whom she had never met.

She alternated between berating Eliot for his weakness in turning to a double-talking Freudian quack and accusing him of having an affair with her.

"You probably do it right on the couch!" Jane would say, although on other occasions she would tell Eliot that she was sure that Dr. Schneider had a mustache and warts.

Eliot and Jane were proof that success did not guarantee happiness. They conducted their increasingly frequent battles in the psychobabble of the mid-Seventies, turning clinical terms into battering rams and the modish jargon of the Human Potential movement into nuclear devices.

"You're a narcissist. You've changed, Jane. And not for the better," Eliot said, his patience frayed by Jane's obsession with herself, her clothes, her career, her image, and her unceasing emotional demands.

Jane now spent hours in front of the mirror before every occasion, trying and discarding outfits, unable to decide what to wear. She exhausted herself and Eliot worrying and fretting over which speaking invitations to accept or reject and what, if she decided to accept, she would say. She demanded one thousand percent support from Eliot for every decision, however minor. She could not choose a new shade of lipstick or even an appetizer in a restaurant without extensive consultation and advice from her husband.

"If I've changed, it's only because I've grown," Jane replied. "I'm famous and I'm sought after. You just haven't kept up with me."

Other arguments were the old-fashioned kind conducted with plain brown wrapper language and stripped-down emotions.

"You came on with Geoffrey Holcomb last night. You had your hand on his thigh. I'm surprised you didn't put your tongue in his ear right at the table. It was blatant and it was embarrassing," Eliot said one bleary, hungover morning after a dinner party. Geoffrey Holcomb was the host of a highbrow current events talk show on public television. He was tall and handsome though slightly beetle-browed. He had been married—and divorced—four times.

"I did not come on with him," Jane said. "I can't help it if men find me interesting."

"You acted like a slut!"

"Geoffrey Holcomb didn't think so! Besides, he can get it up."

Their sex life disintegrated. Using sex as a way to retaliate against Eliot or to prove to herself that she didn't need him, Jane would either pick up a stranger or call an acquaintance for some recreational screwing. She'd return home the next morning and brag to Eliot about her exploits.

"Plenty of men beside you know how to go down on a woman," Jane told Eliot. "Some of them even do it better!"

"I bet you don't know which of our twenty best friends has a ten-inch dick," she teased after an all-nighter that left her with bags under her eyes and beard-burned cheeks.

Jane was not nearly as heartless as she sometimes appeared. She was often embarrassed by the things she said and did. She felt humiliated by her emotional outbursts. She knew she was going overboard but she didn't know how to stop. She had a tiger by the tail and it was turning on her.

Jane made an effort to remember what it was like to be normal but the constant attention and adulation made it almost impossible. Everyone wanted to meet Jane. Everyone told her she was wonderful. Everyone wanted something from her.

"Your book changed my life. It's the best thing I've ever read! I'd love to play Francine in the movie. Do you think you could speak to the producer for me?" gushed a famous television actress who wanted to make the change to films and thought that the leading role in *The F Factor* might be the way to upgrade her career.

"If you ever want a change of pace from your husband, give me a call," said a clearly smitten media baron who slipped his private phone number into Jane's hand.

"I don't know whether to laugh or cry," Jane told Eliot. She had no clout whatever with the producer. The media baron was over seventy.

"Neither," said Eliot. "Why can't you just put it all into perspective?"

"Perspective?" asked Jane. It had become a word from a foreign language. "What's perspective?"

Although she tried to resist, Jane was swamped by stress and pressure. She could not always control her violent mood swings and temper tantrums. She felt terribly guilty for the way she lashed out at Eliot and tried to make amends.

"I know I'm impossible," she told Eliot more than once. "I can't seem to control myself. Success is the worst thing that ever happened to me. But I'll get used to it. One of these days I'll be able to control myself. I'll change. I promise!"

Jane's apologies were often followed by the kind of affectionate, tender sex they had had during their courtship and the early years of the marriage.

"I love you," Jane would say during a hot session in bed.

"Ditto," Eliot would reply.

Other times it was Eliot who would tell Jane that he loved her.

"Ditto," Jane would say.

It was their old formula but, somehow, the magic was gone. Jane's excesses had undermined the relationship.

For a time, though, neither was able to admit it. The marriage, which limped through 1976 on an increasingly insecure combination of memories, habit, and promises did not make it through the year. Even Eliot's sessions with Dr. Schneider didn't help. After all, Eliot reminded himself, Martha Schneider was only an analyst. Not a magician.

"I want a divorce!" Jane shrieked when the Thanksgiving weekend was over. Four days in suburbia with Eliot's money-grubbing family had driven her berserk.

"You've got a divorce!" replied Eliot. Three years with *The*

F Factor and the ups and downs of Jane's ego had driven *him* berserk.

Later on, in Eliot's lawyer's office, they even argued over who had had the idea of getting divorced first.

"I said it first!" Jane insisted.

"Only because I was polite enough to let you finish your sentence!" Eliot retorted.

The judge who handled Jane and Eliot's divorce considered himself an enlightened feminist. He interpreted women's rights as meaning total equality with men—sexual, political, economic. Equality equaled responsibility, the judge wrote in his opinion, and that included financial responsibility.

Jane undeniably had more money than Eliot. Therefore, the judge decided, Jane had to pay. It was the two residences—and Jane's earlier financial terrors—that ended up costing Jane much of the money she had earned from *The F Factor*.

The titles to both the Riverside Drive penthouse and the East Hampton house were in Eliot's name. As soon as Eliot and Jane separated, Jane found that the two places she thought of as "home" and had, in fact, helped pay for were legally owned by a man she now loathed. As part of her divorce agreement, Jane had to buy his share of the house and apartment from Eliot.

"They both went up in value the way Eliot said they would. They cost me a fucking fortune!" said Jane. "What a schmuck I was. When we bought them, I thought I couldn't afford them. In the end, I paid for them twice."

Once, when they were initially purchased. The second time, when under the jurisdiction of a judge who considered himself a champion of women's rights, she and Eliot divorced.

"Thank God I published *The F Factor* under my own name," Jane said a thousand times. "I'd have gone bonkers, if I'd not only helped make Eliot rich but famous besides!"

72
LINCKY

A woman's place is in the house—
and Senate.

—Slogan of the Seventies

1976 was the bicentennial year. It was also the year of Farrah Fawcett, *Charlie's Angels*, and jiggle. The Me generation, getting into high gear, was buying Cuisinarts and Pet Rocks, eating organic food, and shampooing with Herbal Essence. Its members wore mood rings, read Tarot cards, crusaded to Save the Whales, jogged, and signed up for assertiveness training courses while glancing at the passing time on their new digital watches. Anorexia had replaced low blood sugar as the "in" affliction and EST was the hot cure-all of the moment. Linda Carter starred as television's feminist superheroine, Wonder Woman. Faye Dunaway portrayed the macho image of the liberated woman in *Network* while Sissy Spacek personified the wallflower with secret powers in *Carrie*.

Lincky was not a superheroine. Neither was she macho nor a wallflower. She was single and, in her professional life, successful.

"I always wanted to be good at what I did. Time has finally

caught up with me," she told Elly, remembering how, even as a child, she longed to make her parents proud of her.

"People used to call me pushy, now they call me a role model," she told Jane.

Ever since the crash-and-burn of her affair with Josh Butterfield, Lincky had avoided serious romantic entanglements. Although she dated Hank, she lived alone and said that her career was all she needed.

"Bull," said Hank. "I know you better than you know yourself. Always did. Always will."

By the mid-Seventies, North Star was publishing's hot shop. *The F Factor* had set the stage for a series of bestsellers acquired, edited, published, and occasionally even conceived by Lincky. Observing the preoccupations of the times, Lincky published an upscale astrological guide by a Park Avenue socialite who did charts for her friends.

"Everyone in *Women's Wear Daily* swears by her," Lincky said. "I figured that putting her on the talk show circuit in her Adolfo suits and Suga hairdos would be something different. I thought that our astrology book would stand out from the rest of the astrology books."

Lincky was right.

Stars over Park outsold every other astrology guide in its years and stayed on the nonfiction bestseller list for twenty weeks. The paperback rights were sold for just under half a million dollars and the author's next book, *Heavenly Horoscopes*, performed almost as well.

"The Bicentennial is coming up," Lincky told Kathleen van Doren over lunch in late 1974. "I'd love to publish a novel with a bicentennial background. Three women, one family, set in 1776, 1876, and 1976. The first could be the mistress of a Revolutionary War hero. The second an actress and the third a famous model. They'd all be the kind of glamorous women you write about so well. Do you think you might be interested?"

"Absolutely. I've been wanting to write a book with a

bigger canvas," said Kathleen, who lived on mint tea and bacon, lettuce, and tomato sandwiches. "I've been noticing that fat books sell much better than thin ones."

Lincky and Kathleen discussed the characters, the settings, and the overall plot and worked together closely throughout the writing of the novel. The book, eventually titled *American Women*, was Kathleen's biggest seller yet. Hank sold the television miniseries rights, a first for Kathleen.

"Lincky should get part of the money," Kathleen told her agent. "It was her idea."

Lincky also published several mainstream novels about wildly rich but bitterly miserable people as well as a series of spy thrillers by an ex-CIA operative and a bestselling jogger's bible. She continued to publish the psychology books that she had always believed in as well as a series of wine guides and cookbooks that were more and more in demand as Americans ate McFood but dreamed of Taillevent. North Star, thanks to Lincky's editorial eye and Elly's publicity genius, put one book after another on the bestseller lists.

"I'm going to name you president of North Star. For one thing, you've earned it. For another, it would be good for business," Gordon told Lincky in 1976, at the same time naming himself chairman of the board.

Lincky Desmond thus became one of the very first and very few female company presidents in the United States. Her accomplishment was widely reported by media hungry for news of women's achievements and women's progress. The *New York Times*, *People*, and *Time* all gave the story of publishing's new female president prominent coverage. Every writer or reporter doing a story on women—women in business, successful women, executive women, working women— seemed to want an interview with Lincky.

"You're getting as much publicity as any author," Elly remarked, as requests for interviews with Lincky Desmond came in from all over the country.

"If only I were also Jewish, black, and gay, I'd be the perfect all-purpose Seventies feature story," laughed Lincky.

Elly disagreed. "If you settled down and got married, *then* you'd be perfect," said Elly.

"Hank and I have an arrangement," said Lincky.

"An arrangement is not the same as a real relationship," insisted Elly.

"It's better than getting your head handed to you," said Lincky, thinking about Alan Goldmark, Edgar Sanderton, and Josh Butterfield. The accumulation of one disappointment on top of another had undercut Lincky's confidence in herself and her trust in men. She retreated from her anxieties into busyness and activity. She worked almost obsessively, piling one success on top of another, refusing to open herself to the possibility of another betrayal.

"I'm never getting married again," Jane said in the sour aftermath of her breakup with Eliot. "Are you?"

"Never. Once was enough," said Lincky. "Even though women are liberated, men aren't. No matter what they say, most of them still want an old-fashioned wife. Half the men I meet are intimidated by me. The other half think they have to compete with me."

"I know what you mean," said Jane. "Every time I meet a cute guy, he acts as if he's got to prove that he's richer and more successful than I am or else he gets nervous and disappears."

"At least Hank says he likes me to be successful," said Lincky.

Lincky's professional life yielded rewards that went even beyond publishing. She cosigned the loan that helped Becky Reese start her own catering company. She used her clout to help Coral Weinstein get the job as American president of Champs Elysée Perfumes. She made Elly vice-president in charge of publicity for North Star.

"Vice-president?" said Elly when Lincky told her the news. Elly had mixed feelings about the promotion. Ever since she had confronted Owen about his affairs, the marriage had been rocky. Elly was bitter about Owen's infidelities. Owen resented and put down Elly's successes at the office. "I wonder what Owen will say."

" 'Congratulations,' I hope," replied Lincky.

No matter how much Lincky achieved, she always wanted more. If a book made the bestseller list, she wanted it to climb higher. If it was on the list for six weeks, she wanted it to remain for seven. If it hit number one, she wanted it to be number one longer. No matter what she accomplished, Lincky always had other goals in mind.

"You've become insatiable," Peter said. He was proud of Lincky's triumphs but relieved that he was no longer married to her. She seemed obsessively single-minded to him, preoccupied with North Star and her career. He couldn't remember the last time he had heard her laugh.

"Insatiable but in a *good* way," Lincky amended, determined to keep her feet on the ground. She wanted to be a beneficiary of success. Unlike Jane, she did not intend to be its victim. She also refused to see any imbalance in the life she had chosen for herself.

"Success, money, profits. You're becoming a publishing nun," said Hank, for once agreeing with Peter.

"There's always more to be accomplished. Always another record to be broken," replied Lincky.

"You still have a way to go. Barbara Walters is making a million dollars a year," Hank said. Stung by his father's mistreatment at Eagle Paint, Hank *always* kept score.

"Barbara Walters has to put up with Harry Reasoner," replied Lincky. Lincky's salary, although generous, was not in Barbara's league. Publishing was not blessed with—or cursed with—the mega-amounts of money that made television the land of the walking nervous breakdown. "I don't have to put up with anyone."

"Except me," said Hank. "I'm not going to give up and I'm not going to go away."

X

BACKLASH / 1976

"All right, Edith, you go right ahead and do your thing. Just remember that your thing is eggs over easy and crisp bacon."

—Archie Bunker, in *All in the Family*

73
ELLY

1 9 7 6 :

> *Disgraced*: Richard M. Nixon is
> disbarred in California.
> *Disconnected*: Three of five marriages
> now end in divorce.
> *Disinherited*: Numerous will forgeries
> appear claiming the estate of
> Howard Hughes.
> *Discounted*: The repeal of the Fair
> Trade Law prevents manufacturers
> from setting retail prices, thus
> opening the doors to discounters.

EVERY step forward Elly made at the office was accompanied by a setback at home. When Lincky named Elly vice-president of publicity, Owen congratulated her. Then he told her that she was spending her life doing a job that was trivial and stupid.

"Lincky doesn't think it's trivial and stupid. Neither does Gordon," said Elly.

"It's beneath your abilities," said Owen. "You're peddling junk."

"Then what should I be doing? Publicizing books of poetry for Parmenides for a hundred fifty dollars a week?" Elly asked.

"At least you'd be able to hold your head up," Owen said.

"Since when did you get so bitter?" asked Elly. The higher her salary got, the more open Owen became about his affairs.

"I'm not bitter," said Owen. "I just don't like to see you waste your time."

"And I don't like to see you waste *your* time on teeny-boppers," said Elly.

"Oh? Are we going to get into that again?"

"It's humiliating to me, Owen."

"It has nothing to do with our marriage."

"It has everything to do with the way I feel," replied Elly. "You accuse me of doing work that's beneath me. Don't you think your nymphets are beneath you?"

"They're toys," said Owen. "They're playthings."

"Spoken like a true male chauvinist," said Elly, going into the kitchen to check on the children's dinner.

Owen's parade of girlfriends not only hurt Elly's feelings but they were ruining Owen and Elly's sex life.

"You're never in the mood anymore," Owen told her in the middle of 1975.

"How can I be? You're screwing everything that catches your fancy. I don't feel I count anymore. When I make love to you, I feel I'm just one more of your conquests."

"You're not. You're my wife. You're special," Owen said.

"Then why don't you act it?"

"All men need variety," said Owen.

"And women don't?"

"Are you threatening to have an affair?"

"I'm not threatening anything," said Elly. "I'm also not going to make love to you tonight."

One month after Elly was promoted to vice-president of North Star, Owen informed her that he had fallen in love. This time, he said, it was serious.

"Her name is Jennifer," he told Elly.

"What else? Aren't they all named Jennifer these days?"

"I met her at a script conference on the *Badge 201* show."

"What did she do? Bring in the coffee?"

"She's a secretary. She took notes."

"Oh? A real executive," said Elly. "How old is she? Is she out of her teens yet?"

"She's twenty-two." said Owen. He was now forty-five.

"An old hag."

"Being bitchy isn't going to change the way I feel. And it isn't going to change my plans."

"Which are?"

"I'm moving out. Jennifer and I are going to live together," he said.

The next day, a Saturday, Owen arrived at the apartment with his new love. Jennifer Richardson was a Raphaelite vision come to life. She had densely curly auburn hair and huge, saucer-shaped blue eyes. Her pale ivory complexion was smooth and unlined, as smooth and unlined as her soul, Elly thought contemptuously.

Owen let himself into the apartment with his key. Without a word to Elly, he went to the back hall closet and got down the two big suitcases. He carried them into the bedroom, put them on the bed and began pulling shirts, socks, and sweaters out of his bureau drawers.

"Could you give me a hand, honey?" Owen asked Jennifer.

Looking scared but smugly victorious, Jennifer packed the two bags and a Lord & Taylor shopping bag as Owen oversaw the operation, telling her which suits and ties to pack and which to leave behind.

Elly stood silently by as Owen brazenly walked out of the apartment they had once shared, his adoring girlfriend following behind.

"Have a good day," said Jennifer in her little-girl voice as she left.

Elly slammed the door so hard the pictures on the wall rattled and chips of paint floated down from the ceiling.

"Where did Daddy go?" asked Angela, awakened from her nap by the noise and coming into the living room to find her father gone.

"He had to do an errand," said Elly through her teeth. She was so angry she could barely speak.

"Maybe I could go help him," Angela said with a suspicious expression. She did not entirely believe her mother.

"Not now, honey. It's getting dark out."

"Is Daddy mad at us?" asked Brian, who had heard the door slam from the kitchen where he was eating a peanut butter and jelly sandwich.

"He's just a little upset," replied Elly.

"Maybe I could make him feel better," said Brian.

"I bet I could, too," said Angie.

Brian, at six, was a male chauvinist replica of his father, noisily obsessed with aggressive games involving balls (foot-, base-, and basket-), toy machine guns and child-sized rocket launchers. Angela reminded Elly of her mother. At four, Angela was a fashion freak, adamantly refusing to put on any garment that did not please her. She was also fastidiously neat, probably the only child in Manhattan who refused to eat or sleep unless her shelves of toys, sweaters, and books were impeccably neat and perfectly organized. Elly adored them both.

"My children are the one unqualified success of my life," she had once told Lincky.

Owen, who was indifferent to the two children he had had with other women, was surprisingly attached to Brian and Angela. When Brian had the measles, it was Owen who sat up all night with him, giving him medicine, comforting him when he cried and telling him stories to distract him from his fever. When Angela fell in the playground and broke her arm while Elly was at work, it was Owen who had rushed her to the emergency room and hovered over her.

"I'd die if anything happened to them," he told Elly. "I never thought I'd be a devoted father, but I'd kill for my children."

"You just won't live at home to be with them, though, will you?" asked Elly a week after he had moved out.

"I miss them."

"Sure," said Elly. "That's why you haven't seen them once

since you moved in with Jennifer. They're very upset. They miss you. They don't understand what's happened and they don't understand why you don't come home."

Brian had gone on a rampage of destructiveness since his father had left. He had broken his toy rocket launcher, smashed his father's coffee mug and poured a jug of honey into Owen's typewriter. Angie reacted to her father's absence by whining.

"Where's Daddy? When's Daddy coming back? Is Daddy mad at us?"

She did not sleep and wept throughout the night, refusing to allow Elly to comfort her. Agitated by his sister's crying, Brian would often begin to sob, too, bellowing until he threw up.

When Elly told Owen that his children were suffering terribly as a result of his absence, Owen at first said nothing. He looked embarrassed.

"Jennifer doesn't like children," he finally admitted. "They make her uncomfortable."

Jane did not think it such a disaster when Owen moved out to live with Jennifer.

"Owen's a macho shit and you're lucky to get rid of him," Jane said.

"He's a macho shit and I miss him like crazy. So do the children," said Elly.

"You'd feel better if you got mad at him. Really mad," said Jane. "You're too soft on him. You ought to lower the boom on him."

"You're the fighter," Elly said. "I'm too softhearted. Even though I hate to admit it, I'd probably take him back in a minute."

"It doesn't exactly look like he's coming back any time soon," said Jane.

"I'm afraid not," said Elly.

Elly tended to blame herself for Owen's defection. Jane told Elly to stop beating up on herself.

"Men can't stand successful women," said Jane, repeating the conversation she'd had with Lincky. Jane was convinced that the real reason for Owen's defection was that he couldn't handle Elly's success.

"Owen began having affairs when you got your first big promotion. He moved out when you became a vice-president," said Jane, marshaling the evidence in support of her theory.

"That's true. I never quite put the timetable together that way before," said Elly. "On the other hand, my mother's success never bothered my father."

"Your father's successful. Owen's not. He's writing crapola for TV and paperback. Owen thinks he's a flop and he's taking it out on you."

"So what am I supposed to do? Resign my job and go back to being a secretary?" asked Elly, reluctantly deciding that Jane had a point. Would things have turned out differently if she'd remained a secretary or if Owen had been more successful? Elly didn't want to believe it but the sequence of events was irrefutable.

"Hell, no," said Jane. "If you still want the son of a bitch you ought to go get him and drag him back."

It was the same suggestion that Brian and Angela made.

"When is Daddy coming home? Why can't we go get him?" they kept asking Elly.

74
ELLY

1 9 7 6 :

> I'm mad as hell and I'm not going to
> take it anymore.
>
> —from the movie *Network*

JANE'S words and her children's questions had their effect on Elly. Over the next week, Elly felt her long-suppressed anger finally begin to stir. For years, she had downplayed her own achievements and swallowed her disappointment at Owen's failure to live up to his potential. The frozen rage that had kept Elly prisoner ever since the Saturday afternoon Jennifer had smiled and told her to have a good day thawed. Elly, who rarely got mad at anything or anyone, finally got furious at Owen.

"I've been Saint Elly. I've been understanding and patient with Owen," she told Margaret. "Maybe what I've really been is a goddamn fool. I'm fed up with Owen. I'm fed up with myself."

Owen had essentially given up after *Precincts of Childhood*. He wrote paperback thrillers and run-of-the-mill television scripts. He complained that the work was beneath him but made no effort to improve the quality of the projects he took on. When he had too much to drink, Owen rambled on about how he was a better writer than any of the current bestsellers.

"Ludlum? Crap! Robbins? Garbage! Arthur Hailey? Bilge! I'm better than any of them," he said.

"So prove it," replied Elly.

Somehow, Owen never quite got around to it. The big-shot *Newsflash* star had turned into a bitter middle-aged man who chased young girls to prop up his failing ego. Jane's harsh portrayal of Owen as a washed-up has-been in *The F Factor* had come perilously close to life.

By the second week of Owen's absence, Brian and Angela had both gotten into difficulties. Brian got into a fight at school and misbehaved in class throwing erasers, crayons, and staples all over the classroom. He spilled a bottle of ink over a class-mate's new coat and defiantly denied it when a teacher who had witnessed the incident confronted him. Brian's teacher warned Elly of behavioral problems and said that, as a condi-tion of remaining in school, he should receive therapy. If Brian created any more disturbances, the teacher said, the school would have no choice but to expel him. Angela was having nightmares and became extremely clingy, weeping and crying every morning when Elly had to leave for the office.

Both children asked Elly about Daddy constantly. They wanted to know where he was and what he was doing. They wanted to know why he wasn't at home and why he wasn't there to play with them in the afternoon and read to them at night. They were, in turn, hurt, confused, and angry at their father's sudden, unexplained disappearance.

"Maybe Daddy forgot where we live," Angie said on the second Saturday of Owen's absence. "Maybe if we went to get him, we could bring him back."

"I'd do anything to get Daddy back," said Brian. "I'd climb the Himalayas!"

"Would you really?" asked Elly.

"Sure," said Brian.

"Me, too," said Angie.

"Suppose you didn't have to climb the Himalayas? Suppose you just had to go to Twenty-first Street?" asked Elly. She had suddenly remembered what Owen had said—that Jennifer didn't like children, that she was uncomfortable around them.

"I'd go there in a minute," said Brian.

"Me, too," said Angie.

"Even if it was a little scary for a while?" asked Elly as a diabolical scheme presented itself.

"Nothing scares me!" said Brian.

"How scary?" asked Angie.

"Just a little," said Elly. "Just for a while."

"And it would mean Daddy would come home?"

"I can't guarantee but maybe," replied Elly.

"Let's go," said Brian. All action, he went to the closet to get his jacket.

"Can I take Rainbow?" asked Angie. Rainbow was her favorite rag doll.

"Of course you can take Rainbow," said Elly.

"And can I take my machine gun?" asked Brian. "In case I have to shoot someone to get Daddy?"

"Absolutely!" said Elly. The metallic rat-a-tat-tat of the machine gun was one of the most maddening sounds the toy mavens had ever concocted.

Elly bundled Brian and Angie into a taxi.

"Twenty-first Street and Ninth Avenue," Elly told the driver, giving him the address of the Chelsea brownstone where Owen now lived with Jennifer.

"We're going to go get our Daddy," Brian informed the driver.

"He forgot where we live but he'll remember as soon as he sees us," added Angie.

"Now remember," Elly told her children as she paid the fare, "if you get too scared, call me on the telephone. I'll come and get you right away."

Elly rang the bell to the third floor walk-up Owen shared

with Jennifer. Jennifer was expecting a wine delivery for the romantic dinner she planned for herself and Owen that night and automatically buzzed back.

When Elly and the two children got to the third floor, Jennifer had already opened the apartment door. The fifty cents Owen told her always to tip was in her hand. Jennifer's automatic smile for the delivery boy froze as she recognized Elly.

"What are you doing here?" she asked.

"You have my husband," Elly said, gently pushing Angela and Brian through the open door toward Jennifer. "You might as well have my children, too."

Before Jennifer could say another word, Elly turned around and headed down the stairs.

As Elly reached the second floor she could hear Brian's machine gun. As she reached the vestibule, she could hear Angie ask for Daddy and begin to weep. Eventually, Brian would begin to cry, too. If the past were any predictor of the future, Brian would wail until he turned hoarse and his face had turned reddish purple. Once he calmed down, he would spend the rest of the night throwing up.

Angie, on the other hand, would weep steadily and softly, sobbing and sniffling for hour upon nerve-racking hour. Later, she would crawl into her father's bed for comfort.

As Elly reached the street, she could hear Brian rev up into a full-throated bellow.

"Have a good evening," she muttered under her breath, looking up at Jennifer's window.

When Elly returned to her apartment, the telephone was ringing.

It was Owen. Elly had never heard him so angry.

"You bitch! How could you!"

"I thought it over carefully. It wasn't easy," said Elly.

"Jennifer is very upset."

"Tough," said Elly. "She wanted to get involved with a

married man. I thought I'd give her a taste of how married people live."

"Brian is throwing up. Angie is crying. Jennifer is hysterical," said Owen. "What am I supposed to do?"

"If you give Brian some ginger ale, it will settle his stomach. If you let Angie into bed with you for a while, she'll eventually stop crying," said Elly. "I don't know what to do about Jennifer. She's your problem."

75
ELLY

"Breaking Up Is Hard to Do"
"Fifty Ways to Leave Your Lover"

"FAN-tastic!" said Margaret when Elly told her what she'd done. "You finally stood up to him! Good for you, Elly! You were letting Owen get away with murder. It's time you rattled his chain!"

"You don't think I was too rough on the children?"

"Absolutely not," replied her sister. "After all, they were in on it from the beginning. Didn't Brian tell you that he wanted another adventure just like it? And didn't Angie say that she rescued Daddy from that awful girl?"

"Oh, my God, I love it!" Jane said. "Serves the bastard right. What did he say?"

"He called me a bitch," replied Elly.

"Then what?"

"Then he told me Jennifer was upset. He asked me what to do."

"I bet he didn't ask you what to do when he was screwing her."

"You're just great, Elly," said Lincky. "I'm glad you finally fought for yourself."

"It feels good not to be a doormat," said Elly.

"What's going to happen next?"

"I don't know. Owen and I are still working that out."

The morning after Elly had dropped Brian and Angie off at 21st Street, Owen had come to 13th Street. Brian was holding his left hand, Angie, his right.

"Daddy's back!" said Angie.

"I threw up but I'm better now," said Brian.

"Elly, could we have a talk?" asked Owen. He looked pale and tired.

Elly nodded.

"I guess I was a shit," Owen said.

"Guess?"

"Okay, I was a shit. Maybe I shouldn't have moved out."

"You mean you should have had the affair but continued to live at home?" asked Elly. "Don't you think I might have had something to say about that?"

"You never said much in the past."

"I said plenty. You just never listened."

"But you never *did* anything," said Owen.

"You mean nothing I say matters to you? Do you mean that I have to use our children to get your attention?"

Owen looked uncomfortable.

"Jennifer's really upset," he said. "She didn't know how to cope with the children. Brian was throwing up all night and Angie was crying. It was driving Jennifer crazy."

"I don't give a damn about Jennifer," said Elly. "How do you think I felt when Brian was breaking things and getting into fights at school and Angie was having nightmares and crying all the time? Don't you think I was upset?"

"You're their mother," said Owen. "You should know how to handle them."

"You're their father. Why should I have to 'handle' them all alone?"

"What are we going to do?" asked Owen.

"I don't know," said Elly.

"Will you take the children back?"

"So you can go back to Jennifer just like nothing ever happened?"

"I'm in love with her," said Owen.

"Spare me," said Elly. "I thought you were more original than that. You're just like a million other men. You're having a midlife crisis and you call it love. Give me a break."

"Maybe it's just lust. Maybe I'll get over it."

"And I'm supposed to wait around until you do?"

"Elly, do you really think I'm that selfish?"

"Yes."

One week later Owen went to Elly's office. He looked haggard and fragile.

"I spent the last week in a hotel. I've been thinking about what you said," Owen said. "I probably am having a midlife crisis. I'm afraid Jane was right. Maybe I *am* nothing but a has-been. Jennifer made me feel a little better about myself."

"Made? Past tense? Did she throw you out?" asked Elly. Owen looked as if he'd been fighting a war. There were shadows under his eyes and he had lost weight. He looked gaunt instead of lean. His in-control, in-command façade had slipped away. He looked vulnerable and unsure.

Owen shook his head. "It was mutual. When I saw how incompetent she was, I realized that she's just a child. She's completely immature."

"She's twenty-two. What do you expect?"

"Elly, would you take me back?"

"Why should I?"

"I love you."

"Bullshit. You walked out on me. You abandoned your children. You've been a rotten husband and a worse father."

"I know," said Owen. "I want to make it up to you. Won't you think about it? Won't you give us another chance?"

"I don't know," said Elly. "You hurt me. You hurt the children. How do I know you won't do it again?"

"I think I've learned my lesson," said Owen. "Can't we try again?"

Elly thought for a moment. She and Owen had been together for almost fifteen years. Did she want to throw that time away? Were relationships so easily disposable? Did love come with guarantees? No, no, and no. Would she ever meet anyone she would feel about the way she felt about Owen? Probably not. Look at Lincky. Alone. Look at Jane. Alone.

"On certain conditions," Elly said. "Number one, that you work on the high level that we both know you're capable of. Number two, that we have an old-fashioned, closed marriage. No more Jennifers. No more running around. There will be no third chance, Owen."

Owen nodded. He looked very sober.

"I've had an idea for a police story in the back of my head. I'll run it past Hank. Maybe there's something in it."

"Good," Elly said. "And?"

"You're right. A *closed* marriage. No more fooling around."

Elly was surprised to see that he actually seemed relieved.

He did not kiss her. They did not fall into each other's arms. Owen hoped that he could live up to his promises. Elly hoped that she could forget her bitterness. Happy endings were for movies. Real life was not so simple.

76
JANE

MOVIES OF 1976 :

Rocky
All the President's Men
Taxi Driver
Marathon Man
Carrie
A Star Is Born
The Omen

AFTER her divorce, Jane continued to live in the spacious Riverside Drive penthouse she had once thought she couldn't afford and had ended up paying for twice. A recycled, newly single woman of the late Seventies, Jane took advantage of the sexual attractiveness conferred by celebrity. She put on the first high-heel shoes she'd worn in years and went on an erotic rampage. Thirty-five, Jane specialized in young and beautiful men. She considered men her own age "old farts" and rewrote the line of the Sixties to her own specifications: "Never trust any man over thirty. No matter how liberated they seem, underneath they're male chauvinists."

Trading on her image as the compleat sexually liberated lady, Jane met men everywhere: at the lectures she gave, at restaurants, bars and boutiques, at private parties and at gatherings she attended for professional reasons. Jane reveled in her freedom and flaunted her sexual conquests in conversations with friends and acquaintances and in articles she wrote for trendy magazines.

"Why can't a woman be more like a man?" was the title of one. Jane's answer was that there was no reason they couldn't. Just as men got pleasure out of going to bed with women with whom they had no emotional connection, women, Jane declared, could indulge in pleasure, too.

Jane pointed to herself as a case in point. She shared Jacuzzis and champagne, dawn bike rides and midnight sails with blonds, brunettes, and redheads in an orgy of hit-and-run sex. Some of Jane's lovers had jobs and some didn't, some had IQs that (just barely) equaled their ages, some had wives, some had girlfriends and a few had boyfriends. One was living in a halfway house for supposedly recovering drug addicts while another possessed a degree from Cal Tech in astrophysics.

In the heady days following her split with Eliot, Jane saw no reason to say no to anyone for any reason.

"I love fucking!" she told Wilma.

"So what else is new?"

"I'm blocked," she told Wilma. She had begun two new novels and abandoned both.

"That's not new either."

Since her divorce, Jane's perennial problem had come back to haunt her. She suffered from anxiety attacks and an ongoing crisis of confidence. Jane's worst fears of being that most despised creature of all, a one-book writer, seemed to be coming true. During the three years since the publication of *The F Factor*, she had started two novels and abandoned them both.

"I tried to write about my divorce but I kept getting so goddamn mad at Eliot that instead of a novel I was writing a man-hater's bible. No one would publish it. No one would read it," she told Helene Ockent. "Including me."

The second novel was about a woman who murdered her husband and got away with it. Jane just couldn't make the plot work out. "Alfred Hitchcock doesn't have to worry about competition from me," she told Natalie Sher.

Some of the time Jane blamed her utter lack of creative inspiration on her success with her first book.

"I keep thinking I have to outdo myself," she told Wilma. "But *The F Factor* was one of the biggest sensations of the decade. How can I outdo that?"

At other times, she blamed her lack of inspiration on Eliot.

"It's Eliot's fault. He drained me. I spent all my energy fighting with him rather than on my work," she told Elly.

"He also helped you get the idea for *The F Factor*," Elly said.

"Don't remind me," said Jane.

Jane also held her financial anxieties responsible for her dry spell. Jane's expensive divorce had almost cleaned her out. As 1976 was coming to an end, Jane was running out of money. She knew that if she didn't come up with an idea for a new book, if she couldn't write the outline and collect the advance, she was going to have to sell either the spacious penthouse that she considered home or the East Hampton house that she thought of as an escape hatch and sanity saver. She was plagued with recurrent nightmares about crawling back to Glen Sinclair in humiliation and defeat, begging for her old job back.

"I went from millionaire to nillionaire. I know that to someone who's struggling with the rent, my problems are a joke. They're no joke to me," she told Hank. "How can I be creative when I worry about money most of the time?"

"Why don't you talk to Lincky?" he said. "Maybe she can help."

"I keep thinking I have to top *The F Factor*," Jane told Lincky. "I know it's ridiculous and I know it's part of what's blocking me. The trouble is I always want to be the best and I get crazy if I think I'm not."

"I know," said Lincky. "I'm the same way."

"If *The F Factor* hadn't been such a smash, I wouldn't have this problem," said Jane. "Success is what's doing me in. It ruined my marriage. It's ruining my attempts to write a second book. Sometimes, I think it's ruining me."

"Ruined by success?" Lincky asked.

Jane nodded. "Success isn't at all what everyone thinks," she said. "Success brings all the goodies everyone knows about. Money, fame, attention. It also has a down side. At least for me it did. Half the time I felt I didn't really deserve it. I felt I was a cheat. The other half of the time I felt I was God's gift to literature. I was arrogant and obnoxious. Talk about egomania! I can't blame Eliot for wanting out. You don't think I'm really proud of myself, do you?"

"I bet you're not the only one who's been done in by success. It happens to a lot of movie stars and politicians, too. They think they're invulnerable and they go off the deep end."

"Tell me! I sure screwed up. The more successful I got, the more goblins came out. Even though I say I'm better off without Eliot, it isn't really true. I won't admit it, hardly even to myself, but divorcing him was a big mistake," said Jane. "We had something good going and success ruined it. The split was mostly my fault. I drove him crazy and he couldn't take it."

"Maybe that's the idea you've been looking for. The flip side of success," said Lincky. Unlike Jane, Lincky had enjoyed her success. Her success, though, wasn't quite of the public nature that Jane's had been. Lincky had not attracted the disturbed and disturbing sex fantasies of strangers. Lincky had not been looked to as a guru by those in need of advice and sustenance. Lincky's personal life and fantasies had not been exposed. Her success had been anonymous and gradual. She had had time to get acclimated to each new step up the ladder. Jane's success, by contrast, had been public and immediate. She had had no time to prepare for it. She had been swamped by overnight adulation and its vicious backlash.

Jane considered Lincky's suggestion for a moment.

"I could call it *The Bitch Goddess*," Jane said, the title

popping into her head as she spoke. "Do you think people will be as upset by 'Bitch' as they were by 'F'?"

"I certainly hope so," said Lincky.

Jane became obsessed with her new project. She wrote an outline and five chapters in three weeks of fourteen hour days.

"This is dynamite!" she told Wilma. "People are going to realize that success isn't all it's cracked up to be."

"It's even better than *The F Factor*," she told Helene. "It's more mature. Naturally, I blamed Eliot for most of it but I didn't let myself off the hook either."

As always, when Jane knew she was on the right track, she was one of her own most enthusiastic fans. She absolutely loved her new book.

"If I don't like it, who will?" she asked Natalie. "After all, I'm the one who has to write it."

Jane could not wait to give the outlines and chapters to Hank and Hank could not wait to read them.

"It looks like you've done it again," he told Jane when he had finished the outline and early chapters of *The Bitch Goddess*. "Lincky's going to flip!"

"When is she going to flip for you?" asked Jane. Hank and Lincky were a duo. But a duo who lived at arm's length.

"Don't ask," said Hank. "I can negotiate anything. I can't negotiate a deal with Lincky. She keeps putting me off."

"She's crazy," said Jane. "There aren't too many men around like you. Available, heterosexual, dying to settle down. You're one in a million."

"Do me a favor?" Hank said. "Tell Lincky."

77
LINCKY

1 9 7 6 :

"For some reason, self-doubt
appears to thrive in our Bicentennial
year."

—Arthur M. Schlesinger, Jr.

LINCKY left no clothes, no underwear, no makeup, no perfume, not even a comb, at Hank's bachelor apartment in Gramercy Park. She refused to accept a duplicate key and even when she spent the night with Hank, she went home in the morning before work to dress and pick up her mail. When Lincky wasn't with Hank, no trace of her remained.

"My work comes first. You'd be second and you'd hate it," Lincky told Hank.

"At least leave a toothbrush at my place," said Hank. "That way you could sleep later instead of getting up at five to go back to your own apartment."

"I don't mind getting up early," said Lincky.

Whenever Hank proposed, Lincky turned him down.

"Marriage is passé," she told him, pointing to current statistics showing that three out of five marriages ended in divorce.

Hank resorted to bribery. He offered Lincky a floor-through Park Avenue apartment, separate bank accounts, his-and-hers Mercedes, Golden Crown sables, and weekend homes in locales ranging from Connecticut to Capri.

Lincky was offended. "I'm no hooker," she told Hank, turning down one offer after another. "Anything I want, I can buy for myself."

Hank appealed to Lincky's ambition.

"If we got married, we'd be the Clare Boothe and Henry Luce of the Seventies," Hank said.

"You're the one who said we should never get married. You said that you had a lousy disposition and that I'm too uptight," Lincky reminded him.

"That was years ago. I've changed," said Hank.

"I haven't," said Lincky.

Hank had noticed that Lincky was a doting "aunt" to Peter's children by his second wife and to Elly's children, too. She brought them presents and took them out for excursions. She even said how much she regretted not having children of her own.

"If we got married we could do something about that," said Hank.

"No," said Lincky. "I'm too old."

"You're thirty-five. Your mother was thirty-eight when you were born."

"That's true. And I was an only child. I'd never have an only child," said Lincky. "Look what happened to me."

Lincky continued to resist the idea of marriage.

"If we got married, we'd get divorced," said Lincky. "No marriage could hold two Filofaxes as big as yours and mine."

"I'd be willing to give it a try," said Hank.

"Well, I wouldn't," said Lincky. "You fired me once. How can I ever trust you?"

"Hasn't it ever occurred to you that I might have been hurt, too? I was in love with you. You were in the process of changing my life and the way I felt about myself and then you walked out on me. You were brutal, Lincky. If I'm willing to trust you, you ought to be willing to take a chance on me."

"No," said Lincky. "I'm happy the way things are."

"I'm not," said Hank.

Every time Hank proposed, Lincky turned him down and went back to work. She had found that being a woman in a man's world was no longer a disadvantage. In the mid-Seventies, it was often just the opposite. She hired a female investment adviser to handle her money. Because Brenda Thornhill was the only female partner in an all-male firm, she was particularly sympathetic to Lincky's financial needs and goals. Lincky found a female haircutter who, having a busy schedule of her own, understood Lincky's time pressures and didn't keep her waiting.

Lincky hired and promoted women whenever possible and North Star became known as the place for bright and talented young female editors, copywriters, publicity people, and sales staff. Other than Hank and Gordon, the only significant male in Lincky's life was her secretary.

"Aren't you afraid of ending up alone?" Elly asked.

"I'm an only child," Lincky said. "I'm used to being alone."

It was Jane who gave Hank the breakthrough idea he'd been searching for.

"You're a schmuck to keep proposing to Lincky. She's never going to accept," Jane told Hank.

"You mean it's hopeless?"

"No. You're hopeless."

"I am?"

"From Lincky's point of view, you are. From her perspective, you have the wrong image."

"What do you mean? For Christ's sake, I'm rich, I'm successful, I'm powerful. What the fuck does she want?"

"A man who acts that way," said Jane. "Sometimes you talk about yourself like you're a one-man disaster area. You bitch about being from the only Jewish family in town. About how your father was poor, how you didn't get into the college you wanted, how you kept getting rejected for everything. Blah, blah, blah. It's a total drag."

Hank's face turned red with anger.

"It's the truth," he said, defending himself. "My family was discriminated against for being Jewish. My father was the lowest-paid executive in the Eagle Paint company. I was a fraternity-row reject and I got turned down by my first choice of college, not to mention—"

"Big deal. That was a hundred years ago. You act like it was yesterday," said Jane, who had met Hank's parents during one of their visits to New York. "I bet if you changed your image with Lincky, you could change her mind."

78
LINCKY

Dorothy Hamill wins the Olympic
gold medal in figure skating. Her
wedge haircut becomes as popular
as Jackie Kennedy's bouffant and
Farrah Fawcett's mane.

LINCKY blinked when she and Hank visited his parents in
Greenville, South Carolina, in the spring of 1976. Saul and Kay
Greenberg lived in a white-pillared antebellum mansion
straight out of *Gone with the Wind*. There was a cook, a maid, a
butler, and a chauffer to take care of them. Hank's parents also
owned a winter house in Barbados and a summer hideaway in
Maine. They traveled to New York and to London to catch up
with theater, to Paris to sample the newest four-star restaurants, and to Positano for the *ambiente*.

"I thought you said your father was the lowest-paid executive at Eagle Paint," Lincky told Hank after her first evening
in Greenville.

"He was," said Hank.

"What about the rich ones? Do they live in palaces and
drive Ferraris to the supermarket?"

"My father did well in the stock market," admitted Hank.

"Franklin and Marshall offered Hank a full scholarship because of his excellent grades," Kay Greenberg told Lincky the next day at lunch as she indulged in one of her favorite activities—bragging about her son. "Hank was so proud at not having to ask us to pay his tuition that he decided against Columbia."

"He decided! I thought Columbia rejected him," said Lincky, repeating what Hank had told her dozens of times.

"Not with those grades," said Kay Greenberg.

"Don't complain to me about second choice and being rejected!" Lincky warned Hank that evening. "I'm beginning to think I've fallen for a sob story."

"Hank was too nearsighted to make any of the teams, but he became team secretary," Saul Greenberg told Lincky. "He was a damn good secretary, too. Hank also learned that he could wield a good deal of power if he chose to and he chose to. Hank gave out tickets, made the travel arrangements, assigned seats, and handled the press. Everyone in town made a point of getting on Hank's good side."

"And don't let me hear you complain about not making the team, either!" Lincky said.

Everything Hank had said about himself was true. It also turned out that he wasn't telling the whole truth.

Although it was true that Hank had not made the fraternity of his choice at the University of South Carolina, Lincky learned that he *had* been Phi Beta Kappa. Then Hank finished at the top of his class at graduate school and, although the Wall Street firm had in fact rejected him because of his religion, the interviewer was so impressed with Hank that he sent him to his college roommate, the financial vice president of Bell Publishing.

Bell, having no restrictions against Jewish employees, hired Hank immediately. Hank's rise through Bell, his two years as an editor and his career as an agent were marked with one success after another. His agency, although tiny at first, had been profitable from the beginning.

Even the two women Hank most loudly mourned turned out better lost than won.

"The North Shore debutante left her husband for a polo-playing Argentinian. Then she dumped the Argentinian for a Hungarian art dealer and eighty-sixed the Hungarian when she turned gay. She moved in with a butch Italian leather goods designer who cracked the whip over factories in Bologna, Milan, and Florence," Hank admitted when Lincky questioned him about his supposedly miserable love life.

"I bet she did plenty of whip cracking at home, too," said Lincky. "You two would have made a great couple. What about the Park Avenue socialite? What happened to her?"

Hank shrugged. "Lunch at Mortimer's. Fittings at Bergdorf's."

Lincky just shook her head.

By the time Lincky and Hank returned from their visit to his parents, Lincky had a completely different image of Hank.

"You have terrific parents. You didn't have a miserable childhood. You had friends. You did well at school. Even your career was one success after another. You've been lying to yourself all along. And to me! Your silver spoon was straight from Tiffany's just the way mine was!" said Lincky. " 'Poor me'? You're full of shit!"

Lincky braced herself for a Hank Greene outburst. Instead, he smiled benignly.

"That's just what Jane said," he replied in what Lincky could have sworn were dulcet tones.

79
LINCKY

Happy Birthday, U.S.A.!

"HOW does Lincky's calendar look for the July fourth week-end?" Hank asked Sam Lowell, Lincky's secretary.

"She's going to Bridgehampton," said Sam, flipping the pages of Lincky's calendar. Sam ran Lincky's life, seeing to it that she made all her meetings, took time out for vacations, the dentist, and periodic enforced rest days. Although Sam was a hundred percent WASP, he was the Jewish mother Lincky had never had and badly needed.

"Cancel the trip to Bridgehampton. She's staying in the city. Make an appointment for a checkup and tell Dr. Wise to make sure to do a blood test," said Hank. "If she fires you, I'll give you a job. Instead of Bridgehampton, she's going to go to an Op Sail party at Jane's."

When Hank hung up, he made the first of dozens of calls: to a caterer, a band, a florist, a photographer, and a travel agency. He consulted Sherry-Lehmann about champagne and Iron Gate about caviar. He searched for, and found, musicians who could play Rodgers and Hart, Cole Porter, and George Gershwin. He specified white, only white, flowers—tulips, freesia, gardenias, orchids, and roses—and bought two first-class tickets to Paris. Even though the Concorde had started flying to Europe that year, Hank, for once in his life, opted against speed. He wanted to take his time and savor every moment of the surprise he had planned.

When Hank had finished all his calls, he telephoned his unindicated co-conspirator, Jane.

"It's all set. All you have to do is send out the invitations," Hank said.

"You mean the trip to South Carolina worked?" asked Jane.

"Cross your fingers," said Hank.

In that Bicentennial year, New York City celebrated the two hundredth anniversary of the country's birth with a festive Op Sail. Masted sailing vessels, fifteen tall ships, and more than two hundred smaller ones sailed up the Hudson River in a birthday salute to the nation. The terrace of Jane's penthouse provided the ideal viewing angle. The gods of weather cooperated with a picture-postcard clear and sunny day. Tubs of white flowers banked the terrace and Jane had invited sixty of Hank and Lincky's nearest and dearest. She had also invited the judge who had married Elly and Owen.

When the guests were assembled and supplied with champagne, Hank tapped his glass for silence. As soon as everyone had settled down, Hank pulled a small jeweler's box out of his pocket.

"Lincky, would you please marry me?" Hank said.

"You trapped me!" Lincky said. She went pale and then flushed. She took a step toward the door, about to bolt, and tripped over a basket of white roses.

"I'm not *that* bad, am I?" asked Hank, reaching out to steady her.

"How could you?" she asked, looking around. Her friends were smiling. Lincky sighed and tried to smile back.

Then Lincky saw, really saw, the masses of white flowers that filled the air with their sweet scent. The blooms held a message for Lincky. They told her how responsive Hank was and how thoughtful he could be. Then it suddenly registered on her that the champagne wasn't just any champagne but a 1941 cuvée. Hank must have spent a lot of time and money to track it down.

"Two dozen phone calls," he said, reading Lincky's mind the way he sometimes did. "We finally had to have it air freighted from France."

"Because my father put down 1941 for my wedding?" she asked.

"I wanted to observe the family traditions," Hank replied.

Lincky's eyes swam as she realized the lengths Hank had gone to for her. He had transformed himself. For her. He had enlisted her friends, toned down his behavior, and glossed up his image for her. The extent of his desire to please her moved Lincky and caused her to remember that without Hank she might have been just another housewife who'd worked for a few years before settling down to raise a family. It was Hank who had recognized her ability, Hank who had dared her to make the most of herself. Hank had picked up where her parents had left off. He had encouraged her, prodded her, rewarded her, challenged her. He expected the best from her and helped her achieve it.

Lincky recalled her parents' hopes for her happiness and well-being and thought of how much they would have loved Hank. Her father would have respected Hank's intelligence. Her mother would have cheered his determination. They both would have approved his choice of champagne.

"We want you in the family," said Kay Greenberg.

"You'll make Hank happy and you'll make us happy," said her husband.

"So? Will you?" asked Hank.

Lincky glanced at Alvin Hayes. Then at Elly and finally at Jane.

"For Christ's sake, say yes," said Jane.

"Well?" Hank asked.

Lincky looked at him and smiled.

"Well what?" she prompted.

"Please?" amended Hank.

"Yes, Hank," Lincky said. "Yes, I'll marry you."

Hank opened his mouth to say something but he couldn't get the words out. He tried to smile. Instead, unexpectedly, he began to weep.

Several moments later when he had pulled himself together, Hank handed the jeweler's box to Lincky.

"For you," said Hank. "From me."

Lincky tried to open it.

"My hands are shaking," Lincky said. She fumbled with the ribbon and removed the wrapping. When she got the box open, she took the ring out of its dark velvet presentation box. It was an emerald-cut diamond that was big enough to impress anyone, even Lincoln Ten Eyck Desmond.

"Well, are you going to put it on or aren't you?" Hank growled. He had recovered from his tears and did a perfect imitation of himself at his worst.

"Could you help me?" laughed Lincky, holding out her hand and the ring to him.

Hank slipped the ring on her third finger, left hand, and everybody cheered, stamped, whistled, and applauded.

"Good for you, Hank!" said Gordon Geiger.

"Congratulations to you both!" said Charlie Lamb.

"It's not a marriage, it's a merger!" said Glen Sinclair.

"It's time those two settled down," said Wilma.

"I'd thought you'd never change her mind," Becky Reese told Hank.

"It wasn't easy," he replied.

"You're supposed to kiss her," said Ralph Weiss.

"Lincky, kiss him back!" Coral Weinstein added.

To further cheers, applause, and affectionate catcalls, Hank and Lincky obliged.

When the kisses and the cheers subsided, Hank introduced Lincky to one of the few people at the party she didn't know.

"Herbert Englund," Hank said. "New York State Supreme Court Judge Herbert Englund."

Hank and Lincky were married that afternoon on Jane Gresch's sun-splashed, flower-decked terrace overlooking the Hudson River as the brigantine *Gloucester* sailed majestically past. There was dancing and gaiety and laughter. Enough time had passed so that no shadow of grief intruded on Lincky's happiness. Her only memories were happy memories.

"And I didn't even have to pay for the wedding!" she joked later.

"That's because this time you have a real husband," said Hank, holding her protectively. *He* wasn't joking.

Elly sent photos and announcements to the press.

"Please say that friends and family attended the wedding," Lincky asked Elly. For Lincky, her friends had replaced her family and Hank's family, she knew, would soon feel like her own.

Later that evening, as a massive fireworks display lit up the skies of lower Manhattan, Lincky and Hank left for Paris for a three-week honeymoon.

"I did things the patriotic way! I got married on Independence day and pregnant on Bastille Day," Lincky would say later, counting backward.

For a woman who had once said she would never marry again, she looked remarkably happy. For a woman who had made a fetish of keeping her options open, Lincky narrowed her life down to a single, extremely complicated man with layers and layers of mixed motives and convoluted responses.

Hank Greene was an old-fashioned man who had dragged himself into the present. What he didn't know when he married Lincky was that his greatest successes were still in front of him. What he didn't know was that marriage to a modern woman would turn him into a modern man and that the process would be a revelation. The rough surfaces would completely fall away and the diamond that was Hank Greene would finally emerge and shine.

Lincky was no longer alone and Hank could finally be himself.

XI

MAGIC CIRCLE

TURNING FIFTY IN 1987 / 1988:

> Picasso's *Guernica*
> Snow White
> Superman
> Polaroid
> Spam
> The Appalachian Trail
> Nylon
> The Golden Gate Bridge

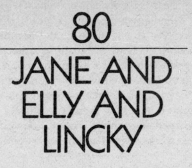

80

JANE AND
ELLY AND
LINCKY

ANNIVERSARIES IN 1987:

Today is 35 years old.
60 Minutes enters its twentieth year.
Woodstock happened twenty years
 ago.
James Bond is twenty-five.
Star Wars is ten.
USA Today is five.

CHAMPAGNE, caviar, and fireworks were traditional at Hank and Lincky's annual black tie New Year's Eve party. As 1987 was about to turn to 1988, they realized that a quarter century had passed since they had first met. Unwilling to let the milestone go uncommemorated, Hank and Lincky decided to embellish the annual tradition. "Who and What" would be the theme.

"This year we want you to bring something or someone who has most influenced your life," they instructed each of their guests.

Elly's decision was easy and she invited her parents to accompany her to the party. Louise Cullen McGrath was sixty-nine years old. Her black, jet-beaded dress came from Armani and her jazzy clear red lipstick from Chanel. Her mother still dressed better than anyone Elly had ever known and she went to work every day at her office at the Manhattan Museum where she was director of the costume collection. Brian McGrath, now seventy-three, was her proud escort.

"Mother and Dad were my inspiration and my standard of excellence. They taught me, without even knowing what they were passing on to me, how to have a career, a marriage, and a family. I learned everything I know from them. Except, of course, for a sense of style. *That* I never learned!" Elly told her sister.

"And I'm bringing your mother," Owen told his children. "She doesn't always see me the way I am. She sees me the way I *can* be."

Lincky's "What" presented no conflicts, no moments of indecision—it was the North Star stock Lincky had bought when the company went public in 1980. Lincky's investment was an investment in a business and in herself. North Star represented a reincarnated Ten Eyck Importing to Lincky. She had created for herself what fate had prevented her from inheriting. On her own and with Hank's encouragement, she had built an outlet for her energy and ability and made her parents' dreams for her come true.

"It's been a vintage year for North Star," Lincky told Hank, explaining her decision. "We bought Raintree Books, which brought us an impressive list of popular bestsellers and complemented our purchase last year of Parmenides. The stock is about to split. I'll make the announcement at the party. It will be still another reason to celebrate."

Jane's choice was not so easy. At first she was going to bring a copy of North Star's first printing of *The F Factor*. Then she decided that bringing an old book—even a book she'd written herself—was conventional and predictable. Jane would rather die than do anything C and P. Instead, she racked her brain trying to think of something much more exciting and much more imaginative.

"Something," she told Wilma dramatically, "much more *Jane*!"

But what? If something was going to screech *Jane!* it had to be original, eye catching, unique, and, if possible, outrageous. What could fit all those requirements? The divorce decree? No. Too depressing. A press clipping of the Bartlett Crispen review that had first propelled *The F Factor* toward notoriety? Nope. Too corny. A hunky boy toy fifteen years her junior to prove how liberated and *au courant* she was? Nah. Too embarrassing.

"Even for me," she told Elly.

Nothing Jane could think of was really superperfect. Finally, she decided to bring the original manuscript of *The F Factor*. Jane thought that people might be interested in seeing the author's own words, corrections, revisions, and second and third thoughts.

She also thought that it would be good for her image if people saw how hard she worked. She knew, after all, that despite her years of success and good reviews, a lot of people still thought of her as a sexed-out whacko.

Jane spent the afternoon of the last day of 1987 rummaging through her files, looking for the original manuscript of *The F Factor*. During her search, Jane found something she didn't even know she still had: the press badge she had worn in Dallas on November 22, 1963.

The once shiny pin on its back had become clouded, the printing on the face had faded, but the fake name Jane had used was still perfectly legible: Pussy Galore. Jane could hardly believe she had once laughed with the rest of the boys at the puerile joke. Knowing a symbol of change when she saw one, Jane pinned the badge to her dress.

As she entered Hank and Lincky's apartment, Jane looked down at the badge for the twentieth time.

"I wore the badge to show how far I've come, how far we've all come," she explained to Lincky.

"And because it's outrageous and you'll get a lot of attention," added Lincky.

Jane had the grace to blush. "That, too," she admitted.

81
NEW YEAR'S EVE

DECEMBER 1987:

Charlie Chaplin, "the little tramp,"
dies, but his legend lives on.

THEY all had put on their party best. Lincky wore black satin trousers that showed off her arrow-narrow figure and a beaded turquoise sweater that exactly matched the color of her eyes. Her thick, butterscotch-colored hair, strikingly silvered, was cut in a sleek, timeless bob that framed her small, strong features. She looked the way she had always looked: modern, racy, built for speed.

Lincky was accompanied by Hank and her three children, two sons and a daughter.

"On the day Hank Junior was born, I reminded Hank that I didn't want an only child," she told Elly. "For once, Hank didn't give me any argument."

Elly wore an unusually elegant navy crepe dress. Even though she had paid a fortune for it at Chanel, one of the crested buttons was hanging by a thread and the hemline wavered uncertainly. Elly and fashion still eyed each other warily. However, the slim figure that had been Elly's bane as a girl was her pride as a woman.

"Don't you ever have to diet?" asked Jane, who was currently subjecting herself to Opti-Fast.

"Never," said Elly, remembering the bust creams and Wate-On aids.

Jane wore an indecently low-cut chiffon gown in gaudy tropical sunset shades. Her breasts were emphasized by a French lace push-up bra. Chandelier-sized rhinestone earrings dangled to her shoulders and her impossible hair, colored somewhere between red and fuchsia, was frizzed out into a messy halo.

Owen, who had always assiduously ignored Jane whenever they had encountered each other socially, finally went up to her. His craggy, lean looks had aged well. What was even more attractive was a bearing of confidence that echoed the younger man but had become more solid and assured over the years. The third in Owen's *Precinct 15* series of novels was on the hardcover bestseller list. The first had just been released as a motion picture.

"I've forgiven you," he told Jane. "I hope you've forgiven me."

"Of course I've forgiven you," she replied sweetly. "You helped make me famous, Owen. How could I possibly be mad at you? Besides, you're the fourth best fuck I ever had."

When the New Year struck, kisses were exchanged, glasses were raised, and toasts were made.

"To a Happy New Year!" said Hank, raising his glass of champagne. He was working on a deal to merge with a large Hollywood agency. If it went through, and Hank thought that it would, he would become even richer, even more powerful. He glanced at Lincky. Only she could make him happier.

"To the future!" said Lincky. The taste of Hank's kiss was

still on her mouth. No trace of bitter mingled with the sweet. Lincky unconsciously touched her wedding ring. To her it was the magic circle, the irreplaceable sense of belonging she had once had but lost and now reveled in once again.

"To love," said Elly, looking at Owen.

"To you," he replied with a possessiveness that was new.

"To nifty fifty!" said Jane, raising her champagne glass highest of all as she realized that she, like her friends, was closer to fifty than to forty. She felt no more than eighteen and most of the time she thought she looked no more than thirty-five.

"Thirty in good light," she told Wilma.

For the first time since she had turned twenty-seven, Jane had not lied about her age to her new boyfriend. And Ted Wight, she noticed, had not died from the shock.

As she made her toast, Jane realized that *Nifty Fifty* was a fabulous title for the new book she and Lincky had been talking about. Fifty, these days, was a gateway for women, a brand-new decade to explore and enjoy. Jane planned to write about a fifty-year-old heroine who was rich and famous and had a fervently monogamous, absolutely eye-popping sex life. The heroine, of course, would be based on herself.

"After all, who else knows more about these things than I do?" she told Lincky as the party broke up and Ted helped her on with her sable cape. Almost floor length, it closed with braided gold frogs and was lined with bright tangerine satin. It had cost Jane fifty grand and she absolutely adored it.

Still, nice as luxuries were, they didn't give substance to life and they certainly couldn't bestow happiness. Work could. *Nifty Fifty!* The more Jane thought about it, the more she liked it. She could hardly wait to get home to her word processor. Boy, was this going to be a book!